FOREWORD

If you've read *Outlander*, then you know something of the Jacobite uprising, but if not, suffice it to say that it's a turbulent time in England/Scotland history. The Battle of Culloden Moor was the last civil war battle fought upon UK soil.

The battle itself was a horrific rout. About 6,000 Jacobites comprised of Highlanders, French, and even English troops faced about 6,000 British troops on a cold spring morning upon the Culloden moor on April 16, 1746. In a nutshell, the Jacobites started first with sporadic cannon fire, which provoked a nasty response from the British. They fired off what were known as canister shot, which were essentially canisters filled with musket balls, turning the cannons into a massive shotgun. Canister shot mowed down entire groups of Jacobites, but it was the Highlanders who got the worst of it. They were fearless as few men are, but they were no match for the superior British forces.

There were piles of dead on the fields of Culloden, Highlanders who were buried where they fell, with the local church doing what they could for the rest of the wounded, English included. The Highlander casualties were somewhere around 1,500 to 2,000, while the British casualties were significantly less – only 50 reported dead. In the days following the battle, the British spared no expense in hunting down Jacobite rebels because, at that point, the wars were over and the Jacobite cause was dead.

Now, imagine the first holiday season after Culloden, that horrible battle that took so many lives. Imagine those in a small village on the road leading to the battlefield, trying to find the holiday spirit in such a year. In fact, a law was passed in 1640 making Yuletide illegal, so surely that only made the season more difficult.

In this collection, we'll peek into the world of the only tavern in the village of Calvine, a place called Balthazar's Inn. The inhabitants are still reeling, as are the visitors, in more ways than one can imagine. There are secrets here, some left untold, some better off exposed, but the spirit of holidays is still there amongst the turmoil. No battle, and no laws, can suppress the goodness, peace, and joy that is the very essence of the holiday season.

It is a time of change in the Highlands of Scotland.

Welcome to A Very Highland Holiday.

A Very Highland Holiday

Kathryn Le Veque
Kerrigan Byrne
Jennifer Ashley
Tanya Anne Crosby
Darcy Burke
Eliza Knight

A Very Highland Holiday Collection…

It's the holiday season of 1746 and the Highlands are snowy. In the village of Calvine, north of Tay Forest along a road that leads straight into Inverness, the only tavern in town is packed to the rafters with travelers.

Eight months after the disastrous defeat at Culloden, the people haven't recovered, nor has the land, and it's a bad winter. But inside the tavern known as Balthazar's Inn, the magic that is the holiday season is about to happen.

A blustery innkeeper, his sensitive daughter, and a cast of unique characters passing through the careworn tavern will bring you six captivating stories of reflection, joy, and enthrallment that is the very spirit of the holidays.

Welcome to an enchanting limited-edition collection you won't soon forget!

The Earl in Winter

By Kathryn Le Veque

Part of A Very Highland Holiday Collection

Part One of The Brothers de Lohr

Text by Kathryn Le Veque
Cover by Dar Albert
Edited by Scott Moreland

KATHRYN LE VEQUE
NOVELS

WWW.KATHRYNLEVEQUE.COM

ARE YOU SIGNED UP FOR KATHRYN'S BLOG?

You'll get the latest news and information on exclusive giveaways, exclusive excerpts, coming releases, sales, free books, cover reveals and more.

Kathryn's blog followers get it all first. No spam, no junk.

Get the latest info from the reigning Queen of English Medieval Romance.

Sign Up Here

kathrynleveque.com

The Earl in Winter

When James de Lohr heads into the wilds of Scotland to discover what happened to his brother at the Battle of Culloden, his stay at Balthazar's Tavern has an unexpected twist. On a night when angels walk the earth, James comes face to face with his very own guardian angel.

AUTHOR'S NOTE

The Earl in Winter is about a descendant of my big Medieval family, the House of de Lohr (de Lohr Dynasty). It's one of my oldest houses, and most popular, and I love the fact that I was able to bring this family forward a few hundred years. They're alpha-male, sword-toting, fun-loving, battle-driven knights (at least, in Medieval times, they are), and it's been really cool to see that the tradition of military service with the family hasn't wavered.

What's even cooler is the fact that the fabulous Kerrigan Byrne has written the companion story to this tale in this very collection – The Earl of Christmas Past. While my tale is about the younger brother, James, Kerrigan's tale is about the older brother, Johnathan. Two brothers, two tales, two earls, and worlds apart (literally).

I hope you enjoy this poignant, tender, and sometimes tearful tale of love – of brotherly love, and also the love between a hero and his heroine.

Happy Reading!

Kathryn

Part One

BALTHAZAR'S INN

December 17, 1746
Calvine, Scotland

ALL HE'D DONE was open the entry door.

That was apparently enough of an invitation for someone to throw a stool at his head.

James de Lohr ducked swiftly, stumbling back out of the door and narrowly avoiding being hit by a man who came hurtling through the opening after him.

But it wasn't an attack – it was because the man had been struck in what was surely a tavern fight to end all tavern fights. He was simply flying with the momentum. James jumped out of the way as another man came flying through the door right after him.

And somewhere in the middle of the chaos, James heard a scream.

There was a woman inside Balthazar's Inn, trapped in the midst of a nasty fight. It was just past sunset on what should have been a peaceful snowy winter's eve and the fists were flying in the low-ceilinged, stuffy common room. All James could see were figures moving about, punching and kicking and grunting. As he stood at the open door, part of a table came flying at him and he deftly knocked it down.

Hell of a party, he thought wryly.

Another scream caught his attention.

This time, the noise was off to his left and, instinctively, he moved towards the sound of distress. He was a military man, an officer, and a very good one. If there was trouble, he was sworn to assist.

Even in the middle of a bar fight.

And then, he saw it.

A woman with frizzy red hair hiding behind a small table as a man grabbed at her. She was using the table like a shield, shoving it at him, forcing him to keep his distance. James grabbed the man by the hair, yanking him away from the woman. As the man stumbled back, James could see that there was a second woman cowering behind the table also.

"C-Come with me," he said over the noise.

The woman balked. "Away with ye or I'll knock the senses from ye!"

James avoided a flying piece of wood. "L-Lady, I assure you, it is only to take you to safety. O-Or do you want to stay in this midst of this tempest?"

The woman paused for an indecisive moment until a candlestick hurled through the air, hitting the wall behind her. That seemed to make her decision for her. With a reluctant nod, she came out from behind the table, pulling her companion with her.

Using his big body as a human shield, James herded the women out of the tavern. It was freezing outside, however, as the snow began to fall more heavily than before. More furniture met its demise as it slammed against the door frame and the women shrieked as wood splintered.

"I-I fear if we remain, we will be subject to more violence," James said. "W-We must find a place of safety."

The woman with the red hair grabbed the woman next to her, beckoning to him. "This way!"

James followed.

Through the slush and snow, they went around to the rear of the tavern. At one point, James slipped in the abundant mud, steadying himself against the stone structure. The tavern itself was unremarkable, squat and thick-walled, with a steeply pitched roof. With snowflakes falling in his eyes, he managed to follow the women through the rear entrance.

They ended up in the kitchen. The heat was like a slap in the face, in sharp contrast to the cold outside. James cleared his eyes, noting the big chamber and roaring hearth. It smelled like roasting meat. As he noted that the door leading into the common room had been shut and bolted, undoubtedly to keep out the insurrecting patrons, the woman with the red hair waved an arm at him.

"Come," she said. "This way."

Again, he followed. In hindsight, it wasn't the brightest thing to do, but he was cold and had come a very long way, and the last thing he wanted to do was stand out in the snow while the common room of the only tavern in town was torn apart.

Therefore, he followed the women into a sculler, and then into a connecting chamber. That chamber had a table, a couple of chairs, and a hearth that was burning low, but it was giving off enough heat to stave off the chill.

James stood in the doorway, looking around.

"W-What is this place?" he asked.

The redhead dropped to her knees in front of the fire and began to stoke it. "This is where my da and I eat," she said. "Sometimes the servants, too. It's not much, but it's warm and dry and away from the madness."

She was referring to the common room. James had two heavy saddlebags slung over his shoulder and he put them on the table.

"W-What happened out there?" he asked. "What started the battle?"

The redhead looked at him, her gaze lingering on him as if to get a good look at him. Tall, blond, and well-built, he was a vastly handsome specimen. "Ye're not from here," she finally said.

"N-Nay."

"Where are ye from, English?"

"Herefordshire."

"Ye're a long way from home."

"I-I am."

Without being invited to, he removed his heavy cloak, revealing another woolen coat beneath that. His gloves came off, as did his tricorne hat. He pulled off the woolen coat, too, hanging it on a peg along with the cloak to dry out. Left in a linen shirt and undershirt, breeches and boots, he sat down near the fire because he was chilled to the bone.

All the while, the redhead was watching him with the expression of a hunter sighting prey. They didn't often see such fine looking men this far north, so the young lord's appearance was a treat for the eyes. She was inherently curious.

Perhaps even a little interested.

"What's yer name, m'laird?" she asked.

He ran a hand through his damp hair. "D-De Lohr," he said. "J-James de Lohr."

"I'm Carrie," she said. "My da owns this place. He's the Balthazar on the sign. Are ye traveling through?"

He shook his head. "N-Nay," he said. "I-I've reached my destination. What was that fight about in the common room?"

He was shifting the subject, unwilling to speak further about himself. Carrie returned to the fire, but she would look for another opportunity to probe him.

"Who knows?" she said. "Someone says a wrong word and the fists fly. Only yesterday, the common room was torn up by a terrible tempest. It even tore up some of the other chambers, too."

James caught movement out of the corners of his eyes, turning to see the second woman in the room as she moved towards the hearth to help Carrie. She had been sitting in the shadows, perhaps stunned from their flight from the common room, and had only now regained her breath. Whatever the case, she was now on her feet.

He took a second look at this lass.

With brown hair, brown eyes, and lush lips, she was worth the second look. She wore a faded skirt that might have been a shade of green at one time, a leather girdle, and a linen blouse. She was also wearing a tattered woolen shawl, something with armholes in it so she could keep it on as she worked and not have it fall away. She was clearly poor in dress, but clean and most decidedly pretty.

Something about her had his attention.

"H-How long have you lived here, Carrie?" he asked, his gaze still on the other woman.

Carrie waved the other woman away as she tried to help, sending her for food and drink. As she left the chamber, Carrie replied.

"All my life," she said. "This tavern has been in my family since the days of my grandfather."

"T-Then you were here when the battle happened."

Her movements slowed. "What battle?"

"Culloden."

"I was here."

"Y-You must have seen the armies coming through town," he said. "B-British as well as the rebels. This road leads directly to the battlefield."

She turned to look at him. "Y-Ye're a long way from home,

m'laird," she said. "In this village, we dunna refer tae our men as rebels. Ye'd do well tae remember that."

He nodded. "P-Point taken," he said. "I-I ask for a reason, however. I will gladly pay you for information."

"What *kind* of information?"

"I-I'm looking for my brother."

Carrie stood up from the fire, brushing off her hands. "Who was yer brother?"

"H-He fought at Culloden," he said, running his hand through his hair again as he sat forward, arms resting on his knees. "H-He was killed in battle and I've come to bring him home. As I said, I'll gladly pay for any information you can provide."

Carrie's gaze lingered on him for a moment. "I see," she said quietly. "I'm sorry for ye, then. 'Twas a terrible day, it was. So many were lost."

"W-What can you tell me?" he asked, ignoring the sympathy in her tone because he didn't want a reminder about the grief he carried around like an anchor. "A-About the English dead, I mean. Do you know what happened to them?"

Her features took on a distant look but she was saved from replying when the woman with the brown eyes entered the chamber, a tray laden with food and drink in her hands. Carrie rushed to help her unburden the tray, setting everything down on the table in front of James. There was bread, butter, boiled pork, stewed turnips, and hard boiled eggs. The drink was a generous amount of ale that had a bitter taste to it.

James hardly cared. He was famished. He, too, forgot about his question as he downed half the ale before plowing into the pork. He was vaguely aware when Carrie and the other lass left him because, at the moment, it was all about stuffing his face and resting his spirit.

He'd finally made it to this horrible place.

He was going to need his strength for what was to come.

Part Two

JAMES

THREE BIG TANKARDS of the cheap ale later, and James was having trouble sitting upright.

He wasn't a big ale drinker, but he'd been forced by necessity to become one when he traveled deep into the Scottish Highlands. That was their favored drink of choice and he'd sampled a wide variety.

He sat in the little chamber in the tavern, watching the fire pop and thinking that he needed to ask for a bed but he was afraid to get up, afraid he would fall right over on his face. As he sat there, he thought he might simply lay his head on the table. It seemed as good an opportunity as any to get some much-needed rest. As he was contemplating that very thing, the chamber door opened.

Instead of Carrie or the other woman who had been serving him, a tall man in an unbleached woolen cloak entered. James didn't pay much attention to him other than to watch him for weapons. Considering the fight he'd just seen in the common room, he wasn't taking any chances. The man had a scarf around his head, which he unwound to reveal a smiling, oddly smooth face.

"May I join you?" he asked.

It was a British accent, so James figured he couldn't be too much of a threat. He nodded, motioning to the other chair. The man pulled off his cloak, his scarf, and hung both upon a peg near the hearth. Pale and slender, he sat in the chair James had indicated.

"'Tis a difficult night for man and beast," he said, holding out his hands to the fire to warm them. "I saw the common room. You are wise to be in this small chamber, away from that chaos."

James tried to nod, but it threw him off balance. "I-I walked into the chaos when I arrived."

The stranger grinned. "It looks as if the entire room has been up-ended."

"T-The ruffians were on the loose."

The stranger noted the remains of the meal before looking to James. "My name is Rafe," he said. "And you are far from home, my lord."

James glanced at him. "H-How would you know that?"

Rafe's smile broadened. "You don't speak like a Scotsman," he said. "Where are you from?"

James sighed heavily. "A-A million miles away."

"English?"

"Aye."

"You are *very* far from home," Rafe said. "Are you simply traveling to see the glories of Scotland in winter?"

James shook his head and nearly teetered off his chair. "N-Nay," he said, grabbing the table to steady himself. "I-I've come looking for someone."

"It must be important."

"I-It is."

"Can I possibly help?"

James was drunk. That was established. Unfortunately, drink had a tendency to loosen his tongue and he didn't stop to think that the man was asking a lot of questions, questions he was quite happily and freely answering. He was speaking to the man as if he had known him, and trusted him, all his life.

"N-Not unless you can bring back the dead," he said quietly.

"I see," Rafe said. "Then I am sorry for you. May I ask who has died so that I might say a prayer?"

The chamber door creaked open and the brown-haired lass appeared, again bringing more food and drink. James assumed it was for Rafe. As she sat it on the table, James leaned back in his chair and nearly fell over. Frustrated, he grabbed at the table again to steady himself.

"I-I have come to find my brother," he said. "B-Before you ask, he perished on the Culloden moor back in April of this year and my mother has not stopped weeping. I promised the woman I would find him and bring him home, and that is what I intend to do. His name is Johnathan should you care to name him in your prayers, but it will not do any good. He was not a pious man."

As the brown-eyed woman began to slowly clean up the remnants of James' meal, listening to the conversation, Rafe was focused on his inebriated tablemate.

"I am very sorry for you," he said with soft sincerity. "It is a sad mission that you are on, then. I'm sure your mother appreciates that you are a good son."

James sighed faintly, chewing on his lip because it was a bad habit of his. When he was frustrated or weary, or both, he tended to chew. His gaze was on the fire but his mind was on the brother he'd lost.

So long ago…

"A-A good son," he muttered. Then, he snorted bitterly. "I-If you must know, I am a terrible son. I was supposed to go with him, you know. My brother, I mean. To Culloden."

"Why didn't you?"

His expression was filled with regret, with irony. "I-I had been struck down by a fever," he said. "I-I could not leave my bed, so he left without me. Like a weakling, I stayed at home while he went north with the Lancaster Foot Regiment. A friend of his returned during the summer to tell us that he had been lost. And do you know *how* it happened? My heroic, foolish brother stepped in to help a failing regiment. They had lost their officers, so he went to help them. It cost him his life, the idiot. And he left me with a burden that is impossible to bear."

Rafe was listening with sorrow. "I am certain he did not do it purposely, whatever it is."

James smacked the table, pointing a finger at him. "T-That is where you are wrong," he said. "H-He never wanted the duties that were expected of him, the burdens that the title would bring him. Did I mention that? He was the Earl of Worcester and hated the trappings. And that's why he hated me."

Rafe frowned. "Hated you? I do not believe one brother would hate another so."

James drunkenly waved him off. "T-That is where you would be wrong again," he said. "H-He hated me because I had freedom he did not. He hated me because I would never know the weight of what he had inherited. But I *do* know because those burdens are now mine. I believe he charged into that battle a-purpose simply to push those burdens onto me."

Rafe had gotten more than he bargained for when he'd asked to share a young lord's table. As he looked at the man, his expression was almost… gentle.

"What is your name?" he asked quietly.

James sighed heavily after his tirade and turned back to the fire. "J-James de Lohr, Earl of Worcester, Viscount Leominster, Warden of the South Marches, Lord Pembridge and Marston," he muttered. "A-As you have noticed, I have a catch in my speech that is unworthy of such a position, as it has been suggested to me. School masters tried to beat it out of me, but it didn't work. When Johnathan and I were young, he would tell me that I sounded like a Billy goat, which would only make it worse and when we would argue, which was frequent, I had to write him notes and letters because he would have me so flustered that I could not speak at all."

Rafe dipped his head in a sign of respect. "My lord," he said. "It is an honor to meet you. As for your brother… sometimes, brothers fight, but the fact that you are here to find his body and bring him home proves that you love him. As I said, you are a good son. And a good brother."

James averted his gaze. "I-I have come because my mother asked it of me," he said. "T-There is no other reason. Even if I cannot find Johnathan's body, I must search for something he had on his person when he came here. Something valuable to my family."

Rafe regarded him for a moment. "If he had something valuable on his person, more than likely, it was stripped of him," he said quietly. "You are a soldier and you know this to be true. Bodies in battle are stripped."

For the first time, James showed a measure of pain in his expression, but he didn't answer. He knew that very unpleasant fact, even if he couldn't speak of it openly. To speak of it would make it real, and as much as he shared a dysfunctional relationship with his brother, he couldn't stand the thought of the man being unceremoniously stripped of his possessions, his dignity…

Everything.

"I-I know," he said, closing his eyes for a brief moment as if to ward off the mere thought. "M-My hope is that Johnathan was removed from the field of battle before the scavengers came. Perhaps there is a chance that the family heirloom is still on his body, though I know there is a good chance it is not."

"What are you looking for?"

"A-A ring."

Rafe lifted his eyebrows as if expecting more of an answer. "Just a ring?" he said. "A signet?"

But James shook his head. "N-Not *any* ring," he said. "A-A family heirloom, passed down from earl to earl. A ring with the head of a lion that has been etched into the purest gold, with rubies set into the ocular cavities as if the blood spilled by the apex predator reflected in its very eyes. At least, that is how the ring is always described, even in old family documents. The lion's head of the House of de Lohr is our mark of excellence. It is a privilege to wear it and, as the earl, it is my right. That is what I am looking for."

Rafe nodded faintly. "Then I wish you well, my lord," he said. "But what if you do not find it?"

James averted his gaze, agonizing over that very possibility. But something moved in the shadows and he looked over, realizing the serving wench with the pretty brown eyes had been in the chamber the entire time. She had cleaned up the meal, but she had never left.

She had heard everything.

Not that he cared. He'd never see her again after this night.

"Y-You, there," he said, avoiding Rafe's question. "I-I need a chamber. I will pay handsomely for the privilege."

The woman came into the light, her big eyes looking at him rather fearfully. "I will speak with Carrie, m'laird," she said. "I think that all the beds are taken, but I shall ask."

James' half-lidded gaze looked her over, the pretty brown-eyed woman who had caught his eye before. "I-I took you from the common room when there was fighting," he said. "Y-You've been like a wraith, moving in and out of this chamber. What is your name?"

"Gaira, m'laird."

"G-Gaira, if you will bring me some blankets, I can sleep right here on this floor."

The woman dashed from the chamber and James turned to Rafe, reaching out to take the last of the man's ale. In fact, Rafe hadn't touched any of the food brought, so James shoved a piece of bread into his mouth.

"W-We shall sleep this night," he said, chewing the bread. "Y-You have asked me of my purpose in this unpleasant little inn, but what is yours? All I have done is speak of myself to no good end."

Rafe didn't seem to mind that James had sucked down the last of his ale. "I am here only for the night, too," he said, avoiding the question for the most part. "I am a healer, my lord. That is my gift and my vocation."

James looked at him with interest. "H-Healer, eh?" he said. "A-A physician? A noble profession. But you are too late for all of those gallant lads at Culloden. They could have used you months ago. My brother could have used you months ago. A bayonet to the neck, I was told. Only there is no recovering from that."

Gaira returned to the chamber with Carrie in tow, both of them carrying blankets and pillows. James' drunken chatter ceased at that moment as the women arranged a pallet for him in the corner, next to the hearth. They didn't bring anything for Rafe and when James started to say something about it, the man waved him off and James let the subject drop. If Rafe didn't want a bed, so be it.

Truthfully, James didn't mind sleeping on the floor. He'd slept on worse. He was grateful for the blankets and the fire, and for the company of a rather silent man named Rafe. He'd spoken more of his brother to Rafe than he had spoken to anyone in a very long time and there was something decidedly cathartic about it. But there was also something undeniably depressing, like a stench of tumultuous brotherhood he simply couldn't shake.

A brother he'd not parted on the best of terms with.

He slept.

Part Three

GAIRA

THERE WAS SOMETHING in her face that suggested… shock.

Surprise?

Astonishment?

Rafe saw it in Gaira's face as she'd listened to James drunkenly spout his tale of woe with regard to his relationship with his brother. James had been oblivious to the fact that Gaira had been trying not to be obvious as she listened to him.

But Rafe was aware.

When James finally fell into an inebriated stupor, Rafe left the chamber in search of the eavesdropping young servant.

Something in her features suggested that she might have known something.

The kitchen was mostly dark at this hour, the only light coming from the wide-mouth hearth that was spitting smoke into the room. As Rafe entered, he spied a big man with a cap on his head bent over a table. Rafe could see that the man was counting money, more than likely the receipts of the day. Rafe moved silently, as he always did, until the man caught movement out of the corners of his eyes and looked up.

"Where did ye come from?" he asked, a mouthful of bad teeth reflecting in the firelight. "I dinna hear ye enter."

Rafe smiled politely. "I did not mean to startle you," he said. "Are you the proprietor?"

The man nodded. "I am Balthazar," he said. "What can I do for ye?"

Rafe looked around the big kitchen to see if there was anyone else in the room that he had missed. "I'm looking for a woman," he said. "She brought food and drink. She also brought…"

Balthazar cut him off. "Oh, *her*," he said. "That's my daughter, Carrie. She's a good lass even if she is a wee bit talkative. Did she tell ye that she's looking for a man tae take her tae London? If she did, then just know I willna let her go. She's been looking for a man tae take her away since she sprouted tits. Eh… I probably shouldna have said that, but ye get my meaning. Ye canna have her."

Rafe was looking at him with a bemused and slightly horrified expression. "I have not had any conversation at length with her," he said hesitantly. "There was another lass with her. Brown-eyed and pretty."

"Ah," Balthazar said knowingly. "That's Gaira. She's a good lass. She's not giddy like Carrie can be. She's got a good head on her shoulders, that one. If ye think she looks different from the rest of the rabble here, she is."

"What do you mean?"

Balthazar leaned back in his chair. "From nobility," he said. "Comes from a family of *mormaer*."

"Rulers?"

"Earldom," Balthazar said. "Her grandfather was the Earl of Forth until the family fell out of favor and their lands taken. Gaira lives with her mother in a home on the edge of town. No menfolk, no armies. Just Gaira and her mother, who cleans chambers for me, although the woman is going tae need more help given the state of my establishment. It looks like we had our very own battle out there in the common room."

Rafe nodded. "I saw," he said. "And that happened only today?"

Balthazar shook his head. "Nay," he said, dragging out the word. "Yesterday we had a war out there. Tore up the room and other chambers as well. We just started picking up the pieces until this happened today. I think I might leave it alone for a few days. Surely someone else is going tae come and try tae tear it up again."

"Why would you say that?"

Balthazar sighed wearily. "'Tis the season for peace and madness," he said. "It seems tae bring out the best and the worst in people. But this year, 'tis particularly bad."

Rafe smiled faintly. "Because it is the first holiday season after the battle at Culloden," he said. "I cannot imagine that those who experienced the battle as you did are finding much peace this season."

Balthazar shook his head, sobering drastically. He suddenly appeared quite weary, as the mere memory was sucking everything out of him.

"It would take a few lifetimes tae overcome what we saw," he said. "We nursed wounded, at least those who could make it here from the field of battle. By the time they reached us, some couldna be helped. Carrie even went tae the battlefield tae look for more wounded, but there were none left. So she collected what possessions she could find and brought them back here so the scavengers wouldna get them. People heard that she was collecting things and some brought her what they'd found."

He trailed off, sadness in his tone, but Rafe was listening intently. "What did you do with all of it?" he asked.

Balthazar lifted a hand in the general direction of the rest of the tavern. "Put it away," he said. "We have a whole chamber full of things from the battle. Someone tried tae destroy it, the same people who ruined the common room yesterday, but the chamber still stands. It still has things from the dead and as long as there is breath in my body, it'll go untouched. Carrie calls it the Chamber of Sorrows. That's what it is, ye know… a place full of sorrow. But it's also a shrine tae the brave dead."

Rafe turned his attention in the direction the old man had indicated. *Chamber of Sorrows*, he thought. A memorial to the dead of Culloden, preserved by an old tavernkeep and his daughter. Rafe thought that perhaps his new friend, James, might find something of his brother there, something from the man that had him so tormented.

But first, he had a woman to see.

"That was kind of you," he said. "Gathering possessions that were important to someone, once. I should like to see them sometime if Carrie will show me, but Gaira… I wish to speak with her. Can you tell me where she is?"

Balthazar allowed himself to reflect on the horrors of Culloden's aftermath for a moment longer before shaking himself, returning his focus to the question at hand.

"She's gone home for the night," he said. "But she just left. If ye hurry, ye might catch her. Her mother's home is down the main road, at the end of town. Ye'll see a two-storied, stone house with a walled yard. 'Tis where Gaira lives."

Rafe thanked him swiftly and dashed out into the night.

The snow was falling lightly and it wasn't difficult to see. Cottages along the avenue were lit from inside, just enough light to see by as Rafe made his way down the avenue, hoping to catch Gaira before she entered her mother's home. But he had a feeling the conversation with Balthazar had cost him time.

Still, it was important he speak with her.

The house Balthazar described came up quickly. There was, indeed, a walled yard, but the wall wasn't any taller than a man's chest. He could see the two-storied home, simple and modest, and faint light emitted from a window on the ground floor. Entering the walled yard, and hoping there weren't dogs to chase him off, he went to the heavily fortified entry door and rapped firmly upon it.

He could hear voices inside. Women's voices.

He rapped again.

"I've come seeking Gaira," he said loudly, hoping they could hear him. "I have no weapons and I mean you no harm. I've come from Balthazar's. He told me where to find Gaira."

More voices. After a moment, someone threw a bolt and the door creaked open. In the dim light beyond, he could see Gaira's suspicious face. Once she got a look at him, however, recognition dawned.

"I know ye," she said, opening the door a little wider. "I served ye food and drink."

Rafe nodded. "You did," he said. "May I come in, please? I'll only stay a moment. I promise that I've not come to harm you. You can see that I have no weapons."

He opened his cloak to show her that he had nothing visible. Gaira inspected him before glancing over her shoulder at something Rafe couldn't see. After a moment, she returned her attention to Rafe and opened the door wider. As he stepped into the warm and stuffy chamber, he could see a woman in the corner with a big ax. Clearly, she was ready to use it if he made the wrong move.

"Thank you for seeing me," he said, keeping his focus on Gaira and not the woman ready to split his skull. "I am not sure how to start this conversation, so I will simply come out with it. You were in the chamber when Worcester was speaking of finding his brother, an officer who perished at Culloden."

Gaira was listening closely but cautiously. "Aye," she said. "I was there."

"You heard the entire conversation."

Gaira wasn't quite sure what he meant. "I heard him speaking," she said. "I dunna know if it was everything he spoke of."

Rafe paused, trying to determine the best way to direct the conversation and not upset her in the process. "As he was speaking, I could see your face," he said. "It seemed to me that Culloden has affected you also. Was I wrong?"

Gaira looked at him for a moment, growing uneasy. "It affected all of us, m'laird," she said. "The battle was a great tragedy."

Rafe could see from the look on her face that he'd hit a nerve. "Balthazar told me about Carrie's Chamber of Sorrow," he said. "He told me that she collected many things from the battle and put them there for safe keeping."

Gaira nodded, averting her gaze as if suddenly unable to look him in the eyes. "I… I know," she said. "I've been in the chamber, many a time."

"Then you know what is in there?"

She nodded.

He hesitated. "Gaira, forgive me for asking, but have you seen something from Worcester?" he asked, almost gently. "I know you heard Worcester speak of his brother, and it occurred to me that you might have seen something from the English. Perhaps something… belonging to his brother?"

Gaira began to blink rapidly, as if blinking away tears. "I… I dunna know…" she stammered. "There are a great many things in that chamber. Men have been bringing them since the battle ended because they've heard of Carrie's treasures. There are many things there."

"Some from the English?"

"The English were at the battle."

"They were," he agreed. "Only fifty Englishmen lost their lives. Surely something of theirs ended up in that chamber."

"Why should ye ask me? Ask Carrie."

She was growing agitated and he realized he was going to lose her because the woman with the ax was about to chase him out. But he made one last plea.

"Imagine if you were searching for your brother, Gaira," he said, making sure he was close to the door should that ax come hurling at him. "If you know something about Worcester's brother, it would be the merciful thing to tell him. This is the season of our Lord, after all. It is the time when Christ was born and angels walked the earth. If you know something, give Worcester that gift. Help him find some peace. He needs you."

That was about all Rafe could say because the old woman with the ax had moved out of the shadows and was coming for him. He quickly opened the door and bolted out into the gently falling snow, slamming the door in his wake.

When he was gone, the old woman with the ax threw the bolt on the door before turning to Gaira.

"*Sassenach*," she muttered with distaste. "He's brave coming here tae ask such questions."

Gaira was struggling to compose herself, struggling not to appear too unnerved to her mother, who could be a hard woman at times. She simply wouldn't understand what was in the tender heart of her daughter.

She never had.

"There's a man at the inn who has come tae look for his brother," she said, realizing her voice was trembling. "His brother was killed there."

"English?"

"Aye."

"Then it was God's will," the old woman said. "Send him tae the church in Inverness. 'Tis where they buried them."

Gaira simply nodded. As her mother went to put the ax away, Gaira headed up to her chamber, up the small, spiral stairs and into a room that was dark but for the soft glow of the hearth.

Shutting the door, Gaira stoked the fire to bring a little more light and heat into the chamber before she went to a wardrobe against the wall. Pulling open the sticky door, there were neat rows of clothing folded inside, with still other clothing hanging on pegs on the door and inside the cabinet. It looked like any other wardrobe.

But this one was different.

It was one of the few things passed down by her ancestors, something salvaged from the Earl of Forth's properties and brought to this tiny village on the outskirts of Inverness. This particular wardrobe had a false bottom to store valuables in secret and Gaira opened the trap door that exposed the contents of the secret compartment.

There was only one thing there.

Carefully, Gaira pulled out a tattered, stained haversack. But it wasn't just any haversack – it was one she'd found in Carrie's Chamber of Sorrow, back in the early days when Carrie was still accumulating her collection.

Gaira had been there when the chamber started to gather shields and sabers and the memories of the lost. This particular haversack had come from a local tradesman who'd gone looking for metal to salvage. He'd brought it to Carrie, trading it for some drink and a meal. Carrie went through it for anything valuable before putting it aside with the other haversacks from the nameless, faceless dead. That was when Gaira had found interest in this particular haversack.

It contained letters.

Gaira could read. Her mother had taught her how and she found more interest in the letters of the dead than in their actual possessions. Several of the haversacks contained letters, and she'd read all of them, but this haversack had been different.

Through those carefully scripted letters, a story unfolded.

It was the story of two brothers.

Carefully, she unbuttoned the three brass buttons holding the haversack closed and opened the flap. Inside were bundles of letters wrapped in hemp twine and she pulled out a bundle to look at it.

Fidelis Semper.

Ever Faithful.

It was the motto of the House of de Lohr.

Gaira could hardly believe the man who had written these very letters had come looking for them. Or, more correctly, looking for the man for whom the letters were intended. She hadn't thought much of the British visitor to the inn until he started talking about his missing brother. She listened more carefully. And then, the name…

De Lohr.

Gaira sank to her buttocks, sitting on the floor with the letters clutched to her breast. She had read every single letter, more than once. Something about them spoke to her in a way she couldn't fully grasp and she had stolen the haversack, keeping it hidden away in her chamber. Carrie didn't even know it was missing because she'd taken anything of value out of the haversack and put it aside, but these letters… they were the *only* thing of value as far as Gaira was concerned.

From the words on the yellowed paper, she'd come to know James de Lohr. There were letters written by James when he was a young lad, all the way until most recently before Johnathan went to war. The earlier letters were from a sensitive, somewhat spoiled young boy, upset with the way his brother had spoken to him or made demands of him. It was usually the same thing, fighting over the way Johnathan had behaved or making mention of a speech impediment.

Gaira had heard that for herself.

But that sensitive, somewhat spoiled young boy had grown into a young man who was still quite sensitive and quite brilliant. He had a gift for words, for writing, and she came to understand that it was because he was self-conscious about speaking. It was easier for him to write than it was for him to speak. But the beauty in his words was something that had endeared her to him.

A man she had fallen for, sight unseen.

But he was here now, a faceless fantasy now come to life.

She could still hardly believe it.

But having heard James speak, she realized there was so much more he didn't know about his brother.

Could she tell him? *Would* she tell him?

Give Worcester that gift. Help him find some peace.

Gaira wondered if she was brave enough to.

Part Four

CARRIE

JAMES AWOKE TO Carrie looking down at him.

Startled, he blinked and instinctively pulled back, bumping his head on the stone wall. Surprised that he had awoken, Carrie jumped back as well.

"I'm sorry, m'laird," she gasped. "Did ye hurt yer head?"

Hand to his head, James frowned as he labored to sit up. "N-No more than it already is," he grumbled, wincing. "W-What are you doing here?"

Carrie's big, green eyes looked at him with concerned. "I came tae see if ye were dead."

"D-Dead?"

"Because ye slept so long. 'Tis midday."

James' eyebrows lifted and he ended up leaning against the wall, rubbing the bump on his head.

"M-Midday, you say?"

"Aye."

He sighed heavily. "I-I'm not dead," he said. "B-But the way my head is throbbing, I surely wish I was."

Carrie retrieved a cup from the table. "Drink this," she said. "It'll help."

He took it, smelled it, and immediately yanked it away from his nose. "B-Bleeding Christ," he muttered. "W-What is that?"

Carrie pushed the cup back towards his mouth. "It'll cure ye," she said. "Drink it quickly. Dunna stop tae taste it; just drink."

James didn't have much choice. She was heavily pushing the cup on him, whatever it was, so he pounded it back like a shot, all in one swallow. But the second the taste hit him, the contents nearly came back up again.

"G-God," he moaned, shoving the cup at her. "What in the hell was in that?"

Carrie set the cup aside, a smile playing on her lips. "Vinegar and eggs."

"*W-What*?"

She nodded. "Vinegar mixed with raw eggs," she said. "It'll cure the pain in yer head. Our customers swear by it."

"O-Or swear *at* it," James mumbled. He wiped at his mouth as if to wipe away the taste and took a deep breath. "W-What does the day look like?"

Carrie went to the only window in the chamber, which was covered with heavy shutters. Unbolting one of them, she pried it open, letting the icy air into the stuffy, smelly chamber.

"More snow from last night, but the sky is clear," she said. Then, she turned to look at him. "So yer brother was at the battle at Culloden, was he?"

He was rubbing his stiff neck at this point, but he glanced at her. "W-Who told you that?"

"Ye did," she said.

"I-I did not."

"Aye, ye did. Do ye not remember?"

Truth be told, James didn't remember a whole lot from last night, but he knew that when he drank, he became rather chatty. He'd give away the secret to the family jewels if he was drunk enough, something his brother often scolded him for. One thing he did remember, however, was the man he'd spoken with the night before and he couldn't help but notice that the man wasn't in the chamber. He seemed to be quite alone this morning but for Carrie.

"A-Aye," he said after a moment. "I suppose I remember."

"And ye asked me what happened tae the dead."

He stopped rubbing his neck. "D-Do you know?"

She nodded. "Mostly," she said. "We're on the road that leads tae the battlefield, ye know. It's two or three days tae the north, but still close enough. Information travels quickly on this road."

"I-I know." When she didn't offer up anything more, he sat forward. "C-Carrie, if you will tell me what you know, I'll make it worth your while. I did not come expecting information for free."

She shook her head. "'Tis not that," she said. "But… many of our lads died there."

"My brother died there."

"Ye dinna come tae dig up the ground, did ye? Because if ye did, I'll not tell ye anything."

James leaned back against the wall, running his fingers through his hair. It was longer, and being that he was blond, people said he had the de Lohr "lion" look. His brother had the look even greater than he did, for Johnathan had the blond mane and the firm jaw. James had more of a refined look, while Johnathan had the look of something that needed to be tamed.

It was a countenance that had ladies eating out of his hand.

James had never quite mastered that.

"I-I swear to you that I do not intend to go digging up the field of battle," he said sincerely. "A-All I want is to find out what I can about my brother's final resting place. He was with the English and I'm assuming they weren't left on the field of battle to rot. That battlefield is sacred Scots ground and they wouldn't leave the English there. A-Am I correct in that assumption?"

Carrie nodded reluctantly. "T-They took the English tae the church in Inverness," she said. "At least, that's what I was told. But… but I may be able tae help ye before ye go all the way tae Inverness. I have something that I want ye tae see."

She stood up from the chair and James bolted to his feet, probably faster than he should have. The world rocked a bit as he regained his equilibrium. There were two doors in the dingy little chamber – one that opened into the scullery and a second door near the hearth. It was through this door that he followed Carrie, into another dingy chamber with two small beds and a wardrobe that took up most of one wall.

As James watched, Carrie went to one side of the wardrobe and shoved. The furniture apparently wasn't as heavy as it looked because it slid easily across the wooden floor. It was then that James realized the wardrobe was covering yet another door, now partially revealed. Carrie lit a lamp on a nearby table and picked it up.

"Come," she said.

There was an element of mystery as James followed her into the room behind the wardrobe. As Carrie held up the lamp to light the small, dark chamber, his eyes widened.

It was a treasure trove revealed.

Shields, spurs, broken blades, parts of muskets, whole muskets, pistols, coats, ruck sacks, and so much more. The chamber was low-ceilinged, with rough stone walls and the old dirt floor, but it was literally packed to the ceiling with things belonging to men.

To an army.

Armies.

James looked at her in shock.

"W-What *is* this place?" he whispered, awed.

Carrie looked around the chamber. "It belongs tae me," she said softly. "I keep these things safe."

James' sense of astonishment grew. He could see the standards – Wolfe, Barrel, Fleming, Sackville – all of them battalions who had fought at Culloden. There were shoes on the floor, neatly lined up, and on a chest sat a stack of sabers. In the corner, a pile of whole and broken targes caught his attention. Some of them had bloodstains, some of them damaged from the musket ball and cannon fire.

Then, there were the flags.

A Saltire lay torn, with holes in it, and on top of that was a British flag that was equally damaged. James stared at the flags, one atop the other, and the shock he experienced transformed into something horrifying. Although he hadn't been at the battle, he was experiencing it through the eyes of the remains.

The smashed, stained remains that still echoed the sickening sound of battle.

He could hear it.

"O-Oh… God," he muttered. "You went to the battlefield and you scavenged all of this, didn't you?"

Carrie was standing inside the chamber, lamp held high. "Nay," she said firmly. "Not scavenge. Some of these things I brought from the battlefield, but other things I was given. They were brought here for safekeeping. I'm protecting them."

James didn't say anything. He had caught sight of the haversacks and he went to them, a dozen or more piled up. Kneeling down, he picked up the first one and peered into it, poking around.

Carrie came up behind him with the lamp.

"As ye can see, their money is still there, if there was any," she said.

"I dinna take their money, but I put any valuables away for safekeeping. I thought that, someday, their kin would come looking for them, so I took these before the scavengers could get tae them. I brought ye here so ye could look through all of this, tae see if there is something of yer brother."

James was on one knee in front of the pile of haversacks. As he looked at them, a lone tear popped from his right eye, falling into the ground. The haversacks were stained with blood, most were badly damaged. He was feeling the concussion of the cannon fire and hearing the wail of the musket balls as they flew over his head. If he closed his eyes, he could feel, and hear, everything. He was in the throes of a battle he'd not attended, but his brother had.

Johnathan had been in the middle of it.

Silently, he moved about the chamber, looking for anything that might have belonged to his brother.

"I've lived in the Highlands all my life," Carrie said, oblivious to his inner turmoil. "I see more of people from all over because of the tavern and I talk tae them. I always thought I understood a great deal, but this battle… I dunna understand it."

James was preoccupied with his hunt. "W-What don't you understand?"

Carrie watched him rifle through a pile of belts and other leather goods. "The British," she said. "They came here tae destroy our lads once and for all. Men like yer brother… why did they have tae come? I dunna understand the needs of war."

James paused. "T-The needs of war," he repeated the words softly. "T-That is a very good question. My family has been fighting for the King of England since Richard the Lionheart held the throne. He's the one who went to The Holy Land and fought against the savages there. His need was to bring Christianity to those men. Every war has a need."

"But what was this need?"

"T-To put down the Pretender, of course."

"And ye believe he's the Pretender? Or do the English fight because they're told tae, not because they believe in the cause?"

James scratched his head. It was an astute question, one without an easy answer. "I-I cannot speak for others, but I fight because that is what I am trained for," he said quietly. "M-My brother and I come from a long line of soldiers. We fight for our king. It is as simple as that."

"Then yer heart isna in it?"

"M-My heart is never in war. I-I don't think my brother's was, either, which makes his death all the more tragic."

Carrie pondered that. "I suppose I want tae know what is in the hearts of men who would come tae Scotland and kill our lads."

"I-It was duty, Carrie. N-Nothing more."

Carrie fell silent after that. As she continued to follow him about, trying to be helpful by holding the lamp, James dug through piles of bloodied and dirty possessions. There was a neat pile of redcoats, torn and filthy, but nothing that belonged to his brother. In fact, he didn't see anything familiar until he returned to the pile of sabers that was by the chamber door. They were on a chest and leaning against the wall, some upside-down, and he took a moment to look through them more carefully.

And then, he saw it.

It was upside-down, and partially covered with another saber, but he recognized it right away. The gorgeous hilt and shield-shaped langet, for inside the langet was a lion's head.

De Lohr.

With a gasp, James pulled his brother's sword forth, staring at it for a moment before feeling tears sting his eyes. The physical and emotional reaction was both unexpected and swift, and he clutched the saber to him as the tears silently fell.

It was something of his brother's he'd not expected to find.

"C-Christ," he gasped. "I-It's my brother's sword. It's Johnathan's. Where did you find it?"

Carrie was trying to get a look at it. "I dunna know," she said. "I found some myself, but others were brought tae me. I dunna know where that one came from."

James didn't press her. He held it up, looking at it, inspecting it with shaking hands before once again clutching the hilt to his chest. He was overcome with grief.

"W-Were you holding this when you died, Johnny?" he whispered tightly. "D-Did you really face all of this alone, without me by your side?"

There were no answers to his questions, only the soft darkness of a chamber that was closing in around him. The ghosts of the men who had owned these possessions were coming forth, looking upon him in judgment because he hadn't been at Culloden and he should have been.

God only knew, James had judged himself just as harshly.

"I-I'm sorry, Johnny," he murmured, closing his eyes as tears streamed. "I-I'm sorry I was not there to hold your hand, to lie to you and tell you that you would survive. I'm sorry that my voice, pitiful as it is, was not the last voice you heard in this lifetime, nor my face the last thing you saw. I'm sorry I failed you when you needed me most. God forgive me, I have done nothing but fail you since the day I was born. B-But I have come to take you home and I swear to God I will not leave without you. I will *not* fail you this time."

It was a deeply painful moment as James struggled with his composure. Behind him, he could hear sniffling and he turned to see Carrie weeping into her dirty handkerchief. It was then he realized that this woman, this stranger, had been witness to his most private pain. She'd gathered these souvenirs of war and now she was seeing a reaction to her cultivated collection.

She was seeing the human side of it.

Feeling foolish with his outburst, James wiped his face, clutching the sword so tightly that his knuckles had turned white.

He took a deep breath.

"I-Inverness, you said?" he asked Carrie. "T-That is where the English are buried?"

Carrie nodded, wiping her nose. "Aye," she said. "The Old High Church. They took some of the wounded, too, I heard. Perhaps ye'll find something more of yer brother there."

James looked at the sword in his hand. "I-I have found this," he said. "Y-You cannot know what this means to me. That you took it and did not let the scavengers get to it… I can never thank you enough."

Carrie forced a tremulous smile. "I'm glad ye found it, m'laird."

James was feeling weary, emotional. "A-As am I," he said. "I-It means everything to me and to my mother. But there is something else I seek, something I am sure you have not seen, but I'll ask anyway. A ring with a lion's head – have you seen it?"

Carrie shook her head. "Nay," she said. "If I had, I would tell ye."

"I-It is very valuable."

"I dinna collect these things for profit. I did it because it was the right thing tae do."

He lifted his eyebrows wearily. "F-Forgive me if I've offended you," he said. "A-As I said, I was certain you had not seen it, but I had to ask."

With that, he turned away, clutching his brother's sword in his left hand and moving like a man who was overwhelmed with life. His brother's saber had been found, but that was not where he would stop. Finding the weapon renewed his determination.

Inverness was his next destination.

Part Five

GAIRA

SHE SAW HIM in the snowy livery yard, baggage in hand. He also had a saber with him, something she didn't remember seeing on him when he arrived.

He was leaving.

Gaira stood at the kitchen door as it opened out into the muddy kitchen yard, seeing a portion of the livery from where she stood. She had come to the tavern at her usual time that morning, but James had still been asleep until Carrie went to go wake him a little while ago. Gaira had been busy in the kitchen, but her mind had been on Carrie and James. Truthfully, *only* on James.

Then, she saw him make his way to the livery.

Give Worcester that gift. Help him find some peace.

Those words had been ringing around in her head all night. She had no idea what happened to the tall, pale man who had come to her home to speak to her of the handsome young earl, but he'd departed and now Worcester was leaving as well. If he left, she might never see him again.

He would never know what she knew.

She knew, deep in her heart, that she couldn't let him leave.

Taking a deep breath, she pulled off her apron and left it behind as she ran across the kitchen yard. Since her home wasn't far, it took her little time to cross the muddy road and into the walled yard. The door to the home was unlocked even though her mother wasn't at home, so Gaira hastened to her bedchamber to retrieve the haversack from its secret place.

Even as she held it, her hands were trembling. The contents of the haversack had been her guilty pleasure, and even a large part of her world, for the last several months. Ever since she'd stolen it from Carrie and kept it hidden so she could bask in those letters over and over again. Letters from a sensitive and tormented young man to his equally sensitive and tormented brother.

So much about Johnathan had been different.

So much about James had been deep.

They simply couldn't find a way to connect.

But James had come for his brother and it wasn't fair for her to keep the letters any longer. She never really thought this moment would come, and she was going to have to explain to him why she had kept them this long, but she would have to face him with what she'd done. Knowing James as she did through his beautiful letters, she felt as if she knew him well. It was strange knowing a man well she'd never actually met.

Until now.

Those letters didn't belong to her, after all.

They belonged to a beleaguered young earl.

Clutching the haversack to her chest, she wrapped herself back up in her simple shawl, one that wasn't nearly enough against the icy temperatures, and ran back across the road and into the livery.

As she entered the yard, she saw James standing just outside of the stable as the groom prepared his mount. It was a long-legged bay thoroughbred, a beautiful and expensive animal. The groom led the animal over to the trough to water the steed while he finished with the tack, leaving James standing by himself.

Gaira's stomach was twisting with nerves as she came up behind him, studying his broad back and wide shoulders. It was the James from the letters, a sweet and angsty young man who was better in the flesh than she could have ever imagined.

"M'laird?" she said, a little breathlessly.

He turned to her and Gaira took a good, long look at his face in the sunlight. Blond, well-built, and excruciatingly handsome, he was quite the perfect young lord.

His sky-blue eyes fixed expectantly on her.

"W-What is it?" he asked.

Her heart began to flutter. "I… I heard ye speaking tae yer companion last night," she said, stepping into the livery. It was quieter in there, out of the elements. "Ye came seeking yer brother."

James' focus had followed her as she'd walked around him and entered the stable. But with the mention of last night's legendary conversation, he grunted and rolled his eyes.

"I-It seems that everyone in this wretched place knows about that now," he said. "D-Don't worry, I'm leaving. It seems that Inverness may hold more answers for me."

Gaira could see how weary he was.

But she was about to change that.

"Perhaps ye'll find yer brother's body there," she said. "But I have his heart here."

With that, she unwounded her shawl to reveal the haversack clutched to her chest. James wasn't certain what he was looking at, at first, but when she held it up to him and he recognized it, all of the color drained from his face. His mouth popped open and something of a groan escaped.

"M-My God," he said hoarsely. "I-It's his haversack. This is my brother's haversack."

Gaira nodded, carefully depositing it into his trembling hands. "It is," she said. "Last night, when I heard ye speak about yer brother, I was certain that this belonged tae ye. Ye see, I've had it for a long while and I… well, I have much tae say about it before ye go. Would ye give me a moment of yer time, m'laird?"

James was unbuttoning the haversack with shaking hands. In fact, he could hardly get it open, but he wasn't so singularly focused that he didn't hear Gaira's soft plea. He nodded so vigorously that his hair wagged about.

"O-Of course," he said, reaching out to grasp her by the arm. "C-Come and tell me everything you know. What is your name again?"

"Gaira, m'laird," she said. "Gaira Dunmore."

"G-Gaira," he repeated, clutching the haversack as he led her away from the livery entry and into a quiet area near the stalls. "I-I remember you. I helped you and Carrie escape the battle in the common room yesterday."

Gaira nodded. "Ye did," she said. "I'm sorry I dinna thank ye for it yet. There's not been the opportunity."

"I-I know," James said. Then, he dropped to one knee and set the haversack down on a pile of clean hay so he could poke around in it. "C-Christ, I can hardly believe you found this. Did you know my brother, then? How did you come by it?"

Gaira watched him pull out a stack of carefully-tied letters. James' question was one with a complicated answer. She was afraid if she didn't tell him everything, and tell him quickly, that she would lose him to the excitement and relief of finding his brother's haversack. He might even chase her away so he could be alone with his brother's memories. Already, she could see that he was distracted with it.

Taking a deep breath, she summoned her courage.

"The haversack was brought tae Carrie by a man who was scavenging the battlefield for metal," she said steadily. "Carrie put it in her chamber with all of the other things she had collected, and as I had done with others, I looked through them. Only this haversack was different. Ye asked me if I knew yer brother, m'laird, and the answer is that I do. I know ye, too. Did ye know he kept the letters ye wrote tae him since the time ye were a young lad until recently?"

James' hands were still trembling, but his initial shock was being overtaking by some confusion. *Bewilderment.* He fingered through the stack in his hand only to realize something.

"B-But… but some of these are very old," he said, peering at one. "M-My God, these are all from me."

Gaira knelt down beside him. "They are," she said softly, looking at his face as he unfastened the hemp string. "M'laird… I read through every single letter. Everything ye wrote tae yer brother. Because of the catch in yer speech, ye wrote him letters when ye quarreled because when ye became upset, the catch grew worse and it was difficult for ye tae speak."

He stopped pawing and looked at her. "H-How did you know that?"

Gaira found herself staring into eyes that were as beautiful as a new day. "I told ye," she said, a hint of a smile on her lips. "Because I read every single letter. Did ye know that yer brother replied tae every letter ye ever wrote him?"

James' gaze was riveted to her. "H-He did not," he said. "H-He never wrote to me."

Gaira's smile broke through as she reached into the haversack and pulled out another pile of letters. She held them up between them.

"He did," she said. "I dunna know why he never gave them tae ye, but for every letter ye wrote him, he wrote one in return. They're all here, in order. I put them in order of the date, or at least as close as I could get."

James' mouth opened in astonishment as he took the stack from her, looking at it. It was a shocking revelation. After a moment, he swallowed hard.

"Y-You read all of these?" he asked.

Gaira's smile faded. "I did," she said. "Believe me when I tell ye that when I first found the haversack, I only intended tae read one or two, tae find out who the sack belonged tae. That was my original intention and I swear that tae ye. But the more I read, the more I wanted tae read. I've read those letters so many times that I've nearly memorized them."

James set down the stack of the letters he had written so that he could focus on the ones Johnathan had written to him. But he made no move to untie the string. He simply sat there and looked at them.

"I-If what you say is true, they were not meant for you," he said after a moment.

She averted her gaze, ashamed. "I know," she said. "I dinna mean tae intrude, but I couldna help myself. There's such a beautiful story in those letters."

He snorted. "I-I am not sure that's possible," he said. "A-Anything I wrote is drivel. I-I don't even know what my brother's letters say."

"Ye need tae read them."

"I-I am not sure I can."

"Why not?"

He glanced at her. "I-I am not sure why I should say that to you," he said. "W-We are strangers, you and I. This is a private family matter and you surely would not care."

Gaira laughed softly. "We are *not* strangers," she said. "I know ye better than I've known most people in my life and I've never even met ye until now. Do ye want tae know what I know of ye? I know that ye're brilliant and witty and sensitive, things ye thought yer brother believed were weaknesses, but I tell ye it's not true. He dinna think that."

"N-Now you're making up lies."

She shook her head firmly. "Indeed, I'm not," she insisted. "Ye can read them for yerself. There's a letter yer brother wrote tae ye six years ago after ye attended a fete given by a family named Summerlin. There was a young woman ye had yer eye on but when ye spoke tae her, she shunned ye. Ye ran off and no one could find ye for two days and when your brother finally found ye drowning yer sorrows at a coach inn, ye scolded him and told him tae go away. Do ye remember that incident?"

James was looking at her dubiously. "I-I do, in fact," he said quietly. "T-The young woman was A-Amy Summerlin."

"Of Blackstone Castle."

When he realized she really *did* know the situation, he became less doubtful. "S-She pretended to be interested in what I had to say when, in fact, I later heard her mocking my speech with her friends and laughing. I-I was humiliated and left the party."

Gaira nodded her head in the direction of the letters he held in his hand. "Ye never let yer brother tell ye that he had avenged ye," she said gently. "In one of those letters, he tells ye that he corresponded with Amy for six months after the incident, pretending tae be a great duke, and promised he'd call upon her. On the appointed day, he never showed up and left Amy greatly humiliated."

James looked at her, incredulous. "I-I think I heard of that," he said. "M-My mother spoke of Amy Summerlin being made a fool of and how she was the laughingstock of her social circle. A-And you're telling me that *my* brother did that?"

"He did."

"For me?"

"For ye. The man had a naughty streak in him tae be sure."

James had known that for the most part. But the fact that his brother had avenged him in a situation where he'd blamed his brother for his problems was astonishing. But that astonishment was coupled with growing remorse.

"H-He tried to speak to me about it, a few times, but I shut him off," he said, thinking back to that time. "I-I never let him speak of it, so he never told me what he'd done."

Gaira watched the regret ripple across his face. "He wrote ye a letter about it instead," she said. "Ye wrote tae him because ye couldna speak, and he wrote tae ye because ye wouldna *let* him speak. I think ye should read the letters, m'laird. I think yer brother was a different man than ye knew."

James sank down to his buttocks, still clutching the stack of bound letters. There was so much remorse and angst in his heart to realize that Johnathan had written him so many letters he never gave to him.

The question was why.

He suspected he knew.

"W-Was I really so difficult to communicate with?" he muttered aloud. "W-Why would he write all of these and never give them to me? Was he so afraid of my reaction?"

Because he sat down, Gaira sat down. "I dunna have the answers ye seek, m'laird, but I'll tell ye what I think," she said. "Yer brother was a proud man. As his younger brother, ye're supposed tae look up tae the man and believe him perfect. Isna that what younger brothers do for the older ones?"

James leaned back against the wall of the stall, his attention returning to the lovely woman with the big, brown eyes. "A-Aye," he said. "B-But I always looked up to him."

"He knew," Gaira said honestly. "And I think that perhaps he thought it would show weakness tae give ye the letters he'd written. Ye'd see that he was a man of flesh and bone and feeling, not the perfect earl who was anything but perfect."

James' brow furrowed. "S-So you're saying that he was embarrassed to give them to me?"

Gaira shook her head. "Not embarrassed," she said. "But a man has his pride. I think pride kept him from showing ye that he was just as sensitive as ye are. Now that he's gone… he knew that the letters would make their way back tae ye and that ye would read him. There's a letter he wrote tae ye the night before the battle at Culloden, in fact. If ye dunna read the others, just read that one. Yer brother took the time tae write it, so it's important that ye do."

James stared at her a moment and Gaira could see the thoughts churning behind those brilliant eyes. With a faint sigh, he looked to the stack of letters in his hand.

"H-Here?" he said. "I-In this group?"

Gaira nodded. "'Tis right on the top," she said. "I organized them by date, so the last one is on the top."

James looked at it. He wasn't certain that he was strong enough to read it, but something inside him was pining for it. The last words from his brother, perhaps a hint of approval or a glimmer of hope for those he left behind.

This was what he'd come for, after all.

Something of his brother.

He untied the twine and retrieved the letter on the top.

The paper was yellowed, the seal broken. It was dog-eared on one side as he opened it up to see the familiar handwriting. It was like a dagger to his heart simply to see Johnathan's carefully-scripted letters, but he fought the grief it provoked.

He continued.

My dearest James –

If you are reading this, I'm assuming that I did not survive the battle. I'm further assuming that some kind Scots family has sent you my possessions, such as they are, and that you realize you are now the Earl of Worcester. Although I am no expert on the post, as I suspect I did not do our family justice, I have no doubt that you will be a much finer earl than I ever was. How do I know this?

Because I know you.

When Mother was pregnant with you, I was a tiny lad, but I knew enough to know that I wanted a brother. I remember praying aloud for a brother and the priest would slap me on the head in the midst of my prayers because of it. That old bastard, Father Bernardo. I know you remember him. I think he slapped you a time or two, also.

And then you were born and I had a brother. Mother would leave you in your bed to cry at night and I would climb in with you to comfort you. I know you do not remember that, but I did. I would lay beside you and tell you what great things we would do together, the both of us. I was convinced we would ride side by side into battle in the morning, vanquish the enemy, and be in the tavern drinking wine by evening. I was convinced we would be inseparable.

I think, in a way, we are.

In my possessions, you'll find a stack of letters that you wrote to me. Every single letter you ever wrote to me. I have always kept them with me, even on a battle match. There was one in particular that I kept in a pocket next to my heart because it meant a great deal to me. When I came to Culloden without you, the letters came with me. Whether or not you knew it, you were by my side with every step because I knew that no matter what happened, you would be there for me in spirit if not in presence. Those letters are you, even more than if you were with me in the flesh. In them, you have entrusted me with your fears and hopes and insecurities. I take that trust very seriously.

James, I know I have not been the easiest man to know. I can be aloof. I can be quick to temper. I was always jealous of you and the freedom you had, unencumbered with the de Lohr expectations as I was. You were young and brilliant and your laughter… James, I can still hear it. Your laughter is so easy. I don't know how you do it and I always envied it so. But you are also annoying and insufferable at times and sometimes I want to kick you squarely in the fart hole.

Still, you are my brother and I love you.

I know I never told you that, but I do. I always have. Tomorrow, we are facing six thousand rabid Scots and their allies and although we are better armed and better prepared, there is still a chance I will not make it out of this alive. If I do not, I want you to know that it has been a privilege being your brother. I could not have asked for a greater honor. You will be standing beside me tomorrow as I fight the enemy and if I should fall, know that you will be among my final thoughts.

James, I have always adored you and reproach myself most stringently for never telling you so. But I know that my death will be quite devastating to you and as the reverend prayed for the regiment tonight, I prayed that God would send a guardian angel to watch over you after I am gone. I suppose that I was your guardian angel while on earth, but after I am gone, I pray another will take my place.

Do not grieve overly for me. Do not let Mother grieve overly. Take care of her and of yourself, and I wish you joy and happiness all your life. You are my brother, James, and most worthy of the de Lohr name. I have no final wish or instructions except for one – there are many brave men who will fight tomorrow and I consider it an honor to serve with them. Bring my body home, if it is possible, but leave something of me with my men in the place we have fallen. Not everyone will have the opportunity to return home, so leave something of me behind to watch over them.

Your mercy is appreciated.

Your loving brother,
John

Tears were running down James' face as he finished. Still holding the letter, he put a hand over his face, giving himself the luxury of indulging in his grief if only for a brief moment. He pictured his brother, writing the letter by candlelight on the eve of a great battle. There was no fear conveyed in the letter, no cowardice or remorse. Simply a man wanting to ensure his affairs were in order and that his brother, the most important person in his life, understood what was in his heart.

He had been right.

James *was* devastated.

"I'm sorry if this has reopened a wound that was trying tae heal," Gaira whispered, breaking into his thoughts. "But I saw the letter and I knew that ye should, too."

James wiped at his face quickly, struggling to compose himself. "Y-You were correct," he said. "I-I am glad I saw it. I only wish… well, my brother and I were not the type to speak affectionately to each other. We could laugh together, drink together, and argue quite well, but when it came to speaking of our feelings… it simply wasn't done. T-That is why this letter means so much to me."

Gaira smiled timidly. "I am glad."

There was so much more she wanted to say to him, so much that wouldn't come. Now simply didn't seem like the right time. Before her was the man she'd fallen in love with through his letters but, at the moment, this was not about her or her feelings. This was about James and the loss of a brother.

She didn't feel right saying anything more.

She had done what she'd come to do.

"I… I suppose ye'll be leaving now," she said. "I've heard they buried English officers in Inverness, so perhaps that's where yer brother is. I do wish ye well, m'laird."

She started to stand up, but James stopped her. "W-Wait," he said. "P-Please… wait. I am coming to think that without you, none of this would have been possible."

Gaira paused, realizing that she was close to tears at the thought of leaving those letters behind.

Leaving James behind.

"I'm sure someone would have found them and sent them tae ye," she said. "The Highlands are full of good people, in spite of what the English think."

James was looking at her closely, as if seeing her through new eyes. "P-Perhaps someone would have," he said. "B-But it's equally possible they would have ended up in a hearth somewhere, burned to ashes, and I would have never known what you have been able to give me. It is the greatest kindness anyone has ever bestowed upon me."

Gaira was trying hard not to weep so she lowered her gaze. "Ye're welcome," she said tightly. "As I said, I came tae know ye and yer brother very well. Ye deserve tae have peace between ye."

"I-It is most thoughtful of you to say so," he said, eyeing her. "B-But why do you seem so troubled now?"

Gaira couldn't help it; she broke down in tears. "It's foolish and it shouldna matter," she said. "I'm only a serving wench at a place called Balthazar's where patrons piss on the floor and try tae pinch my backside. I'm no one."

James could see that she was upset and his focus shifted from his own grief to the woman's obvious distress. "Y-You are wrong," he said quietly. "Y-You are the woman who brought my brother back to me.

That makes you very special."

Her head snapped up and she looked at him, wishing with all her heart that his statement was true in a romantic sense. That wish removed any sense of restraint as she spoke. She figured that she'd never see the man again, so whatever she said was of little matter.

But she had to say it.

"I've lived my entire life in this dingy little village, with no excitement, no prospects, and no hope," she said. "But my family wasna always impoverished. My grandfather was the Earl of Forth, a great advisor tae King James until he fell out of favor by taking one of the king's mistresses as his own. My family was stripped of everything and we came here tae live, far away from king and court. My grandfather and father were learned men, so they eked out a life here, but when they died, it was only me and my mother and we do what we can tae survive."

James was listening intently. "T-Then you're the heiress to the Earldom of Forth?"

Tears were falling faster than she could wipe them away. "If it still belonged tae my family, aye," she said. "I just thought ye should know that, once, our family fortunes were much as yer family's. We were powerful and wealthy. The earldom had been in our family for centuries and it was taken away in the blink of an eye. I was educated by my grandfather, so I'm not like the other women in this village. I'm different. 'Tis a difficult existence here, much like yer own existence with yer brother. It is… complicated. 'Tis clear by yer letters that ye never felt as if ye fit in, or were worthy, and that's something I can relate tae. I… I suppose in a sense, that's why I felt drawn tae ye both through those letters. But I was drawn tae ye most of all."

His expression softened. "W-Why me?"

She shrugged, unable to look at him. "Because ye're tender," she said. "The things ye wrote tae yer brother speak of a tender heart, a dreaming heart, and of a man who wants tae do right in life. So many men are hardened and cruel, but ye… ye have a soul. Ye've had challenges, but ye've not let them define ye. Do ye want tae know the truth? Yer letters took me out of my hellish existence and, for a moment, I could be by the side of a man who tried tae live the life he was born tae live. I dunna know if that makes sense, but it's the truth. I fell in love with ye and I dunna even know ye, but now that I've met ye, I feel as if I've known ye all my life. I wasna going tae give those letters back because they were so important tae me, but I see now that they're even more important tae ye. I'm sorry I kept them as long as I did and I pray ye can forgive me."

She was looking down at the straw as she finished, preparing for the response sure to come. He would probably thank her for her candor and leave just as fast as he could. Only a madwoman would declare her love for a man she'd only come to know through letters.

But something strange happened.

Suddenly, he was sitting next to her and his fingers were under her chin, lifting her face to his. Gaira found herself looking into eyes the color of the sky, the slightly-bearded face creased into a smile. For a moment, he simply looked at her before kissing her gently on the cheek.

"L-Lady Gaira," he addressed her formally, as would have been her right as an heiress. "T-The fact that the letters between my brother and me mean so much to you tells me that you are a woman of great depth and understanding. You knew what I needed when I did not even know. I feel that it would only be right to allow me to come to know you as you have come to know me. My brother said that he prayed for a guardian angel to watch over me. Do you think he meant you?"

She flushed a dull red, her heart thumping so forcefully against her chest that she could hardly breath. "Probably not," she said, fighting off a grin. "I've never been called an angel before. A devil, perhaps, but not an angel."

He smiled because she was. "I-I will call you an angel," he said softly. "Y-You have become mine by reuniting me with my brother's belongings."

"But… but I should have done it sooner."

"I-If you had simply sent them to me, I would not have had the honor of meeting you."

There was that sweet man, the one she'd come to know in the letters. As she had told him, he had a tender side.

"Then perhaps everything happens for a reason," she said. "Perhaps the reason was so we could speak."

"I-I believe so," he said. "A-And I believe something else."

"What?"

"T-That you should come to Inverness with me," he said. "A-After all, it seems to me that you have almost as much invested in this situation as I do. You read Johnny's letters and you know the man, as you've said. Would you like to see this through? I am going to find the man in those letters you so carefully kept."

Gaira was nodding her head before he even finished. "I would," she said, incredulous that he should even ask. "Oh, I would!"

James took his hand off her chin, his eyes glimmering with mirth. "I-I am assuming that your mother would not be too keen on you accompanying me to Inverness, unchaperoned," he said. "I-I would, of course, give you my word that I will behave respectfully and politely, but I would hazard to guess that your mother might not believe the word of a Sassenach."

He said it with the perfect Gaelic inflection and Gaira grinned. "I'm a wicked lass for saying this, but she doesna have tae know."

He cocked an eyebrow. "Y-You would lie to her?"

She shrugged. "Sometimes, I sleep at the tavern, in Carrie's chamber," she said. "Especially when it's cold and we have an early morning the next day. My home is across the road, so 'tis not far, but sometimes it's easier – and warmer – tae sleep in Carrie's chamber. There have been times when I've not been home for a week."

"A-And your mother does not miss you?"

The warm inflection on her face faded. "My mother and I dunna have a close relationship," she said. "She goes about her business and I go about mine, although she does clean at the tavern once in a while. I'll simply tell her she's not needed and tell Balthazar she canna come, so she willna know I'm not there."

She sounded confident, but James was still dubious. "I-It is at least two days to Inverness and two days back," he said. "And the weather is snowy. Are you certain you can do this?"

The warmth was back as she looked at him. "'Tis for Laird Johnathan, after all," she said quietly. "I wouldna miss this for the world."

Within the hour, James and Gaira were heading north, along the road to Culloden.

Part Six

INVERNESS

The Old High Church

JAMES LOOKED AT the man in shock.

"*Y-You*?" he said. "I-I was wondering what happened to you, but now I find you here? In Inverness?"

Rafe had been standing at the entry to the Old High Church that had stood for centuries. The brown stones and high tower faced out over the River Ness, guarding the city both literally and figuratively. It was the spiritual center of the town, but it also served as a prison. Some dark things had happened within the walls of the old building.

Rafe stepped forward, greeting James amiably.

"I knew you would be coming here," he said. "The English dead were buried here, so it was a natural assumption. I came ahead of you. I thought I would help you look for your brother."

James had been on the road for almost three days. The snows hadn't returned, but the roads themselves had been in bad shape. More than that, he'd taken it slowly for Gaira's sake. Standing behind James, she was bundled up in one of his coats against the icy weather.

Hearing Rafe's explanation, James' surprise turned to confusion.

"Y-You thought to...?" he repeated. "B-But why should you do that? Although I appreciate your initiative, my brother's fate is not your concern. Surely you have better things you could be doing."

Rafe shook his head, motioning him and Gaira into the church, which wasn't much warmer than it was outside, but at least it was out of the elements.

"I told you that I am a healer," he said. "This is where I am meant to be at the moment. I came ahead and made some inquiries about Johnathan de Lohr and I believe I found someone who can help you."

James' features registered shock. "Y-You did?" he said. "*H-Here*?"

Rafe nodded. "As I said, the English were brought here after the battle," he said. "Wounded, prisoners, and dead. All of them were brought here. The battlefield is quite close, in fact. You passed it on your way into town."

James scratched his head, turning to look out into the churchyard as if to see the battlefield beyond. A chill ran over him. "I-I was not aware."

"It is true," Rafe said. "But I spoke to a priest at length here when I arrived. He told me that the British army brought the dead and wounded here and then executed the Jacobite prisoners. If you look into the southeast corner of the churchyard, you will see a mass grave."

James was starting to pale, his breathing deepening when he realized what Rafe was telling him. "M-My brother is in a mass grave?" he clarified. "I-Is that what you are saying?"

Rafe held up a finger, begging patience. "Wait," he said. "Let me find the priest who knows. I shall return quickly."

With that, he wandered off into the dim church, leaving James standing in the entry, feeling as if he'd just been kicked in the gut. He caught movement out of the corners of his eyes, knowing it was Gaira but afraid to look at her.

Afraid he might break down if he did.

He hadn't come this far to discover his brother's remains were jumbled up with a bunch of strangers.

"I'd heard the same thing," Gaira said softly, putting a gentle hand on his arm. "I dinna want tae tell ye. I dunna know it for certain, but word travels. We had heard the English executed prisoners here and buried their dead."

"B-But they wouldn't have buried them with the prisoners."

"Nay."

"D-Does that mean all of the English are in a mass grave, then?"

"Perhaps the priests can tell ye the truth."

Her voice was soft, lilting. *Comforting.* Funny how he couldn't remember when she hadn't been around him somehow – beside him, in front of him, behind him. The past three days with Gaira had been some of the most unusual and important of his young life. As she stood next to him, he put a big arm around her shoulders and pulled her against him.

He drew strength from her.

In fact, she had become so much more to him than a woman who had read his letters and it had all started with this journey. Gaira had been an ideal traveling companion – never complaining, keeping up a steady stream of conversation to make the travel pass more pleasantly. The days had been long and the nights has been… interesting.

Though James had kept his promise and had behaved like a gentleman, by the second night, they were far too comfortable sleeping in the same room with each other. The first night they'd stopped at an inn, which had been full because of a large family traveling south. Their horses crowded the livery and they even had a carriage that had been parked in the yard. James had managed to negotiate a small bed in the servants' quarters for Gaira, but he ended up sleeping on the bench of the coach because there simply wasn't any other place.

Somewhere in the middle of the night, however, Gaira had come outside with a pillow and two blankets she'd stripped off her rented bed and found him. He'd slept upright against the side of the carriage with a pillow between him and the cab wall, while she'd slept on the bench beside him, her head in his lap.

It wasn't exactly proper, but it had been warm and there had been a great comfort in the fact that they were in the same spot. James, in particular, felt comforted that she wasn't out of his sight. It was odd how attached he'd become to her even in the short time he had known her. They'd left at dawn the next morning after breaking their fast, continuing on as far as they could until they were forced to seek shelter because the night had been so cold.

The second night had been spent on the floor of a farmhouse, in front of the hearth, surrounded by the family's dogs. James had awoken with his arm wrapped around a snoring hound and Gaira had awoken surrounded by dogs who had slept up against her for warmth. It hadn't been the most comfortable sleep, but it had made for a great story.

And now, they were in Inverness.

"James?" she said softly. "Did ye hear me?"

She'd began calling him James yesterday. No longer "m'laird" because, frankly, they were beyond that. He didn't like to hear her address him so formally, so he had asked her to call him James.

She had complied.

As he heard her softly uttered words, he was lashed back to the painful world of reality, a world where his brother was dead and now possibly in a common grave. The impact of it cut through him like a knife.

"I-I heard you," he said after a moment. "I-I suppose we shall discover the truth, but I pray that my brother did not end up in a grave with other dead. He did not deserve that."

Gaira's left arm was around his waist and he felt her squeeze. "Dunna give up hope."

James paused, his thoughts turning from his brother to the tall, pale stranger who seemed so determined to help him.

"W-What I would like to know is why Rafe came," he said. "I-I seem to remember him asking me if there was anything he could do to help me find Johnny, but I did not expect him to go out of his way to do it."

Gaira held his hand tightly. "'Tis a rare man who would be so kind and helpful," she said. "He's a wanderer. I dunna want tae say that he has nothing better tae do, but he doesna seem tae. Perhaps he is looking for a purpose."

James turned to look over his shoulder at her. "H-Helping a man he does not know?"

"Helping a man who needs it."

She had a point. James squeezed her shoulders affectionately and returned his focus to the church, watching for Rafe's return.

It wasn't long in coming.

Rafe emerged from the darkness with a small man at his side. Clad in a rough woolen coat and breeches, his hair cut short against his skull, the man came into the light, his gaze fixed on James. Before James could say a word, the man spoke quietly.

"Ye have his look," he said quietly. "Ye have his eyes."

James eyed him curiously. "W-Who?"

"Yer brother," the man said. Then, he shook himself. "Forgive me. I am Reverend Essich. I… I simply canna believe that ye came, m'laird."

James stared at him a moment before taking a deep, steadying breath. "You knew my brother?"

Reverend Essich nodded. Then, he motioned to James. "Come," he said. "Quickly."

James followed, pulling Gaira with him. Rafe walked alongside as they followed Reverend Essich into a small alcove off the main sanctuary. It was private here, the stone-cold darkness pierced by banks of prayer candles.

Reverend Essich cleared his throat softly.

"Eight months ago, those loyal to Stuart were executed by the English out in the churchyard," he said. "Though their cause has greatly died away, there still may be some who would like to see an Englishman dead because of it. Ye took a risk coming here, m'laird."

James nodded. "I-I know," he said. "B-But I have come looking for my brother. It seems to me that you know of him."

Essich nodded. "I do," he said, glancing at Rafe, who nodded encouragingly. "But when he came here, I dinna know his name. When yer friend told me that ye were looking for a man who had been bayonetted through the neck, I thought it might be him and now that I see ye, I know that ye are his brother because ye look just like him. I never even knew his name."

"J-Johnathan," James said without hesitation. "J-Johnathan de Lohr, Earl of Worcester."

Essich smiled faintly, revealing yellowed teeth. "Worcester," he repeated. "The man was nobility."

"He came from a great line of soldiers."

The reverend nodded. "No doubt," he said. "Yer friend says that ye seek the truth about him. I was here on that terrible day when the English were brought here. My fellow brothers and I fought tae save those we could, but in yer brother's case, it was of no use."

James braced himself. "T-Tell me, please," he said. "T-tell me everything you know."

Essich began to wring his hands in a nervous gesture. "I want ye tae know we tried very hard, m'laird."

"I-I understand."

Essich sighed faintly, hoping that was the truth. He hoped the man really did understand because he had much to say.

"The English were brought here by the wagonload," he said. "There were dead and dying men on the wagons, all piled in together. My fellow parishioners and I separated the dead from the dying as Cumberland's men took the Jacobite prisoners and executed them in the churchyard. We could hear the muskets firing regularly. Meanwhile, a group of prisoners had been forced tae dig their own mass grave in the corner of the churchyard."

It was cold-blooded, but such were the perils of war. It didn't usually bother James, but with his brother involved, he was feeling quite emotional about the whole situation.

"G-Go on," he said.

Essich continued. "We thought yer brother was dead when he was brought here, but he wasna," he said, watching James close his eyes tightly. "He dinna die on the field of battle if that's what ye were told. He was brought here in a pile of men and when we realized he was alive, we quickly took him away and put him in the dormitory with the other wounded."

James sighed heavily and hung his head, slumping against the wall behind him. As Gaira and Rafe and Essich looked on with concern, the reverend continued quickly.

"Yer brother had taken a bayonet through the neck," he said. "I dunna know how he survived as long as he did, but he was a strong man because he lived for a full night after he was brought here, and during that night, he never awoke. I made him as comfortable as I could, m'laird."

James had a lump in his throat as he listened. "H-He never regained consciousness?"

Essich shook his head. "Nay," he said. "There were times when I thought he might, but he never did. He wasna alone when he died, if that's of some comfort tae ye. I was with him. I said a prayer for him."

James could feel the tears but he fought them. This was perhaps the best ending he could have hoped for, considering the circumstances. "I-I am grateful," he said. "W-What… what did you do with him?"

"We buried the dead on the other side of the church, opposite the churchyard," Essich said. "Yer brother was buried in his own grave, dressed in the clothing he was wearing, but before we buried him, I removed what possessions he had in the hopes that I could discover who he was."

James was losing the battle against the tears. "What did you find?"

The reverend dug into a pocket of his threadbare coat and pulled forth a meager handful of things. One looked like it was a folded document of some kind, while there were two other items that became evident when Essich opened his hand and extended it to James. The first thing James saw was the Eardley Norton pocket watch that Johnathan always carried, one that had belonged to their father.

The second thing was the ring.

Ruby eyes glimmered weakly in the candlelight.

"G-God," he gasped, grabbing the ring. "Y-You have it. The ring; *you have it*!"

Essich nodded. "The only thing inscribed on it was *Fidelis Semper*," he said. "Had there been a name, I might have been able tae find ye, but there wasna. Not on the watch and not even on the letter."

James was still reeling over the reclamation of the de Lohr ring. The relief he felt was indescribable, the family heirloom that thankfully wasn't lost as they'd all feared. Now, he had it, and it was his. He slipped it on his finger as he looked up, seeing that Essich was extending the folded paper to him. Hesitantly, he took it.

"H-He had a letter on him?" he asked.

"Aye," Essich nodded. "From someone named James. I found it in a chest pocket, right against his heart."

With the ring on his finger and the watch in one hand, James looked at the letter, feeling the impact of the reverend's words. It was just as Johnathan's letter had told him, how he kept a certain letter close to his heart in battle.

There was one in particular I kept in a pocket next to my heart because it meant a great deal to me.

Swallowing hard, James opened it up to see which letter it was that meant so much to Johnathan. The first thing he saw was a childish scrawl and he knew that it was a letter written by a very young boy. He recognized his own writing.

Lifting it into the light, he began to read.

You are a very mean boy, Johnny.

I want to cut you with my saber and slash you and kill you. If I sound like a Billy goat, then you look like a horse's arse and I don't care if you tell Mummy. You say very mean things to me and I don't care because I am going to kill you. Someday you will be dead and I will be happy. I will draw a picture of me laughing and when you are in the ground, I hope the worms eat your eyeballs. Then I will dig you up and put more worms on you. When you go to heaven, God will see all of the worms in your eyeballs and when I go to heaven, I will see them also. Wait for me when you get to heaven so I can see the worms. If you do not wait for me, I shall be very angry.

Your brother who hates you,
James

Startled by the petulant message in a letter that Johnathan should keep so close to him, James started to laugh. He laughed so hard that tears streamed down his face, but these were tears of delight. That his brother had kept that querulous, silly letter with him, keeping it close to his heart through the years, meant the world to him. It literally meant everything. It was incredibly representative of their childhood, but it was also representative of the bond they shared throughout the insults and bad feelings and torment. It began to occur to James why Johnathan had kept the letter so close.

Wait for me when you get to heaven.

God… so ridiculous, yet so poignant. Johnathan kept a young boy's plea close to his heart because it spoke of James' true adoration for the brother he very much loved.

When he faced battle, that little request had fortified him.

"What does it say?" Gaira asked timidly. "Will ye tell me?"

James was still chuckling. "H-Here," he said, handing it to her. "Y-You can see for yourself."

Gaira took it and read through it, giggling as she came to the end. "Did ye really send such nasty things tae yer brother?" she gasped. "Ye were a naughty lad."

James nodded, taking it from her and carefully folding it. "I-I was," he said. "A-And he loved me for it, so I suppose I wasn't as naughty as I thought. To see that this silly little letter meant something to him… it is a feeling I cannot begin to describe. All I know is that I love it."

Gaira smiled at him and he winked at her before returning his attention to the reverend. When he looked at the man, his chuckles started anew.

"I-I am the James of that letter, as you may have guessed," he said. "I-I wrote that letter to my brother when I was around six or seven years of age, I believe, and he was nearing twelve. We had quarreled because he told me that I sounded like a goat when I spoke. I'd forgotten that I'd even written him that letter. How surprising to find that it meant so much to him."

Essich was smiling, mostly because he was pleased that something in this horrific circumstance had brought James pleasure.

"The bond between brothers is unique and powerful," he said. "It would seem that ye and yer brother shared that bond."

James' smile faded. "We did," he said. "T-The strange thing is that I did not even realize that until I came to find him. I-I always thought we did not understand one another, but I was wrong. So very wrong. The important thing is that I have found my brother and I intend to take him home."

Essich nodded. "I'm glad," he said. "But the ground is frozen now. 'Twill be difficult to dig him up. Can ye wait until the spring when the ground is softer?"

James looked at Gaira. The idea of spending the next few months in the Highlands, with her, was not a dismal one. In fact, he was rather pleased by it.

"I-I suppose I'll have to," he said. "I'm not leaving without him, so I shall make do until the time comes."

"Do ye have a place tae stay?"

The corner of James' mouth twitched as he and Gaira smiled at one another. "I-It is possible," he said, inferring that she was part of those future plans. "I-I'll find somewhere to stay and something to occupy my time. Meanwhile, I can have a casket built for my brother so we can transport him south. It will give me time to make the necessary preparations."

The man actually seemed a good deal more at peace than he had when he'd first entered the church. He knew where his brother was, he'd been told of his relatively painless passing, and he had recovered items that were precious to him. That was a great relief to Essich, who stepped out from the alcove and motioned to the group.

"Come with me, then," he said. "Some warm drink and bread tae celebrate the life of Johnathan de Lohr before we make the necessary preparations."

Gaira was first, following the reverend, with James and Rafe bringing up the rear. They passed through the cold, candle-lit church and through a door that was near the nave. Exiting into what used to be the cloister centuries ago, James found himself looking up into the clear night sky.

"I-I don't recall ever seeing the stars so bright," he said. "S-Somehow, the world seems a little brighter tonight."

He paused, and Rafe with him, both of them looking up into the sky.

"Feeling better?" Rafe asked.

"A-Aye," James said. Then, he pointed to the sky. "L-Look, there; that star is bigger than the rest."

Rafe could see the one he meant. "*When they saw the star, they rejoiced exceedingly and with great joy*," he said. When James looked at him, he smiled weakly. "That is from the Bible. It is nearing the time of day of Christ's birth, in fact. It seems to me that you have been given the greatest gift of all this holiday season."

James nodded, thinking on his journey to Calvine, to Inverness. "O-Of everything I thought it would be, it was none of those things," he said. "I-I don't know what I expected, but this journey has been most unexpected in many ways."

Rafe looked over James' shoulder, seeing Gaira as she stood down from them on the walkway with the reverend. "I'm glad she told you what she knew."

James turned to look at Gaira before returning his focus to Rafe. His brow furrowed. "W-What do you mean?" he asked. Then, realization dawned. "Y-You knew about my brother's haversack? You knew she had it?"

Rafe shrugged. "I suspected," he said. "I did not know for certain, but on the night you and I sat together, she was in the chamber. I saw her face as you spoke of your brother and I suspected she knew something. I told her to tell you what she knew and I am glad she did."

That explained it a little better and James turned to look at her again, his gaze lingering on her. "I-I am glad she did, also," he said. "S-

She is a thoughtful, warm woman, one I intend to get to know quite well."

Rafe's eyes were glimmering with mirth. "Another gift you have received this holiday season," he said. Then, he looked up at the sky again. "Tell me something, James."

"W-What?"

"Do you believe in miracles?"

James started to speak but stopped himself. Then, he chuckled wryly. "I-I never thought so until I came to the Highlands," he said. "B-But it seems to me that everything that has happened with regards to my brother has been some sort of miracle. I came to know things about my brother that I hadn't known before and I found a woman who knows him, and me, very well. I-I know that sounds odd considering I'd not met Gaira before I came to Calvine, but she's quite… special."

"I know."

"M-My brother left me a letter that was found in his haversack and in the letter, he mentioned praying for a guardian angel for me," James went on. "H-He said that he was my guardian angel on earth and he prayed that God would send me another in his place. I think… I think that Gaira may be that angel. I feel something for her that I cannot describe, but it has something to do with comfort and understanding and…"

"Love?" Rafe interjected.

James grinned, lopsided. "P-Perhaps," he said. "I-I am hopeful."

Rafe smiled faintly, watching James as the man gazed up at the stars again. This wasn't the same young lord he'd met at Balthazar's Inn several days ago. That young lord had been tormented and bitter. The man before him was full of peace.

It was, after all, a season of peace.

Rafe looked back up to the sky and to the bright start in particular.

"Do you know your archangels, James?"

James shook his head. "I-I am afraid I am much like my brother was," he said. "Neither of us were very pious."

The corner of Rafe's lips twitched. "I know that about you," he said. "If you don't know your archangels, then let me explain to you that Raphael is the archangel of healing, both physical and emotional. This is a season when angels walk the earth, a time of miracles. Your brother's prayers were heard, James. Johnathan exchanged one guardian angel for another. And, yes, he is waiting for you in heaven, but not with worms in his eyeballs."

James had been daydreaming as he gazed up at the stars, but Rafe's odd statement caught his attention. "A-Ah, yes," he said. "W-Worms in his eyeballs. I think that was something I wrote to him on more than one occasion when I was younger, but… hold a moment… *how* did you know about that? Did you read that letter, too?"

Rafe grinned, patting him on the shoulder as he turned and headed back towards the church. "That bright star will be gone tonight," he said, pointing upwards. "And so will I."

Confused, James took a few steps after him. "B-But where are you going, Rafe?"

"To find others that need healing. And, James?"

"What?"

"The name is Raphael."

With that, he turned and disappeared into the church. Literally, he disappeared into the darkness. Bewildered, James went after him only to be faced with a vacant church. There was no tall, pale man in white woolen clothing anywhere to be seen. Baffled, James turned towards the door again, processing what he'd been told.

What had happened.

Raphael is the archangel of healing, both physical and emotional. This is a season when angels walk the earth, a time of miracles.

That's what Rafe had said.

The name is Raphael.

Startled, James came to a halt, realizing what he'd just been told. Rushing out into the cloister, he looked into the sky to see that, indeed, the bright star had vanished. Now, it was simply a velvet black sky covered with a sea of diamonds, all of them twinkling brilliantly.

It was an evening full of beauty.

Oddly enough, he didn't doubt Rafe in the least. Now, the man's presence made sense. Everything he had done made sense. The recovery of Johnathan's sword and haversack and letters and the ring made sense. Even Gaira made sense. James hadn't been a man to believe in miracles as he'd said, but tonight, he did.

The pieces of the puzzle had all come together.

On this night of nights, James realized that he had come face to face with his very own guardian angel.

When Gaira asked him later what had become of Rafe, James simply told her that the man had to leave.

Perhaps there were some miracles better kept to himself.

Part Seven

JAMES AND GAIRA

Year of Our Lord 1747
The month of April

JAMES' FACE WAS buried in Gaira's neck, smelling the sweet musky scent that had the ability to arouse him like nothing else. He could feel her soft breasts against his bare chest, experiencing the sensual movement every time he thrust into her.

Gaira's legs were wrapped around his hips but he unwrapped them, holding them behind the knees, giving him more freedom of movement as he continued to thrust into her sweet and yielding body.

His wife.

Gaira had her hands on his lower back, stroking it, stroking his smooth buttocks as he made love to her. She loved it when he slowed his pace, withdrawing completely only to plunge into her again, slowly. Her hands drifted between their bodies, putting her fingers on his phallus as he joined his body with hers. Nothing seemed to fuel James' desire than her fingers on his manhood.

His climax was instantaneous.

It was the second time that morning he'd taken her, as he'd taken her every single night since the day he'd married her two months earlier. At the Old High Church in Inverness, Reverend Essich had performed the ceremony joining Gaira Dunmore, former heiress to the Earldom of Forth, to James de Lohr, Earl of Worcester. Carrie had been in attendance along with Gaira's mother, who sobbed loudly through the entire thing. When all was said and done, Lord and Lady Worcester signed the parish registrar's book as man and wife.

Much had gone on in the past four months in preparation for returning Johnathan de Lohr to Lioncross Abbey, home of generations of de Lohrs. James had rented a little cottage in Inverness, right on the River Ness, a place for him and his wife to stay while he made the necessary arrangements.

Gaira's mother, Helen, chose to return to Calvine after their marriage, to the home she had shared with her husband for many years, leaving her daughter to start her new life as the Countess of Worcester. Gaira and James quickly integrated into the Inverness community, with Gaira becoming popular with the locals. She was bright, educated, and entertained an excellent crowd, and the women of the village tittered over her handsome husband.

Truth be told, so did Gaira.

It was the life she never thought she would have.

But, God, did she love it.

This morning, however, would prove to be their last morning in Inverness, as preparations for digging up Johnathan's grave were coming to a head. In months past, a beautiful coffin had been built of Scots pine, heavy and well-made as befitting the former Earl of Worcester. The man who made it was also the wheelwright in the village, and his skill had been beyond compare. He'd carved beautiful lines into the coffin and, at the strange request of the current Earl of

Worcester, managed to carve some worms up near the head of the coffin.

He was being well paid, so he didn't ask questions.

But to James, those worms meant everything.

Now, the lined coffin was waiting for its occupant and arrangements had been made to begin the digging at sunrise. Spring had come early this year and the ground was already softened enough to dig. As James lay next to his naked wife, his arms wrapped around her, he could see that it was about sunrise now. Face in the side of her head, he groaned softly.

"T-They will be waiting for me," he mumbled. "I-I cannot keep my brother waiting."

Gaira yawned. "Do ye want me tae go with ye?"

James opened his eyes, thinking on what this day would bring. "I-I would like you to," he said softly. "T-This is why we came to Inverness in the first place. Let us greet Johnathan together. I can tell him of our marriage."

It was a very big day in their lives, one that Gaira knew her husband was both looking forward to and dreading. She smiled, trying to lighten the mood.

"Would he approve of ye marrying a serving wench, then?"

James chuckled. "S-She's not a serving wench," he said, lightly slapping her bare buttocks. "S-She's a countess. A veritable goddess. Aye, he would approve."

Gaira laughed softly, wrapping her arms around him and hugging him tightly. She kissed him gently with her soft lips, feeling him grow amorous in an instant, ready to take her again. But there wasn't time and she pushed him away.

"Get up, my bonny lad," she said, sitting up with the coverlet held to her naked breasts. "Today is a big day and ye mustna be late."

With a heavy sigh, James sat up beside her. There was something in his manner that suggested he was becoming moody towards what he was about to face and Gaira looked at him with sympathy.

"It will be all right," she said softly. "Dunna fret over what ye must do. It has tae be done."

He nodded faintly. "I-I know," he said, sounding resigned. "T-This is the day I have waited for, yet there is something about it that is inherently sad. I am going to see my brother today."

"I know."

"I-It will be his body, in whatever state it is in."

"And ye dunna feel ready for it?"

He shrugged. "G-God knows, I should be," he said. "S-Since it has been so cold, he should be well preserved and I have been prepared for this moment ever since we were told of his death, but still… seeing him will make all of this a reality. My brother is truly dead."

Gaira smiled sadly at him putting a gentle hand on his cheek. "He is," she said with quiet finality. "But he met his death well. Ye know he did. It's time tae bring him home."

James held her hand against his face, turning to kiss the palm. "A-And I shall," he said. But then, he grew quiet. "I-I have been thinking of something else."

"What of?"

"F-From his last letter to me," he said. "J-Johnny asked that I leave something of him behind to watch over the brave men who would never make it home. He wanted to ensure they were protected. I have been thinking long and hard about that request."

"And?"

He lifted his left hand, the one with the de Lohr signet ring on it. He gazed at the heirloom for a long, intense moment.

"C-Carrie told me that when she went through the things that were brought to her, she removed any valuables away for safe keeping," he said. "Y-You said the same thing."

Gaira leaned against him, looking at the ring as well. "In her Chamber of Sorrows," she said. "She has hole in the floor where she keeps a box of the valuable things she has found."

"W-What is in there?"

Gaira reflected on the small, square wooden box shoved into its little niche in the floor.

"Gold," she said. "Gold coinage and other valuables. It seems strange that men would carry such precious things to a battlefield, but they did. There are gems in the box, rings and the like. Why do ye ask?"

James held up the ring, inspecting it in the weak light.

"B-Because I am going to leave this in the box, too."

Gaira's eyes widened when she realized what he meant. "The signet ring?" she gasped. "But… *why*? Ye came all the way tae Scotland for the thing. It belongs tae ye. Why would ye leave it behind?"

James was studying the ruby eyes, the golden lion face. "I-I am not sure I can explain, but I will try," he said. "J-Johnny was wearing this when he died trying to save men. Everything inside me tells me that I have no right to take it away from this place. He asked me to leave something of him behind to watch over the brave dead, and it seems to me that this ring is the most logical thing to leave behind. The power of the de Lohr crest can watch over those men who fought, and died, by Johnny's command. Does that make sense? I feel as if, by all rights, the ring should remain here with those who died for it. For Johnny. I have no right to take it away from them."

There was that tender soul again, the one Gaira loved so well. Perhaps she didn't exactly understand it all but, then again, men in battle shared a special bond. Brothers shared a special bond. Clearly, this meant a great deal to James and she knew he hadn't made the decision lightly.

Leaning over, she kissed him on the cheek.

"If that's what ye want tae do, then do it," she said. "At least ye'll know where it is, for always. It willna be lost, but simply standing watch over the dead of Culloden in Carrie's chamber."

"E-Exactly," he said, looking at her. "I-I knew you would understand. One of the many things I love about you. And who knows? Maybe one day, a de Lohr will wear the ring again. But for now, it belongs to Johnny and that room full of ghosts. That is where it shall stay."

"And ye feel confident with that decision?"

"I-I do. More than anything."

Gaira kissed him again and, for a moment, they smiled at one another, feeling the warmth and love between them that was stronger than anything on earth.

Stronger than death.

Stronger than a ring.

In the days to come, the de Lohr signet ring found a home in a dingy little box buried in the floor of Carrie's Chamber of Sorrows. Exactly thirty-one days later, Johnathan de Lohr was laid to rest in Lioncross Abbey's great chapel, taking his rightful place among his ancestors as his brother, his brother's wife, his mother, and several de Lohr relatives witnessed the interment.

But not before a letter from James was packed against Johnathan's stilled heart before they closed the lid forever.

A letter from one brother to another.

My Dearest Johnny –

And so, our letter writing campaign comes to an end.

From your petulant, ridiculous younger brother, you have my deepest thanks for the path my life has taken. It seems odd to say such a thing, but in your death, I found my life and my purpose. I pray that I can live up to your example, for it is one I shall always worship.

What I should have told you in life, I will tell you in death. If you do not wait for me in heaven, I shall be very angry, for it will be my greatest honor to tell you how much I love you the moment I see you again. How much I have always loved you, my brother. I am sorry I wished worms in your eyeballs. I did not mean it.

Much.

Until we meet again,
James

ઌ THE END ഓ

About Kathryn Le Veque

KATHRYN LE VEQUE is a USA TODAY Bestselling author, an Amazon All-Star author, and a #1 bestselling, award-winning, multi-published author in Medieval Historical Romance and Historical Fiction. She has been featured in the NEW YORK TIMES and on USA TODAY's HEA blog.

Kathryn's Medieval Romance novels have been called "detailed", "highly romantic", and "character-rich". She crafts great adventures of love, battles, passion, and romance in the High Middle Ages. More than that, she writes for both women AND men – an unusual crossover for a romance author – and Kathryn has many male readers who enjoy her stories because of the male perspective, the action, the passion, and the adventure.

Kathryn loves to hear from her readers. Please find Kathryn on Facebook at Kathryn Le Veque, Author, or join her on Twitter @kathrynleveque, and don't forget to visit her website and sign up for her blog at www.kathrynleveque.com.

Please follow Kathryn on Bookbub for the latest releases and sales.

The Earl of Christmas Past

By Kerrigan Byrne

Part of A Very Highland Holiday Collection
Part Two of The Brothers de Lohr

The characters and events portrayed in this book are fictitious. Any similarity to real persons, living or dead, is purely coincidental and not intended by the author.

The Earl of Christmas Past

A solstice blizzard drives Victorian photographer, Vanessa Latimer, to a crowded Highland Inn where the only available room is haunted by the ghost of a fallen warrior unwilling to give up his side of the bed.

Chapter One

Calvine Village, Highlands, Scotland – 1891
Winter Solstice

FATE HAD BEEN Vanessa Latimer's foe since she could remember.

She was the most unlucky, ungainly person of her acquaintance, and had resigned herself to an early death. However, she always imagined said death would be glorious, as well.

Or at least memorable.

Something like tripping and accidentally sacrificing herself to a volcano in the Pacific Islands. Or perhaps becoming the unfortunate snack of a Nile crocodile or a tiger in Calcutta.

Meeting her end as a human icicle in the Scottish Highlands had never made it on the list.

Not until the angry blizzard turned the road to Inverness treacherous, and something had spooked the horse, sending the carriage careening into a boulder the size of a small cottage.

The driver informed her that the wheel was irreparably damaged, and that she must stay in the carriage while he went for help.

That had been hours ago.

When the dark of the storm became the dark of the late afternoon on this, the shortest day of the year, the temperatures plummeted alarmingly. Even though Vanessa had been left with furs and blankets, she worried she wouldn't survive the night, and set off along the road with a lantern and the most important of her luggage.

Now, huddled on the landing beneath the creaking shingle of Balthazar's Inn, she clutched her increasingly heavy case to her chest, shielding the precious contents with her body.

The surly innkeeper's impossibly thick eyebrows came together in a scowl as he wedged his bulk into the crack of the open door to effectively block any attempt at entry. Even the gale forces didn't save her nostrils from being singed by his flammable scotch-soaked breath. "As ye can see, lass, ye're not the only traveler stranded in this bollocks storm, and I let our last remaining room to the other rank idiot not clever enough to seek shelter before the storm fell upon us. So, nay. Ye'll have to try elsewhere."

"Was that rank idiot a shifty-eyed man in his fifties named McMurray?" she asked, forcing the words out of her lungs like a stubborn bellows to be heard over the din. The wind buffeted her skirts this way and that, plastering them to her trembling legs.

"Aye," he said with a self-satisfied smirk as he also managed to leer. "But doona think to be offering to share his bed; we're a reputable establishment."

"Never! I wouldn't—that isn't—what—" Vanessa gaped and shuddered for a reason that had nothing to do with the cold. Her driver had left her out there to freeze to death while *he'd* purchased a room with her fare? She should have listened when her instincts had warned her off hiring him.

Her case, growing heavier by the moment, threatened to slide out of the circle of her arms and down her body, so she bucked it higher with her hips and redoubled her efforts to hold it aloft with fingers she could no longer feel. "Is there somewhere nearby that might take me in?" she called, coughing as a particularly icy gust stole her breath.

"Aye." He jerked his chin in a vaguely northern direction. "The Cairngorm Tavern is not but a half hour's march up the road." He said this as if the angry wind did not threaten to snatch her up and toss her into the nearest snowdrift.

Swallowing a spurt of temper and no small amount of desperation, Vanessa squared her shoulders before offering, "What if *this* rank idiot can pay you double your room rate to sleep in the stables?" She pointed to the rickety livery next to the sturdy stone building. 'Twas the season and all that. If it was good enough for the baby Jesus, who was she to turn her nose up?

At this he paused, eyeing her with speculation. "Ye'll pay in advance?"

A knot of anxiety eased in her belly as she nodded dramatically, her neck stiff with the cold. "And triple for a warm bath."

He immediately shook his head, his jowls wobbling like a winter pudding. "Doona think I'll be spending me night hauling water for ye and yers."

"J-just me," Vanessa said, doing her best to clench her teeth against their chattering. "N-no m-mine."

"No husband? No chaperone?" For the first time, he looked past her as the storm finished swallowing the last of the early evening into a relentless chaos of white snow and dark skies.

"I'm—I'm alone." Vanessa told herself the gather of moisture at the corner of her eyes was the sole fault of the untenable weather. *Not* her untenable circumstances.

A banshee-pitched shriek sliced through the wail of the storm. "Rory Seamus Galbreath Balthazar Pitagowan, ye useless tub of guts and grog!" The door was wrenched out of the innkeeper's hand and thrown open to reveal a woman half his height but twice his width.

She beat him about the head and shoulders with a kitchen towel, the blows punctuated by her verbal onslaught. "Ye'd leave this child to freeze to death? And the night of the solstice? If no one were here to witness, I'd wake up a widow tomorrow, ye bloody heartless pillock! Now go make up Carrie's chamber, lay a fire, and heat water for this poor wee lass's bath."

Mr. Pitagowan's arms now covered his head to protect it from the stinging abuse of his wife's damp towel. "Carrie's chamber? But…me love…it's haunted. And what if she—"

"I'm sure the bairn would rather sleep with a ghost than become one, wouldn't ye, dearie?"

At this point, she'd sleep next to the Loch Ness Monster if she could get warm. Besides, the very idea of a haunted bedroom in an ancient structure such as this one couldn't be more tempting. She would be warm *and* entertained. "Oh, I don't really mind if—"

"And tell young Dougal to put a kettle on!" Mrs. Pitagowan hollered as her husband plodded away, looking a great deal shorter now that his wife had cut him down.

Arms truly trembling now, as much from the weight of her burden as the cold, Vanessa took a step toward the door, which remained blocked by a large body. "Do you mind very much if I come insi—?"

"Are ye hungry, lass?" Mrs. Pitagowan's hand rested atop her ample belly, which was accentuated by the ruffles of an apron that might have struggled to cover a woman two stone lighter.

"I'm actually colder than any—"

"The wee mite is starving to death, just look at her!" she shouted after her husband, snatching the case from Vanessa before she could so much as protest. "So, make sure to set aside a bowl of stew and bread!"

Panicking about her case, Vanessa held her arms out. "Oh, do be careful, that's ever so fragi—"

"Well I doona ken why ye insist on standing out there in the cold, little 'un, come in before I can snap yer skinny wee arms off like icicles." The round woman carried her burden like it weighed a bit of nothing as she waddled into the common room.

Vanessa shivered inside and closed the door behind her, struggling with the ancient latch. She knew she was a rather short and painfully thin woman, but at eight and twenty, she'd not been addressed as *child, bairn, wee mite,* or *little one* for longer than a decade.

If ever.

Turning to the common room, Vanessa swallowed around a lump of anxiety as she noted that, indeed, the place was filled to the exceptionally low rafters with wayward travelers.

Most of them male. All of them staring at her.

A glow from the over-warm room rolled over her as a blush heated her stinging cheeks.

"G-good evening," she stammered, bobbing a slight curtsy before brushing quickly melting snow from her cloak.

The only other woman looked up from the table where she tended her husband and four unruly children to send her a pinched and sour glare. No doubt she made assumptions regarding Vanessa's vocation due to her lack of chaperone.

She was aware unfortunate women traveled to such taverns looking to pay for their lodgings with their company and favors. And after what Mr. Pitagowan had said in front of the entire assembly, Vanessa couldn't exactly blame the woman for her speculation.

Besides, she was used to it.

Her attempt at a smile was rebuked, so she turned it on the handful of men clustered in overstuffed chairs around the hearth, nursing ale from tankards that might have been crafted during the Jacobite rebellion.

"Bess!" a kilted, large-boned man crowed, wiping foam from his greying, ill-kempt beard with the back of his hand. "Tell 'er if she's afraid to bed down with the ghost, I'll be happy to offer an alternative arrangement." His eyes traveled down Vanessa's frame with an uninvited intimacy that made her feel rather molested. "One that would keep the wee lass warm, but I canna promise ye'd be dry."

As she was wont to do, Vanessa covered her mortification with all the imperious British pomposity she could muster, lifting her nose in the air. "You needn't speak as if I were not standing right here. I am capable of understanding you exceptionally well, sir. Correct me if I'm wrong, but I highly doubt you've ever had a woman accept such a crass and ridiculous proposition. One you didn't have to offer recompense, that is."

The men gathered around the fireplace all blinked at her, dumbstruck.

"I thought not," she said. "Now I'll thank you not to make such ill-mannered and indecent suggestions in the presence of children." She gestured to a grubby lad of perhaps eight, who promptly tossed a piece of bread into her hair.

The boy's father boxed his son's ears, and the child let out an ear-splitting wail, setting her teeth on edge.

"English." A thin, pockmarked highlander harrumphed the word into his ale glass. "The night's too cold for a frigid, prickly wee bundle of bones, Graham," he said to her harasser.

"Aye, she's hardly worth the trouble." Another spat into the fire, and the resulting sizzle disgusted her.

"Ye barbarous Douglasses behave!" Mrs. Pitagowan thundered over her shoulder as she turned sideways to squeeze herself down the aisle created by the six or so tables in the common room. "Or ye'll find yerselves arseways to a snowdrift and make no mistake! Now follow me, lass, and let's get ye out of those wet clothes."

Vanessa turned to obey, cringing at the Douglasses' disgusting noises evoked by the innkeeper's gauche mention of her undressing.

She passed a long bar, against which two well-dressed men in wool suits picked at a brown stew and another grizzled highlander wore a confounding fishing uniform in the middle of winter and leagues away from the ocean.

She'd heard tell the Scots around these parts were an odd lot, but she'd underestimated just how truly backward they might be.

Balthazar's Inn, at least, was charming. Though the pale stone walls were pitted with age, a lovely dark wood wainscoting rose from the floor to waist height, swallowing some of the light from the lanterns and the fireplace to create a rather cozy effect. In observation of Christmas, boughs of holly and other evergreens were strewn across the hearth and over the doorways, tied in place by red ribbons. Similar braided wreaths moated the lanterns on each table, filling the room with the rather pleasant scent of pine.

"Thank you for taking me in, Mrs. Pitagowan." Vanessa remembered her manners as she followed the woman through a chaotic scullery.

"Call me Bess, everyone else does," the lady sang.

Vanessa jumped out of the way when Bess's grumpy husband threw open an adjoining door and stomped past them carrying an empty cauldron and muttering in a language she'd never heard before.

"Bess, then. I appreciate your generosity—"

Turning in the doorway, Bess narrowly missed smashing the case against the frame, causing Vanessa to blanch. "Doona get the idea I'm being charitable, lass. I heard ye offer thrice the room rates. And I'll be needing payment afore I ready the room."

Right. Vanessa sighed, digging into the pocket of her cloak for her coin purse. "How much?"

"I'll take half a crown what with the bath and stew."

Vanessa counted out the coin, fully aware she'd pay half as much at any reputable establishment in London, but she was beyond caring, what with a bath and a hot meal so close at hand. "You called this *Carrie's room* before," she mentioned, more to make conversation than anything. "Is Carrie the name of the apparition who will be keeping me company?"

A dark, almost sympathetic expression softened Bess's moon-round face as she used a free hand to tuck a pale lock of hair back into her matronly cap. "Oh—well—that's just a bit of local superstition, isn'it? Nothing to worry about. A lady like ye'll be perfectly safe."

Local superstition was exactly what drew her to the Highlands for Christmas, but Vanessa thought it best not to disclose that to Bess just now.

What had the woman meant, *a lady like her*? Someone wealthy, perhaps? English? Or female?

Either way, fate had left her little choice but to find out.

Chapter Two

JOHNATHAN DE LOHR was awoken from his blank torpor by the sound of a delicate sneeze.

It was time again. The solstice maybe, when the sun flared and tugged at the planet in such a way the tides became wilder. The storms became more violent. The creatures of the earth more feral.

Untamed.

And those dead like himself, cursed to still inhabit this plane, were called to be restless.

Reminded what it was to be human.

Only to have it ruthlessly taken from them again.

He materialized—for lack of a better word—by Carrie's old bed in time to have a dust sheet snatched right through his middle by a large, apple-cheeked woman in a matronly apron.

He didn't recognize her at all.

"We've a water heater but no piping to the rooms, far as we are from civilized Blighty," she said, snatching the last of the covers off a tall wardrobe as a portly man with wild tufts of greying hair dumped an empty metal basin on the floor with a derisive clang.

Ah, *there* was Balthazar, or at least one of his kin. John had known generations of them to come and go, but this iteration he'd seen when the man was younger. Much younger.

The innkeeper stomped out with nary a word and was replaced by a lad of maybe fifteen with longish unkempt dark hair and a cauldron of steaming water, which he poured into the tub.

Wait, they'd let the room? *His* room? This was not to be tolerated.

He could make himself visible, of course, on a night like tonight, could take to wailing and thundering and all manner of ghostly things. He might even be able to summon the energy to touch or move something. To breathe on or even grab at someone with icy fingers, terrorizing them away so he could regain his own tranquility.

It took so much from him, though, exerting his will in the realm of the living.

Waking always discombobulated John. For a moment, the chaos of the round woman's tidying, the noise of a full inn and the water crashing into the metallic basin, along with the press of three or more bodies in such a small chamber overwhelmed him. A storm screamed and battered at the ancient window, the snow knocking like the very fist of a demon in gusts and surges.

The blasted woman—whom he assumed was the current Balthazar's wife—had tossed the dust covers out the door and was now rushing toward where John stood in front of the bed, with a fresh pile of sheets and new pillows.

He didn't like the odd sensation of people walking through him; it rankled like that odd tickle one felt when bashing their elbow, but without the pain.

Unable to easily avoid the rotund woman in the cramped space, he retreated a few steps until he found himself standing inside the wardrobe, his vision hindered by the closed doors and the darkness inside them. Much better. Was this piece new? He tried to remember if he'd seen it the last time he'd lingered here. They'd no doubt procured it to cover the door that led to—

Another small sneeze interrupted his thoughts. "Forgive me," begged a British female voice before a delicate sniff. "Dust always makes me sneeze." She cleared her throat. "It *is* kind of Dougal and Mr. Pitagowan to draw a bath. I feel it is the only way I'll ever be warm again. And the room is really so charming, I'm certain I'll be comfortable here. I might not have survived a march to the Cairngorm Tavern."

John closed his eyes as a strange, incandescent vibration shimmered through him.

The new feminine voice was husky and smooth, like smoke exhaled over the most expensive brandy. It slid between his ribs like a smooth assassins' blade, nicking at a heart that hadn't ticked for at least a century. It both stirred and soothed him in equal measure.

"Like I said earlier, miss, this isna kindness, it's a service. One ye paid generously for, so enjoy it with our blessing and warm yer wee bones before ye shiver right out of them."

John had always been an appreciator of the Scottish brogue, but *this* woman's pitch could likely offend sensitive dogs. It was especially jarring after the crisp, clear notes of British gentility.

He poked his head back through the wardrobe doors to find who belonged to such a sound, and realized immediately why he'd missed her before.

Dressed in the most peculiar plain grey wool cloak that'd been soaked through, the slip of a woman had flattened herself against the grey stone wall just inside the door, her skirts protecting an oddly shaped brown case on the floor beneath her. A plain, dark felt hat shadowed her features in the room only lit by two dim lanterns, but he could tell it had obviously not kept her ebony curls dry. The impression of a sharp jaw and shapely lips above a thick black scarf drew the rest of him from the wardrobe to investigate.

She'd been out in that bastard of a storm? This waifish girl? No wonder the Pitagowans had interrupted his peace to prepare the room for her. The laws of Highland hospitality—if there still was such a thing—would not have allowed them to deny anyone sanctuary.

"You have my gratitude all the same, Mrs. Pitagowan," the woman said.

God, how he had missed the dulcet pronunciations of the gently bred ladies of his homeland. It'd been so long. He wanted to bid her to speak, to never stop.

"I told ye, call us Bess and Balthazar, everyone else does." The innkeeper trundled over to the door and accepted a tray of tea, which she set on the small stand next to the bed. After, she squeezed around her husband, who'd returned with yet another cauldron of water, to the small brick fireplace on the far wall. Rolling up her sleeves, she squatted to arrange a fire.

"You must call me Vanessa, then."

Vanessa. John tested the name on his tongue, and he thought he saw the woman tense beneath her layers.

Could she hear him already? The sun hadn't gone down yet.

"Where are ye from, lass?" Bess asked, carrying on the conversation.

John found himself equally curious.

"My family resides in London, mostly," Vanessa answered. "Though I am compelled to spend most of the time at our country estate in Derbyshire."

John thought her reply rather curious, not only the phrase but the bleak note lurking beneath the false cheer she'd injected into her voice. Compelled. An interesting word.

If Bess thought it odd, she didn't mention. "Where were ye headed in such a storm, if ye doona mind me asking?"

"Not at all." Bending to drag the case with her, Vanessa rested it by the tea-laden table, out of the way of Balthazar's and Dougal's stomping feet. "I was on the road to Fort Augustus on Loch Ness when the blizzard overtook us." She poured herself a cup of the steaming brew as she answered.

"Is yer family there?" Bess turned to cast a queer look at her. "Will they be fretting after ye?"

The lady didn't bother to sweeten the tea; she simply lifted it to her soft mouth and puckered her lips to blow across the surface before taking a sip.

A strange, hollow longing overtook John as he watched her shiver with delight as she swallowed the warm liquid and let out an almost imperceptible sigh.

Christ he'd give his soul to taste tea again.

"My family is in Paris for Christmas this year," she answered vaguely after the silence had stretched for too long.

"And ye're not with them?" Bess prodded, catching flame to a bit of peat she'd laid beneath the kindling.

"No. No, I am not invited to—that is, I don't travel with them, generally. I am more often occupied by my own adventures."

An awkward silence fell over the room like the batting of a moist blanket. The lady sipped at her tea, retreating deeper into her cloak and her thoughts as the tub was filled.

Once Bess had built the fire to a crackling height, she added one more extra-large, dry log from the grate next to the fireplace, and stood with a grunt. She reached in to test the water and flicked it off, wiping her hand with her apron.

"A strange trunk, that." She nodded to the ungainly square case. "Not quite a trunk, I suppose, and not a satchel either."

"It's a camera." Vanessa abandoned her empty teacup to the tray to stand over it. "I was to be on a winter photography expedition at Loch Ness before the storm hit. I left my trunk with my belongings on the abandoned coach."

A camera? John squinted at the case. He'd never heard of such a thing.

Bess clapped her hands together in delight. "Och, aye? Now's the time to find Nessie, if there ever is one! No doubt ye caught wind of the Northern Lights this year. We could see them snapping across the sky afore the clouds covered them. 'Tis, no doubt, the reason this storm is so powerful. All things are intensified during the *Na Fir Chlis*. And during the solstice, and Christmas after that..." She let the words linger, winking conspiratorially. "All things are possible, are they not?"

"That was my hope." Vanessa smiled broadly, and John felt a catch in his throat, as if the very sight of that smile had stolen something from him.

"Well, here's ye a toweling and some soap. Though perhaps not as fragrant and fancy as ye're used to."

"It'll do perfectly," Vanessa assured her with a kind smile.

John had always appreciated a woman who was kind to those beneath her in rank, stature, or wealth. It had been one of his greatest irritations when a shrewish lady was demanding or unfeeling to the help.

"I'll leave ye, lass," Bess said with a smile. "I'll see if I canna find ye something to sleep in. Get warm and dry and then come to the common room for some supper."

The moment the door latched, the woman, *Vanessa*, locked it and immediately grappled with the knot on her scarf. Unraveling that, she hung it close to the fire, pulled the pin from her hat, and discarded it, also.

John was stunned into stillness at the unfettered sight of her face.

Lord, but she was lovely. The structure of her visage delicate enough to be elfin, pale and sharp, even in the golden firelight. Her eyes, he was pleasantly surprised to find, were as grey as a winter sky.

On many women, such dramatically precise features appeared to be cold and fathomless. But not so in this case. She seemed to glow with this sort of…radiant luminescence that was initiated behind her eyes and spilled over the rest of her like a waterfall.

What was the genesis of such a phenomenon? he wondered. What would he call it?

Life, he realized. An abundance of it.

As someone who hadn't been alive in—well he couldn't remember how many years, precisely—he was drawn to the way it veritably burst from her. Like such a diminutive frame could barely contain it all.

Damned if he didn't find that alluring as hell.

After bending to unlace and remove her boots, she turned her back to him, facing the fire. She shucked her woolen cloak and hung it on a wall peg close to the heat to dry.

Then, she went to work on her blouse.

Bloody hell and holy damnation. This desirable creature was about to strip bare and bathe. *Here.* In the room that had been his prison for so damnably long.

Her movements were harried and jerky, as if made clumsy by exhaustion and the cold.

John had been bred a gentleman in his day. Over-educated and imbued with codes and creeds and ratified rules of behavior. That breeding tore at him now. He should turn away. He should leave her to wash and dress. This interloper upon his dark, abysmal existence—if one could even call it thus. This tiny creature of light and life.

He might have done the noble thing…

If he hadn't hesitated long enough to watch her peel her blouse down her arms, uncovering shoulders smooth as corn silk and white as rich cream.

Lord, but he was transfixed. Even though he technically levitated above the ground, his feet were as good as pegged to the floor.

He watched her unlace her own corset that knotted in the front and wondered when that had changed over the years. Her chin touched one shoulder to glance behind her, as if sensing the intensity of his regard. She looked straight through him, which was a blessing, because if he'd been visible, she'd immediately notice that he sported a cockstand large and vulgar enough to offend even a courtesan.

His conscience prickled. He *shouldn't* watch her…but in this bleak and lonely hell so far from home, she was an oasis of beauty. An English rose among Scottish thistle.

The firelight silhouetted the fullness of her slightly parted lips, the pert upturn of her nose, and the astounding length of her lashes in stark relief.

He was helpless to do anything but appreciate the vision.

Sighing and shaking her head slightly as if to ward off her own silliness, she fiddled with the buckle of a wide belt and pushed her skirt from her hips, drawing down a thin white cotton undergarment at the same time.

Had he knees, they would have buckled. Had he a fist, he would have bitten into it to stave off the hollow groan of longing fighting its way up his chest.

As she assumed she was alone, she was neither self-conscious nor was she self-aware. This was no slow, practiced uncovering of a mistress, meant to tease and titillate. And yet, the sight of her heart-shaped bare ass as she bent to step out of her clothing was enough to unravel whatever matter remained of him.

If she'd been facing the light and not away from it, he would have been granted a peek at the intimate cove between her thighs.

The gods were not so kind.

She straightened, peeling a simple white chemise from her body with a shivering stretch, and turned toward the bath in the center of the room.

Toward *him.*

A watering mouth was the first thing that alerted him to the fact that he would slowly, with infinite, infuriating increments, regain a semblance of corporality.

He would have welcomed the sensation, if he wasn't so utterly distracted by the sight of her in all her nude glory.

Christ. She was a masterpiece, someone crafted by a loving artisan from some other material than the minerals and mud that forged the rest of man. Every other woman now seemed a clumsy clay attempt at the marble-smooth perfection of her.

Though her form was diminutive, her shoulders were not; they were straight and proud, held so by an erect spine and practiced posture. Said posture displayed her tear-shaped breasts to perfect effect, their nipples, peaked and puckered with cold, the same peach hue as her cupid's bow mouth.

God but his hands ached to touch her. To explore every creamy inch of her. To find the places that made her gasp and tremble.

To discover where else she might be peach and perfect.

As if she was loath to leave the warmth of the fire, she took up the soap and her underthings, and tiptoed to the edge of the bath.

The crude basin only came up to about past her knees, so she barely had to lift her leg to test the water within. She dipped a toe, then engulfed the delightfully feminine arch of her foot before wading in to her shapely calf.

John had never been jealous of an inanimate object in his life, but as she hissed and sputtered whilst lowering her chilled body into the hot water, he would have changed places with the liquid in an instant.

It's not as if he was exactly solid.

Though, he was getting *hard…*

He crouched when she did, his eyes unable to leave her as she drew her legs into her chest and settled into the heat with a sibilant sigh of surrender.

He'd give what was left of his soul to coax a sound like that from her. Especially now that he knew what she looked like with naked pleasure parting her lips, and the dew of steam curling the tendrils of her hair that she had yet to take down from its braided knot.

Abandoning her soap and undergarments to the side, she did little but enjoy the heat of the water for a moment, cupping it in her hand and pouring it over what parts of her chest, breasts, and shoulders, she couldn't completely submerge.

God, he remembered what that felt like, sinking into a hot bath on a chilly night.

He'd give anything just to feel warmth.

John made himself dizzy trying to follow every bead of water that caught the firelight along the tantalizing peaks and valleys of her body. Though she was a woman in a crude basin on a packed floor on the edge of the civilized world, she might as well have been a winter goddess bathing in a dark pool.

Would that he could attend her. That he could follow the little bejeweled droplets with his tongue and find the intriguing places they would land.

Would that *he* could make her wet.

She eventually gathered up her undergarments, which were still rather clean all things considered, and scrubbed at them with the soap.

He remembered that she'd mentioned she had no trunk with her, and would likely need to wear them again tomorrow until her things could be fetched.

That finished, she wrung them out and set them aside before taking up the soap once more.

John had been no saint as a young man. He'd frolicked and fornicated in the presence of his young and noble mates, sharing courtesans and the like. He'd enjoyed watching women. What they did to each other, to other men.

To themselves.

But he could truly never remember gleaning as much intimate enjoyment as he did watching her start at her foot, and lather a bit of coarse soap up her leg to her thigh and in between them before working her way back down the other side.

Had he not been dead, he might have expired from the length of time he held his breath.

Restless, aroused, John drifted in circles around the tub as she washed, humming an unfamiliar tune softly as the firelight danced across her skin.

He found himself behind her as she ran a lathered hand over her shoulders and did her best to reach her back. She was about to get suds on a dark velvet curl that had escaped her coiffure and reflexively, John's hand made to brush it aside.

Knowing he couldn't. Understanding that his hand would pass through her before it actually did.

Even so, his body was helpless but to reach for her.

Which was why her muffled shriek startled them both.

Chapter Three

AS GRACEFULLY AS a gazelle, the woman surged to her feet, snatched the towel, and leapt from the bath to retreat as far away from him as possible.

John was almost too shocked to much lament the fact that she wrapped her torso in the towel and clutched it to her clavicles, protecting most of her lovely figure from view.

He looked down at his hand, pleased to note that it had become visible, or at least the transparent shadow of it, a flesh-colored outline through which he could see the floor beneath, interrupted only by the cuff of his crimson regimental jacket.

"Holy Moses," she gasped, breathing as if she'd run apace. Enough of her skin was still visible to notice that she rippled with tiny goose-bumps. "You're a—shade. A man. A..."

"A ghost?" he politely finished for her.

She blanched unbelievably whiter, pressing a hand to her forehead as if to check for a fever. Apparently not finding one, she lowered her palm, unveiling a wrinkle of bemusement.

"You're not Carrie," she accused, her diction slow and uncertain.

"An astute observation," he answered wryly.

"Did you know her?"

"Know her?" He found the question odd and out of place.

"You're in her bedroom. Did you haunt her?" Brows lifting impossibly higher, her gaze shifted to the cobalt coverlet on the bed, and the spider-web thin lace of the curtains, no doubt making certain scandalized assumptions.

He opened his mouth to dispel them, but what came out was, "What year is it?"

She blinked back at him in mute confusion. Her eyes all but crossed and uncrossed as she looked at him, and then through him, and then at him again. "You're English," she said rather distantly. "But here…haunting the Highlands. Why?"

John drifted around the basin toward her. "Pay attention, woman, what bloody year is it?"

She swallowed, retreating from the bed and inching around the basin to keep it between them. "It's eighteen ninety-one."

He froze as his calculations astonished him. "I've been asleep for thirty-five years this time."

"My," she breathed, bending down to retrieve her undergarments from the edge of the tub as she backed toward the fire. "You must have been awfully knackered."

He scowled at her, not understanding the word. "You're quite calm for a woman being haunted. Why are you not running out of here, screaming for help at the top of your lungs?"

She seemed to consider his question carefully, letting go of one side of the towel as she tapped her chin in a contemplative posture. The towel slipped down her chest a little, and John felt his composure slip right along with it.

"For one, I'm not dressed. And for another, Bess warned me I'd spend the night with a ghost. I suppose it was my erroneous assumption that apparition would be female."

He allowed her to keep the basin between them, even though he could have passed right through it and not even disturbed the water.

Not yet.

"I do apologize if I frightened you, miss," he felt compelled to say. "Let me assure you I am a mostly harmless ghost."

"That's a relief to hear. Though I'll admit I was more startled than frightened…almost."

His scowl suddenly felt more like a pout, which irked him in the extreme. "I'll have you know, the mention of my very name has struck terror in the hearts of entire regiments. And you expect me to believe you are so bold as to be fearless? I am a bloody apparition after all. You're not even having a mild crisis of nerves?"

"I'm sure you were *very* terrifying, sir," she obligingly rushed to soothe his ego, which helped not at all. "But I'll admit I'm rather too elated to be scared."

"Elated?" He couldn't believe what he was hearing. Was the woman mad?

She nodded, her lips breaking into a broad smile, her slim shoulder lifting in an attractive and apologetic shrug. "I've always believed in ghosts, and I've never been lucky enough to meet one. I have so many questions. I could cheerfully murder myself for leaving my notebook back at the carriage." She said this as a muttered afterthought before looking up at him with a winsome smile. "Do you mind, awfully, turning around so I can dress?"

"I don't see the point," he challenged, crossing his arms over his chest and lifting a suggestive brow. "You act as though I haven't been here the entire time…watching you."

"How *dare* you?" she gasped in outrage, her notice flying to the bathtub as if it'd just dawned on her that he could have been present without her knowledge. Her color heightened as a comely blush crept up her chest and neck from below the towel.

He was coming to hate that bloody towel.

John bristled, but only because guilt pricked at him. "I *dare* because I'm dead and have been imprisoned in this godforsaken structure since before your grandparents were born, no doubt. What have I to do but observe the goings-on here? Most people are none the wiser."

Her eyes widened as she, no doubt, imagined what he'd borne witness to in so long a time. "That isn't excuse for your ghastly behavior! You are—were—a Lieutenant Colonel?" She raked her eyes over his form, a few more colors of his crimson regimentals lit by the fire at her back. "This is conduct unbecoming an officer, I say."

"Take it up with my superiors, then," he snorted, leaning in her direction with eyes narrowed until he willed himself to disappear.

"Wait!" Her panicked quicksilver gaze scanned the emptiness, hopping right over him. "Come back," she pleaded. "I'm sorry. I won't scold you. I promise. I was just—"

He reappeared paces closer to her, standing on her side of the basin now.

She made a little squeak as he did, hopping back as close to the fire as she could get.

An inconvenient conscience needled him again. He was behaving badly, but a century of isolation tended to strip a man of his manners. "Tell me. Would you have behaved differently were our places reversed? Would you have looked away? Maintained my modesty, my privacy?"

Her gaze traveled down the length of him, and a very masculine sense of victory burned through his veins when he spied the glimmer of appreciation as it dashed across her features. An acute awareness of their proximity. Of his proportions in contrast to hers.

She was a woman.

He was a man.

They were alone in a room together with very little clothing between them.

And if he were naked, the warmth in her gaze told him she would drink in the sight of his body.

Just as he had.

"I cannot say what I would do in your case," she admitted, her voice lower, huskier. "But if you asked nicely, I *would* turn around."

He could refuse. What would she do then? But even as the thought flickered through him, so did another indisputable fact. One hundred and fifty years later, he was still a nobleman, one tasked to uphold honor.

And she was a lady deserving of his respect and deference.

Goddammit.

He bloody turned around.

The rustles of her unseen actions intrigued and tempted him, but he clenched his fists and forced himself to stay right where he was.

"I'm Miss Vanessa Latimer."

He heard the towel hit the ground and this time was able to bite into his fist. Death, it seemed, did not diminish desire.

"Johnathan de Lohr," he finally gritted out. "Earl of Hereford."

"I don't think so," she laughed over the sound of her belt buckling.

"Do you presume to tell me I don't know my own name?" he asked crossly.

"Not at all, but I've been introduced to Johnathan de Lohr, Earl of Hereford at the Countess of Bainbridge's ball a few years past, and have it on good authority that he's very much alive. As far as I know, there was not an Earl of Hereford who died at Culloden."

He frowned, bloody irked by the entire business. "And how would you know that?"

Her rueful sound vibrated through the dimness. "My mother always wanted me to marry a peer, so I've studied *Burke's* more than the Bible, the encyclopedia, and most literature combined. More's the pity. I find it tedious in the extreme."

"I was hardly Earl long enough to make it into the annals of Burke's." Hope leapt into his chest. News of his kinsmen never traveled to this place, and he always wondered about the fate of his family. "Tell me about him? About the Hereford you met."

"Well..." She drew the word out as if it helped her retrieve a memory. "He's attractive but not in that charming, handsome way of most gentlemen. More like brutally well-built. Tall and wide, golden haired like a lion. His hand was warm and strong when we were introduced. And his eyes...his eyes were..." She drifted off, though the little sounds of friction and fabric told him she still dressed herself.

"Blue?" he prompted after the silence had become untenable. De Lohr eyes were almost invariably blue.

"Yes. But I was going to say empty."

"Empty?" he echoed.

She made a melancholy little sound. "He stared at me for a long time, and I could sense no light behind the eyes. They were cold and hollow as a hellmouth, I'm afraid." She seemed to shake herself, her voice losing the dreamy huskiness and regaining some of the crisp starch his countrywomen were famous for. "But worry not, he's possessed of an impeccable reputation and an obscene fortune, so you should be proud of your legacy, all things considered... When were you the Earl, my lord?"

"Please, call me John," he requested. "I've technically no title now; I died during the Jacobite rebellion of seventeen forty-five. My brother, James, became the Earl after I perished at the battle of Culloden."

"You had no heir?"

A bleak and familiar ache opened in his chest. A void that existed whenever he thought of the life he didn't have the chance to live. "I had no wife."

She made that noise again, one that made him wonder what she was thinking. That made him want to turn around to search her beautiful face. Her remarkability was evidenced in the description she'd made of his kinsman. Most people, when asked, would recount reputation and accomplishments, not impressions of one's soul behind their eyes. Miss Vanessa Latimer observed the world in a different way than most.

"It remains strange to me," she was saying, "that you are here. Culloden is miles and miles away."

"Yes. Well. I've gathered from listening to locals that we English won. That Scotland is firmly beneath the rule of King and Crown."

"Queen," she corrected. "Queen Victoria."

"Still?" he marveled. "Surely she's dead by now."

"She's ruled for fifty-three years. Though, while we're on the subject, I don't know many Scotsmen who would deign to call themselves British, though we are technically united under one sovereign. It's no longer a blood-soaked subject, but it's still a complicated one, even after all this time."

Of that, he had no doubt. "I always respected the Scots. I fought because it was my obligation. I was no great supporter of the Stewarts or the bloody King. The de Lohrs prosper regardless of what idiot ass sits on the throne, but we do our duty by our birthright, and sometimes that means going to war."

"Why, then, do you think you're stuck here haunting a small village inn some seventy miles from Culloden?"

He shrugged. "It's been a mystery I've been grinding on for one hundred and fifty years."

"Maybe I could help you," she offered, her voice bright with optimism.

"How could you possibly?"

"I'm stuck here too now, aren't I? At least until the storm blows over, and I love a good mystery. You're obviously not going anywhere, so why not?" She emitted a short sigh one might after completing a task. "There. You can turn back around."

The first thing he noticed when he did was that her damp undergarments were pinned to the fireplace mantle, drying in the heat.

Which meant beneath her clothing she wore… nothing but her corset. Somehow that knowledge was just as arousing as the idea of her completely naked.

Well. Almost.

He locked his jaw, glaring at her strange garments as if he could see through them. As if he'd never seen them before. The skirts of this decade were odd but ultimately flattering, spread tight and flat over the hips and flaring like a tulip toward her knees. A wide belt with an ornate buckle accentuated her impossibly small waist, and the bodice was made of some fabric other than silk. Something lighter that bloused out at the shoulders and bust.

Suddenly he wanted to know everything there was to know about this strange and extraordinary woman.

She peered up at him rather owlishly. "Goodness, I can see more of you now."

And he could see less of her, he silently lamented.

"You have color," she noted, as if to herself. "Your hair is as gold as your namesake's. In fact, you rather look a great deal like him."

Did he? And she'd called him handsome.

Sort of.

He did his best not to preen. "The fault of the solstice, it seems, and the strangeness of the Northern Lights at such a time of year. There's maybe been five such occurrences in the past one hundred and fifty years, and if this is anything like those, I'll become more corporeal as the night goes on."

Her eyes flew wider. She opened her mouth, no doubt to ask a million questions, inquisitive minx that she was.

So, he headed her off at the pass. "What sort of weapon is a *camera*?" He said the word carefully, tasting the syllables, trying to dissect its root words as he drifted toward the case. "You said you were going to take a *photo* with it. Do you really think to battle the Loch Ness Monster in the middle of winter?"

She blinked, moving in front of the case as if to protect it from him. Her delicate features, once so open and intrigued, were now closed, defensive.

Perhaps a bit reproving.

"Photo is the abbreviation for photograph," she informed him stiffly.

He searched his education of the ancient languages. "Photo meaning light. And graph meaning…something written."

"Precisely."

"I couldn't be more perplexed," he admitted.

"I'll show you." She crouched down to open the case, undoing buckles and straps and throwing it open to unveil the strangest contraption he'd ever seen. She didn't touch it, however, but took a flat leather satchel from where it was tucked beside the machine. What she extracted after opening the flap stole the next words from him.

Perching on the bed, one knee bent and the other foot still stabilizing her on the floor, she placed a strange and shiny piece of paper on the coverlet. And then another. And another. And several more until they were all splayed out in wondrous disarray.

John could have been blown over by a feather.

With unsteady fingers, he reached out to the first photograph, a portrait of the Houses of Parliament in London, but this depicted it with a cracking huge clock tower built. The edifice glowed and reached into the sky taller than anything he could imagine. The rendering was nothing like a painting. Colorless and with only two dimensions. But it was *real*, as if the moment had been captured by some sort of magic and…

"Written by light," he breathed.

She nodded, watching him with a pleased sort of tenderness as he discovered a modern miracle that she probably considered quite pedestrian. The next photograph was of the Westminster Cathedral. Another a close-up of a tall lamp. The flame fed by nothing he could imagine, as there was no chamber for wood nor oil. It was as if the fire floated on its very own.

He was about to ask after it when something else caught his eye.

"What the bloody hell is this?" He smoothed his hands over a rather terrifying-looking automaton comprised of arms, levers, whistles, and wheels.

"A locomotive engine. We call it a train, as it can pull dozens of boxcars behind it endlessly at astonishing speeds. I left England on the seven o'clock train last night and arrived in Perth early this afternoon."

He shook his head in abject disbelief, aching to see the real thing. To discover how his empire and world had changed in so long. "How does it work, this locomotive?"

"I'm no engineer, but the engine is powered by steam created with coal fire." She put up a finger as if to tap an idea out of the sky. "You'll be interested to know, ships are powered by steam and steel, as well, rather than wind and wood. We can cross to America in a matter of six days."

"America?" He scratched his head. "Oh, you mean the colonies."

Her lips twisted wryly. "Well…that's a long and rather disappointing story. But the short of it is, they are their own sovereign nation now."

He narrowed his eyes at her. "You're having me on."

"I am not. Declared their independence in seventeen seventy-six. They've their own parliament and everything."

"And what royal family, I'd like to know?"

"A democratic republic, if you'd believe it. A society whose aristocracy is chosen from the best capitalists."

"Not landowners, then?"

She shrugged, gathering back a few of the portraits from the bed into a tidy pile. "Some. But mostly industry giants and war heroes. Machines, factories and the like have changed everything. England's like that too, now. The new century will belong to innovators rather than aristocrats, I'd wager."

"Good God, what I wouldn't give to see that." He couldn't decide what would be worse, dying before his time and missing what might have been. Or existing past his death and learning what he was still missing. What if the Empire rose and fell, and he was still sitting here in the bunghole of Blighty, watching generations of Balthazars raise, eat, and sometimes bugger sheep?

Her eyes brimmed with sympathy, as if she could read his thoughts. "I wish you could see it all. I plan to. I haven't been to America yet, though I'm dying to visit New York. I think I'll go there next if my journey to Constantinople is delayed."

"You're traveling to Constantinople? With whom?" He looked pointedly at her ring finger, which he noted was bare.

Why that ignited a little glow of pleasure in his chest, he couldn't say. It wasn't as though he could speak for her. It wasn't as though he knew he would. They'd been acquainted for all of five minutes.

"Oh…haven't decided yet," she hedged, glancing away and plucking at a loose thread in the coverlet.

"You mentioned your family wanted an advantageous marriage for you, but you didn't introduce yourself as nobility."

His observation seemed to displease her. "No. But my father owns a shipping company, and the thing to do is marry off rich heiresses to impoverished lords."

He made a sound in the back of his throat that he wished didn't convey the depth of his derision on that score. It wasn't that he thought women shouldn't marry above their rank.

It was that he instantly and intensely hated the idea of *her* being married.

She was young, but old enough to have been made a mother many times over. Maybe twenty and five or so…So why wasn't she spoken for?

John allowed his notice to drift to another photograph, this one of a woman in a dark dress seated in a velvet chair. She posed like one would for any master of portraiture, looking off into the distance. Her features carefully still.

From her place at his elbow, Vanessa said, "This is my eldest sister, Veronica. The Dowager Countess of Weatherstoke."

"A Countess. How fortunate for her."

"I wouldn't have traded places with her for the entire world." The melancholy note in her voice made him glance up at her, but her faraway expression didn't brook further discussion.

He saw the resemblance between her and the woman in the portrait. Hair the color of midnight. Bright eyes, a heart-shaped face, and elegant, butter-soft skin.

"My family is visiting her in Paris, where she lives among the beau monde," she said, her voice injected with a false, syrupy insouciance. She picked up the photograph as if to hide it from him, examining it with a pinched sort of melancholy. "Veronica is the beauty of the family."

"No," he insisted more harshly than he meant to. "No, she is not."

She peered up at him oddly, her gaze had become wary and full of doubts he dared not define. "Yes, well…the photo doesn't do her justice."

"It doesn't have to. She doesn't hold a candle to you."

Chapter Four

VANESSA'S FOCUS HAD been arrested. Nay, seized and held captive.

The air thickened between them and the storm seemed closer now. The wild chaos of it slipping into the night. Invading the space between them. Prompting her instincts to prickle and her hair to stand on end.

She was a kitten who'd stumbled into the den of a lion. Nothing more than a light snack. Something he could pick his teeth with.

So why did she have the very feline urge to arch and glide toward and against the lithe strength of his form?

To search for warmth. For protection.

His body, as iridescent as it still was, radiated as much heat as the firelight. His shoulders were wide and his arms long and thick beneath the fitted lines of his crimson jacket.

His features were distinguished, compelling, the product of centuries of such ancestors breeding his sort of perfection. His eyes weren't just blue, they held a startling lapis brilliance, as if backlit by something electric, like lightning. His spun gold hair was caught behind him in a queue. It shone lambent, as did his gauzy specter, barely able to catch the light that pierced through him rather than reflected off him. The square chin above his high, white collar framed a wide, hard mouth that curled in such a way, she might have called it cruel.

His eyes were kind, but that mouth was most certainly anything but.

The word *depraved* came to mind.

A corner of his lip lifted as she stared at it rather rudely. Not quite a smile, but the whisper of one.

The ghost of one.

He cleared a gather from his throat and turned away, dispelling the tension as he drifted over to the camera.

"So, this device is what you use to capture these photographs? This...camera?"

She would never not smile at the way he said that word.

Shaking off whatever had held her mesmerized, she hopped to engage. "Yes. Would you like to see how it works?"

"Very much."

Vanessa had to stop herself short of clapping her hands like a delighted child. Photography was one of her passions, and while many people were curious about it, she'd never had the chance to show it to someone quite so captivated.

Or, rather, captive. But who was she to split hairs?

His feet levitated some six inches off the ground, and his hands locked behind his back in a posture befitting an officer of his class. He looked down at her from over his aristocratic nose and she had the sense he mentally *disassembled* her for examination whilst she *assembled* her tripod.

"I eavesdropped on you and Bess before," he admitted.

"Oh?" She wasn't quite certain how she felt about that, so she remained silent on the topic.

"I'm given to understand you didn't go to Paris with your family because you'd rather stand on the frigid shores of the deepest lake in the world and try to photograph a creature that only exists in folklore?"

She glanced up from where she screwed on the mounting bracket. "And?"

He gave a rather Gallic shrug. "It can't be astonishing to you that someone might remark upon the decision. It seems…rather out of the ordinary."

Vanessa tried not to let on that his assessment stung, as if she weren't aware that her behavior was remarkable. That she was doing what she could to make the most of her exile without advertising it. She didn't allow herself to look up at him as she pulled the accordion-style lens and box from her case with a huff. "I'm a woman who is only interested in extraordinary."

"Evidently."

She cast him a censuring look as she affixed the camera to the tripod. "So says the iridescent apparition levitating above me."

"Touché." He twisted his mouth into an appreciative sort of smile as he studied her. "So, you believe in ghosts and lake monsters. What else? Fairies? Vampires? Shapeshifters? Dragons?"

"And why not?" She crossed her arms, wishing he didn't make her feel itchy and defensive. "Did you know a woman, Mary Anning, found dinosaur bones the size and shape of the long-necked mythos of the Loch Ness Monster only decades ago? Which means creatures like Nessie *have* existed, and perhaps still do."

She held her hand up against his reply. "And if you go to church, they'll tell you about angels and demons. Saints and spirits. Like you, for example. I've done extensive readings on the supernatural, and the stories are eerily similar across all sorts of nations and civilizations. If the native peoples of Australia and also the Scandinavians have similar myths of flying serpents and dragons, doesn't it seem like their existence might be possible? Probable, even?"

His mouth pulled into a tight, grim hyphen, even as his eyes twinkled at her. "Historically, I'd have said no, but at the moment it does seem ridiculous to argue the point."

"'There are more things in heaven and Earth, Horatio, Than are dreamt of in your philosophy,'" she quoted, wagging a finger in the air like some mad scientist as she bustled around her camera, checking bits and bobs. "Truer words were never written."

When she looked back up at him, he'd drifted close. Too close. Close enough that the fine hairs on her body were tuned to him, to the inevitability of his touch.

A touch that never came.

"People still quote Shakespeare?" he murmured.

She swayed forward, and had he been real—or rather, alive—she'd have bumped into him. Instead, her shoulder sort of just...passed through his and she was fascinated with that same odd sort of sensation she'd had in the bath.

Not contact but—but what? An impression?

She swallowed around a dry tongue. "Always. People will *always* quote Shakespeare."

Ye gods, it had been a long time since she'd been alone with a handsome, virile man. One who looked at her like that. Who crowded her and invaded her space in a way she didn't find the least bit irritating.

Overwhelming, yes. But in the best of terms.

She'd forgotten the heady experience of it. The places in her body that would come alive, and demand attention.

Once again, he retreated, floating backward to give her space to work. "What do you call yourself? A mystic investigator of some sort? You travel the world looking to make these realistic portraits, these...photographs of the unexplainable?"

"Not exactly. I travel the world searching for adventure. I just like to capture these adventures in effigy. Because it's sort of like capturing a memory, isn't it? Sometimes that means a Grecian ruin or a Galapagos tortoise, and sometimes…" She snatched the dark cover she had to put over her head in order to see through the lens. "It means a ghost or a relic of something supposedly extinct."

He made a deep, appreciative sound in his throat. It plucked a chord inside of her that vibrated deep. Deeper than church bells or bagpipes or the crescendo of the most tragic opera. Deeper into the recesses of her body and soul than she dared contemplate just now.

She retreated beneath the dark cloth, looking through the lens of the camera, turning the dial to focus it.

When she spied him, she let out a little sound of triumph. "Put your hand to your lapel," she directed. "And levitate perhaps…three more inches toward the ground."

He leveled an abashed look somewhere above the lens, then tried to peek around it as if looking for her. "You're not—trying to photograph *me*, are you?" He seemed as if the idea had curdled his cream.

"I've heard any number of mediums have photographed ghosts. They say you can capture ectoplasm in photographs, and that's supposed to be a gelatinous sort of goo left by spirits and ghosts. You're ever so much more than goo."

"Do try to contain your effusive admiration." His voice could have dried the Amazon into the Sahara. "I'm endlessly flattered to be placed above ectoplasmic *goo* in your estimation."

She giggled, a mischievous part of her wanting to trap the pinched and offended look on his savage features for posterity. "Come now, don't be missish. You look so smart in your uniform. Handsome, I'd dare say."

He straightened a bit, blinking this way and that as if looking for somewhere to place her compliment for safekeeping. "You think so?"

She looked him over, from his chagrined expression to his shiny boots. He was so tall and broad, almost offensively so. No one would call him elegant; he was too ferocious for that. But no one could call him wild; he was too regal for that.

So, what was he? *Who* was he?

So many questions almost choked her mute until one was allowed to spill out.

"How did you die?"

He stalled.

She poked her head up from beneath the camera. "Oh, lands. I'm sorry. I didn't mean to be uncouth. I just… Well you don't look at all injured. I'd have assumed your coat would be riddled with bullets, or you'd have some ghostly axe sticking out of your head. I suppose I read too many penny dreadfuls."

He didn't move, except to tug at his collar before he returned his hand to rest on the lapel of his jacket. "It was a bayonet to the neck," he informed her with almost no inflection at all.

"Oh…" Vanessa was sorry she asked. But his neck didn't at all look—bayonetted. So that was lucky for them both, she supposed. He would have made for ghastly company. "Don't move," she directed before pointing the flash at him and shooting.

He flinched.

"I thought I said not to move," she admonished him.

"You didn't bloody warn me it would be as loud as a musket blast," he muttered. "Can I move now?"

"You might as well," she sighed.

She was going to have to get used to the silent way he sort of—floated around her. It just wasn't seemly for a man of his stature.

"When do I get to see the photograph?" he asked, a boyish sort of anticipation making him appear years younger as he peeked over her shoulder.

A frown tugged at her lips as a heavy stone of sadness landed in her belly. "Well, you won't. After a few minutes, a negative impression will appear on a pane of glass, and I can get that developed into a photograph when I go back to the city. But—you'll only see shadows and light on the glass. I'll bring the photo back here, though, if it actually captured you."

"Perhaps it did," he said blithely with a smile that didn't at all reach his bleak, sapphire eyes. "For I am just like your negative…shadows and light."

A knock at the door saved her from bursting into tears. Vanessa shooed at him as she hurried to unlock it and opened to an anxious Bess.

"I heard the blast!" she fretted. "I came to make sure the ghost hadna gotten to ye."

"The ghost and I are getting along just famously," Vanessa said with what she hoped was an encouraging smile. "I was merely testing the camera to make sure the storm hadn't damaged it."

"Aye, well." Bess itched at her cap. "Would ye like to come through to the common room for stew, so Balthazar and Dougal can haul your bathwater away?"

"Of course, thank you." She turned to the ghost. The Earl…

John.

"I'll be right back," she promised him.

Bess leaned into her room and eyed the device warily. "Ye're really attached to that contraption, aren't ye? Talking to it and the like."

"Oh, no, I was talking to—" Vanessa looked over to see that he'd disappeared. "Well, actually, yes. It's my most prized treasure."

Bess regarded her askance, but ultimately shrugged. "I talk to me oven sometimes," she admitted. "It's a mite smarter and more useful than me husband and less temperamental, too."

Vanessa laughed merrily as she followed the woman through the adjacent storeroom and toward the front. "You called your husband Balthazar, but I heard you refer to him as Rory not too long ago."

"Aye well, the keepers of this inn have had Balthazar in the name since back when this part of the world was Caledonia. Since it is the name of the place, they all seem to take it on."

"I see," she murmured, not seeing at all.

Because the Douglasses were getting even more drunk and sloppy by the fire, Vanessa eschewed the mostly empty tables for the bar, at the end of which the two gentlemen in fine suits were nursing drinks and playing cards.

Bess placed a steaming bowl of stew in front of her and hovered as Vanessa tucked into it immediately.

"How do ye like it?" the proprietress asked, pretending to shine a glass.

"Oh, this is…" *Delicious* wasn't the word. She luckily had some incredibly fibrous and gamey meat to chew as a stall tactic. "It's really filling and—erm—flavorful."

"Aye, it'll put some meat on yer bones." Bess winked. "I gave that driver of yers something extra in his stew. He'll be up all night heaving into a chamber pot for leaving ye in the storm like a blighter."

Vanessa suppressed both a giggle and a spurt of sympathy for the man while she reminded herself never to get on Bess's bad side.

Even after only a moment away, Vanessa was antsy to get back to her room.

To Johnathan. However, she thought this an excellent time to do a little sleuthing for his sake. "So, Bess, you were saying, about the inn. It was here during the Jacobite rebellion? And the battle of Culloden?"

"Och, aye!" Bess said, obviously delighted to have someone to tell, as she was a natural raconteur. "Like many crofts and castles around here, it was a safe haven for the Jacobites, to be sure."

"But, not the English?"

Bess's features wobbled as she narrowed only one eye at her. "Well, no offense to yer countrymen, but after the battle at Culloden, the

English were everywhere were they not? They stayed at the inn, to be sure, as it was sedition to deny them entry. But, they never found our secret spots, did they?" She tapped her head as if she'd thought of those secrets herself.

Vanessa perked up. "Secret spots?"

"Just so. Like Carrie Pitagowan's Chamber of Sorrows."

"Chamber of Sorrows?" Vanessa echoed. "Now that sounds deliciously ominous."

Bess leaned closer, her chins wobbling in agreement. "Aye, Carrie worked beneath these old rafters during the days of Culloden. A saucy minx she was. Curious, like you. Always looking for something more."

Vanessa winced. Was she that obvious?

Bess seemed not to notice, continuing with her story. "Carrie would go to Jacobite battlefields and strip the English soldiers of their treasure. It was about this time of year back then, another blizzard, another *Na Fir Chlis* when 'twas said she cursed that room. Warned all who would listen that a lion lived there and would devour any who stayed."

Chills spilled over every part of Vanessa, and she took another bite just to distract herself from them.

Oblivious to her discomfiture, Bess continued, "Of course each new generation doesna believe in Carrie's lion, but every time we try to let that room, the occupants are haunted right back out of it again."

At this, Vanessa frowned. "Why let it to me, then?"

Bess cast her eyes down as she drew her fingernail through the pit in the wood of the bar. "I doona ken, lass, if ye want the honest truth. I couldna leave you out in the storm and…something told me the Chamber of Sorrows would welcome ye, and the lion with it."

Vanessa swallowed the dry meat in a lump that made its uncomfortable way down her esophagus, and drank a long swallow of dark ale to force it down.

She could see Johnathan de Lohr as a lion. Fierce and golden haired. Not only a conqueror but commander, ruler of all he surveyed.

And well he knew it.

"Ye've known a bit of the longing that lives in that room, I wager." Bess lowered her voice to the decibel of confidants. "And yer fair share of sorrow, too. Else why would ye be here alone what with Christmas bearing down on ye? If ye doona mind me asking, why's yer family in Paris without ye?"

Her pitying look speared Vanessa through the ribs as she cast about for an answer. "Well I—"

"Tell me the young, cheap whisky isn't making me see things, Priestly," a nasally, masculine, *British* voice slurred with a bit of a lisp. "Tell me this isn't little Vanessa Latimer, wot?"

Vanessa turned to see that the men who had been playing cards at the edge of the bar now crowded close around her, effectively trapping her onto the tall stool upon which she perched. They each had an empty glass in their hands, and the one who'd addressed her swayed, dangerously.

"By Jove." His dark-haired friend—Priestly, she presumed—might have been passably handsome but for sporting a pathetic, thin mustache. He leered down at her from marble-dark eyes held way too close together. "I thought she looked familiar when she blew in, but she was in such a state of disarray I didn't care to look at her. She cleans up rather well, though. I could almost believe she was respectable."

"Yes," the first one intoned, combing his hands through fair hair made greasy with too much pomade. The scent of it was nearly overpowering. "Quite respectable. But we know better, don't we?"

The food turned to ashes in her mouth. Vanessa locked everything down just as she'd taught herself to when preparing for just one such encounter.

"Gentlemen," she greeted soberly. "I don't believe we've been introduced and, therefore, it is not polite to approach me thusly."

Priestly's eyebrows shot up. "My, aren't we all grown up and putting on airs? What do you say to that, Gordie?"

Gordie's watch chain gleamed as he leaned in obscenely close, his breath reeking of scotch. "We've heard tell you spend your time galivanting to exotic places. Learning, no doubt, *exotic* skills."

Priestly all but tossed his glass to Bess. "I'd take a whisky, but not the kind that tastes like we've licked a peat bog. The good stuff you're no doubt hiding back there. And I'll make a bloody ruckus if you water it down."

Vanessa let out an outraged breath, ashamed of her countrymen. "That's beneath you, gentleman, talking to a proprietress like that."

Gordie leaned even closer, forcing her to bend over backward to escape him, which caused her to bump into Priestly. "I'd rather *you* were beneath me."

"I beg your pardon!" she huffed. She'd been heckled before, but not so publicly. Nor so rudely.

"Really, Gordie, don't be vulgar; we're sharing a room in this shitehole, there's not privacy at all."

Gordie's suggestive expression caused the gorge in Vanessa's stomach to rise into her throat. "We can share other things. We've done it before." He raked her with a glare miraculously overflowing with both disdain and desire. "Woman like her will let you put it anywhere you like."

Before he even finished his last word, her entire bowl of stew lurched from the table and was heaved into his face, the scalding gravy latching onto his skin.

A shrill scream erupted from him as he clawed at himself, trying to wipe it off.

Vanessa's hands were still clenched at her sides. She'd never even reached for the bowl.

She looked across the bar at Bess in time to see that the whisky bottle she'd retrieved was snatched from Bess's hands and smashed over Priestly's head. The jagged neck hung in the air as if brandished by an invisible hand, ready to plunge into the man's throat.

"Sweet Christ in heaven." Bess crossed herself and made a few other signs against evil as well.

It was her ghost. Even though she couldn't see him, there was no denying it.

"John," Vanessa gasped into the empty air next to the floating bottle. "Johnathan, don't."

The bottle dropped.

Priestly turned on her. "You putrid slag! You're worth no more than a—"

His entire body flew back as if it had crumpled. He landed on the table by the fireplace, splintering it and scattering half a dozen drunk and slightly dozing Douglasses.

The highlanders launched into action, leading with their fists, assuming, no doubt, they'd nearly missed a tavern brawl.

Gordie managed to wipe mutton out of his eyes in time to catch a fist to the jaw, dropping him to the floor immediately.

Vanessa whirled to Bess, who wiped her hands on her apron and reached beneath the bar. "Go back to yer room, dearie. I'll restore order here." When she extracted a plank the size of an oar, Vanessa quickly retreated. She passed Balthazar on her way, grinning and rolling up his sleeves as if eager to join the fray.

Picking up her skirts, she ran to her room, dove inside, then shut and locked the door behind her.

Her skin burning with humiliation, she went to the window and threw it open, letting the cold air steal her breath in a welcome blast.

Johnathan appeared, his color heightened and sharpened as his entire form slammed into the room like a mountain of muscle and wrath. "Those bog-faced sons of a whore! Were I myself, I'd wrench his arm from his socket and beat him to death with it, and then I'd decapitate his friend just so I could piss into the empty cavity where his spine used to be."

"Please, calm down." Vanessa let out a few shaken puffs into the blizzard, pressing her freezing hands to her burning cheeks as the storm pricked her with crystals of ice.

She could stand it no longer than a few seconds, so she wrestled the window closed and latched it.

John paced the length of the bed next to her, his fists white with unspent rage. "Are all gentlemen in this age such smarmy, weak-limbed dandies? Makes one wonder how many cousins had to fornicate to produce such a slithering strop of a rubbish heap and call it a man. I have a few regrets in my life, and my afterlife, but not slicing him open with that bottle is going straight to the top."

Even as she pressed her forehead to the cool windowpane, she fought a sad little smile at his vehemence. "Yes, well, none of that was necessary, but thank you all the same."

"He called you a slag!" John roared.

"It doesn't matter," she whispered, her breath spreading in an opaque circle in front of her.

Even though his motions made no noise, she could sense that he stopped pacing. "Doesn't. Matter?" he said with a great deal of emphasis on all the T's.

She closed her eyes. "I've been called that and worse. I'm used to it."

"How is that bloody possible?" he thundered. "You're…well you're—"

"I'm ruined," she said gently, finally gathering the strength to turn around.

She had expected to see him be incredulous, but not his head cocked to the side in doglike befuddlement. "What? Ruined?"

She breathed in a deep breath through her nose, preparing to lose his respect and regard. Mourning it already. "This is why I am not with my family at Christmas. Or any holiday, really. I'm *persona non grata* in the eyes of society. My reputation couldn't be lower if I actually sold myself on Whitechapel High Street."

At that, he became impossibly still.

"It happened long ago," she explained, already exhausted. "I fell in love with William Mosby, Viscount Woodhaven. He gave me a ring with the largest diamond I'd ever seen. We made love beneath the Paris sky…"

"And then?" he growled.

"And then he married Honoria Goode, the daughter of my father's shipping rival, for her dowry was ten thousand pounds more obscene than mine."

"He broke his word to you." The statement was murmured softly, almost without inflection. "Did he break your heart?"

Vanessa couldn't bring herself to look at him.

"Well…not irreparably at first. Not until he—until he published a pamphlet scoring the lovers he'd had. Prostitutes, mostly. But I was on the list, and my score wasn't very favorable. *Pathetically eager, but impossible to please,* he said. He called my… my um…" She looked down, wondering why it was so difficult to say. Why she'd stopped feeling ashamed so long ago, but was suddenly afraid of the opinion of a dead man. "Well he said I am broken."

The rickety chair at the bedside shattered against the far wall.

"Have you no brothers?" John thundered. "Your father didn't kill him in a duel?"

She stared at him in open-mouthed astonishment for a moment. He was magnificently angry. His muscles seemed to build upon themselves as he heaved in breaths to a chest she could still mostly see through to the fire on the other side.

The effect was rather apropos, as the flames licked at his chest, seeming to ignite the scarlet coat with the same inferno that blazed in his eyes.

"Well," she answered somewhat demurely. "Duels have been illegal for some time now."

He gaped at her. "You're joking."

"I'm afraid not."

"You mean to tell me, there is no recourse to besmirched honor?" He gestured broadly as if he couldn't comprehend the idiocy. "Any blighter can walk around and say whatever they might to defame an innocent, and others do what… *believe* them?"

It did sound rather ridiculous the way he said it. "If they're a man of influence, they are believed," she answered. "That seems to be the way of it. I mean, there are libel laws, but…that recourse is rarely taken."

He made a disgusted face and threw a gesture at the door toward the chaos on the other side of it. "This age isn't enlightened, it's barbaric."

"I don't know about that. Fewer people die in duels, so…I suppose you might call that progress."

"Not in my opinion. Not this bloody—" He whirled on her. "What was his name again?"

"William Mosby."

"William… I'd cheerfully murder the ponce myself. I'd strike his entire legacy from the annals of time until—"

"No need." Vanessa held her hand up against him. "Truly. He's…well, he's met his fate. What's done cannot be undone."

Suddenly. Miraculously. His features softened as he looked down at her, his arms dropping to his sides as he lingered close. Closer. His hand reached out as if to lift her chin, but he never quite managed. "I am sorry that you suffered."

She summoned that false-bright smile for him. The one she'd learned so well. "I am lucky, in many respects. I still have a generous stipend from my father, to assuage his guilt, I imagine, for keeping me away from them socially. And with it I plan to see the world. I go on adventures like this one. And, reputation-wise, I've nothing to lose, so I may do what I please."

His brow furrowed in consternation. "But you're alone. Why not have a companion to take on such adventures with you?"

She let out a very unladylike snort. "The idea of compelling someone to keep me company with coin never appealed to me. Besides, then I'd be responsible for them, wouldn't I? And, if I'm honest, very few would consider an association with one as besmirched as I a very desirable position. No one would consider my references a boon."

The look on his face caused her own to fall. She couldn't bear the tenderness. Or the pity.

"It is not so much suffering," she all but whispered. "When there are so many in the world who know such pain, my bit of shame and isolation seems rather small in comparison."

He dipped his head, his lips hovering above her forehead. "Suffering can be profound or prosaic, but it is suffering all the same. Yours is not inconsequential."

His words melted her like honey decrystalizing in the summer heat. His presence washed over her like silk flowing in a breeze. Insubstantial, sensual, and yet compelling.

"You're not broken," he said. "You're not ruined. Not to me."

"You're being kind," she choked out over a lump of emotion lodged in her throat.

"I mean it," he said fiercely.

She ducked away from him, turning to hide the burn of tears, pinching the bridge of her nose against their ache. She was too proud for this. She could not come apart in front of a veritable stranger.

"What?" he asked. "What's wrong?"

"You—have a ruthless side," she admitted breathlessly. "It—um—it makes my blood rush around a bit."

He was close again. Right behind her. His presence a relentless affectation. "I frightened you?"

"No! I mean. Not entirely. You're the only person who has ever stood up for me before," she admitted, moving toward the fire and smoothing her dress down her thighs in a nervous gesture.

"Then why retreat from me?" he persisted.

She could tell the flames nothing but the truth. "When you touch me I…Well, actually, you don't *touch* me. But you were able to hold on to inanimate objects. To do a man violence."

He let out a long breath. "I'm little better than an awareness most of the time. Something I could slip in and out of at will at first, but the longer I tarry, the more I spend in the void. But there are holy days—solstices and equinoxes where, if I concentrate very hard, I can become something like corporeal. At least, for a moment. I can will things to move, but it depletes me. On nights like *Na Fir Chlis* I am the most visible, but I cannot sustain contact for long."

"I see," she whispered.

His voice ventured closer, until she could almost feel his warm breath against her ear. "When I reached for you in the bath, my hand went through you… You felt that?"

"I feel—something. Not your skin, per se. Something else. It's like…" She cast about for the word. "A tingling. No, stronger than that. A vibration, perhaps."

He made an amused noise deep in his chest. "Really?"

"It's disquieting."

"Does it cause you pain?"

"No. No, quite the opposite."

"The opposite?" He drifted around her, standing so close to the flames a normal man would have caught. "The opposite of pain is pleasure."

She retreated a step. "So it is."

He advanced, his eyes liquid pools of carnal promise. "Does my touch pleasure you, Vanessa?"

"I don't—I don't know how to answer that."

"Why?" he pressed. "Why after being so fearless, is it pleasure that scares you? Do you fear your desire for it?"

She swallowed. "Yes. Maybe. I couldn't say." She feared the ruin it had already brought her. The derision of another lover. Another man she thought she might care for. Who might profess to care for her. She feared the strength of her feelings, her desires, after only knowing this man for the space of an hour.

His hand reached out, a tremor visible in the long, rough fingers. His palm caressed her face, but not in the way she wished it would. It was there, but it wasn't. The warmth of his touch lingered; a callus might have abraded her soft cheek. *There.* Right there. But also, just out of reach.

It was both bliss and torment. The vibrations of his energy, of the very striations etched into the palm of his hand, were tangible. But whatever touched her was not flesh. Not exactly.

It was enough to make her weep, the longing she sensed in the gesture. The cavernous pain she read etched into the grooves branching from his eyes, and in the tension of his skin stretched tight over his raw, beautiful bones. "I haven't touched a woman in a lifetime. In a handful of lifetimes."

"Do you want to?"

"Is that an invitation, Vanessa?" His voice was like liquid velvet, his eyes twin azure flames. "If I could, would you let me?"

"I—Um…" She was a quivering, boneless puddle of sensation. Of desire. Her loins ached, moistened, bloomed for him. Her lips plumped and her skin burned to be touched.

Her entire body was one thrumming chord of need.

Was she the only one undergoing this torture? "John?" she whispered, turning her head out of his palm, if only to spare them each more impotent longing. "Can you *feel* desire as you are?" she queried. "Can you—erm—manifest it? Physically?"

His lips actually stirred her hair as he growled against her ear. "I've been hard as a diamond since the moment I watched you undo your buttons."

Chapter Five

JOHN LEANED BACK and let his admission crash into the space between them, overflowing it with heady, carnal, unspoken reveries. His. Hers. All amalgamating into one frustrated frequency of need.

All the chaos of the common room had gone quiet, no doubt Bess had kicked everyone to their beds. In this abandoned corner of the structure, he and the comely Miss Latimer might have believed they were the only two people in the whole of the Highlands.

John watched her intently as she stared—or rather—glared at him. Unblinking. Her chest rose and fell beneath the high-necked blouse as she very distinctly did not allow herself to look down.

She'd have found the answer to her question if she had, straining against the placket of his trousers.

However, after what he'd just discovered about her, he realized he might have been too forward. Might have overwhelmed a woman who'd only just been harangued by undesirables.

He closed his eyes and stepped back, allowing her space. "I shouldn't have said that."

Squirming with shame and regret, she instantly buried her face in her hands. "No. That is—the fault is mine. I asked you the vulgar question. I don't know what's gotten into me."

"I order you to stop feeling shame," he said with a stern frown.

She looked up at him askance. "You can't command emotions, that's not how they work."

"I can and I will," he shot back, looking to goad her past her mortification. "I insist the blame for our—indelicate interaction be placed on my shoulders. I've forever been a man too plain of speech. Too blunt and coarse and forbidding. It made for a successful Lieutenant Colonel, a mediocre nobleman, and well… ripe shit at relationships."

The tremulous tilt at the corner of her mouth told him his candor was working. "Which relationships?" she queried, her relentless curiosity returning. "With women, you mean?"

"'Twas doubtless why I remained a bachelor at five and thirty. I assumed one took a wife like one took a hill in combat. It was all strategy and espionage, if not an all-out battle. I was built to win, not woo, and I frightened many a maidenly noble lady into the arms of some gentler, more civilized man."

She wrinkled her nose at that rather adorably. He wasn't certain how to interpret the expression, but that didn't stop him from continuing, if only to put conversational space between their previous fraught interaction.

He marched around her, exploring the space of his chamber with his hands clasped behind him. He did his best not to prowl like the predator he was. To draw his tense shoulders away from his ears. "My social ineptitude reached past the fairer sex to anyone, really. My parents. My brother, James. Even after everything, he came to claim my remains all those years ago. Or perhaps he only returned for the ring, and taking my benighted bones back to the de Lohr crypts was an afterthought, though I couldn't say I'd blame him."

"The ring?" She grasped onto the one subject he'd only mentioned as an afterthought.

"A de Lohr signet. Given to my templar ancestor—the Lion Claw, they'd called him—by his ladylove so many generations ago."

John summoned a picture of the piece into his mind. The head of a lion had been etched into the precisely crafted purest gold; rubies set into the ocular cavities as if the blood spilled by the apex predator reflected in his eyes.

"Surely your brother came to collect *you*, and the ring was the afterthought."

"You underestimate the significance my family put on that ring," he said gruffly. "And you didn't know my brother. We did not part on the best of terms. I regretted that. I was a hard man to know, and I did not understand his impulsive passions. His depth of emotion. And, if I'm honest, I envied him his freedom as the second son, his shoulders unencumbered by the weight of the de Lohr name." Unbidden, John looked into the past, seeing the familiar face of his brother, the disappointment in his eyes the last time they spoke. "I am confident James made a better Earl than I might have. At least, I hope he did."

"The Earldom of Hereford is still one of the most wealthy and respected titles in the Empire," she explained gently. "If that is any condolence to you."

It was, actually. "You're kind to say so. I don't get word of such things up here. It's mostly clan gossip and peasant revelry."

Something about that elicited a giggle from her, and when he looked, her silver eyes were twinkling like the little diamond bobs in her ears. "We don't call them peasants anymore. Not that it should matter to you much, I suppose."

He chuffed out his own sound of mirth. "Yes. A more enlightened age, you've mentioned." He was about to ask her to tell him about it when she began to pace as if puzzling something out.

"So not even your remains are here in Scotland. I still find it extraordinarily peculiar that your bones should rest in the de Lohr crypts but your spirit should be *restless* here of all places. Did you visit this inn before you died?"

"Never."

"Perhaps you killed the previous proprietor in the war?"

"No, I'm certain it has something to do with Carrie Pitagowan and her blasted curse." He'd been over and over it in his mind, and he wasn't exactly excited to rework it with her. "Do you happen to know any witches who might be able to break it?"

She ignored his dry sarcasm. "What about her Chamber of Sorrows?"

At the mention of the room, he went still.

She continued, pacing the length of the bed. "I asked Bess, and she told me that Carrie went to Jacobite battlefields and took things, especially from English officers. I've noticed you have no saber nor hat nor medals upon your jacket." She whirled on him, ceasing her pacing as she held her hands up in a motion that might stop the entire world so it might listen to her next sentence. "John! What if she took your ring?"

Christ but she impressed him. She'd been here all of five minutes and she'd discovered what it'd taken him decades of eavesdropping to find out.

"I have no doubt my body was looted after the battle, by starving, angry highlanders. But I've searched the Chamber of Sorrows. Nothing in it belongs to me."

John had done many distasteful things in his life as a soldier, and also in his short tenure as the heir to an Earldom, but smothering the enthusiastic light shining from Vanessa Latimer's open, upturned face had to be the worst.

Still, he could tell he'd not defeated her as the wheels and cogs of what he was coming to understand was a sharp and restless brain didn't cease their machinations. "Can you take me to this Chamber of Sorrows?"

"Certainly, though it's not far." He motioned to the wardrobe, a piece of furniture almost as tall as he was. "The Pitagowans have merely covered the door with this."

She circled the thing, tapping on her chin as she was wont to do. Testing its heft with a little push. "I don't know if I can move it."

John didn't know if she could either, which meant he'd have to. "I'll do what I can to help you."

Clearly heartened, she gifted him with a brilliant smile that sparked a little flicker of joy in his guts before she flattened her back against one side, bracing her feet on the ground to pit her entire weight against the thing. It scraped and budged, but only an inch or so.

John joined her, levering over her and bracketing her head with his arms. If someone walked in at this moment, that person would do well to assume they were about to kiss.

Or had just finished doing so.

As if she'd read his thoughts, her eyes dropped to his mouth. Her tongue snaking out to moisten her own lips.

John's lids slammed closed as lust roared through him. "Goddammit, Vanessa. *Push.*"

The wardrobe gave way beneath their combined efforts, and he all but leapt away from her and retreated to the opposite end of the room.

It'd been a long time since he'd asserted himself onto the world of the living so often in one night. It tired him. Weakened him in so many ways.

The chief among them his self-control. In one respect a heavenly thing, and in others, pure hell.

He willed his inflamed libido to cool and ordered the heart that'd begun beating again to stop. He commanded his soul to stop yearning. To cease aching for what should not—what could *never*—be.

"That took a lot from you, didn't it?" she observed.

He looked down at his own outline and noted it was thinner, more translucent, the features blurred.

"I'll be fine," he sighed. "Though I'll hope you forgive me for not opening the door."

Vanessa took one of the oil lamps from the sideboard and pushed open the doorway that was really no bigger than a cupboard. Even someone as petite as she had to duck to get inside.

John merely went through the wall.

He found himself watching her more than noting any of the treasures in the dusty old place. Pure, unadulterated awe slackened her jaw, parting her lips as she twirled in the center of the tiny antechamber as if trying to take in the entire glory of the Sistine Chapel.

She all but floated to the haphazard shelves and rickety cases lining the long chamber.

As one could never do in a museum, she reached out trembling, elegant fingers and tested the sharpness of a saber mounted on the wall or threaded them through the plume on a hat. It was as if she could see with her eyes, but never truly had a vision of anything until she'd experienced it through touch.

John found himself wanting to trade places with inanimate objects as she caressed them with the reverence of a lover. Buckles. Buttons. A rifle, a medal of valor, irons for captives, chains and whips and other implements of violence and war.

She didn't belong in this place, this so-called Chamber of Sorrows. She was a creature of light and joy. One to whom melancholy and sorrow did not attach itself for long.

What must it be like to move in the world in such a way?

Vanessa Latimer had transfixed him like nothing or no one had done before.

Everything she did, every gesture she made was attractive to him.

From the way she blinked the fans of her eyelashes, to the swift, almost sparrow-like movements of her graceful neck as she tried to look at everything all at once. The sway of her skirts soothed him, drew him toward her as she ventured deeper into the long chamber, which was actually more a corridor that ran the length of the inn.

She paused at a small table upon which letters and miniature portraits of women or children were stacked neatly. As if understanding they might disintegrate if she touched them, her hands hovered like butterfly wings above the loops of writing often stained with blood.

He'd known her for such a short time, and yet he understood that she burned to stop and read every word, absorbing it into her memory.

Eventually, she glanced back at him, her gaze brimming with so many things. "Have you read these?" she asked hopefully.

Once again, he hated to disappoint her. "This is maybe the third time anyone has ever brought a light in here when I was awake. I've rarely been able to truly examine these things, and when I could I was searching for something that might belong to me. For letters my brother, James, wrote me. I carried them with me everywhere, even into battle. They were a testament to his bravery and strength he never even knew he possessed."

The sound she made conveyed both regret and admiration. "I wonder if they were sent home to him."

"I hope so," he sighed, not wanting to dwell on a hope he couldn't verify.

"You need light to see?" The very idea seemed to surprise her.

He felt his features soften, the sadness melting into an endlessly amused half-smile. "I'm a ghost, not a vampire."

She rolled her eyes at his teasing, swatting at him with no real heat. "How should I know the rules? I mean, you float above the floor and you can walk through walls."

"Sadly, I cannot see in the dark." Or through things. Like her clothing.

She made a noncommittal noise as she moved further along the chamber. Her ankle rolled beneath her skirts and she nearly lost her footing.

Reflexively, he reached for her, but she righted herself before he could do anything.

Clearing her embarrassment from her throat, she pointed beneath her and offered an abashed explanation. "The floor is uneven."

He nodded his head, his heart too much in his throat to reply.

She returned to examining every single treasure. "Are you *sure* none of this is familiar? These sabers, a hat, perhaps? Even a button?" She sounded almost desperate now.

He shook his head. "No, none of these are mine. Though I recognize a few of them as belonging to compatriots."

Ones he mourned for many years.

She ran her hands across a bayonet, testing its edge. "You said you sleep a great deal. Is that truly what it's like to be…" She made an uncomfortable gesture at his general personage.

"Dead?" he clipped.

"Well I didn't want to seem indelicate."

She was so delicate, she'd never seem anything but.

"It's just I have so many questions. And I am afraid to ask them, but when else will I get the chance? Is there a light anywhere like people have claimed, at the end of a tunnel perhaps? Have you met others like yourself? Or angels? Or—or anyone else out of the ordinary? Out of our limited mortal understanding, I mean."

He wished he could spin her a hypnotic yarn that would make death seem less depressing, but he was an honest ghost, and a boring one, evidently.

"I've met no other apparitions and my torpor, it's—not even like sleep, exactly. It's nothingness." He almost hated to admit it, because sometimes the void terrified him. "I want to say darkness, but it's not even that tangible. I am gone, and then I surface. I am here, but I have no part of myself. I have nothing but a vague sense of who I am. And each time I go under…I stay for longer. There are days I fear I'll become one with nothing, and every part of who I was will be lost."

What he didn't say was that each time he went under, he was always disappointed to be brought back. He would rail and stomp and use what little power he had to throw things. To rattle the bedposts and windows and make the stones of his cage tremble. He'd frighten people just to do it. Because now that he'd found himself again, he'd have to dread the next time he was lost.

She blinked watery eyes up at him, her sharp chin pitting and quivering with emotion. "How do you endure it?"

"How can I do anything but?" he replied, his finger aching to smooth an unruly tendril of hair away from her furrowed brow.

Her throat worked over a difficult swallow. "I wish I could save you, somehow."

A tenderness welled in him in that moment and threatened to spill over into emotion he had no idea what to do with. What a Countess she'd have made. So small and yet regal. So soft-spoken and yet brave. Independent. Unbiased. Kind. Honest.

God. He'd have offered for her hand after one chaperoned meeting. He'd have claimed her and planted children inside of her, creating an undeniable legacy of which any man would be proud.

It was almost worth one hundred and fifty years of loneliness to have met her.

She'd brought him back to himself, somehow.

Whatever she saw in his eyes caused her to step in toward him. And, once again, she stumbled.

Catching herself this time, she lifted her skirt to examine the packed earth beneath her.

Whatever she found caused her to gasp.

"Hold on." Rushing past him—nearly rushing through him had he not moved out of the way in time—she retrieved the lantern from the entry and plucked a bayonet from the wall.

Returning, she shocked him by placing the lantern on the ground, kneeling down in a pool of her skirts, and using the bayonet to scratch and dig into the dirt.

"What the devil are you about?" He hovered over her, worried that she'd finally reached the edge of her sanity.

"This floor has a dip right here about the size of my shoe," she said around the labor of her digging. "After I tripped this last time, I thought, if Carrie was a clever girl, she might *bury* her most prized possessions to make certain they weren't discovered. Even if the Chamber of Sorrows was."

Something within him ignited. He wished he could grab something and rake at the earth next to her. That he could reach into it and pull whatever might be down there above ground. But the bland weight of weakness still tugged his limbs until they were heavy, and he began to admit to himself that the torpor was calling to him.

Every moment he spent with her cost him, dearly.

But the darkness would have to drag him away. He'd not go willingly. Not while he could bask in her presence for one more moment.

She worked until she was winded, and the helplessness he felt made him want to throw things. To shake his fist at whichever angry god cursed him to such an existence.

Until a hollow sound announced the bayonet had struck something.

Their eyes met for a breathless moment.

Then, she attacked the ground around it with renewed vigor, scraping out a small, square wooden box. She stood, and John could hear Vanessa's heart beating hard enough for the both of them as she opened the simple container.

Every jewel inside the box glittered gem-bright in the golden glow of the lantern.

But it was the twin rubies he found that suffused him with a lightning bolt of sensation.

"Vanessa. The ring."

With trembling fingers, she plucked it out and held it up so they could both gawk at its magnificence.

He could feel it pulsing with a magnetism no inanimate object should possess. The lion stared at him from hot ruby eyes.

Claiming him. Calling to him.

He thrust his hand between them, splaying his fingers. "Put it on."

Her forehead crimped. "What if it doesn't work?"

"*Vanessa.*"

She nodded, lowering her hand to slide it onto his finger.

His boots hit the earth with a heavy thud. He had weight. He had mass. The air bit at his cheeks and filled his lungs with a cold incredible breath. His heart threw itself against wide ribs and his muscles corded with strength. Veins pulsed with blood.

With need.

His hand gripped hers. Slim, cold fingers trembled against his flesh. His skin.

Her eyes were wide and watery as she stared at him without blinking.

"John?" she whispered.

He was almost sorry.

Almost sorry that a strangled groan was all the warning she had before he crushed her to him and captured her already open mouth.

Chapter Six

HIS KISS WAS a sweet violence. Both a conquest and a claiming.

Vanessa welcomed the assault on her senses as this *man*, this solid, starving, sexual man clamped her entire body to his and devoured her mouth as if her kiss could restore his very life.

The sensation of his lips—his skin—was more than a tingling suggestion now. He was tactile. Warm. Almost as if fed by lifeblood.

Almost.

She still detected that the feel of his flesh was imperfect. A vibration persisted where the smooth whorls of his fingerprints should be. It was at once more than an ordinary touch, and not enough.

It didn't matter. She'd take whatever she could get.

He had a scent now, cedar and leather and the faintest trace of gunpowder.

It tantalized her endlessly.

Her hands clutched the lapels of his crimson wool coat, reveling in the coarse fibers abrading her fingertips because it meant he was *real.* Tangible. She suddenly wanted to explore everything. Everywhere. Every hot, smooth and strong inch of him.

He kissed like a man denied a hundred and fifty years of pleasure. Of pain. Of desire and release. There was a savage wildness in it, an untamed urgency that sent little thrills of anxiety and anticipation pouring down her spine and spreading into the deep, empty recesses of her womb.

With a strong, hot lick, his tongue parted the seam of her mouth and dipped inside to sample her flavor.

He tasted like a wicked sin. Like every drink too masculine for her to sip and every dessert to decadent to be indulged.

His arms felt like iron shackles around her, and she became his willing prisoner there in the Chamber of Sorrows. Surrendering to the inevitability of what he was about to do to her. Of what demands he would make of her body.

The very thought made her legs puddle beneath her until she feared she couldn't remain standing.

When she went all but limp against him with a sibilant sigh into his mouth, his kiss unexpectedly gentled, his lips sweeping across hers in featherlight drags. The contrast was her undoing as she lifted onto her tiptoes to seek more.

His large, rough hands drew up her arms and shoulders until he bracketed her jaw in his palms and tilted her face up, pulling back to look down at her with agonizing tenderness.

"My God, you are so pure and perfect," he marveled in a harsh, breathless tone.

His words evoked a hot blush that spread up her chest and heated the cheeks he cradled so reverently in his hands.

Vanessa's lashes swept down over eyes pricked with tears, as a familiar shame swamped her, dousing the flames of her ardor a few degrees. "You know I am not so pure. Not in the sense of the word that seems to matter to most people. I'm no virgin. No *ingenue*. But neither am I a whore. Do you understand that?" She worried the knowledge he had made her seem more accessible to him, and another part of her fretted that he would think less of her.

"Woman," he growled, his breath coming in agonized pants, his azure eyes smoldering down at her like the core of a flame burning too hot to be contained. "I'm about to do things to you that would make a virgin faint. I'm going to worship you in ways that would offend a whore. So, I suppose we should both be grateful you are not either of those things."

She gaped up at him, astonished by his wicked candor. "What sort of thing—Oh!"

He snatched her off the ground with unsettling strength and swept her out of the chamber in a few strides. This time, he had to duck to get through the doorway and deposit her on the bed.

Vanessa was glad for the sturdy wood of the frame rather than creaking brass as he ripped his coat from his heavy shoulders and joined her there.

She had a feeling they would have woken the entire inn with what they were about to do.

He prowled up her prone body like a great cat until he settled fully upon her, his weight a delicious press as he took her mouth once again.

Ribbons of desire unspooled within her as she wound her hands around his neck, tugging the leather thong that caught his long hair into a queue. Releasing it, she twined her fingers into the silky mass at his nape, curling them into claws and nipping at his lip.

His lips tore from her with a ragged sound. "Fucking Christ, Vanessa, if you do that, this won't last long."

Vanessa tried to appear contrite, but she very much doubted she mastered the look if his urgent response was anything to go by.

He broke away from the circle of her arms to unlace his shirt, reach back and pull it over his head and down his arms in one graceful move.

Had she been less mesmerized by the magnificence of his figure, she might have been curious about the odd workings of his historical trappings as he divested himself of them.

But he loomed like Apollo above her, his skin like gold and honey poured over solid sinew and steel. The cords and veins in his arms danced and flexed as he worked his belt and trousers free.

Vanessa's fingers lifted to the buttons at her throat, but he stopped her with a curt order as he bent to kick away his boots.

"The thought of your bare ass beneath that skirt has teased and tantalized me all night," he said in a low rumble. "Now you'll let *me* be the one to decide when to undress you."

Dominance from any man had always caused a tight ball of frigid defiance to form in her chest, immediately freezing any warm feelings she might harbor toward him.

But *his* command released a flood of hot, liquid desire from her loins as she veritably bloomed beneath the intensity of his regard.

Vanessa let her hands fall demurely to her sides as she lay back on the coverlet. It was an excruciating exercise in a discipline she'd never actually possessed.

Her eyes touched him everywhere she could not, drinking in the fantastic breadth of his shoulders and the vast mounds of muscle that comprised his torso. She counted the obdurate ripples of his ribs and the corrugated plane of his abdomen before boldly following the vee of his hips to where his arousal jutted from a corona of dark gold hair.

Vanessa realized belatedly that one measly lover could never have prepared her for a man like Johnathan de Lohr.

She swallowed hard.

He groaned low.

And then his hands were upon her, circling her ankles and prying her legs open so he could fit between them. Rough palms rasped up the smooth swell of her calves, lifting the hem of her skirts, tracing those otherworldly sparkles of sensation in their wake.

He bent to kiss her in strange places she'd never imagined so seductive. The delicate skin on the inside of her knee, for example, as his questing fingers inched up her thigh.

Aroused and overwhelmed, she reached for him, tugging at his shoulders, needing the safety of his weight again. Craving the comfort of his kiss.

He obliged with a silent look of tender understanding, his lips returning to hers, one arm bracing his weight as his other hand resumed its wicked discovery of her.

She clung to him, greedy for more of the sensation sweeping like wildfire from his lips. From his fingertips as they glided over the thin skin of her inner thigh.

How could she have thought she'd known desire before? Never had it been like this with William. He'd been all charm and coaxing, evoking a maidenly curiosity from her born of innocence and not a little insecurity. This encounter was nothing like the weightless little butterflies he'd set free with his artless caresses and quick fumbles in the dark.

This. *This* was a tempest as powerful and encompassing as the one raging outside. Her belly quivered, her limbs trembled, and her breath caught on little gasps of need that he took into his own lungs as if to lock parts of her inside of him.

His kiss was ferocious where his fingers were not. He dominated her mouth once more, his tongue flexing and exploring in decadent strokes reminiscent of the act itself.

Gentle fingers petted through the intimate hair at the apex of her parted thighs, finding abundant moisture there.

They gasped against each other's mouths when he split the silken center of her with one lithe stroke.

Reflexively, her thighs clamped together, imprisoning his hand there.

William had struggled with her pleasure, had become frustrated with how complicated sensation had been to evoke from her body. He'd written about it. Told the world she was impossible to please.

That the fault had been hers.

And she'd believed him.

She understood now it was because she never wanted him like this. She never felt anything close to this unleashed frenzy of mindless, animalian need.

Sparks already threatened to take her over the edge as she realized that whatever miracle of magic and energy that made John corporeal also produced that strange, indescribable vibration wherever his skin connected with hers.

Against the sensitized flesh of her sex, it was an ultimately unparalleled sensation.

His finger slid easily between the slick ruffles, testing the damp folds and swirling her liquid desire around the little bud that throbbed with such fervency it bordered on pain.

"John," she implored against his lips.

"So wet," he groaned, his eyes unfocused as if he didn't mark her plea.

"John, I'm already going to—"

"Yes," he agreed fiercely. "Yes, you are."

With a couple expert flicks of his finger, he blew her entire world apart.

Vanessa felt as if the storm outside now originated from somewhere within her. The climax whipped her this way and then that, pushing and pulling her in powerful gusts of pure extasy.

Hoarse cries were ripped away from her throat as she threw her head back into the mattress, whipping it from side to side as if to escape the overwhelming intensity of the pleasure.

He seemed to instinctively understand when it became too much, and he slowed his lithe ministrations, bringing her back to herself in slow increments.

She lay sprawled out for a moment as his hands remained beneath her skirts, soothing and petting her. Cupping her as he crooned soft encouragements into her ear, nuzzling her neck and exploring it in little nips before soothing them with a glide of his tongue.

Vanessa wasn't certain what she expected from him, then. Perhaps that he would rip her clothing from her, spread her wide and sink inside of her for a few barbaric thrusts. Lord knew he'd earned it.

But no. He reclined away from her, covering her with her skirts.

His eyes glittered with masculine mischief as that cruel mouth spread into a dangerous Cheshire grin.

"What?" she queried with an anxious little gasp.

He gave her one dark command that both startled and stymied her.

"Kneel."

It occurred to her to explain to him that she wasn't one to be ordered about…as she obediently scrambled to her knees.

Yes. Just as soon as they finished, she'd certainly tell him so.

Curious anticipation dispelled whatever languor had stolen into her blood after her initial release, and she found that excitement began to build at this new and unique encounter.

In a moment he was behind her, fiddling with her skirts.

She had the idea that she knew where this was going, and the thought rather disappointed her. Not that she *minded* being taken from behind, especially not by him. She just didn't think that their first time would be in such a position.

"Would you like—that is—should I bend down?" she ventured.

"Stay as you are until I move you."

She did. Kneeling straight like a penitent at prayer as he rustled and disturbed the bed a bit.

And then his hands were on the insides of her thighs, prying her knees wider to make room for…

His shoulders?

Her eyes peeled wide as he maneuvered himself on his back beneath her skirts, his hands splaying her thighs wider, charting her bare backside as his breath grazed the intimate flesh splayed open over his face.

Her knees nearly lost their starch.

Thoroughly scandalized, Vanessa leaned to one side, meaning to wriggle away, when his long, unyielding arms clamped around her thighs.

Oh dear God. She blindly grabbed for anything, her fingers grasping the headboard.

"I—I don't think we—"

"Don't think for once, Vanessa," is what she thought he muttered, though the words were a bit muffled by her skirts.

Clearly, he didn't know her well. Which meant they should not be doing something so astoundingly intimate and immoral. "I just—"

He stole her words with one wicked kiss. One wicked, carnal, wet, and languorous kiss to lips that had never before known the mouth of a man.

Suddenly the entire world was very far away. Anything and anyone she'd ever known might never have existed. She was not herself. He was not a dead Earl. They were not in Scotland on a snowy winter night trapped by a gale and perhaps by fate.

There was only what *his* mouth did to *her* sex.

First, he supped and sampled in teasing little tucks and twirls, using only his lips, causing her body to respond with little flinching twitches as the pleasure ebbed and flowed beginning at her core and sparkling through her entire body. She'd have not been able to support herself in such a position if it weren't for his arms winched around her thighs, taking the crux of her weight.

His tongue joined the fray before too long, eliciting a sharp gasp of delight from her as her knuckles tightened on the headboard. His mouth was relentlessly skilled as he slipped and slid around and through the petals of her flesh with inquisitive delight.

It was an exquisite torture. An excruciating bliss.

She wondered dimly where the distant, pathetic, demanding little mewls and gasps were coming from. Surely not her. She'd never dream of making such sounds.

Then, *oh then*, merciless monster that he was, he cleaved her with the flat of his tongue. Tasting the entirety of her topography, he laved at the little bud at the aperture of her sex with a relentless pressure that catapulted her into the stars.

Her fingernails scored the wood of the bed frame as he centered all his attentions on her core, his muscles tightening around her thighs as she bucked and writhed, arched and contracted against the onslaught of pulsating pleasure. She rode his magnificent mouth as unadulterated bliss rolled over her like a tide this time, slamming into her with the strength of a rogue wave and drawing her under. Each time she threatened to surface, the wave in the distance was upon her and again she would be dragged beneath it, helpless against the fluid potency.

And yet he was her anchor, his unfailing strength gifting her with the precious knowledge that she would never be lost. Not while he held her.

He unlatched himself from her with a noisy sound before the storm of her climax had truly passed. She made a plaintive sound in her throat as his strong hands held her legs open and he maneuvered himself into a sitting position. Resting his back against the headboard, he split her legs over his lap while she still shuddered and twitched in the aftermath of an orgasm woefully interrupted.

He stared at her for a moment, and Vanessa scrambled to find her wits so she could fathom what she read in his eyes.

But she never had a chance, not when he lowered her to where the hot, blunt head of his cock rested against the flesh still quivering with release.

Before she could beg him to do so, he lowered her onto him, filling her with one long, slow impale.

Chapter Seven

If John wasn't already dead, joining with this woman would have killed him.

The wet velvet sheath of her was a heaven in its own right as it welcomed his cock, giving way only in incremental inches as her intimate flesh pulsed around him.

He set his jaw against the storm of a release already gathering at the base of his spine.

It was why he'd not undressed her.

Of course, he'd wanted to see her body again. To unwrap her like God's very own Christmas gift. But also, he found her prim, high collar stitched with simple lace unwaveringly erotic when her sex was currently pulling his straining shaft into her body somewhere beneath her skirts.

It would last longer like this. Without the added tantalization of watching her unbound breasts sway in front of his eyes.

It'd been longer than a century since he'd been with a woman, goddammit, and a man could only take so much.

But she took all of him. And she gave as well, holding nothing back as he made his erotic demands of her.

God, she was magnificent. Her lips bee-stung from his punishing kisses and her silver eyes a gunmetal grey, dark and dilated with passion and the aftershocks of a pleasure he was about to resurrect.

There wasn't a man alive who deserved her.

And neither did he.

Lodging himself to the hilt, he held her there for a moment, flexing within her, kneading the soft globes of her ass with restless fingers.

When he could stand it no longer, he arched away, lifting her up to enjoy the soft pull of her channel as it clenched at him.

She was so fucking small. So tight. So perfect. He couldn't use the word enough. Vanessa Latimer was the perfect woman. His perfect match.

He'd only had to die and wait a century and a half to meet her.

It had been worth it.

His every muscle clenched and corded with tension as he released her hips to run his hands down her smooth thighs.

Trembling as they were, she took over, her knees gripping his hips as she lowered her body to meet his relentless upward thrusts.

Of course they found a perfect rhythm immediately. Of course they did. Of course they *would*.

Even as they gathered speed, he reached behind him to unlatch her fingers from the headboard and nudged them to grasp his shoulders.

He wanted to feel the bite of her nails as he made her come one more time.

Licking his thumb, he reached beneath her skirt and found slick places where they joined—his hardness, her softness—and he thrummed the little peak of her pleasure, knowing her climax still lingered there because he'd left it at the ideal crest to make it crash upon her once again.

Her mouth fell upon his, open and gasping. And the moment he felt her silken sheath clench around him, drenching his cock with yet another release, he threw open the gates and allowed the storm of his own pleasure to devour him.

It took him with more force than even he expected, locking every muscle into a paroxysm of bliss. His skin caught fire, his veins constricted then released, filling his blood with an inferno of pure, carnal power.

One word swept through him as he released an agonized groan into her mouth, clenching her to his arching, straining body.

Mine, he thought, a wave of melancholy following on the wings of the most powerful pleasure he'd ever taken with a woman.

His woman.

Mine.

It was a fact. She was his. He'd claimed her just now.

And it was also a lie, because they could never be.

They stayed locked like that for an eternity, or perhaps only a few moments, it was impossible to tell in the dark.

She collapsed against him, her ear to his chest. John took entirely too much delight in wrapping one of her ringlets around his finger, uncurling it, and starting again.

Finally, after the silence had stretched between them for too long, she said, "I can feel your heart beating."

"Really?" he murmured. Because he could only feel it breaking.

She sat up, miraculously still joined with him as she blinked languidly with her doe-bright eyes. "But you're not—returned. I can feel you fading. I can see that you're diminished."

She swallowed what he knew was a lump of tears and summoned a brave smile for him, even though anguish shined in her eyes.

"I know." He lifted his knuckles to run them against her downy cheek, realizing that he could almost see her skin through his hand. He was tied to the ring, and it had given him precious time…

But it wouldn't be enough to keep her.

Slowly, with infinite care, he finally got around to undressing her. His fingers appreciating every button, buckle, and clasp. Delighting in every slip of skin he uncovered.

She lifted off him and they found a fresh ewer and towel left by the innkeepers, and washed themselves before sliding into bed like a couple long used to each other's nearness.

Like it was the most natural thing in the world.

He tucked her against him, her back to his front, and he rested his head in his hand so he could gaze down at her. Commit her face to his memory.

For who knew if he would ever see her again after tonight?

She snuggled into him with unabashed relish, greedily drawing from his warmth.

"You should rest," he murmured. Pressing a kiss to her temple as she covered a yawn with the backs of her knuckles.

"I'm not going to sleep," she mumbled, her eyes opening a little less each time she blinked. "I'm not going to miss one moment with you."

"I know," he said against her hairline. Pressing little love kisses to her eyebrows. Her lids, feathering his lips across them, tasting the salt of the tears she refused to let fall. He didn't want to say goodbye, either.

"Will you do something for me, Vanessa?"

"Anything."

He slid the ring that belonged on his pinky onto her ring finger. "Return this ring to Lioncross Abbey for me. Perhaps it can put me to final rest."

She curled her fingers into a fist. "Perhaps, if I keep the ring with me, I'll keep you, too," she slurred, half asleep. "You could be my ghost. You could haunt me."

Somehow, he knew it wouldn't work, but he didn't have the heart to tell her so. His fingers worked over her face, as if learning her features like a blind man. Smoothing at her brows with featherlight touches until her jaw cracked on a yawn.

"Don't make me sleep." She fought it valiantly as a recalcitrant toddler. "I haven't shown you your photograph yet. The glass negative."

"Tomorrow." He said the word like a promise. A promise he already knew he would break. "I love you, Vanessa."

She mumbled something he thought might be the reply he hoped for. It didn't matter. As much as he desired her heart, he also wanted it free. Because she would live the most extraordinary life, and he was just lucky to be a part of it for one memorable solstice night.

Chapter Eight

Christmas Day—Lioncross Abbey

VANESSA LET OUT a violent sneeze as she once more descended into the dust of the de Lohr crypts, her body and her heart recoiling from what she was about to do.

She'd infiltrated the de Lohr crypt, a monolithic cavern beneath the granite cliffs upon which the incomparable stones of Lioncross Abbey lorded over lush and verdant lands.

If the noble family had been in residence, there'd be signs of life, but as she circled the grounds on horseback, she'd spied none. No gas lamps lit the predawn light, nor did even so much as a drape twitch in the tower.

The castle itself was an impenetrable fortress, but sometime over the past hundred years or so, an enterprising Earl had added on a lavish manner home to the keep and landscaped it in such a way that the gardens at Versailles would weep with envy.

The crypts, fortunately for her, were situated on a dark corner of the grounds and were accessible enough if an enterprising body didn't mind clipping away vines of ivy and squeezing through the slats of an iron fence that would have kept out an invading army.

But not one enterprising slip of a woman.

She'd eschewed her skirt for the mission, donning a pair of lad's trousers and a coat that swallowed her to the knees. She'd pinned her hair high on her head and hid it beneath a cap.

Frost had crunched beneath her feet as she crept across the outer bailey to the mausoleum-like crypt entrance. She descended a few of the spiral stairs down below the frosted earth, before lighting her lantern. She tiptoed past the stone slabs covering many a de Lohr ancestor until she came to the one marked the year of Culloden, chiseled with the same name as was etched into her heart.

She pulled the chain upon which the ring rested from beneath her blouse, and wrapped her fingers lovingly around it, letting it burn against her palm. Could she do this? Could she uncover his bones and not fall to pieces at the sight of them?

She'd only known him one night. And that was all it took to fall.

Whatever shame and sadness she wore as a coronet before was no comparable tragedy to the past few days she'd spent waiting for him to appear.

Awaking in the sunshine after a Scottish storm, alone in the bed they'd shared, had just about broken her spirit.

He was lost to her, of that she had no doubt. Lost so soon, when she'd only just found the one man to whom she'd consider relinquishing both her name, her hand, and her heart. A man who'd transfixed and teased her. Who'd pleasured and protected her. A man to whom true honor meant more than reputation.

He'd only ever asked one thing of her.

But it was a cruel thing.

She closed her eyes and took a fortifying breath, filling her lungs with the loamy scent of earth and frost and a hint of decay. She released the ring, letting it settle between her breasts, a comforting weight around her neck.

One she'd have to give up.

She could do this. She'd done difficult things before.

She set the lantern onto the earth and discarded her gloves beside it before placing her hands on the stone slab above his coffin and pushing with all her strength. She groaned and strained, even let out a few curses, but it didn't budge.

Blast. She'd need leverage. Perhaps a—

Strong arms seized her from behind, drawing her back against a body as hard as iron. One arm locked beneath her breasts, the other around her throat.

"I'll give you two breaths to tell me what you are doing here, before I snap your neck." The growl was ferocious, arrogant, and alarming.

And no sound had ever been so dear.

"John?" she whispered around the tightness of her heart throbbing in her throat. She turned her face to the side, instinctively searching for his warmth. "John, is it really you?"

"A woman?" As quickly as she was seized, she was released. Cast away from the embrace she craved with the strength of an opium fiend.

She turned to see him, drinking in the sight of him with the thirst of someone finding an oasis in the desert.

Before her glowered a man of pure flesh and blood. Sinew and strength. His golden hair was cut in neat layers, even though it now spiked in wild disarray, as if he'd rolled out of bed only minutes prior. It suited him, the lord of Lioncross. The structure of his body was achingly familiar. The same long frame, the same wide shoulders and tapered waist accentuated by a dark wool coat thrown over a hastily buttoned shirt.

Aside from deeper brackets around his hard mouth and longer sideburns, he *was* John.

Except.

His eyes were perfectly dull and flat. So empty a blue as to almost be called grey as they assessed her with all the emotion one might attribute to a shark.

"You address me so informally, madam," he said over an imperious look.

Her heart gave one powerful, painful thump, before sputtering and dying. "I'm sorry," she gasped. "I can explain."

One golden brow arched over a look of recognition. "We've met before."

"Y-yes," she stammered. "At Lady Bainbridge's fete."

Recognition flared in the dim lantern light. "You're Veronica's sister."

Just when she thought her heart could sink no lower. "Yes. I am."

He made a rumbly, pensive sound, half between a purr and a snarl. "I still don't understand why they call her the pretty one."

"What?" Suddenly it was impossible to breathe.

He shook his head, blinking as if trying to clear it. "Sorry. Do you mind telling me what the bloody devil you're doing in my crypt on Christmas?"

"I um…" She itched at her hair beneath her cap, wondering just how to get herself out of this predicament without being thrown in an asylum. "You wouldn't believe me if I told you."

He leveled her a droll look, propping his shoulder against a stone wall. "Try me."

She gazed at him a long time, at the lantern light splashing deep hollows beneath his chiseled cheekbones. Something in the imperturbable stillness of his gaze told her she could say anything.

So, she attempted the truth.

"I took refuge at a place in the Highlands of Scotland called Balthazar's Inn on solstice night. While I stayed there I…met…" She sputtered and stalled out a bit. It was impossible to express her experience without choking up, so she reached behind her neck and unclasped the chain, letting the lion head ring slip from it into her palm. "I happened upon this, and was told it belonged to Johnathan de Lohr, the one who was lost at Culloden. I was…tasked to return it."

Those heartless, ruthless eyes affixed on the ring, and she thought she might have read a spark of life in them.

But only just.

"The Lion's Head." His voice had become deeper, like a monk's at prayer. "All this time. All these many generations have searched for it…and it just walks into Lioncross at Christmas." He reached for it. Paused. And flicked his eyes back to hers. "May I?"

"It's yours." She offered it to him reluctantly, loath to let go all she had left of her lover.

He handled it as if it were made of spun glass, tilting it to unveil an inscription on the inside, which she'd never noticed. "Ever faithful."

She leaned over to take a closer look, immediately aware that if either of them tilted their heads a fraction, their lips would meet.

"I've seen so many drawings. We've always assumed the ring was lost at the battle of Culloden. This was crafted in the Holy Land and gifted to the Lionclaw to always adorn the hand of the Earl of Hereford. In fact, a replica was never made because this one meant so much. They said there was a bit of magic crafted with it."

Swallowing a surge of grief, Vanessa looked longingly at the coffin behind her. "I suppose I should have given it to you. I just thought…Well I wanted to return it to its rightful owner."

The corner of his mouth tilted, and for a moment she thought she might burst into tears.

"That is good of you." He hesitated, drawing a hand through his mane in an attempt to tame it. "It's freezing out. Might I invite you in for some warm tea?"

She shook her head, needing to lick her wounds. Unwilling to have to look at him in the brilliant winter sun. "Oh. I don't want to take up any of your—"

"Please," he murmured, capturing her hand. "It's a rather large castle, and it's just me, now. The last de Lohr…well of my line, anyhow. You'd be doing a solitary man a kindness on Christmas."

She swallowed a spurt of pity and called it ridiculous. He was one of the most eligible bachelors in the Empire. If he wanted companionship, he'd only have to crook a finger.

"I'm no sort of company," she argued. "And not someone you'd want to be seen socializing with, besides."

The tiniest hint of an azure flame flared behind his eyes, causing them to glow like black sapphires in the dark. "I'm a de Lohr. I do as I fucking wish."

Worry crimped her forehead. "Perhaps you haven't heard about me."

"Oh, I heard," he said meaningfully. "I saw the pamphlet that blackguard, Woodhaven, passed around my club." His voice took on a savage bite to match the ferocity of his features. "I burned them all and got his bloody membership revoked."

She smiled at that. "Well…maybe one cup of tea."

He took up her lantern and turned away, so she followed his shoulders up the stone steps, blinking against the brightness of the morning.

Which was why she bumped into him.

It was like running into a boulder.

Jostled by her, he dropped the ring, and it rolled between his feet as he took a few steps before he realized.

Vanessa bent to pick it up, and a snowflake landed on the tip of her nose as she straightened. She blinked and looked around, mesmerized by the drifting crystals of frost dancing toward the earth. It was as if the sky had released little diamonds, and they'd chosen to land in the Lioncross gardens, adorning them with indescribable wealth.

"Odd," he remarked, tilting his neck up. "It wasn't snowing when I followed you down here. In fact, it was a clear morning."

Something gripped her at the sight of his throat arched to the sky. Something both foreign and familiar, and she cleared her throat to dislodge any gathers of emotion and the odd impulse to fall upon it like a vampire.

"Here," she offered, taking the ring between her thumb and fingers and reaching for his hand.

He looked down at her and relinquished his hand to her grip. It was so similar to the one she'd become acquainted with, she thought she might expire. A few different marks and calluses, but nothing remarkable enough.

She slid the ring over his knuckles.

A perfect fit.

She wanted to rip it off again. To claim it for her own. Because it didn't belong to him, this man with the empty eyes and kind, familiar smile. It belonged to John. *Her* John. The ghost who'd been somehow more full of life than even this magnificent specimen of a man.

She wanted to go back down into the crypt and sit with his bones. She wanted to go back to Scotland and sleep in the bed she'd shared with him. And mourn. Wail. Cry.

She knew it was pathetic, and she couldn't bring herself to care, because he was gone. She could feel not only his body but his soul missing the moment she'd awoken after the solstice.

Perhaps he was finally at rest.

"Vanessa."

She jumped at the sound of his voice. Looked up into his face.

His face.

The hollows had disappeared and...the eyes! The *eyes* were the same. No longer a grey/ blue but sharp with that familiar larkspur brilliance.

His name escaped her on a choked whisper.

John.

She jumped into his arms and he caught her against his chest, sweeping her around in the cheerful flurry before setting her back down.

"How is this—? What are—? Is he still—?" She couldn't seem to finish a sentence, she was too incandescently happy.

He put his hand to his temple and then threaded it through his hair, testing locks much shorter than his had been. "It isn't just him. That is, it's me. But also him."

"I don't understand," she croaked, fighting tears of hope and disbelief.

His smile could have eclipsed the sun. "I can't say I do, either. All I can tell you is…when we, you and I, met at the Bainbridge ball all those years ago, I wanted you then. But I'd already planned not to marry because I didn't have a heart nor a soul to give to a woman, and you deserved everything of that and more."

Johnathan de Lohr, the Earl of Hereford lifted his face to the sky once again, allowing snowflakes to gather on his eyelashes as if he enjoyed the sensation for the very first time.

"I was born empty," he told the clouds. "It would scare my mother to look into my eyes. She said she didn't think I had a soul. It was why she never had more children. And I felt it too…"

"And now?"

He captured her with his gaze. "Now, I think I was always a vessel. I *am* Johnathan de Lohr. Perhaps was *meant* to be him—me—whatever. I still have my memories." He gave her a hot look that threatened to scorch through her trousers. "I have his memories, as well."

She tried to believe it, though her mind couldn't seem to grasp just what was happening, and then she realized. "I never told you my first name."

"Vanessa. I *am* the man you spent solstice with. You showed me photographs of locomotives and of what I now understand to be gas lamps. You stood with me in the Chamber of Sorrows and made love to me while a tempest raged around us."

A tear slid down her cheek as the marvelous truth of it slammed into her with all the power of that locomotive at full tilt.

Vanessa's entire body stilled. Her lungs froze in her chest and her heart forgot to beat as one word settled into her soul, looking for a home.

Made love.

Love… Dare she hope?

His expression was so full of tenderness it threatened to melt her into a puddle of pure, blissful sentiment. "It's as if for one hundred and fifty years, one hollow note was playing in my ear, driving me mad, and then you blew in on a blizzard and brought with you every symphony I could hope to hear. You are my match, Vanessa. I never needed more than a moment to know it with unquestioned absolution. And I want to see the world with you, if you'd let me."

He captured her hand and held it to his lips, pressing a worshipful kiss into her palm before he continued. "Like I said, I am *that* Johnathan de Lohr, and *this* one, who also lived an entire lamentable life without you. Since the moment I met you, you haven't been far from my thoughts. I might not have the same body you became acquainted with, the same scars or history. I don't have the hands that touched you. The mouth that tasted you, not exactly. But I have the soul that adored you from the first moment I laid eyes on you."

Eyes. Ye gods what immaculate and incandescent light beamed at her from those eyes.

What life.

"I like *these* hands," she whispered, fondling the ring, then she lifted it to her own lips to return his kiss, before peeking up at him from beneath coy lashes. "I would not mind acquainting myself with the rest of you. It is not as if my reputation can't handle going into your castle unaccompanied."

"Wait." He stopped her, held her back from marching toward Lioncross. "I would invite you in only with the understanding that my intent is to carry you across the threshold as my Countess as soon as possible. I would defend your honor, Vanessa, and restore your good name."

A smile engulfed her entire being, even as snowflakes landed on her heated cheeks like chilly little blessings from heaven.

"Let's start with tea and see where that takes us," she teased, knowing that the moment he proposed properly, she'd have no other answer for him but yes.

Yes. Forever yes.

"Kiss me, Vanessa," he growled, dragging her against his inflamed body. "Kiss me because it's Christmas and you're in my arms. Kiss me because I'm the luckiest soul to ever live and then live again."

Yes, she thought as she was swept away by the potency of his kiss. Entranced by the same magic she'd experienced that first time in the Highland storm.

It *was* Christmas.

And never would a gift mean so much as the soul of the man she loved.

THE END

About Kerrigan Byrne

Kerrigan Byrne is the USA Today Bestselling and award winning author of several novels in both the romance and mystery genre.

She lives on the Olympic Peninsula in Washington with her wonderful husband and Willow the Writer Dog. When she's not writing and researching, you'll find her on the beach, kayaking, or on land eating, drinking, shopping, and attending live comedy, ballet, or too many movies.

Kerrigan loves to hear from her readers! To contact her or learn more about her books, please visit her sites:

www.kerriganbyrne.com
twitter.com/Kerrigan_Byrne
facebook.com/kerrigan.byrne.9
Instagram: @kerriganbyrne

Fiona and the Three Wise Highlanders

By Jennifer Ashley

A Mackenzies / McBrides Christmas Novella
Part of A Very Highland Holiday Collection

The characters and events portrayed in this book are fictitious. Any similarity to real persons, living or dead, is purely coincidental and not intended by the author.

Fiona and the Three Wise Highlanders

Fiona MacDonald is overjoyed to see Stuart Cameron alive and well after his imprisonment by the English, but her worries are not over. Stuart Cameron owes his safety to a pair of smugglers who have come to collect on their debt, and Stuart will need her help to win himself free.

Chapter One

Kilmorgan Castle, 1892

"PAPA."

Ian Mackenzie, at his desk in the attic room he'd turned into his private study, warmed as he heard the voice of his youngest daughter, Megan. He looked up from a letter he'd been transcribing, one from the 1350s that described his ancestor, Old Dan Mackenzie, and his feats at the Battle of Berwick. All thoughts of the past, the battle for Scotland, and Old Dan's reward of a dukedom, fled.

Megan was ten, with the glossy brown hair and blue eyes of her mother. She loved books and music, happy to sit reading or playing sweet notes on the piano. She was also as interested in the family's history as Ian.

Ian said nothing, waiting for Megan to tell him why she'd come. She was shy, as he was, but she spoke up firmly when she had something to say.

"What happened to Stuart Cameron, Papa?" Megan crossed the room to stand beside his desk. She had a bow in her hair, a blue one to match her eyes, and it rose above her head like fairy's wings. Ian had the sudden impression that she *was* a fairy, and she'd fly away from him if he weren't careful.

"Papa?"

Ian forced his gaze from the bow and settled it on her eyes. "Aye, lass. Stuart Cameron. Will Mackenzie's best mate."

A few days ago, Ian had regaled the younger Mackenzie generation with the tale of Alec Mackenzie, brother to their ancestor who'd survived the Battle of Culloden. Alec had rescued the family friend, Stuart Cameron, from captivity and certain death.

Ian carefully folded his papers and pushed them aside. Old Dan would have to wait. He lifted his daughter to his lap, his arm around her waist to hold her steady.

"Stuart Cameron traveled to France with Alec and Will after escaping from prison," Ian began without inflection. "He returned to Scotland in December of 1746, where he met Fiona Macdonald—"

"No, Papa." Megan gazed up at him reproachfully. "That is not how you begin a story."

Ian felt a trickle of mirth. His family believed him a stickler for procedure, but whenever he deviated from it, *they* grew bewildered and guided him back.

"Aye, 'tis so." Ian held Megan closer. "I will start again."

He leaned back in the chair and closed his eyes, bringing to mind the exact words of the letters he'd read, plus the diary of Fiona Macdonald, great-great-great-great aunt by marriage to his mother, Elspeth Cameron.

"Once upon a time …"

Near Inverness, December, 1746

THE THREE MEN who swaggered into Balthazar's inn were bundled in drab thick coats, boots that must have squelched through every patch of mud from here to Aberdeen, drenched hats pulled down to their ears.

Fiona Macdonald sat very still in the warm corner near the fireplace, feet buried in the straw on the floor. Beside her, Una, her maid, long-time companion, and fellow conspirator, stiffened, ready to become a guard dog in an instant. Una was not happy that Fiona had to rest in the common room, but the inn was crowded tonight, and a chamber was being readied for her by the innkeeper's daughter.

"We come bearing gifts," the smallest of the men sang out. He was a disreputable fellow, who removed his hat to reveal sun-bleached brown hair. His skin had the tough brown hue of old leather, but his smile was wide, his teeth whole if stained. "Is that not what ye do when ye see a star guiding ye to an inn at Christmastide? Is there a wee babe in the stables we should visit?"

The men in the smoky common room laughed. Through the din, the innkeeper, Balthazar, stroked his beard with his fingers. "There's already one wise man here, Gair Murray, and I'd not let ye within ten feet of a wee babe."

"Ye know me, then?" Gair's smile widened. "And ye bandy me name about, do ye? Worth a free jar, I'm thinking."

"Everyone knows ye, Gair. You're among friends here."

Not likely, Fiona thought as she wrapped her hands around her cooling mug of tea. Gair Murray, a smuggler, had no true friends, not really. He did favors for men up and down Scotland, but for pay, at the same time on the lookout for anything he could lift for himself.

His only friend in the world, if he could be called so, was the thin but much taller man next to him. Padruig looked out at the world with one gray eye, the other, lost in some long-ago battle, covered with a leather patch.

Both men wore cloaks over their coats, Padruig's black, Gair's brown with a stripe that made it appear suspiciously like an old tartan. Fiona hoped he wouldn't be caught wearing a forbidden plaid.

Padruig, as usual, said nothing as the more garrulous Gair bantered with the innkeeper.

Fiona regarded the third figure with growing tension. He was a huge bear of a man, a Highlander without doubt, his hair a strange shade of black. Soot, she realized as a streak of it came off when he removed his hat. He was trying to disguise the true color.

He was muffled to his ears in a plain gray scarf, he the only of the three not to have a cloak wrapped about him. He hunched his back as though trying to conceal his height, but he did a poor job of it. This was a man used to standing straight, proud, arrogant.

Perhaps his spirit had been broken, as so many of them had been. Fiona had once been a proud Highlander herself.

And still am. We are defeated, not gone.

The man had to pull down his scarf to drink the tankard of ale Balthazar shoved onto a table for the three men. More soot smeared from his hair, which shone like a streak of sudden flame.

Only one man had hair that brilliant shade of red. But he was dead, captured by the Hanoverians after Culloden, taken prisoner, vanished. Fiona's heart had died that day. He'd have been executed by now. Fiona's nightmares had showed her his death so many times in the last eight months that she was certain of it.

Until the man turned his head and looked at her.

Blue eyes like summer skies skewered her, and the firm mouth that had once kissed like fire pinched into a frown. He rose from the stool he'd just taken, as though unable to stop himself.

Stuart Cameron.

Her brother's enemy and the man who'd stolen her peace before he'd run off to join the doomed army of *Teàrlach mhic Seamas.*

PADRUIG EYED STUART in concern, though Gair continued telling the men next to them some tale he was inventing about their travels. Gair's constant banter kept people mollified until too late to recognize his perfidy.

Fiona Macdonald shouldn't be sitting in a wayside tavern in the middle of the Scottish Highlands with English soldiers hunting down any they even thought smelled like a Jacobite. She should have taken ship months ago to France or the Low Countries, or at least be home with her brother, anywhere she'd be safe. It was typical of her to decide not to flee or hide.

Stuart could not stop himself crossing the tavern to her. The room was crowded, so much so that none paid much attention to another weary traveler pushing through their midst.

The eagle-eyed maid, Una, glared up at Stuart as he approached. So she was still with Fiona. Loyal of her. Fiona sipped tea as though she noticed no one.

Stuart knew Fiona had seen him and recognized him. Best to corner her before she burst out with his true identity … not that the Fiona Macdonald he knew would do such a thing, although she might in her surprise. Or Una might, indignant at his return.

Stuart came to a halt next to Fiona, pretending to warm his hands at the fire. His heart thumped with Fiona's nearness, the fire nothing to the slow heat that churned through his body.

It had been so long since he'd seen her, touched her, simply enjoyed her presence. He'd dreamed of her, the image of her face, her smile keeping him from the very bottom of despair.

"What are ye doing here, lass?" Stuart asked in a quiet voice.

"What are you?" Fiona's answer came as quietly. She rested her mug on her lap. "You're alive, I see."

"Aye. Barely."

"What happened to ye?"

"A guest of his majesty." Stuart shrugged, trying to maintain the stance of a servant who mooched along after Gair and Padruig. "Then France."

Fiona's eyes widened slightly. She had the loveliest eyes, green like jade in sunlight, which set off her very dark hair. He saw her realization that he'd been a prisoner—and she'd never know all of that horror if Stuart could help it. Escaped by the skin of his teeth—and with the help of the Mackenzie brothers—over the Channel to France. He'd rested and recovered there, but he'd soon longed to be back in Scotland, and so had hunted up the expert smugglers Gair and Padruig, and hired them to provide him passage.

"Ye should have stayed." Fiona's voice was barely above a whisper.

Did she mean in Paris or prison? Stuart let the corner of his mouth pull into a half smile. "Missing home."

"Home isn't safe."

"Is it safe for you?" Stuart countered.

He saw the flinch Fiona tried to hide, though Una didn't bother to smother her scowl. Not much older than Fiona, Una had the flaxen hair of a Viking and the demeanor to match. She guarded Fiona like a lioness. For that, Stuart would forgive her scowls.

"Safe enough," Fiona said. "The soldiers don't always stop a woman."

"More fool they." The greatest fault the Hanoverians had was to underestimate Scotswomen. The English kept their own women so sheltered and subdued they assumed their northern neighbors did the same. "I thought ye'd be on a ship heading across the seas." *Without your waste of a brother,* he finished silently.

"Broc is ill," Fiona said, the gleam in her eyes telling Stuart she knew what he was thinking. "He never recovered after his injury at Falkirk."

"Does he still claim it was me who shot him?" Stuart allowed the smile to form.

Broc Macdonald, who'd stubbornly thrown in his lot with King Geordie, had suffered a leg wound at the Battle of Falkirk and had been carried, wailing, from the field. So Stuart had been told. He hadn't witnessed the injury.

"Yes." Fiona's own smile flashed then vanished. "Though I told him ye couldn't have."

"Loyal woman."

"'Tisn't loyalty. I know the truth."

Stuart barely heard her. Fiona's smile transcended her drab garments, shawl, and the faded cap she wore under a broad-brimmed hat. The ensemble made her look like an ordinary farm woman, instead of the laird's sister she was. Her beauty was like a breath of air in this musty place, returning the memory of her laughter, her quick wit, her sparkling eyes.

He recalled dancing with her in her brother's house not long before Prince Teàrlach marched on Edinburgh, her warm hand in his, her lithe grace as they moved in the patterns of the reel.

He recalled her red lips that neared his as they turned, hand in hand, then moved tantalizingly out of reach. The kiss on the terrace after that, when he'd wrapped his plaid around her and warmed them both.

"Still," Stuart made himself say, "kind of ye to put in a word for me."

"You didn't shoot him because you were keeping Duncan Mackenzie alive." Fiona's sudden frown almost matched Una's in severity. She hadn't liked Duncan's recklessness and had feared he'd be Stuart's death. Duncan had perished on Culloden Moor, the poor bastard. He'd had all the arrogance but not the quick thinking of his younger brothers.

"For my sins." Stuart leaned closer, returning to the pretense of warming his hands. "But what are ye doing *here*, lass? In the middle of nowhere the day before Christmas Eve?"

Fiona glanced behind Stuart and folded her lips. *Hmm.* She didn't want to say in front of anyone who might hear. He saw none but Highlanders in the room, but one couldn't be certain which way any man's loyalty lay.

If she were any other lady, Stuart would shrug and not pursue it. But this was Fiona Macdonald, and she never did anything not worth learning about. He'd have the secret out of her. Perhaps later, in a dark chamber, with the door locked …

A distinct presence made itself felt—or smelled—at his side. Both women winced, and even Stuart took a step away. Gair rarely bathed, and the heat of the close room made him ripe.

"The question I ought to ask," Fiona said, pretending to ignore Gair. "Is why are you in such disreputable company?"

"Ah, she breaks me heart," Gair said with a dry chuckle. "We're saving his life, lass, is the answer. Spiriting him across the land to his home."

"Spiriting?" Una wrinkled her nose. "Ye couldn't spirit anything but whisky, Gair Murray. From the smell of things, ye've had a lot of it."

Gair laughed without malice. One thing Stuart liked about the man was that he knew exactly who he was and had no aspiration to be anything else.

"A fine reunion ye're having," Gair said. "But it's time to pay the piper. Not that I play the pipes. Can't abide the things."

Stuart straightened in puzzlement. "I paid ye, Gair. In advance. Every bit of silver I had. Ye insisted, I remember." He still felt the sting of handing over the last coins he had in his sporran. He hoped the king's armies hadn't stolen the rest of what he'd stashed at home.

"Aye." Gair returned the look without shame. "That was *my* payment. Now for Padruig."

Bloody man. Stuart had always known he couldn't trust Gair. To smuggle Stuart into Scotland and across the country without betraying him, yes. With his money? No.

"Ye don't share your take with Padruig?" Stuart asked, as though surprised. "I'd reconsider, Gair. He's a dangerous man."

He and Gair glanced as one at Padruig. The man leaned his left elbow on the table near a large tankard of ale, while he amused himself twirling a dagger in his right hand. His lank and long hair, worn leather eyepatch, and the concentration in his good eye did not lend reassurance.

Gair's humor didn't fade. "Oh, he's happy with what I give him. This is something special, he tells me."

The innkeeper had vanished, tending to whatever innkeepers tend to, but the common room remained crowded. A few lads ran about serving the loud Highlanders, while the window grew dark with the cold midwinter night.

Stuart smothered a sigh and gave Fiona and Una a truncated bow. "Excuse me, ladies."

Gair guffawed and followed Stuart across the room to the table. Padruig flipped the blade through competent fingers and let it land, point down, buried a half inch into the wood.

"The landlord won't be happy with that," Stuart remarked as he slid onto a stool.

Padruig said nothing. Where Gair could talk the hind leg off a mule, Padruig was silence itself.

"What do you want?" Stuart asked him. "I'll have no more money until I reach home, and even then I might have nothing. The bloody English will have confiscated everything." Possibly not the cache of jewels he'd hidden well before he'd left to join the Jacobite army, but Stuart wasn't fool enough to mention jewels in front of Gair. "Take your share out of Gair's hide."

Gair went off into gales of hilarity, but Padruig's face remained impassive.

"'Tis nae coin I want."

Padruig so rarely spoke, that when he did, he drew attention. Even Gair ceased his laughter. Padruig opened the tankard and took a loud sip of ale.

"What then?" Stuart asked impatiently.

Padruig sipped again, set down the tankard, and wiped his mouth on his sleeve.

"A *sgian dubh*."

Stuart's brows climbed. "A knife? Is that all? Cumberland's men might have taken all of those from my home as well, but likely I can find one stashed somewhere."

"No." Padruig's harsh word dried up Stuart's relief. "One particular *sgian dubh,* lost at Culloden Moor. Bring me that, and your debt to me will be paid."

Chapter Two

FIONA NEARED STUART'S table in time to hear Padruig's words. She ought to have remained quietly in the corner—Una hissed for her to remember what they were there for—but Fiona was drawn to Stuart like an arrow to its mark.

Even hunched into his coat, his hat restored over his awful hair, he held a power that filled the room. Fiona could no more keep from him than she could cease breathing.

"Oh, aye?" Stuart demanded as Padruig studied him. "Ye wish me te crawl about on me belly in the grass at Culloden, pushing aside the bones to look for an eating knife?"

"Perhaps it is special to him." Fiona slid onto a stool next to Stuart's.

Stuart jumped, but Gair and Padruig, who'd seen her come, accepted her without comment.

"'Tis." Padruig nodded at Fiona.

Gair shrugged. "First he's told me of it. But if he wants a *sgian dubh*, I suggest ye find it for him," he said pointedly to Stuart. "He won't let you loose from the bargain without it."

"Then I never will be," Stuart growled. "What ye want is bloody impossible."

The anguish in Stuart's voice as he talked about searching Culloden Moor was similar to what she'd heard in other Highlanders she'd spoken to since that battle. They'd seen horror, and while they'd survived, they'd never completely recover from it.

"Not necessarily." Fiona set her mostly empty tea mug on the table. "The innkeeper's daughter has collected things from the moor and keeps them in a room here. She calls it her Chamber of Sorrows. Perhaps she's found your *sgian dubh*."

Stuart's blue eyes skewered her. Fiona wished she still held her mug so she could hide behind it. Stuart gazed straight into her soul.

She hadn't quite adjusted to the fact that he'd returned. Alive. Part of her was in shock, believing him a ghost who'd vanish as soon as she touched him. The other part sang in heavenly thanks, that Stuart had escaped and was whole. A quarter of an hour ago she'd been mourning him. Now he was here, and joy was burgeoning. When the shock faded, she'd be giddy and incoherent.

What they'd be to each other after a year apart, if anything at all, remained to be seen, but for the moment, it was enough that Stuart was here.

Now he continued to stare at her as though he had no idea what she was talking about.

"Oh, aye?" Gair answered her.

"I'll ask her if you can look," Fiona offered. "She's an agreeable young woman, I'm finding. Though be careful, Gair. She has made no secret of the fact that she'd like a husband."

Gair burst out laughing, which had the unfortunate consequence of him spitting droplets of ale across the table. "No fear on that score, lass. Gair's not the marrying kind."

Fiona had spoken in jest. Carrie, the innkeeper's daughter, had made it known she'd prefer an Englishman who could take her to softer living, so Gair was safe, but she did not explain. None of the three men at this table would have any use for Englishmen at the moment, even theoretical ones.

"You do that, *chaileag.*" Gair took another slurp of ale. "Padruig will be grateful. I imagine this one will be too." He jerked his thumb at Stuart, carefully not calling him by name.

Fiona said nothing about Gair addressing her as *girl,* or of him using the forbidden Erse tongue. It was not easy to cease conversing in a language you'd spoken all the days of your life.

Stuart kept his gaze on Fiona. Unnerving, that. She longed to ask him what had happened to him, how he'd escaped, how he'd survived. And to tell him what she'd been doing since the day last year when they'd parted so stormily at her brother's house. She'd been travelling the Highlands too, though she'd returned home from time to time to rest and plan. But she'd tried to stay away from her brother as often as and for as long as she could. Handy to know so many women in the Highlands with sentiments similar to hers.

They couldn't discuss such things, though, not here, in a tavern any traveler might enter.

I missed you, Stuart. I feared for you, my heart.

Fiona lifted her tea mug and drank the last bitter dregs, but she couldn't avoid Stuart's scrutiny.

STUART FOLLOWED FIONA into the Chamber of Sorrows located in the rear of the inn—Fiona had somehow persuaded the landlord's daughter to admit them. Though Stuart hadn't heard what Fiona had said to Carrie when the young woman had returned to the taproom, he wasn't surprised Fiona had arranged it. She had a way with her, did Fiona Macdonald.

When she'd said *sgian dubh*, the words soft on her tongue, Stuart's entire body had become incandescent.

Fiona was a true lady of the Highlands, her speech holding the unmistakable lilt. Far gentler than the harsh voices of the men he'd been surrounded by, her consonants almost a whisper against the liquid vowels.

Stuart had missed her until he ached. He hadn't realized how much until he'd been trussed up in that dark building in the farmlands of southern England, unsure whether he'd live or die. The thought of never seeing Fiona again had been almost as bad as the creative torture the English bastards had inflicted on him.

To find Fiona here, in this wayward place, far too close to the field where so many of his friends and family had perished was … odd. Why was she here? Fiona never did anything without a reason, and Stuart would have to pry out of her what that reason was.

The chamber was filled with sorrows indeed. Swords and pistols hung on the walls, and tables and boxes held knives, buckles, and other smaller relics. So much. A testament to the many who'd fallen.

Stuart halted just inside the door as the noise and stench of the battle suddenly poured back to him. The crack of gunfire, the acrid smell of powder, the screams of the dying, the blood-pounding rage that had kept Stuart fighting, followed by the intense grief of watching Duncan Mackenzie fall, his brothers and father swallowed by the smoke.

Gair pushed past as Stuart froze on the threshold, unable to move.

Fiona was already following the red-haired Carrie through the room, gazing at the assortment, her footfalls hushed.

Gair, who'd raided battlefields, beached ships, burned-out houses, and the like, had no qualms about examining the collection. He kept his hands behind his back much of the time, as though vowing he'd not filch anything, though Stuart noticed Fiona keeping a close eye on him.

"'Tis not here," Padruig announced after he and Gair had scanned the room for about half an hour. Carrie remained in the corner, letting them look but making certain they didn't nick anything.

As far as Stuart could tell, Padruig hadn't done much searching—Gair and Fiona had picked through boxes and studied objects on the shelves.

"Plenty of knives, though." Gair gestured at a case full of them. "Ye could find a good one. I'm sure the lass would give it to ye for a fair price."

Padruig, more stoic than usual, shook his head. He turned his back on Gair, pressed past Stuart, and made his way through the outer chambers to the noisy taproom.

Gair shrugged and began to follow. Fiona hurried to the door to stand beside Stuart and block Gair's path.

"Put them back," Fiona said evenly.

Gair gave her an innocent stare. "What are you on about, lass?"

Gair was a small man, and Fiona could look him straight in the eye. "Please." The word was firm, no pleading in it.

Gair's cheeks stained red. He heaved a sigh, sent Stuart an aggrieved glance, and pulled three buckles, a knife, a ring, and a few coins from his pockets. As the innkeeper's daughter watched, hands on hips, Gair returned them to the last basket he'd been sorting through.

Astonishing. Stuart hadn't seen him pocket anything, the sly sod.

"Is that all?" Fiona asked.

Gair let out another sigh and dropped two more coins into the basket. He lifted his hands. "That is all. Sorry, lass." He flashed Carrie a grin and slid past Stuart and out.

Stuart still couldn't move. The sorrow in the room pressed at him like a wave of chill fog until he could barely breathe.

Fiona laid her hand on his arm. Her touch, the warm pressure of her fingers, cut through the coldness, and the air began to clear. Stuart's feet came unstuck. He drew a long breath and stepped aside, giving Fiona room to leave the chamber.

Her hand slid from his coat, her face turned up to his, her green eyes searching. Stuart swallowed, suppressing the sharp need to enfold her in his arms and crush her to him. He remained still, which took all his strength. Fiona at last ducked around him, her expression unreadable.

Carrie remained, not offering to see them out. When Stuart glanced back, he saw her straightening the things Gair had displaced, her movements gentle.

Stuart caught up to Fiona and grasped her elbow, intending to take her aside where they could speak alone, but a maid hurried to her and said, "Chamber's ready, milady."

Of course, Fiona would want to trade the smoky and crowded outer room for privacy and relative comfort. She thanked the maid and started to follow her.

"Fio—" Stuart stopped himself as the maid gave him and then Fiona a curious stare. "Miss Macdonald."

"Thank you for your assistance, sir," Fiona said, maintaining her serenity. "Good night."

Damn and blast. Stuart could only bow like a good servant. He watched as she disappeared into one of the large chambers they'd just walked past to reach the collection. Una, with a severe scowl, shut the door.

Stuart glared at the blank wood for a few moments then gave up and returned to the taproom, remembering to shuffle like a lackey.

A harried maid slammed fresh tankards in front of Gair and Padruig as Stuart resumed his seat. Stuart had not had a chance to drink his first tankard, but Gair and Padruig were experts at putting away ale.

"Macdonald," Padruig said.

Stuart took a fortifying sip. The ale wasn't bad, as far as ale went, though he'd had better. "What Macdonald?"

"The lass's brother."

Stuart had thought that was who he meant. "Broc. A complete arse. Stay away from him."

Over my dead body will my sister run off with a Cameron and a rebel! Broc had shouted it at the top of his voice, and Fiona had quietly told Stuart he'd better go.

Broc Macdonald had inherited his father's lands, becoming laird of the surrounding glen. He had an ancient castle that had been made comfortable with modern furniture and carpets. So why was Fiona not there, warm and snug, even if she'd have to look after the ungrateful swine, and instead out in the deep cold between Inverness and Culloden Moor?

"He has it."

Stuart snapped back to Padruig. Even Gair ceased his drinking to frown at his partner. "Who has what?" Gair demanded.

"Broc Macdonald has the *sgian dubh*."

"Oh, aye? We just spent half an hour picking through that dross, and ye tell me it's for nothing?"

Stuart eyed Gair calmly. "You only think it a waste because Fiona caught you nicking half of it. Why do you think he has your knife, Padruig?"

"Worth a chance, wasn't it?" Padruig said. "The young Macdonald lass put me in mind of her brother. He happily watched his kinsmen be slaughtered then picked them clean. I saw him doing it." Padruig folded his thin lips together, having made the longest speech Stuart had ever heard him utter.

Stuart hadn't been aware Padruig and Gair had been anywhere near Culloden during the battle, but he said nothing about that. They'd been on hand to help the surviving Mackenzies flee to France in Gair's rickety ship, true, but he hadn't realized they'd come in from shore.

"What are ye saying?" Gair asked Padruig. "Ye want the lass to go home and tell her brother to give it up to ye?"

"I'm saying *he* should." Padruig flicked a bony forefinger at Stuart. He lifted his tankard. "And we should go along with them."

Gair regarded his partner in amazement. "When did ye become so daft? It's Christmas in a few days, and I planned to put me feet up here and wait for Hogmanay."

Stuart lifted his hand for attention. "What makes you think Broc Macdonald will even let me near his house?"

"Ye have his sister," Padruig said.

Stuart shook his head. "I haven't seen the woman in more than a year. That's nae *having* her, Padruig."

Padruig shrugged as though that was something Stuart needed to work out.

"I agree with Gair," Stuart said. "You've run mad. I've never heard ye once mention the name of Fiona's brother or this *sgian dubh* ye want."

"The lass brought it to mind."

So calm was Padruig, as though what he asked was a trifle Stuart could fetch for him in five minutes.

"Help me understand." Stuart tried to keep his voice steady. "Until I find it for you, I'm to be in your debt and follow you about Scotland like a hostage to your clan?"

Padruig pursed his lips as he thought this through, then gave Stuart a slight nod.

"And if I refuse?" Stuart hadn't battled for months against King Geordie's armies, Butcher Cumberland, and the Black Watch, nor survived weeks imprisoned and tortured, to succumb to the whims of Gair and Padruig. "Ye don't want to cross me, man," he said to Padruig.

Padruig's one good eye went icy and the hand that rested on the table tensed. Stuart kept his focus on that hand, which he knew could draw a knife in a flash.

Gair laughed, the sound lost in the general noise of the tavern. "I don't know why he's so set on retrieving this knife, lad, but Padruig don't set on a thing often. Best indulge him."

Stuart *could* fight them both—he'd taken on larger and tougher men. But together, Gair and Padruig made a formidable team, especially because they fought dirty, knew more tricks than a pair of weasels, and would not give up until they defeated their foe. They'd not survived this long without that sort of doggedness.

Stuart opened his hands in a gesture of surrender, pretending to relax, though the thought of facing Broc Macdonald and so many memories chilled him. "So be it."

Padruig's fist softened and the frost left his eye. He took a silent sip of ale.

"I warn you though, 'twon't be easy." Stuart directed his statement to Gair. "Fiona will want to keep a sharp eye on you."

"Aye." Gair deflated, his laughter dying, he probably imagining Fiona's eagle gaze fixed on his every move. "I thought as much."

FIONA'S STOMACH GROWLED as the savory odor of food being carried into the chamber wafted to her. She had her back to the door, only glimpsing the servant trundling in as she tidied her bag of belongings. She pushed the men's shirts and breeches she'd arranged to be left here with Carrie beneath her own clothes, so that anyone having a peek into the bag would see only her spare petticoats and stockings.

Una poked at the fire, not trusting the inn's staff to build it to her liking. The small room was gloriously warm, defying the snow swirling outside the dark window.

"Thank you," Fiona said to the servant. "Leave it on the table, and we'll have at it."

"Aye, miss," came the gravelly reply.

Fiona swung around. The servant, hunched in a homespun wool coat, glanced up at her, a twinkle in his blue eyes.

"Una," she said. "Will you wait outside a moment? Ask Carrie to give you something to eat."

Una took one look at Stuart Cameron bending over the food tray, folded her arms, and plunked herself onto a stool by the fire. "Nay," she said. "I'm staying."

Chapter Three

FIONA WEIGHED THE perils of Una remaining—she'd have to argue long and hard to send her maid away for a private moment with Stuart. Stuart clanked the plates on the tray, also making no move to leave.

Fiona, resigned, stepped past Stuart and closed the door.

"Your reputation, ma'am," Una said, aghast.

"Is beyond saving by this time," Fiona returned briskly. "Either everyone pities me as the sister of Broc Macdonald or they believe me a hussy, and nothing will change their opinion. It scarcely matters these days, does it?"

Stuart lifted his head. "When did you grow so cynical, love?"

His soft lilt threatened to shatter Fiona's heart. "When Highlanders died and my world was destroyed."

Stuart rose to his full height, his feigned obsequiousness falling away. "Why are you truly here, Fiona? Traveling alone?"

"Nothing I can tell you now." Fiona shivered as she indicated the walls and one small window. Anyone could listen, anyone could be in the pay of the Hanoverians, or hate the Jacobites for their own reasons.

So many scores were being settled in the Uprising's aftermath.

Stuart nodded his understanding. "Will ye be returning home then?"

Fiona went to her bag and buckled it closed. "I don't know." Go back to Broc for Christmas and pretend to dote on him? She'd been gone for months this time, her travels ostensibly to visit friends all over the Highlands, which was partly true—she simply didn't mention what she and her friends got up to. Broc thought her a frivolous gadabout and had upbraided her the few times she'd returned. She hadn't been home now since June.

Stuart pushed his hair from his face in the endearing way she remembered. He was so tall, his broad shoulders in keeping with his size. He was a crazed fighter—she'd seen him do battle—and yet, the blunt hands that wielded a claymore and pistol so deftly could be gentle …

Stuart's fingers left a sooty streak on his cheek. "When ye do go, I have a boon to ask." He darted a glance at Una, who fixed him with a scowl. "Take me with ye."

Fiona came out of her daze. "To Castle Mòr? Are ye mad? If Broc sees ye again, he'll kill you. He said so." She put her fists on her hips, her slim panniers swaying. "I recall *you* saying the same about him."

"Aye, but Padruig wants to go there. He thinks your brother might have this dagger he's searching for. The pair of them sent me in here to persuade you."

"Oh." Fiona tamped down her sudden disappointment. She had no reason to believe Stuart would want to rekindle what they might have had if Prince Teàrlach hadn't arrived in the west. They'd only begun a few tendrils of passion, and then hell had come to them.

"If I find this bloody knife, I can go about my business," Stuart said. "Debt paid."

"Ye trust them?" Una asked in amazement. She'd never learned that retainers weren't to interrupt their employers—Una was a distant cousin, in any case, a member of Fiona's clan.

"Not really," Stuart answered. "But I'm ready to be shot of them. Gair isn't helping me out of the kindness of his heart."

"Aye, well, it might end in shooting," Una said darkly.

Gair and Padruig were no strangers to casual violence, Fiona knew. She also knew they would never betray a Jacobite Highlander. They might bleed that Highlander of all he had and steal anything left, but they were loyal Scots to the bone.

"I've come to beg ye." Stuart made a show of going down on his knees, which only made him slightly less tall.

Fiona's breath caught. She could go to him, place her hands on his shoulders, lean down and kiss him …

She sucked in air and nearly choked. "Aren't the Butcher's men looking for you?" Her words were cracked and dry. "It's dangerous for you to be in Scotland. Their men hunt everywhere."

"Aye, but I've come this far. 'Tisn't many more miles to your brother's home. And I'll continue playing the servant, a beast of burden."

Stuart was so far from being a beast of burden that Fiona wanted to laugh. "You might hide from Cumberland, but not from my brother," she pointed out.

"No matter. I'll discover if he has the dagger, give it to Padruig—or let Padruig convince your brother to let it go—and be off."

"Going where?" Fiona could barely voice the question.

Stuart shrugged. He climbed to his feet, towering over her once more.

How had Fiona come to be so close to him? She didn't remember moving, but now she stood only a yard away.

"Home for now." Stuart's words filled with emotion. "Back to my own lands."

"Where you'll be caught and captured."

Another shrug. "I'll do everything I can to prevent that, but I need to see to my house and people before I leave again. If I do. I'm tired of running, Fiona." His weariness touched her.

She closed her hands so they wouldn't tremble. If Stuart continued to stand so near and say her name like that, she'd be lost.

"I can't take ye to Broc. He'll kill ye."

Stuart rubbed his forehead, leaving another black streak. "Well, I'm going with or without ye, love. Be easier with ye."

Her irritation rose. "Bloody stubborn Scot."

"Aye, that's me." Stuart was inches from her, his big hands clasping hers and lifting them to his lips. "Come with me, Fiona. Ye were so angry when I left ye, that ye might enjoy watching your brother trying to best me."

Never. Fiona had worried herself sick about Stuart from the moment he'd ridden away from the castle, laughing, rushing off to war.

Fiona pried her hands from his, hoping he couldn't see how much she was melting. "Never mind. I'll come with you. My intervention might keep ye alive." She tried to glower.

Stuart shot her a grin that was like sunshine breaking through clouds. "Even if it doesn't, I'll enjoy arguing with ye on the way." He made an exaggerated, courtly bow. "Ladies. Good evening. We leave on the morrow."

He turned up his collar, hunched himself down, opened the door, and tramped from the room, becoming one more servant in an inn full of travelers. The door closed, shutting out the noise.

"Ye aren't truly going to go to Castle Mòr with him, are ye?" Una asked in alarm.

Fiona checked her bag once more, making certain it was securely fastened. "Aye, that I am. What we have to do is on the way, anyway. Stuart or my brother might die if I don't go with him, and if I have a chance to prevent such a thing, I will."

"Humph," Una muttered, but thankfully said no more.

THE NEXT MORNING, Christmas Eve, was bitterly cold but clear. Stuart, with Gair and Padruig, waited in the yard until Fiona and Una emerged. Una was bundled to her ears in misshapen wraps, Fiona in a loose dark skirt, long coat, and scarf.

Gair was ready to set off, clutching a long staff to trudge out of the yard, but Fiona forestalled him. "I must wait for my mount."

"Ye brought a horse?" Gair asked in amazement.

"I'm certainly not trudging through the snow on foot, sir." Fiona's green eyes widened over her scarf, and Stuart smothered a laugh.

One of the lads from the inn brought out a horse from the livery, a shaggy and sturdy mare. The lad moved to boost Fiona into the saddle, but Stuart reached her first. She gave him a startled look as he cupped his hand for her to step into, but she let him grasp her leg and lift her lightly to the mare's back. Fiona swung her leg over the saddle, revealing leather breeches beneath her skirt, riding astride like the resilient Scotswoman she was.

The contact with her shapely thigh and calf, even through the layers of clothing, warmed Stuart's blood. This was a woman made for loving, for lazing in bed with on a cold winter's day.

He'd take steps to ensure that happened once he was finished with Gair and Padruig. The war was over, Scotland in ruins. Fiona should not stay here. After he discovered whether his house was in one piece and retrieved some items from it, he'd take her to France, and they'd wait for time to pass. Together. His heart wrenched at the thought of leaving Scotland again, but he thought he could weather exile with Fiona.

Stuart gave Fiona's leg a pat. She glanced at him then quickly away. Stuart couldn't see her cheeks beneath her scarf, but her forehead went a pretty pink.

Before Stuart could turn from her, Una more or less used him as a climbing tree to hoist herself behind Fiona, riding pillion. Stuart grunted as Una kicked him—surely she hadn't meant to do that—as she settled herself behind the saddle.

Stuart made certain both women were steady before Fiona took up the reins. She spoke softly to her mount, who flicked her ears at Fiona's voice. The beast had a wooly brown winter coat and a lighter brown mane and tail. A horse, not a pony, as rugged as the hills around them.

The stable boy tried to hand Fiona's bag to Una, but Stuart intercepted it and slung it over his shoulder. Fiona pretended nonchalance, but Una's silent concern was palpable. Interesting. What was in the bag they feared he'd see?

Stuart settled it on his back with his own small sack of belongings, and at last, they set off.

The bulk of the Macdonald realms lay on Scotland's western coast and the islands, which was why those clans had been among the first to support Prince Teàrlach—the prince had arrived on the islands and worked his way eastward, recruiting his army along the way.

Not all Macdonalds had joined the cause, which had created a bitter split in the clan, dividing families and friends. Fiona's brother had firmly stood against supporting the prince, and had finally taken up arms against his fellow Highlanders.

Broc Macdonald's castle lay south and west of Inverness, some twenty miles distant. Very near the lands of the Camerons. They were neighbors, if uneasy ones.

They couldn't skirt the long lake south of Inverness, because they'd run too close to Fort Augustus and other strongholds of the Hanoverians, who were still hunting Highlanders. Stuart doubted they'd give up even for Christmas.

No matter. Stuart knew these glens well, probably better than Gair and Padruig, who preferred hugging the coast so they could slip off over water. Stuart also knew the people in each village, though whether they'd hide him if asked, Stuart couldn't say. Too much fear lay in these lands, and no one wanted to be caught with one of the rebel Scots.

Fiona rode serenely along, gazing at the surprisingly clear sky, the hills rising to their right. Stuart walked next to Fiona's horse, where he could grab its bridle if the mare tried to bolt, though the horse seemed tame enough.

Gair, who walked a few paces ahead, following Stuart's directions, took them up a path that rose through woods, avoiding the more habitable places along the lake. Padruig brought up the rear. Unlike Gair, he used no walking staff and had strapped his small pack to his back, leaving his hands free.

Roads in the Highlands, once off the main thoroughfares, were more like wandering tracks made by cows sometime in the Middle Ages. Stuart's boots were coated in snow, ice, and mud before they'd gone a few miles.

"I see why ye're up there," he grumbled at Fiona. She hadn't said much except for bland remarks on how lucky they were in the weather. As this time of year was usually full of pissing rain or blinding snow, Stuart couldn't argue.

"It is drier on horseback, I grant," Fiona said. "And Piseag is so warm." She sank her gloved fingers into the horse's fur.

Stuart rumbled a laugh at the name. "Ye call her 'Kitten'?"

"What's wrong with that? She's gentle and soft."

"When I was a lad, a kitten climbed me and scratched my face all over."

Fiona's eyes crinkled as she studied him. "Poor Stuart. I don't see any scars on you. Well, it toughened ye for the army."

"Aye, Geordie's men were no match for that cat. She'd have had them begging for mercy."

"How did ye manage to have yourself captured, then?" Fiona asked, as though inquiring about why he'd been late for tea one afternoon. "If ye were so hardened by your cat?"

"Oh, you know. Helping a friend." The aftermath of Culloden rose in Stuart's mind. Jacobite soldiers were fleeing, after those who'd surrendered and laid down arms were slaughtered where they stood. His childhood friend, Calum, had been half dead, unable to run. Stuart had lingered to drag him away when four of Cumberland's men had surrounded them. Calum, already dying, had flung himself at the soldiers, and they'd cut him down. Stuart had attacked, bellowing a fierce cry, and had fought, enraged, before he'd been felled by a blow to the head.

"Still don't know why the soldiers didn't kill me outright," Stuart said, lightening his tone to hide his anger. "But they tied me up and took me off, first to an outbuilding, later marching me to a ship to journey south. Ended up in prison with Willie Mackenzie. Good thing. His brother Alec and the lady he married wrested us free, and I fled with all of them to Paris."

"Mackenzies?" Fiona asked in surprise. "I thought Will and Alec perished, along with the rest of the family."

"So did I, but there was Alec, opening the door of my cell, and Will chivvying us all out. Indestructible, is Will Mackenzie."

"It appears you are too." Fiona's voice lowered, "I read your name on the rolls. Captured. I was sure you'd be hanged."

"As was I, lady. But here I am."

She frowned at him, though she blinked, her eyes moist. "Walking right back into danger."

"I intend to stay out of it. Find Padruig his trophy and be about my business."

"Ah."

Stuart glanced quickly at Fiona, hoping he heard regret in her voice.

He did not tell her that when he next vanished, he'd ask her to come with him. If she said no, he'd simply have to convince her, and he could come up with some very creative methods …

"Another reason for riding a horse," Fiona interrupted his thoughts. "Is that I can see farther than I can on foot. For instance, a few Black Watch and one English soldier are waiting for us around the next bend."

Chapter Four

FIONA'S HEART PUMPED faster as Stuart put his hand on Piseag's bridle to halt her, and whistled softly between his teeth. Gair hurried back to them, and Padruig gathered close.

Fiona tried to stay calm, forcing herself not to beg Stuart to hide, to flee back to the inn. He could blend in with the throng there and escape during the Christmas revelry.

Stuart's face set in stubborn lines, his blue eyes quiet as he withdrew into himself. Fiona watched him leave the carefree, laughing, impetuous Highlander behind and become the honed and deadly soldier.

They stood in a thick stand of trees, the land sloping sharply upward on their right, downward on the left. At the scrape of boots of the approaching soldiers, Stuart left the track, fading noiselessly into the uphill woods, his dark coat blending with the black rocks and boles of trees among the snow.

Padruig seized Piseag's bridle, and Una moved restlessly behind Fiona.

The soldiers rounded the bend and stopped in surprise. No officers, Fiona thought with relief. Just infantrymen, possibly heading for their camp or perhaps even Balthazar's inn, anticipating a warm room and a draught of ale.

No worries that the soldiers would search her bag, Fiona reflected. Stuart still had it on his back and he was gone.

The three Black Watch, in their kilts—the tartan ban did not extend to them—looked more annoyed than worried when they beheld Fiona and party. Fiona's idea that they were heading to camp or the inn to go off-duty solidified.

The Englishman with them, in the red coat of Something-or-Other Foot, appeared as anxious to push past them as the others, but it was his duty to stop and question any Scots person on the road.

The four formed a barrier across the track, the Englishman slightly to one side, as though ready to let the Black Watch deal with any trouble.

One of the Black Watch soldiers lifted his rifle from his shoulder and aimed it vaguely at them. "No farther. Who are ye, and what's your business on this road?"

"I don't call it much of a road." Gair spat to the side of it. "We're taking this lady safely to shelter. It's brutal cold, if ye'd not noticed."

The man had the sharp blue eyes and fair hair of a Highlander, his accent putting him from the north and east. "What lady, and what shelter?"

"This lady." Gair jerked his thumb at Fiona. "Whatever shelter we can find. Any houses the way you've come?"

"Only burned ones." The man smiled a little over the barrel of his rifle.

Fiona lost her temper. These were Scotsmen who'd turned on their own people, burning homes of those suspected of hiding Jacobites, throwing entire families out with nowhere to go.

She dragged her scarf from her mouth, letting the cold burn her lips. "I see you there, Iver MacGregor," she said to another of the Black

Watch who hovered behind the man with the rifle. He was thinner than the others, with brown hair under his bonnet, and scraggly whiskers on his face to match. "What would your mother say about that beard? Ye should grow it out or cut it off entirely."

Padruig remained stoic, but Gair shot Fiona an alarmed look, trying to silence her. The Englishman and the soldier who hadn't spoken struggled to hide grins.

"Fiona?" Iver bleated. "I mean ... Miss Macdonald? What are you doing out here in the weather?"

"Trying to get *out* of the weather. But you and your friends are blocking my way."

Iver's mouth popped open, which was its usual position. Iver MacGregor lived in the next glen from Fiona's family home, and he and Broc had played together as children. Iver looked perpetually bewildered, had even when he'd come out of his shell enough to dance with Fiona one Hogmanay, before he'd joined the Black Watch.

"We can't let none pass," Iver explained as though Fiona hadn't heard about the Uprising. "Rebels about."

The Black Watch leader lowered his rifle but didn't move, seeming happy to let Iver speak for all of them.

Fiona made a show of looking around. "I see no Highlanders here. Only these men I hired to see me through. You know them. Gair Murray and Padruig."

Iver flushed, and the others shuffled, uncomfortable. Most people in the Highlands had bought smuggled goods from Gair and Padruig. The minute Gair was arrested, he could reveal what he'd sold not only to every soldier whose duty it was to stamp out smuggling, but to their superiors as well, all the way up the chain of command.

Iver stepped closer to the horse, on the side opposite Padruig, and peered up at Fiona. "Ye trust them?"

"I do to lead me true until they receive their pay at the end of the road. I'm only going home. My brother is ill, as you might have heard."

Iver nodded, brow furrowing. "Aye, he took injury at Falkirk, I recall. Give him me best."

"I will. Now, shall you let me pass?"

The Black Watch leader roused to life. "Sorry, ma'am. Orders. Everyone on the road is to be searched."

"Very well." Fiona nodded to Una, who started to slide down. Padruig caught Una and set her on her feet, but Fiona swung off herself, not waiting for assistance. "Be quick about it. I'd like to be indoors before nightfall."

Thank heavens for Stuart. She could be serene, knowing the soldiers wouldn't find the extra clothes and food she carried, would never realize what she intended to do with them.

Gair was less sanguine. "Ye can see I'm not carrying guns or a casket of gold, can't ye? Will ye rob me of the few coins I have? I'm reduced to escorting a woman across the Highlands for pay. Take pity on me."

Iver winced. "Sorry, Gair. I'll make it quick."

Iver found four knives, two flasks of whisky, and a few English gold sovereigns in Gair's pockets, but nothing that seemed to alarm anyone. Padruig had one knife and a flask and that was all.

With Iver's persuasion, they allowed Una and Fiona to turn out their own pockets, showing they carried only dried meat, bread, and cheese for the journey.

The leader clicked Gair's two gold coins together. "We might have to confiscate this. Could be the spoils of smuggling."

"Now, hang on—" Gair blustered.

"Give them to him, Gair." Fiona kept up her air of an inconvenienced highborn lady as she turned back to her horse. "I'll give you the cost at journey's end."

She allowed Padruig to give her a leg-up into the saddle, settling herself and paying no more attention to the men, as Una was lifted on behind her.

The leader grinned, and the coins disappeared. Gair snarled. Padruig stepped to Gair and simply looked at him. Gair subsided.

"Give my best to your mum, Iver," Fiona said graciously. "Good day, gentlemen."

Padruig grasped the bridle again, though Fiona held the reins, and led the mare past the soldiers. The Englishman and the two other Black Watch seemed pleased with their chance encounter. Iver saluted Fiona wistfully.

"Take care, Fiona. Perhaps I'll see ye at your brother's at Hogmanay?"

"Perhaps." Fiona nodded down at him, as though it made no difference to her.

She managed to remain composed as Padruig led her on, Gair following, but her mouth was dry, her limbs trembling. She adjusted her scarf over her nose, its warmth welcoming.

Would the soldiers see Stuart? Hear him? Shoot him outright? And where had Stuart gone? He knew these woods and valleys better than most. Would he vanish over the mountains, never to be seen again?

Her heart pounded, and her fingers twitched. She wanted to urge Piseag to run, run, run, so she could find Stuart but knew that would be the height of foolishness.

They rounded the bend. The soldiers did not follow, though Fiona did not risk glancing back to see whether they watched.

Padruig and Gair kept up a steady but not rapid pace, Gair raising his voice in a badly out of tune song. Another mile went by, and another. They saw no more soldiers, and Fiona began to relax.

Fiona also did not see Stuart. They traveled for an hour, the road leaving the hills and striking over a glen toward mountains beyond and the castle where Broc Macdonald had retreated, nursing his injury.

Clouds began to blot the sky. Fiona would have to turn aside soon, as she'd promised, though how she'd fulfill her mission without the bag Stuart had taken she did not know. She could only do her best.

They stopped in the shelter of a tree to water the horse in the nearby stream, Padruig breaking ice with his boot. In a low voice, Fiona explained to the two men what she meant to do. As predicted, Gair argued, but Padruig gruffly agreed and stared Gair to silence. Then they went on.

Fiona saw no sign of Stuart as the clouds gathered, and she realized as the miles went by, that he was truly gone.

STUART, WHO'D BEEN shadowing Fiona and party, pulled his coat close against the growing wind. He knew they were heading for Broc's castle in the next glen, so he could simply hurry there and wait for them. But leaving Fiona to the mercy of Gair and Padruig, not to mention any Hanoverian soldiers lurking about, did not appeal to him.

Stuart was surprised, then, when Fiona turned off the small road that would take her to her brother's castle, and wended her way up a path toward a tiny crack between two tall mountains.

Chapter Five

STUART FOLLOWED AT a discreet distance as Fiona's horse went higher into the foothills, around a stand of snow-covered boulders, and out of sight.

There was nothing back there. Stuart knew every nook and cranny of this part of the Highlands, especially so close to his own lands. No one lived in that bleak area of the mountains, and no road led through the rocks. It was a dead end.

The phrase made him shudder. Stuart scanned the open ground between himself and the boulders, then sped his steps to cross the snowy valley, not slowing until he'd reached the rocks behind which Fiona had ridden.

The bag he carried weighed on his back. He'd had a look inside and found Fiona's things, but also men's clothing, secondhand and worn, the kind laborers would wear. Several sets of them. He'd studied them in puzzlement—why on earth was she riding around the Highlands with such gear?

Stuart reached the outcropping in time to see Fiona, the horse, Una, Padruig, and Gair, vanish in a cleft in the rocks. Stuart skirted the snowy boulders and approached.

When he started into the black shadow between the rocks, he suddenly found himself staring down the tip of Padruig's knife. Stuart halted, the point against his nose.

Padruig recognized Stuart, blinked, and relaxed. "Ye'd better come in."

A blanket had been tacked between tall rocks, forming a door of sorts against the cold. Behind it, Stuart found Highlanders, half a dozen of them.

The men had grubby, bearded faces and weariness in their eyes. Stuart recognized a few of them, the rest he did not. Retainers and men, foot soldiers of Prince Teàrlach's army. Those who'd fought and then fled for their lives when the word came down that no quarter was to be given.

Fiona glanced at Stuart. "Good. You've come."

She might have been welcoming him to a small garden party she'd arranged. Saying nothing more, she reached for the bag Stuart slid from his shoulder.

Fiona plunked the bag down and opened it, digging past a flash of women's underclothes to pull out breeches, shirts, and coats. Una busily helped.

"I should have things to fit everybody," she said as she laid out the garments. "The coats might be a bit small, but they're the best that could be found."

"Aye, well, I'll have me tailor sew me a new one." One Highlander flashed his teeth in a grin. "Next time I visit him in London."

A few guffaws sounded, but mostly these men were exhausted.

"Gair," Stuart said quietly. "Hand round your flask."

Gair turned innocent eyes to him. "What flask is that?"

"Do it, lad," Padruig growled.

Gair immediately pulled a battered tin bottle from his pocket. He opened it, releasing the pungent odor of whisky.

"*Uisge beatha*," one man said in reverence. "Thought I'd never taste fine malt again."

"And ye won't now, I wager," Stuart said.

The man took the flask, drank, and coughed. "You're right, there. Tastes like me gran's washing-up water."

The others laughed but they reached eagerly for the flask in turn. Fiona handed them the food she'd purchased at the tavern for the journey, all of her share. Stuart moved to stop her, but Fiona's face was set, and he knew he'd only begin an argument.

The mystery of why she carried the clothing was solved. Now to the mystery of how she'd known these men would be here.

"We encountered Black Watch about seven miles to the northeast," Fiona told them as they ate. "They were heading toward Inverness. Tonight will be a good time to slip out and make your way to Kinloch Hourn. A ship will be there to take ye to Skye."

"Straight through your brother's lands," one man pointed out. "Skirting them, anyway."

Fiona nodded. "I will keep Broc occupied, and he'll never notice. I'll burn down the castle if I have to."

More laughter. "I believe ye," the man continued. "Why don't you come with us, lass? We could use a soft face to light our way."

Amid nods from the other men, Fiona jerked her thumb at Stuart. "I have to help this one out of trouble first. Will take all my skill, I think."

"Aye, Stuart Cameron is nothing but trouble," the man said. "Where've ye been, lad? Haven't seen ye since Culloden. Thought you were dead."

"I was helping His Majesty discover how many knives can cut into a Highlander before he betrays his fellows."

Fiona glanced at him, her eyes glittering in the darkness.

"And what is the answer?" the Highlander asked.

Stuart shrugged. "Don't know. I never let them get to the end. I decided to quit playing and legged it."

The chuckles came again. Most of the men were happily eating the meager meal, shared exactly between them.

Padruig, who'd been standing guard at the door, ducked inside. "We should not linger."

"True." Fiona re-latched her bag. "Any messages for your families, lads?"

They all had something to say, though more than one begged Fiona not to endanger their loved ones by revealing where the men would go.

"Never worry," Fiona said cheerfully. "I am quite discreet."

"We thank ye, lady," the lead Highlander said. "We hate to take your charity, but sometimes a man grows desperate."

"Not charity," Stuart broke in. "It's Christmas."

"Aye, and that makes us the three wise men," Gair said. "We come bearing gifts, as I like to say."

"But you're about to go see King Herod," the leader returned. "Broc Macdonald, who once pretended to be a friend."

"A friend to all of us," Stuart said. "I think, when he discovered I had designs on his sister, he went a bit mad." Fiona flushed but did not correct him.

"He was mad before that," the Highlander said. "I've known him all me life. Don't wish him well from me. My apologies, lass."

Fiona shook her head. "The times have changed us all. My brother is an arse. I *will* tell him that."

Laughter rang out, softened at the last minute. "God bless ye," another man said. "Happy Christmas."

"Happy Christmas." Fiona bathed them all in a warm smile and slid out of the shelter, Stuart holding the blanket for her.

The leader caught hold of Stuart before he could go. "Take care of that one," he murmured, his breath sharp with Gair's whisky. "She's an angel of mercy. But if she's caught helping men like us …"

"I won't let her be," Stuart said with conviction.

He waited until Gair retrieved his empty flask, then followed him out.

Padruig was about to assist Fiona onto her horse, but Stuart waved him off. Padruig ducked aside, taking the bag from Una under her very watchful eye.

Stuart turned Fiona to him, the two of them resting against Piseag's warm flank. Before she could speak, he tilted her face to his and kissed her.

THE KISS TOOK Fiona's breath away. She'd missed Stuart with every beat of her heart in the long year since she'd seen him last, and his presence now both elated and weakened her. His arms hard on her back kept her upright as his tongue tangled hers, he tasting of whisky and the bracing cold.

But his mouth held heat, his breath scalding her cheek. Fiona dug her fingers into his coat, the rough wool laced with his warmth. Her body ran with fire, need squeezing her, as well as joy that he was here, unhurt, and alive.

She felt the gazes of Padruig, Gair, and Una on them, none of the three ready to politely turn away. Stuart didn't seem to care. He scooped Fiona up into him, kissing his fill. Piseag remained solidly at her side, as though the mare understood Fiona needed her to prop her up.

A sharp blast of wind made Stuart lift his lips from Fiona's. He gazed down at her, his blue eyes like pieces of aquamarine. He was

Scotland, its sky and bluster, its strength and wildness.

He slowly released her, his breath coming fast. "Are ye well, lass?"

Fiona didn't know. She never would be, not until Stuart was completely safe.

"Yes," she whispered.

Stuart traced her cheek. His leather glove was coarse against her skin, but his touch was gentle as could be.

He abruptly stooped down, grasping Fiona's booted foot to boost her up into the saddle. He lifted Una behind her, while Una gazed over her scarf with all the scorn of a Viking queen.

Stuart caught Piseag's reins and turned the horse. "Come on," he said to Gair and Padruig. "We should get ourselves indoors before nightfall."

THE FIRST WISPS of snow began to fall as they crossed the last open valley and into the fold of mountain where lay the Macdonald family home.

Fiona eyed the glen with mixed feelings. She'd played here in her happy girlhood, knew sorrow with the deaths of first her mother then her father, and grew frustrated when she realized her brother saw her as a commodity to be married off. A clanswoman could be used to strengthen ties with other clans. Broc hadn't intended for her to fall for a Cameron, especially one with Jacobite sympathies—Broc believed that being loyal to King Geordie would help him rise in profit and status.

Stuart had said very little to her since his impetuous kiss, resuming the trek through the cold wind. Fiona hadn't quite recovered, and wasn't certain she would. The kiss had staggered her, opening up places she'd forced closed.

Her thoughts went back to the last kiss she'd shared with Stuart,

September of the previous year, before Teàrlach reached Edinburgh and took it over. They'd had a grand ball at Castle Mòr, Broc's way of saying he wasn't afraid. He'd invited both Jacobites and loyalists, as though daring anyone to make trouble. The Camerons had come, Stuart in their lead, and with him had been Mal, Alec, and Will Mackenzie.

Fiona had laughed and danced with them all, knowing in her heart disaster was near. Those supporting Teàrlach were too confident, those opposing too scornful. Their arrogance would clash violently, and she'd been right.

Stuart had swung her out of the Scots dance and into a hall outside the ballroom. He'd leaned her against a wall, his fiery hair loosening from its queue, his body warm in the night.

"Come with me, lass," he'd whispered. "When all this is over and Scotland ruled by its own king, come home with me. We'll have a grand celebration, with you as my lady."

It wasn't exactly a proposal of marriage but Fiona had known that was what he meant.

They'd kissed, long and passionately, Stuart's hands on her waist, one coming up to cup her breast. The taste of him had lingered from that day to this, brought to life once more by their kiss outside the shelter.

Fiona hadn't given him an answer that night. The future had been so uncertain, and she hadn't wanted to upset Broc.

Stuart had come to her one more time before he'd left to join Teàrlach's army, and Broc had threatened to kill him.

Ye think I'll let me sister run off with a bloody Jacobite? What will ye drag her to, a hovel while you hide as a traitor?

'Twill be a damned better fate for her than being forced to marry one of your toadies, Stuart had growled. *Have the grace to follow Teàrlach and die like a man for your lands. Let Fiona be laird—she'll be far better at it than you.*

Broc had let out a snarl of fury and drawn his dagger. Fiona, in alarm, had stepped between the two men.

I'm going nowhere, she'd shouted. *With either of you!*

She hadn't dared storm from the room, or Broc might have gone at Stuart. Stuart would have defended himself, and blood would have been spilled.

Stuart had rounded on Fiona, his red and green plaid swinging. *Come with me, lass, away from this rotten bastard who'll drag ye into the muck with him.*

He'll drag ye to a Jacobite dunghill, Broc had countered. *Go with him and be damned to ye. You'll both be hanged soon enough.*

Behind his bluster, Fiona had seen Broc's fear, his pain from the death of their parents that time had not erased. Broc worried for Fiona, sure that Teàrlach would lose, and she being with Stuart would doom her. He didn't want to lose Fiona as well.

Stuart had glared at Fiona, his fury at Broc plain. Behind it, he also had fear—that he'd never see Fiona again.

I can't, Stuart. Fiona had let her voice go soft. *When it's over, and if you're alive, you come back to me.*

It will be over swiftly, Stuart had promised. *In weeks, lass.*

In weeks, you'll be dead, Broc had declared, his head up, his arrogance high.

Stuart had laughed. *Then I'll never have to see you again.*

If I do see ye, *I'll kill ye.* Broc had pointed his dagger at Stuart, determination in his eyes.

Stuart had laughed again, spun on his heel, and was gone, the sound of his boots ringing on the stones.

Fiona hadn't worried much, not then. Stuart had been correct—Teàrlach had already been poised to take Edinburgh, and then he'd quickly won at Prestonpans. Stuart would come marching back soon, and Fiona would leave her home to be with him. She imagined that once the Jacobites had the upper hand and Teàrlach's father was installed as king, Broc would switch sides with blinding rapidity.

But none of that had happened. France's promised support had vanished in the fickle wind. Teàrlach's army had eventually been crushed, so many men dying, and for what? For a callow young prince who'd proved he had no idea what he was doing against a force that far outnumbered his.

Now proud Highland men hid in makeshift hideaways, dependent on the charity of Fiona and women like her.

Stuart hadn't returned to her. She'd read of his capture, knew he'd soon die, and tried to bury the anguish in her heart.

Until she'd glanced up at the inn yesterday afternoon, and beheld him.

This time, she knew, she could never let him go.

STUART EXPECTED, AS they approached the castle, that the giant door would open, and a dozen soldiers, egged on by Broc, would pour out and surround them. They'd not even bother arresting Stuart—they'd stab him through immediately, or wait a bit while they built a gallows to hang him. But nothing like that happened.

The castle, as good castles that had survived from the 1400s were wont, squatted on a hill overlooking two valleys. A long road wound to it, the approach visible from the tall windows.

The castle itself was a square tower that rose five floors, with a two-story addition built in the 1600s in front of that. The newer wing held the great hall, where Stuart had danced with Fiona in happier times.

Gray-brown stone made the castle appear to be yet another rock thrusting up through the snow. Stuart saw no light in any window, no sign of habitation.

Perhaps Broc had given up cold drafts and moved to a more solid house in Edinburgh—Stuart couldn't help hoping. Fiona would take over the castle and liven it up. Stuart always said she'd be better at running the place than Broc.

He glanced at her, but she'd pulled her scarf over her face again, a hood covering her hair. He couldn't see her in the darkness, couldn't tell what she thought of bringing Stuart to her home.

Would Broc kill Stuart right away? Or philosophically reflect on how much life had changed both men?

Stuart stifled a laugh. Broc wasn't the reflecting sort.

No one challenged them as they slogged on. The castle loomed high, and Stuart's breath quickened as they climbed the steep hill toward it. Were they walking into an ambush? Or would they find an empty and deserted castle?

A gate in the center of the outer wall led, Stuart remembered, to a courtyard and the great hall. The gate was closed, likely bolted for the night.

Fiona nudged Piseag, turning her flank to the gate, which Fiona pounded with her fist.

Stuart squashed his hat down on his head, pulling up the collar of his coat. With any luck, he would still pass for Gair's lackey. He'd find Padruig's knife—or convince the man it wasn't here—and move on to his own house.

After a long wait, Gair moving restlessly, the gate creaked open, and a pale face peered out. "Who's there?" a hoarse voice asked.

"Marcas?" Fiona sounded astonished. "Why on earth are you answering the door? Where is everyone?"

"Miss Fiona." The name was exhaled in relief. A thin man with graying red hair pushed open the door, his lined face eerie by the flickering light of his lantern. "They've all run off, miss. Well, most have. Terrified they'll be taken as Jacobites. Or killed by Jacobites."

"Truly?" Fiona asked in indignation.

Stuart wasn't very surprised. Broc had never engendered loyalty, the man being so distrusting himself. Stuart wondered, with a qualm, if he'd find the same situation at his home.

"Aye. It's a sad state of affairs," Marcas said. "Not long after ye left the last time, they decided they'd had enough, and up and went. Come in—the laird will need to see you."

Not *will want to see you* or *be happy to see you*, but *need to. Hmm.*

"Then we'll go to him right away. *Tapadh leibh*, Marcas."

She'd merely said *thank you*, but Marcas peered up at her in worry. "Never speak Erse here, Miss. Ye know the laird doesn't like us to."

"Nonsense. Where is he?"

Una had already dismounted, and now Fiona swung her leg over the saddle. Stuart caught her and lifted her to the ground. Fiona glanced at him gratefully and stepped inside the gate, leaving Stuart to handle the horse, as a servant should.

The courtyard was deserted. Even this late, with snow starting, Stuart would expect to see it a hive of activity. Broc was a laird, which meant he was the main landholder in this area. He'd not only have tenants but all the workers who kept the castle running—gamekeeper, farm steward, blacksmith, cooks. Various other servants should be there to make certain the laird and his family had plenty of food and firewood this cold winter's night.

No one but Marcas, whom Stuart remembered was Broc's valet, appeared. Marcas ushered them across the silent courtyard. Stuart broke away to take Piseag to a stall inside the walls, quickly stripping off her saddle and bridle, and making sure she had food in her manger.

He caught up to Fiona and party as they entered the new addition of the castle and the empty great hall. His footsteps echoed as they crossed the slates where Fiona had danced with Stuart to the merry tunes of fiddles and the thump of drums.

"*Everyone* is gone?" Fiona asked.

"All but me and a few others." Marcas sounded tired. "I tell the laird he should go, to Edinburgh perhaps, or London, but he doesn't listen. His cousins say the same."

"Cousins?" Apprehension filled Fiona's voice.

"Aye. Neilan and Tavin Macdonald have been coming and going some months now. Just yesterday they arrived for Christmas"

"Oh, no." Fiona turned from Marcas and fled the great hall, hurrying into the dark passageway beyond.

Chapter Six

FIONA HASTENED THROUGH the short corridor that connected the new hall to the old castle, built so the laird would not get wet or too cold traveling from his private chambers to the public area.

She went up another flight of stairs in the old building to the inner hall, which was much smaller than the new one, about twenty feet long and ten wide. The ceiling had been renovated in the last century and now contained dark carved beams that lent some warmth to the gray stones.

Or would lend warmth, if there was any light or heat to the place. A smudge of rushlight glowed at one end of a table, haloing the faces of three men—Broc and next to him, the cousins, Tavin and Neilan, reprobates and parasites. They being here could not bode well.

"Broc?"

At the sound of Fiona's voice, the man at the head of the table jumped to his feet. He tottered, grabbed a stick next to him, and hobbled forward.

"Fiona?" Relief tinged his voice. "Is it you? I'd given up."

Fiona grew cautious, but Broc sounded genuinely glad to see her.

He stumbled toward her, leaning heavily on the stick, and caught her in an embrace.

"It is a happy Christmas indeed," he breathed in her ear.

"Cousin Fiona." Tavin rose from the bench he'd been sitting on and made his way to her. His brother Neilan also rose but remained at the table. "Welcome. How fortunate."

"Fortunate?" Fiona's suspicions immediately rose. The last time she'd seen Tavin, he'd been trying to convince her that marrying him and giving him all her money was a grand idea.

"Aye. We're trying to persuade Broc to take ship for the Americas. Better for him than limping around here. He can start a new life in the colonies."

"Can he?" Fiona skewered Tavin with a gaze. Tavin was tall and admittedly good-looking, and he thought much of himself. He dressed in the English style—breeches and brocade frock coat that was far out of place in this ancient setting. He wore a wig, white and sleek over his true dark hair.

"And what happens to Castle Mòr if my brother leaves the country?" Fiona asked as though merely curious.

"Well." Tavin attempted affability. "We're the closest male heirs, you know. If you go with Broc, we'll take good care of it. If you stay …" Tavin took a step closer to her, and Broc had to move out of his way. "The castle is yours, of course. But you'll need a husband, won't you?"

One more step, until Fiona could smell the powder on his wig. She heard a rumble, and then Stuart was there, his hands full of Tavin's coat, hauling the man away from Fiona and to the nearest stone pillar.

Neilan, who was even more of a fop than his brother, his wig decorated with four green silk ribbons, squeaked, and Broc hastened back to Fiona. "See here, you. Unhand him. Fiona, who is this man? I can have him arrested."

Stuart raised Tavin halfway up the pillar and let him go. Tavin landed on his feet, but his high-heeled shoes turned under him, and he staggered, grabbing for the pillar to hold him up.

Stuart turned around, pulling off his battered hat and throwing it to the ground.

"*Feasgar Mhath*, Broc Macdonald. How have ye been keeping yourself?"

AS HAD THE creaky retainer, Broc cringed as Stuart bade him a good evening in the Scots language. Stuart thought Broc was more upset about hearing his mother tongue than seeing Stuart Cameron returned from the dead. The Macdonald cousins were equally dismayed by the words, but Stuart saw no recognition in their eyes.

"What are …" Broc trailed off and swallowed. "Fiona?"

"'Tis not my doing." Fiona unwound her scarves, though it was scarcely warmer in here than outdoors. Her face appeared, flushed with cold. "I found him on the way home. Now—it has been a long journey and I am hungry. Is there food? Lights?"

"Everyone has gone," Broc said. He did not look well, his face pale in the flickering rushlight, and he clutched the stick as though it was all that kept him on his feet. He shot a fearful glance to Padruig and Gair, who'd followed Stuart in. "Deserted me. Only three are left—the gamekeeper, Donia in the kitchen, and Marcas."

Fiona's eyes went wide. "Good heavens. Only three people to have the caring of you? Can ye not shift yourself to the kitchen and carve a bit of bread and cheese? I assume Donia is doing the cooking. She was kitchen assistant when I left."

"Yes, she is carrying on." Broc's voice was a near whisper.

"Sit down, man," Stuart advised. "'Tis clear ye can barely stand.

There's no shame in it. Ye took a hit in battle."

Broc sank to his high-backed wooden chair—the laird's chair. All else around the table were benches. Tavin, who'd finally recovered himself and brushed off his coat, smirked at Broc. Tavin hadn't fought in the war, had likely never picked up a musket in his life.

"What about our tenants?" Fiona asked. "Are they well? Sitting in warm, snug houses, or ones with holes in the roofs?"

"Don't know. Most have gone. Marcas says many have turned to the cities to find work and won't be coming back."

He was a broken man. Stuart again wondered if he'd find his own home like this one. Deserted, empty, all having fled in fear.

"Which is why *we* should take it over," Tavin said. "Ye don't need farms, ye need sheep. Wool fetches a nice price, and sheep don't fuss over their roofs. Times are changing, Broc. King George beat the Scots idiots who want to live in the dark ages. *You* picked the right side. Go off to the colonies and leave it to us. You'll see."

"This is my home," Broc said weakly.

"And mine." Fiona fixed Tavin with her steely gaze. "Make yourself useful, you two. Go down to the kitchens and see what's to eat."

"Ha," Tavin said. "We're not lackeys."

"Very well. I'll go." Fiona tossed down her scarves and turned toward a door that led to the stairs.

Tavin started after her. Stuart gave him a cold stare, and Tavin quickly backed away. Stuart ducked into the stone stairwell Fiona had entered, holding the walls to steady himself as the stairs spiraled downward.

He'd left Padruig and Gair in the hall, but he did not fear for them. With any luck they'd terrify Tavin and his brother into disappearing into the night.

Stuart caught up with Fiona in a passage that connected storage rooms to the kitchen.

"Are ye all right, lass?" he asked in a low voice.

"They're leeches," she said furiously. "Sucking us dry."

"I see that. Family can be hell." Stuart cupped her shoulders. "It's been a long ride, and ye've done much." He brushed a finger over her smooth cheek. "Your compassion astonishes me."

Fiona shrugged, but he saw a flicker of darkness in her eyes. "I can't not help Highlanders who are trying to survive. They fought so bravely, while my cousins sit on their cushions, eat sweetmeats, and tend to their wigs."

Stuart flashed her a grin. "Ye have hidden depths."

"They need to stay hidden, don't they? Or I'll be arrested and those lads hunted down."

"Aye, as you say. How many others have ye helped while I sat on my … cushion … in prison?"

"I don't know. Dozens."

"How do ye find them? If you'll let me ask? How did those lads come to hide in the rocks near Càrn Eige?"

"They were sent word." Fiona kept her voice quiet, still wary of being overheard. "And I received word that they were there. No one pays much attention to what women get up to. It's wives and sisters and mothers all over the Highlands who find the men and make sure they're fed, clothed, and provided a path to safety. Supplies are left by those who can obtain them at places like the inn where you found me. I and a few others coordinate it."

Stuart lightly caressed her shoulders. "They are correct—you are an angel of mercy."

Fiona's face softened, and she rested her hands on his chest. "If I'd known you were in prison, I'd have tried to find out where and have you released. I'm so sorry."

Stuart stared down at her in amazement. "If ye'd poked around, ye might have been arrested, or … King Geordie's soldiers got up to terrible things. I'm glad ye didn't know. But it's all right now."

"Is it?" Fiona's eyes sparkled with tears. "I've always thought of my home as a refuge, even with the arguments I have with Broc. Now it's too sad. Broc …"

"Aye, he's not well. He needs to be somewhere warm where he can heal."

She stiffened. "Not Antigua. I'm not letting Tavin send him off to the colonies."

"I meant warm and snug, not hot and malarial."

"Oh. Then what…?"

Stuart forestalled her words by tilting her face up and kissing her. He couldn't resist with her standing so close, she shrugging off her sacrifices to assist defeated men, never mind the grave danger to herself.

He got lost in the kiss, Fiona rising to him, her arms going around his neck. Fiona held on, her body flowing to his, her lips parting. Stuart kissed her leisurely, tasting her, letting the wanting he'd bottled up surge through him.

Fiona gave and gave of herself, assuming a brisk air to keep others from wounding her. So few gave to *her*.

But Stuart was here for her now. Coming to this castle and seeing Broc Macdonald had revealed to him exactly what he needed to do.

He eased away from the kiss, tracing her lower lip with a gentle thumb.

Fiona drew in a breath. Stuart expected her to berate him, but she only met his gaze with a steady one, opening herself to him.

He read Fiona's hurts and fears over the last year as she'd watched Scotsmen and Scotswomen become intoxicated and then destroyed by Prince Teàrlach's cause, saw her brother come home wounded, his spirits ebbing.

She'd also believed she'd lost Stuart—he saw the sharp devastation his disappearance had caused. He pulled Fiona close, burying his face in the curve of her neck.

"Never again," he whispered. "We'll never be parted again."

Fiona's relieved sigh made his heart sing. Her arms came around him, enclosing him, shielding him. Stuart had missed her with a mad intensity.

After a long time, he lifted away. "That is, unless ye want to see the back of me."

He kept his words light, but he waited in trepidation for Fiona to agree.

Fiona touched his face, running her fingertips over his unshaved whiskers. She laughed softly, dissolving his fears. "'Tis the front of you I like seeing." She sent him an arch look and took his hand. "Though the back of ye can look well too. Now, I am truly hungry. Shall we feast?"

THEY DID NOT find much in the larder, but even the meager pickings of bannocks and drippings, slices of cold mutton, and a few wilted greens seemed a feast after the long day of travel.

Donia, the cook's assistant, had taken over and was not happy about it. "I want to go live with me mum," she said. "But I hate to leave the master. He's all in, the poor love."

Fiona had never heard her brother called a "poor love." Broc had always been arrogant and commanding, even after his injury, but tonight, she'd found him a pathetic wreck.

Una, who'd entered the kitchen after taking Fiona's things to her room, began assisting Donia without a word.

"We'll feed him up," Fiona promised. She took the tray that Donia had piled high with food and crockery, but Stuart immediately relieved her of it.

"You're good to stay, Donia," Stuart said. "I'm thinking the others will return when the countryside is calmer. The cities are full of smoke and hardship, no place to raise a family."

"I tried to tell them." Donia's eyes filled. "I hope you're right, sir."

"I am." Stuart strode from the kitchen with all the confidence Fiona remembered. If he said a thing would happen, it would.

Stuart led the way up the stairs, carrying the heavy tray as though it weighed nothing. When they reentered the hall, Gair was busy trying to interest the two cousins in purchasing a silver snuffbox in pristine condition. Fiona did not want to know where he'd obtained it. Possibly a perfectly legal transaction, but then, this was Gair.

Broc's eyes brightened when the tray landed on the table and Stuart began handing out dishes like a trained servant. Tavin and Neilan hadn't quite worked out yet who he was.

"Thank you, sister," Broc said. "I could use some grub."

"Not too much," Tavin said quickly. "You're weak. Broth is better for a man in your condition."

"Bollocks." Stuart plunked a good portion of the mutton and bannocks onto a plate and slid it in front of Broc. "He needs feeding up. Have you been starving the man?"

Broc lifted his knife and started sawing at the mutton, using the tip to shovel the meat into his mouth. "Been a long time since I had a full meal."

Fiona turned her glare to her cousins, but spoke to Broc, "Well, you needn't worry any more about that. I've come to look after you."

"As you should." Broc's automatic reply made him sound like his old self, the high-handed laird certain Fiona should obey his every command. She'd never understood why he'd assume she'd listen.

Stuart dished out a plate for Fiona and himself and also for Gair and Padruig, who had no qualms about joining them at the table. Neilan continued to gaze covetously at the snuffbox. Neither cousin noticed Stuart wasn't serving them until Stuart sat down and began eating.

"Steady on, man," Tavin said. When Stuart ignored him, Tavin let out a growl and reached for the food—what was left of it. He took as much as he could for himself and shoved the mostly empty platters toward Neilan.

Stuart had found a carafe of whisky in the kitchen and now poured a dollop for everyone at the table except Tavin and Neilan.

They ate in silence for a time, during which Padruig shot a hard look at Stuart. Fiona wondered why Padruig wanted the *sgian dubh* he sought, and why he thought it would be here. He'd claimed Broc had taken things from Culloden Moor—Broc had gone to observe even if his wound had precluded him from fighting—but so might have many a man in the king's army.

"Sister," Broc said after he'd eaten his fill and drunk a little of the whisky. "I'm glad you are home."

"I am happy as well," Fiona said cautiously. It was a rare day Broc didn't follow a kind word with a demand.

"Tavin is right that I should go away from here. I doubt I'll ever have an heir." Broc had not married. The lady he'd set his eyes on had chosen another, and he'd nursed resentment and wounded pride in the five years since. "If you marry Tavin, you can both live here, and you'll bear the Macdonald heir."

Broc spoke woodenly, as though the speech was rehearsed. Fiona could guess who'd coached him.

She turned a sweet smile on Tavin who was trying to persuade Gair to hand him the whisky. Gair would begin to and then stop and pour more for himself or Padruig.

"No, thank you, Tavin," Fiona said clearly. "I will not marry you."

Tavin gave her a sour glance. "You might not have a choice, cousin. Broc won't sire any sons, thanks to his injury. You are his only hope. I am the logical man for you to marry. Neilan is the younger—he'll run our lands, while I take over here."

"Won't sire any sons?" Stuart's large rumble interrupted. "He was shot in the leg, not the balls. He'll sire sons just fine."

Broc's face went crimson. "Dinnae mock me, sir."

"Not mocking. 'Tis a fact. What have these idiots been filling your head with?"

"They talk a lot of sense," Broc said, though Fiona glimpsed a silent plea in his green eyes. "I won't be able to be laird much longer. A stronger man should take over."

"I see I came home just in time," Fiona began, but Stuart held up his hand.

"I crave a boon, Macdonald," Stuart said.

Broc flicked his tired gaze to him. "What?" He took a large sip of whisky, like a thirsty man who'd just found water.

"I'm searching for a *sgian dubh*. One lost on Culloden Moor. Do ye have such a thing? If ye can find it for me, I promise I'll rid ye of your unwanted guests and restore ye to your power."

Chapter Seven

BROC FROWNED, MORE bewildered than interested. "A *sgian dubh*—?"

Padruig spoke the first words he'd uttered since they'd arrived. "Plain hilt. Crest of MacNab on it."

"I heard ye were light-fingered on that battlefield, Macdonald," Gair added. "Arrived to watch the slaughter and then retrieved weapons and things. Stashing them to bring home with ye."

Broc blinked. "Confiscating. They were the weapons of a fallen enemy and had to be secured."

Gair took a noisy sip of whisky. "Where did ye secure them to?"

"My strongroom. Until they're wanted. They'll be melted down, I think."

Padruig's silence was far more unnerving than Gair's snort. Stuart decided he'd better interrupt.

"It's one knife among many," Stuart said. "King Geordie will never miss it."

"They're not mine to give away—"

"They weren't yours t' take," Padruig said in his firm voice.

"Did ye hear my terms, Broc?" Stuart asked. "The *sgian dubh*, and your cousins vanish into the smoke and leave ye be. You are laird, you'll recover, find a bonny lass to marry ye, and have a score of bairns. These lummoxes have filled your head with tales."

"Now, look here—" Tavin began.

"God's balls, but ye sound like a Sassenach," Stuart growled. "Why don't ye take yourselves to England and have done?"

"We are *loyal* to England—to Britain." Tavin spoke as though he explained to a child. "We have land here, that we will keep arable or for sheep, and pay taxes we owe. In return, His Majesty leaves us alone. That's the sensible road to take these days. No popping white cockades on bonnets and believing the Stewart kings will rise again."

"Land, aye." Stuart nodded. He finished up his bannocks, which were crumbly and oat-y as he liked them. "But it's a lawless time. Ye never know what will happen to your lands if ye leave them for too long."

"That is why Neilan will go home and tend the estate," Tavin said patiently. "While I stay here and help Broc."

"Should go soon, the pair of ye," Stuart said. "I happen to know quite a few Highlanders not happy with those who turned on them. Ye never see them, but they're about. Wouldn't be surprised if ye find your fields burned, your houses taken down brick by brick, your tenants and retainers gone …"

Neilan looked nervous, but Tavin bristled. "Marauders will be arrested, hanged as traitors and looters."

"If ye can catch them." Stuart calmly sipped whisky. "I know many men, throughout Scotland, and even England, in fact, who wouldn't mind stripping Hanoverian sympathizers of all they have."

"You never would," Tavin said, though he took on a note of uncertainty. "I'd arrest *you*."

"Oh, I won't go near your lands. Nothing to do with me." Stuart sent Fiona a wink.

Fiona gazed back at him, her eyes a beautiful green. She had no idea what he was doing, but her smooth face betrayed nothing.

Neilan spoke up. "What do you mean?" The silver snuffbox rested at his elbow, which meant Gair had successfully persuaded him to buy it.

Stuart leaned toward the cousins, enjoying himself. "Have ye never heard tell of the *brollachan* that did so much damage to the enemy camps during the Uprising? Oh, I beg your pardon, I mean loyalist camps, full of Highlanders happy to bow to King Geordie and pay him taxes."

"A *brollachan*?" Tavin scoffed. "Don't be daft. There is no such thing."

Neilan nodded, his eyes round. "I remember the tales."

"It was never a ghost," Tavin said loudly. "It was one of the Young Pretender's men playing tricks."

At that moment, a huge clatter sounded. Neilan leapt to his feet, and Tavin rose slowly. Broc jumped and stared. An empty pewter plate Gair had set on a smaller table had fallen for no apparent reason. Neilan gazed at it in terror, and Broc also looked stunned.

"Children's stories." Tavin resumed his seat with a thump. "Sit down, Neilan. Ye look like a half-wit."

Neilan resumed his seat, continuing to stare at the platter, as did Broc. Padruig, who'd knocked it to the floor while Stuart had held the cousins' attention, continued to eat.

"Mebbe." Stuart shrugged. "Whether 'tis men or ghosts, ye stand to lose everything. Can ye afford to? Is that the true reason you're here, trying to pick Broc's pockets?"

Neilan flushed guiltily, but Tavin bristled. "You're mad. If men are terrorizing the lands of loyalists, they'll be taken. Or shot."

"As I say, *if* ye can find them." Stuart tapped the side of his nose. "Now, I can put in a word for you with the *brollachan*, tell it to leave ye be."

"Because you're one of them?" Tavin asked. "Perhaps we'll have *you* arrested."

"'Twould be inhospitable," Stuart pointed out. "As I'm a guest in the house you wish to be yours."

Tavin began to splutter, but Fiona shushed him. She, like Padruig, had not jumped when the plate had fallen. It lay on the floor even now, the burnished pewter winking.

"It is an interesting point," Fiona said serenely. "Why the desire to take over Broc's lands, Tavin? Everything not well at home?"

"Of course everything is—"

"Stop lying." Neilan threw down his spoon and rounded on his brother. "We're skint. All our tenants ran off too. But everyone knows *ye* have the better lands, Broc. Tavin wants them. And Fiona. Notice it's me who has to stay home and try to eke out an existence while he takes over the laird's castle."

"Shut it, ye cretin." Tavin balled up his fist. Stuart reached across the table and caught Tavin's wrist before he could bash his brother.

Tavin extricated himself from Stuart's grip and sat down, red-faced. Neilan quickly rose and moved away from the table, coming to rest next to a stone pillar.

"I don't notice Fiona saying she'll marry ye," Neilan snarled at Tavin.

"A very good observation," Fiona said. "I turned you down a few minutes ago, Tavin, if you recall."

"You'll have to marry me." Tavin's polite affability disappeared. In its place was the hard ambition of a man who'd waited years to take what he wanted. "Look at Broc. He's dying, or as good as. He'll never walk right, never catch a bonny lass, as this lackey says, never have sons. You'll never command as a woman, Fiona, even if ye do become laird. Ye need the might of men behind ye, and they've all gone, haven't they?

I'll take over as laird, and if you don't marry me, I'll turf ye out. You'll have nothing, nowhere to go. So ye have no choice, woman."

Fiona reached for her glass of whisky. "Ah, what a lovely proposal ..."

Stuart's rage rose until his vision tinged with red. Tavin, with his round, pale face under the irritating wig, reminded him strongly of some officers Stuart had faced in battle, men who'd come out of their tents to fight only when they absolutely had to and then killed those who'd thrown up their hands in surrender.

"She'll not be marrying ye." Stuart's statement was flat, hard, and rang through the hall.

"Are ye going to stop her?" Tavin's smirk tempted Stuart to reach for the knife in his boot.

"Aye." He turned his gaze to Fiona, who had grown silent, her amusement gone. "Because she's marrying me." Stuart softened his voice as he held Fiona's stunned gaze. "If she'll have me."

The room went very quiet. Gair and Padruig ceased their noisy chewing and turned their way, interested.

Fiona's chest rose with her sharp breath. Stuart held his, waiting for her to laugh, to dismiss him with a wave, to say she needed no man. Fiona was a strong woman, who could stand on her own, no matter what her foolish family thought.

Fiona's eyes, the color of jade in sunshine, glistened in the lamplight.

"Yes," she whispered.

FIONA'S QUIET WORD, which she said with all her heart, had a different effect on all present. Gair appeared highly amused, Tavin incensed,

Neilan surprised, Broc shocked. Only Padruig remained stoic.

Stuart's grin spread across his face, her wild Highlander coming to life. He leapt from his seat, knocking the bench over behind him, and was around the table before Fiona could gasp.

He hauled her up and into his arms. "Ye mean it, love?"

Fiona clutched Stuart's coat, happiness flooding her. This was *right.* She never should have let him go when he'd walked out a year and more ago, never been so complacent that she could see him whenever she wished.

She'd hang on now, wherever the road took them.

Tavin's hands landed on Stuart's shoulders. "Traitor! I'll kill you …"

The polished veneer Tavin strove to paste over his Highland ancestry had fled. His face was mottled red, his wig sliding sideways as he attacked the boulder that was Stuart.

Fiona ducked out of the way as Stuart swung on Tavin. Broc, to her astonishment, came to his feet and hobbled to Fiona, putting himself between her and the two fighting men. Protecting her.

Stuart lifted Tavin, crushing him between his large hands. Tavin flailed and fought. He must have studied pugilism somewhere, because his punches were tight and swift, each jab landing on Stuart's body.

Stuart flung Tavin away. Tavin stumbled but gained his feet, his wig falling to the floor to reveal his shaved head, dark with stubble. His face was twisted with a snarl, an enraged Highlander denied what he considered his.

Neilan stood stupefied as his brother toed off his impractical shoes and rushed Stuart. Stuart met Tavin in the middle of the wide room, a roar issuing from his throat. He must have yelled so at Prestonpans, where he'd captured English artillery, and again at Culloden, when he'd fought to the bitter end.

Tavin's arms flashed as he struck, Stuart defending blow after blow.

Stuart was a larger man, but Tavin was quick and treacherous.

A knife flashed in Tavin's hand. Fiona cried out, but Stuart was already moving. He locked a strong grip around Tavin's wrist, bending the arm around Tavin's back. Tavin punched with his other fist, catching Stuart on the cheek, splitting it open. Blood spattered just as Tavin screamed, and Fiona heard a thin crack of bone.

The next instant, Tavin was on the floor, sobbing and hugging his arm, as Stuart kicked away the knife.

Stuart stood back, gathering his hair from his face, most of the soot having fallen away. The red gleamed in the half light, Stuart a grim giant over the fallen Tavin.

"You broke my arm, you bastard," Tavin ground out.

"Forgive me, lad." Stuart dragged in a long breath. "I'm tired of men sticking knives into me."

Fiona stepped from her brother and thrust a handkerchief at Stuart, who took it dazedly and touched it to his cut cheek. "Brawling in a laird's hall. I'm amazed at both of you."

Her voice shook, her bravado failing. She knelt next to Tavin and gently probed his arm. Tavin cursed and wept, the savage Highlander fading once more into the spoiled boy Tavin had always been.

"'Tis a clean break," Fiona said crisply. "I'll wrap and splint it for ye, and you'll be healed in a few weeks. I suggest ye go home and rest, and not venture out for a time."

"Aye, I'll take him." Neilan sounded relieved.

"I'm not leaving." Tavin scowled up at Fiona and Stuart. "Not until I have what I came for."

"My lands?" Broc stumped over, moving more quickly than Fiona had seen him do in a while, his stick ringing. "My home, my sister—everything? Get out, Tavin. Ye're not welcome here. Go back to your house and stay there. I, as your laird, command it."

"Ye have no authority over me." Tavin's words were a gasp.

"Aye, that I do. I'm head of this family, and now that ye've shown your true colors, I'll do whatever I can to keep ye from inheriting. I'll marry whatever lass will have me and sire as many children as I've got years left in me."

Stuart's eyes twinkled with mirth over the blood-streaked handkerchief. "Better not say that when you're proposing, lad. Might put a lady off."

Broc ignored him. "On your feet, Tavin. Let Fiona see to your wound, and then you're gone."

Tavin finally looked worried. "In the night, and the snow? Have some pity, Broc. It's Christmas."

"'Tis not Christmas until tomorrow. I don't want ye here. Ye have a perfectly fine house ten miles away. Go before I find some way to throw you out of that too."

Tavin snarled. He swung his free hand at Fiona, but found it caught in Stuart's fist.

"I went easy on ye, lad." Stuart lowered his voice to deliver the warning. "But if ye try to hit Fiona again, I'll break every bone ye have."

Tavin gulped and subsided. Gair and Neilan emerged to flank Tavin. "Come on, you," Gair said, one hand under Tavin's arm. "Best ye retire from the scene of battle. I know how to set a broken bone."

Tavin threw a terrified glance at Gair and a beseeching one at Fiona. "Go with him," Fiona said. "I'll be in to look after you soon."

Stuart released Tavin into Gair's care. Tavin had no choice but to let Gair walk him out, Neilan quivering behind them.

Broc let out his breath. "I thank you, Stuart Cameron. I should never have let Tavin crawl under my skin. But I've been so afraid …"

Fiona slid her arm around her brother, and he leaned into her gratefully. "Never mind," she told him. "I'm sorry I stayed away so long this time. I didn't realize ye needed me."

"No, I drove ye from me." When Broc decided to become morose, he could be a master of it. "I'm glad ye returned, love. Stuart." Broc offered his hand, the other resting heavily on his stick. "Thank you. I am in your debt."

Stuart accepted the handshake, and he clapped Broc on the back. "Ye owe me nothing. Your blessing on my nuptials with Fiona and the *sgian dubh* I need, and all is cleared."

"I think Fiona will do well with you," Broc said graciously. "As for the *sgian dubh*, you are welcome to search through what I have found. If this knife is important, it should be returned to its owner."

He glanced at Padruig, who'd remained on the edge of the conflict and reunion. Broc shrank a little behind Fiona as Padruig gave him a keen look from his one sharp eye.

"I no longer need it," Padruig said.

Fiona blinked, startled. "Pardon?"

"Padruig," Stuart said with exaggerated patience. "What are ye talking about, man?"

"I have the *sgian dubh*." Padruig reached into his coat and removed a knife, holding it up to catch the light.

Fiona saw a plain dark steel blade, worn from years of use. The hilt was wrapped in a strip of leather, and a crest had been melded to it. Fiona clearly read the word *MacNab* on top of the shield.

Stuart growled. "How long have ye had that?"

"Since Culloden." Padruig calmly sheathed the knife and returned it to his pocket. "I took it from my dead brother."

Fiona caught her breath. "Your brother? Padruig, I'm so sorry."

"We were never close. But he was my kin." His nod at her sympathy said the matter was at an end.

Stuart's fists balled. "If ye have the blasted *sgian dubh*, why did ye give me the rigamarole about finding it for you? Making us search the lass's chamber at the inn, dragging us here? Through the snow? In the coldest part of December?"

"Ye needed to come here." Padruig flicked his gaze to Fiona. "*She* needed to. Ye were pining for her, Cameron. When I saw her at the inn, it put the idea in me mind."

Fiona shared Stuart's exasperation. "To trick us into traveling home?" she blurted out. "Did ye know my cousins were here?"

"No. That was luck." Padruig shrugged. "All's well, isn't it? You're betrothed and will soon be man and wife. And now that Stuart helped your brother, he'll not betray you." Padruig's lips twitched into a faint smile, something rare to his face. "Gair likened us to the three wise Highlanders, the daft sod. Come bearing gifts. This is my gift to you." He lifted his whisky glass. "*Slàinte.*"

He'd barely taken a sip before Fiona flew at him, grabbing the startled Padruig in a hug and kissing his stubbly cheek.

"You're a wonderful, wonderful man." Fiona clasped his arm while Padruig peered down at her, his gaze softening. "Thank you."

Chapter Eight

STUART ESCORTED FIONA up the stairs to the private chamber where Gair had retreated with Tavin—he could hear Tavin yelling all the way—to find that Gair had done a competent job of bandaging Tavin's arm.

Fiona studied Gair's work, ran skilled fingers over the splint, and nodded. "'Tis well done. You'll heal fine, cousin, so cease your wailing. Broc has kindly allowed you to stay the night, but you'll be off in the morning."

Stuart did not like the idea of Tavin spending one more evening in this house—what would he get up to, even injured? But Fiona, smiling sweetly, gave Tavin a thick liquid to drink, explaining it would ease his pain.

It must have eased it quite a lot, because after Tavin downed it, he slumped onto his brother, who reposed worriedly on the edge of the bed, and fell fast asleep. Gair, chuckling, retreated from the chamber and went back downstairs.

After a moment, they heard Gair's voice rise from below. "What? Ye bastard, ye dragged me across frozen Scotland and nearly got me shot and ye had the bloody *sgian dubh* all along?"

"Shut it." Padruig's growl made Gair's bluster fade. "The whisky's good."

Gair trailed off into mutters, and Fiona smothered a laugh.

She rose, but her legs immediately folded, as though she'd drunk the potion she'd given Tavin.

Stuart caught her. "You're all in, love. Come with me."

With a curt good-night to Neilan, Stuart half-guided, half-carried Fiona up the next flight of steps to the rooms two floors above the hall. Here Broc and Fiona had their private chambers, spacious quarters high in the tower. The view, Stuart recalled, over the glens and to the mountains beyond, was worth the steep climb.

The vista was hidden by darkness now, the windows black. Stuart had been inside Fiona's sitting room before, and had kissed her in it, but he'd never ventured into the room beyond that, her bedchamber.

He took her there now, and Fiona did not stop him. The chamber held a tall bedstead with delicate posts—very modern—as well as brocade-upholstered chairs, a bookshelf filled with leather-bound tomes, a soft carpet, and hangings and paintings on the stone walls. Fiona had taken a cold room in an ancient stone castle and made it comfortable.

The fire had been lit, its small heat already permeating the room. Someone had turned down the bed as well, and Stuart saw the lump of heated bricks at the foot of it. The efficient Una, he guessed, looking after her mistress while the men brawled at the supper table.

Stuart shut the bedchamber door one-handed and clicked the key in the lock. "Lass."

Fiona turned in his arms, lacing hers around him. "Stuart."

Silence surrounded them as Stuart kissed her. Their lips met, parted, met again. Fiona loosened in his arms, her strength returning. She rested her hands on his back, and as he kissed her, she inched her touch down to his hips.

Stuart broke the kiss. "Lass." This time the word was tinged with laughter.

"I missed you." Fiona pulled him close. "I feared you gone forever."

"Nay." Stuart kissed her cheek, her throat. "I knew I had to live, to be free. To see my love again."

"Love?" The word warmed his ear.

"Aye." Stuart raised his head and cupped her face. "I love you, Fiona."

Fiona's answer was an unintelligible gargle as she launched herself at him. Her next kiss burned, her lips parting his. Stuart started when she suckled his tongue, then he deepened the kiss, letting her do what she would.

They were betrothed, in front of witnesses. No matter it hadn't yet been proclaimed to the world or announced at the nearest kirk. Fiona was his, and Stuart belonged to her.

Stuart slid off his coat, glad to be done with its weight. He unlaced Fiona's stomacher and eased her bodice open. Both of them wore many layers of clothing against the cold, and they came off one by one, the two of them starting to laugh as they unbuckled, unbuttoned, and untied endless garments.

Finally they stood together near the heat of the fire, body to body, nothing between them. Fiona traced his cheek.

"I love *you*, Stuart Cameron. Thank you for coming back to me."

"Ah, lass, I couldn't have stayed away from ye."

The next kiss erased all past sorrows. Stuart ran his hands down Fiona's pliant body, rejoicing in the silken smoothness of her skin.

He lifted her and carried her to the bed. Stuart climbed over her, and as the clock on the mantel chimed midnight, Stuart slid inside his love. His heart eased for the first time in a year, as Fiona's eyes softened, and she welcomed him.

Outside snow abraded the window, and inside, Christmas glided in amidst love and newfound joy.

GAIR AND PADRUIG offered to escort Tavin and Neilan home the next morning. Broc sent them off after a hearty breakfast that Una, Donia, and Fiona managed to create between them.

"He *is* a wise man," Fiona said as she and Stuart waved off the small party. The snow had ceased falling and lay in drifts under a clear blue sky. "Padruig, I mean."

"So he claims." Stuart sent Fiona a warm smile that trickled another frisson of desire through her.

She felt very different this morning, washed clean, and thoroughly loved. Fiona and Stuart had lain together throughout the night, drowsing at intervals before finding each other again. She'd wept in his arms, realizing anew how close she'd come to losing him. Stuart had kissed away her tears and held her with comforting strength.

"Will Gair and Padruig return, do you think?" Fiona asked.

"Probably not." Stuart guided her inside to the warmth of the main hall, Broc behind them. "Once Gair is paid, he vanishes. On to the next mark—I mean job."

"I heard him suggest they travel to a cove near Kilmorgan," Broc said. "And fetch their ship. Isn't that the seat of the Mackenzies?"

"It is," Stuart said. "Deserted now. But I imagine the Mackenzie brothers will find their way home. They always do."

Broc looked downcast. "I'd meant to pay you back by finding the *sgian dubh*. I was imagining presenting it in triumph."

"Take Padruig's gesture as a sign of peace between us," Stuart said. "All is well."

Fiona watched the two men shake hands, and impatience twinged her. "All is well? Nae so, Stuart Cameron. You're still a wanted man." She faced her brother. "If ye wish to pay back Stuart for ridding us of our greedy cousins, clear his name. Write to all your cronies in England and the army, and wherever else, and tell them Stuart is not to be touched. Say he was listed as a rebel by mistake. Something. Anything. I'm to marry the man—I don't want to worry the rest of my life that soldiers will come in the night and take him away."

Broc was already nodding as Fiona ran out of breath. "It shall be done. I dinnae want my sister married to an outlaw either."

"Excellent. Shall we adjourn to your study so you can begin your letters?" Fiona took Broc firmly by the arm and turned him toward the stairs.

Stuart gave a shout of laughter. "Better do as she says, lad."

"Aye." Broc shot Stuart an ironic glance. "You see what you're marrying?"

"I do," Stuart said with warmth. "And I love her dearly for it. She truly is an angel of mercy."

Stuart's words and smile heated Fiona from head to toe. She guided her brother out, Stuart following, his laughter and his very presence the best Christmas gift she could have wished for.

Epilogue

Ten years later

HOGMANAY OF 1756 arrived with all its bluster. Stuart Cameron gazed about the hall of his own house, which was filled with revelers.

When he and Fiona had reached the Cameron home the day after Christmas ten years ago, it had been as deserted and silent as he'd feared. But when word went out that Stuart had returned, his retainers and household staff emerged from all corners of the glen. They'd hidden after they'd heard of Stuart's capture and likely execution, but now reappeared to welcome home their laird and his new lady.

Ten years on, Stuart gazed across the wood-beamed ceiling at his wife, Fiona Cameron, who busily helped their oldest daughter, Alina, string garlands. A fiddler and a drummer practiced in the corner, ready to break into song. It was Hogmanay, and when the First-Footer arrived, the dancing would begin.

Alina, their first-born, looked so much like her mother, sharing her dark hair and green eyes. Likewise did their oldest son, who'd come two years later, Stuart Michael—they called him by his second name. The third son was Broc, named in honor of Fiona's brother. He was all Cameron, a strapping lad with bright red hair and blue eyes. Innis, the youngest daughter, also a redhead, had arrived two years ago. She played with empty spools at the moment, watched over by a smitten Una, the babe excited by the celebration.

Ten years of hope, happiness, and recovery. Ten years of love. The house was warm, full, laughter and music echoing from every corner. Broc had kept his promise and had used his influence in the government and military to clear Stuart's name. No more fear of the Butcher's men chasing him through every corner of the country. When Malcolm Mackenzie had been restored to the dukedom of Kilmorgan, he had added his assistance to make certain Stuart, the Mackenzies' old friend, lived undisturbed. Even so, Fiona and her network of ladies had continued aiding Highlanders who needed to flee Scotland, and Stuart had been happy to help her.

Broc had found a lass for himself—not a sad dowager who'd leap at the chance to marry any man, as he'd feared, but a fine woman with fire in her eyes. She'd nursed Broc back to health and borne him three dark-haired sons. Broc had been transformed.

Tavin and Neilan had wisely decided to try their luck in France, and had departed Scotland's shores, so far never to return. Broc, as their nearest relative and their laird, had taken over their property, keeping it in trust for his younger sons.

Fiona swirled by, stooping to kiss Stuart on the lips. His body stirred, craving another morning like this one had been, he with Fiona in their large bed, wrapped around each other.

Fiona winked at him as she hurried on, knowing his thoughts.

"The First-Footer!" Michael shouted as someone pounded on the massive door below.

He and his brother raced down the stairs. Stuart caught up Innis and followed, Fiona and Una coming after him with Alina.

The clocks were striking twelve. If the first guest in the door had dark hair, they'd have good luck all the year. If he or she were blond …

Michael, impatient, shoved open the bolts. A man, slight and small with white-gray hair pushed inside, snow swirling after him.

"About time ye opened up. Me balls will freeze off."

"Gair!" Fiona eyed him reproachfully even as she pulled him inside. "You're the First-Footer. It was supposed to be Broc or one of his sons."

"He's pulling his children off the horses—takes him a while." Gair beamed a broad smile. "'Tis no matter. Me hair was black as tar when I was a boy."

"Very well," Fiona said, resigned. "Upstairs to the hall with you. But nothing goes in your pockets, mind."

Gair widened his eyes. "I don't know what you mean."

Padruig pushed in behind him. "Shut it, Gair." He turned his gray eye to Fiona. "I'll watch over him."

Padruig and Gair appeared scarcely any different. Same weather-beaten faces, same scruffy clothes. But they'd filled out, well-fed, and their coats, though salt-crusted from the sea and mud-spattered from their journey, were of fine brocade and velvet. Rumor had it that they'd stumbled across a treasure—possibly even the French gold that was supposed to have come to aid Prince Teàrlach. No one could confirm this rumor, and Gair and Padruig had never mentioned it to a soul.

"*You* are welcome," Fiona said to Padruig. "As always."

Padruig gave her a nod. "Thank ye, lass." He handed her a small silk bag that clinked. "A gift for ye and your wee ones."

Fiona took the bag with a smile, loosened its drawstrings, and peered inside. Her face lost color. "Padruig …" she said in awe.

Padruig closed her hand over the bag. "Never ask."

"Of course not." She slid the bag into her pocket.

The fiddles and drums upstairs began to play. Broc, with his wife and children, sailed through the door, Broc no longer needing the stick to hold him upright. A slight limp was all that was left of his wound from Falkirk.

Fiona hugged him and her sister-in-law and nephews. Amidst the greetings she took her children's hands and led everyone upstairs while music poured around them.

"A fine Hogmanay," she called above the fiddles to Stuart. "Complete with my three wise Highlanders."

Stuart leaned to her. "And my bonny wife. I love ye, Fiona Cameron."

"I love you too, Stuart."

The drums sped, the fiddles played, and Stuart swept his wife and children into the first dance, his world complete.

"AND THEY LIVED happily ever after."

Ian Mackenzie concluded the story with the expected phrase, and Megan sighed happily.

Ian had become aware, as he told the tale, that the other Mackenzie children, Ian's brothers, and Beth had crept in to listen. Jamie, his son, as unlike Ian as could be—thankfully, in Ian's opinion—was the first to ask questions. This was usual.

"MacNab. The name on Padruig's *sgian dubh*. Wasn't the mum of Old Malcolm Mackenzie a MacNab?"

"Allison MacNab, aye." Ian gave him a slow nod. "She was Padruig's kinswoman. Distant. In the same clan."

"Did Gair and Padruig really have the French gold?" Ian's oldest daughter, Belle, asked.

Ian shrugged. "So Will Mackenzie believed. Fiona's journal doesn't say what was in the bag Padruig gave her."

"It was some of the gold," Jamie declared. "I'm sure of it."

"How can you know?" Belle asked. "If no one has said for certain?"

"Because Gair and Padruig were old scoundrels. Of course they wouldn't confess they had all the gold from the French king." Jamie's older-brother scoff was firm.

Belle, who had plenty of fire, began to argue. The discussion was taken up by other Mackenzies, including Ian's brothers Mac and Cameron, all having an opinion to share.

Ian let them go on while his gaze went to Beth, her blue eyes shining in merriment.

Ian enjoyed the stories of the past, when his ancestors had fought to survive, using cunning and craftiness to keep themselves and their families safe. They'd lived and loved with intensity in a time when Scotland had been untamed.

As Ian glanced about the full room, he decided that as interesting as the past must have been, now was better. Ian was surrounded by his family and his wife—who loved him and whom he loved back with vehemence.

They'd saved his life, especially Beth, who bent down to kiss his cheek. She'd made certain Ian could sit in peace, surrounded by warmth and love.

That was the truest gift of all.

THE END

About Jennifer Ashley

Thank you for reading! This novella is a part of the Mackenzies / McBrides series, which begins with ***The Madness of Lord Ian Mackenzie***. For more information on this series and others, see the website: www.jenniferashley.com.

New York Times bestselling and award-winning author Jennifer Ashley has more than 100 published novels and novellas in romance, urban fantasy, mystery, and historical fiction under the names Jennifer Ashley, Allyson James, and Ashley Gardner. Jennifer's books have been translated into more than a dozen languages and have earned starred reviews in *Publisher's Weekly* and *Booklist*. When she isn't writing, Jennifer enjoys playing music (guitar, piano, flute), cooking, reading, hiking, and building dollhouse miniatures.

To keep up to date on her new releases, sign up for her
email blasts here:
http://eepurl.com/47kLL

One Knight's Stand

By Tanya Anne Crosby

Part of A Very Highland Holiday Collection

One Knight's Stand

Bound for a marriage she hopes will save her cousin from the gibbet, Lady Elizabeth Louise Wolfe finds herself en route to Scotland to marry the younger son of a known traitor to the Crown. Fate intervenes when, on the way, she checks into an inn and registers as the "MacKinnon's bride." Presumed dead at Culloden, Callum MacKinnon, stops by the inn as well, intending to clean up before his return as the prodigal son. Imagine his surprise to discover his "bride to be" has already procured a room. And more—the feisty sassenach everything he never realized he desired.

Chapter One

December 31, 1746

Lady Elizabeth Louise Wolfe fidgeted in her seat, feeling the tension mount in her shoulders as the carriage wended its way closer to their intended destination: Chreagach Mhor, a no-man's-land eight months after Culloden.

The old laird had been executed, the elder son as well—traitors to England, so she'd been told. Now, if only to further someone's notion of justice, she was consigned to wed the younger son, who was only too callow to reveal himself a traitor… as yet.

What was he? *Fourteen? Fifteen?*

Young and malleable, Lachlan MacKinnon was to be "softened" by Elizabeth and then mentored by her Uncle. If she succeeded, England would have itself a new northern "friend."

If she failed…

She would be married to an undesirable at best.

A traitor, at worst.

But that alone wasn't what bothered her most. Rather, she appreciated men and women who followed the dictates of their hearts and stood up for causes they believed in—like her. Or at least she liked to believe they were like her. And really, it took courage even to distribute pamphlets to rouse interest for the defense of runaway slaves—as her mother had done.

In fact, perhaps she would be well in Scotland, though she knew her uncle was sending her away, in part, to remove her from the influence of "that motley crew of ne'er do wells."

Still, it didn't help her mood all that much to know that she must do this alone, with only her chaperone for company. Wasn't a wedding supposed to be the grandest thing ever?

It was the worst.

Her father couldn't be roused from his travels to join her, her uncle and aunt were too busy celebrating the Twelve Nights, and not even her cousin James could be swayed from his noble duties—what had he said? He had some debt of honor to pay?

To whom.

And why couldn't his debt be left for another occasion?

Why must he, too, leave Elizabeth to face this alone?

Worst of all, how was she supposed to face that poor child?

She was twenty-three, and he just a boy. How was she supposed to denude herself, and perform wifely duties, when he was a child, with more hands than sense?

And, dear God, how in the name of England was she supposed to help mend a rift between their nations? Wasn't that putting too much on the shoulders of women conscripted for this effort? Mind you, that's precisely what this was, yet another form of compulsory service. It would be one thing if she had adopted this cause all on her own. It was another thing to force a woman—any woman—to lie back and do her duty for the sake of England… *in bed.*

And nevertheless, it wasn't so much that she didn't wish to… explore. It was merely that she wished it to be her own choice—not that of her uncle's or cousin's.

Upsetting herself more and more with dark thoughts, she considered that she was being used for a crusade not her own. While, in truth, she didn't have any meaningful opinions about The King Over the Water, neither did she feel invested in the Forty-Five Rebellion—not for its cause, nor its resolution. These were men's wars, and in Elizabeth's estimation, women would never agree to put their sons on a battlefield with swords at each other's throats. It was no more than a dangerous game of King of the Hill—one minute this king, the next another. What they really needed was a woman on that throne—one with sensibilities something like her own.

Tapping her fingers impatiently, she flicked a glance at Mrs. Grace—the only person in her life who had ever truly understood her, except for maybe her cousin, James, although he, in fact, was the very author of a misery.

"It will be good for you to get away," he'd said.

"You'll be lady of a great house," he'd said.

"Think of it this way," he'd said.

"Your affiliation may well save a good family from ruin."

Bollocks.

That family was already ruined. They'd lost both a father and a brother and for all intents and purposes, their lands as well. And in the meantime, it stood to be seen as to whether Elizabeth would even have a complete roof over her head. Many of the Scots' homes had been razed, if not seized. And what was she supposed to do if she arrived to find the place in shambles? What would her mother have said, if only she'd lived to see this day?

Plenty, Elizabeth was certain.

Like Elizabeth, her mother had been painfully outspoken.

Unfortunately, her father didn't appreciate Elizabeth's forthright nature. The very instant her mother kicked up her toes, he'd foisted her upon an aunt and uncle who scarcely had time for their own progeny, much less an annoying niece who was a champion for the poor and oppressed. Neither did they understand her. Only her cousin James had ever cared much for her welfare; although now, so it seemed, even he was against her.

What was he thinking?

Did he expect she wouldn't speak up if she found the situation untenable? After all these years, did he believe she would turn a blind eye to the atrocities her compatriots were inflicting? Indeed, she was not to be trusted to hold her tongue, and what then?

She, too, would be branded a traitor…

Did they execute women?

At the best of times, Elizabeth was not the one they should assign to such a delicate mission. No matter what her country of origin, she tended to call things the way she saw them. So then, what now if she should happen to agree with her husband's family?

Lord only knew, not even her uncle could save her then.

She sighed portentously, annoyed all over again, and hardly in the mood to arrive in the dead of night at some wreckage in the wilds of Scotland.

"It won't be long now," said Mrs. Grace, with a forbearing smile.

Elizabeth smiled back at her chaperone, wondering if she knew how close Elizabeth was to shouting for the driver to halt… so she could run away, screaming.

But there was this small bit of curiosity that kept her seated: Why did her uncle feel such responsible for this particular clan, when, to the best of Elizabeth's knowledge, they were perfect strangers? Simply because James was the one ordered to execute the elders didn't make her Uncle Edward responsible for their reintegration. No doubt, it was a nice gesture, but her mother's brother simply didn't have the same sense of charity as his deceased sister, and, in fact, he really liked to make the point that it was her mother's audacious personality that put her in the "wrong place at the right time"—in front of a speeding carriage, with a sign in her hand.

"How much longer?" Elizabeth relented, ending her long bout of dissenting silence.

The elder woman peered out of the carriage. It was snowing harder, and the carriage was slowing down. At this pace, they would arrive at Dunmore on the Twelfth Night, not the First.

"I don't know," said Mrs. Grace, as the voices outside grew louder and louder.

Finally, the carriage came to a complete halt, and they heard their driver scuttle down, muttering a curse—shocking words no lady ought to overhear, but Elizabeth snickered and Mrs. Grace shook her head. After a long moment, the driver—one Mr. Hadley, who by the by, appeared to be smuggling spirits, judging by the suspicious sounds coming from their luggage rack—appeared at their door, pulling it open and giving Elizabeth only the briefest of glances before addressing her companion. "The bridge north of Calvine lies buried," he said, brows pinched. "Won't be passing through t'night, mayhap not even tomorrow."

"Oh, good grief," said Mrs. Grace. "What would you have us do, Mr. Hadley?"

"Welp," said the driver. "There's an Inn here in Calvine."

"Insufferable," complained Elizabeth, though not because the thought of stopping aggrieved her, but really, she didn't appreciate that Mr. Hadley's question wasn't addressed to her, considering that it was her interest being discussed. She was not a child—unlike her betrothed.

For her outburst, the driver cast her a disgruntled glance and Mrs. Grace reached out to pat Elizabeth's hand, as though to say, "Quiet, dear."

"Can you please take us there?" Mrs. Grace inquired.

"Sorry mum," said the driver. "You'll see when you get down. The road's full of travelers, all stuck on account of the weather. I'm guessing most'll be waking the new year in their coaches."

"Stuck?" said Elizabeth. "What do you mean *stuck*?"

"Stuck," repeated the man, with a sniff, then, again, he turned his face to her and spoke to Mrs. Grace, as though he couldn't bear the thought of addressing her.

"Really!" she exclaimed. Although she knew him not at all, she wondered if he might be lying, or… scheming. He had some look about him she simply didn't trust.

"Ask for Balthazar," said Hadley. "He ain't got much room, but I'll warrant if there's a bed to be let, he'll give it to ye if you tell him I sent ye."

"Oh, thank you," said Mrs. Grace, kindly, and the man departed.

"I don't like that he assumes to ignore me," complained Elizabeth, her brow furrowed.

"My dear, don't be so ready to take offense." Mrs. Grace patted her arm yet again. "You're quite direct, at times, and tis off-putting to some. Alas, not to worry," She said. "I will see to it that we are settled. And, of course, Elizabeth knew that to be true. Mrs. Grace might not be overly fierce, but she was infinitely patient and persevering—two traits Elizabeth sadly did not share. Twenty minutes later, they were both standing with valises before a grizzled, snaggle-toothed old man who was far too preoccupied with combing his beard to note the two of them standing before his counter. But, of course, Mrs. Grace was hardly inclined to disturb him, so they waited "patiently," while he gently worked at a Lilliputian tangle, and Elizabeth stood melting—quite literally. She had snow in her shoes, snow in her hood, and even more snow in her hair, all of it thawing and making her damp. She could feel those wild little curls losing their shape and tickling her nape. Nevertheless, she held her tongue, inspecting the interior of the inn.

The pale stone walls above the waist-high wainscoting were pitted with age. In observation of the holiday, there was a Christmas Crown hanging from a high ceiling—a wreath of sorts, woven with small branches of ash to ward away bad spirits. Additionally, there were boughs of holly strewn across the hearth and over every doorway, tied in place by striking red ribbons.

But the fire in the hearth was the most curious thing of all. It changed colors, from green to gold to violet—a striking display that the boffin in her longed to explore. Naturally, it had the effect of drawing every drunkard's eye in the tavern, sedating them as would a hefty dose of laudanum—very clever, she thought. The mistress of this inn was brilliant—unlike this oaf standing behind the counter. Alas, the longer they stood, the more attention they garnered.

Most disconcertingly, there were a number of male occupants in the crowded tavern, some eyeing Elizabeth with undisguised disapproval—perhaps because they were Scots?

A few eyed her with arched brows and veiled smiles. Regardless of how they felt about it, no doubt two proper English women traveling alone on a holiday was no common sight.

Beneath her feet lay a carpet of sticky straw, a rather primitive application that was no doubt cheaper than carpet, considering the way the guests sloshed ale up over their heaping cups—all the while they drunkenly repeated the same two verses of the Boar's Head Carol.

The boar's head in hand bring I,
Bedecked with bays and rosemary.
I pray you, my masters, be merry…

The boar's head, as I understand,
Is the rarest dish in all this land,
Which thus bedecked with a gay garland.

"Pardon, madam," said Mrs. Grace as a sweet-looking woman passed them by with a tray full of foamy ale. "Can you please direct us to one Mr. Balthazar."

"John!" screamed the woman, surprising them both with the tenor of her voice. The tray in her hand threatened to overturn its burden as she cast a glance at the man behind the counter who, inconceivably, was still combing his beard.

"No, we are looking for Balthazar," said Elizabeth. "We were told—"

"John Joseph Pitagowan!" screamed the woman again, and Elizabeth gave Mrs. Grace an alarmed glance, to which her chaperone responded with an admonishing nod, as though to say, "I told you so. Please leave it to me!"

"What?" said the man, to which the woman slid her chin forward—like a hen—and said, "Can't ye see we've guests tae tend? Leave off with the whiskers already, else ye'll find yourself on the morrow wi' your chin bald as your head!"

The man flushed brightly. "We're full to the rafters," he explained.

"Oh, but, sir, our driver," interjected Mrs. Grace very sweetly. "He said to tell one Mr. Balthazar that Mr. Hadley sent us."

"Hadley?" said the goat-chinned man, a smile crinkling the corners of his eyes. "Why didn't ye say so! Did he say if he brought—"

"I really don't know," said Mrs. Grace. "But I do suspect the answer to your question might be yes, because he does, indeed, have a package for someone ensconced with our luggage." And this they knew, because Mr. Hadley had steadfastly refused to carry a second trunk for Elizabeth. And therefore, she'd been forced to pack away her entire life in one small suitcase and a tiny valise. Her uncle had promised to send the rest.

Exasperated, the tavern woman threw up a hand and hurried away, perhaps nettled by the name Mrs. Grace provided, or else she was certain now that they would be well cared for. Clearly, Mr. Balthazar or

Mr. Pitagowan—whatever his name might be—was infinitely pleased to hear from their driver. "Good ole Hadley," he said, tugging at his beard. And then he gave a nod toward the woman who'd disappeared. "That's me wife," he explained. "She's no' much for good ole Hadley, but he's a good chap." And then he launched immediately into what sounded as though it might still prove to be a dismissal. "Thing is, we've only got one bed left." He eyed both of them circumspectly. "Belongs to my daughter, though, as it happens, she's away for the evening, so I believe I can let it. She likes to get away now and again. But," he said, inclining his head. "There's still only one bed."

"Oh, dear," said Mrs. Grace. "Have you nothing else at all?"

He shrugged. "A cot and a blanket in the stable," he said. "But, don't worry, it's all perfectly partitioned."

Mrs. Grace waved a hand at him. "That' good enough for me," she said. "You may assign Lady Elizabeth your daughter's room, and I thank you kindly."

"Oh, no!" said Elizabeth, but Mrs. Grace held up a hand in that way she had when matters were already settled. "I'll be fine," she said. "You take the room, dear."

"But—"

"No buts," said Mrs. Grace. "I'll be perfectly fine. And anyway, I can hardly tolerate my own snoring. If we share, you'll be baggy eyed and fit for no one's company, much less prepared to meet your darling groom."

"I would be happier to share," argued Elizabeth.

"No," said Mrs. Grace. "I won't allow it. How much?" she inquired of the innkeeper.

"Half a crown for the both o' ye. Supper'll be extra."

"Very well," said Mrs. Grace, and with that, she removed the proper remuneration from her reticule and asked, "Shall I pay you directly?"

"Oh, no," said the man. "Gi' all remittance to Mrs. Pitagowan, else she'll put my arse in the snow with Hadley." His blush returned, as he pointed toward the woman who'd already yelled at him once. "Bess," he said. "She's o'er there."

Mrs. Grace pointed as well, and he nodded, then her faithful companion grasped Elizabeth by the arm and squeezed gently, and said, "Sleep well, dear." And suddenly she was away, leaving Elizabeth to deal with the innkeeper.

"So ye're going tae meet yer groom?" he said, once again tugging at his beard.

Elizabeth nodded. "Yes, sir."

"Inverness?"

"Yes, sir." The man was entirely too forward; still Elizabeth held her tongue, looking wistfully over her shoulder at Mrs. Grace, who was now conversing quite amenably with "Bess" "o'er there." It never failed to impress her that Mrs. Grace could so easily get along with anyone—unlike Elizabeth, who hadn't a good conversational bone in her body. But it really mustn't be entirely unexpected, when she'd been left to fend for herself for most of her life.

And anyway it was never on her own behalf that she became nettled; nothing ever got her dander up more than the disaffection of others.

Elizabeth waited whilst the man searched the myriad of keys on his belt, and then he smiled congenially and led the way into a scullery, where he hollered to a young boy to light the fire in Carrie's room, and to change the bed sheets. Afterward, he led Elizabeth into another smaller room, then stopped before an old, iron-banded door.

"So, then, who's the lucky groom?" he asked as he slid a big black key into the lock. "Is it Douglass?"

Elizabeth shook her head.

"Mackintosh?"

"No sir. I'll be pledging my..."

"Ach, now, dinna tell me, it must be MacKinnon!" He shook his head sadly, and said, "Poor bastard." He jiggled the knob, then opened the door to let her in.

The room itself was quite cozy, with a small brick fireplace and an adjoining door at the far side of the room. "Is that perhaps another guest room?" she asked, hopefully.

"Nay," he said, shaking his head. "Tis my daughter's closet."

"May I use it to store my valise?" She lifted the heavy bag in her hand, only belatedly realizing that he had never once bothered to offer to carry it—not that this itself should bother her overmuch. Elizabeth had long been of the mind that a woman could carry her own bag. It was rather his unhelpful demeanor.

"Nay," he said again. "Tis locked. We've had some guests snooping of late, and my daughter's no' too keen on it. Also," he said with a lift of his brow. "No baths. Ain't no one about to draw you any water. And if you want tae sup, ye'll be more'n welcome in the hall. Mrs. Pitagowan makes a fine stew, and I believe she's got some frumenty as well."

"Frumenty?"

"Pudding," he said, "wheat boiled in milk, with cinnamon, nutmeg and ginger, made special for the holiday, all very expensive!"

"Thank you," said Elizabeth, and then he was gone.

Still, she wasn't alone. She waited patiently for the young man who'd rushed in after them to finish lighting the hearth fire, and then change the bedsheets. After he left as well, Elizabeth closed the door. As weary as she was, she set down her valise in the middle of the room and went to test the bed, considering how hungry she might be—perhaps not enough to brave the randy lot in the tavern. And anyway, she doubted she would see Mrs. Grace again this evening. Her companion was not the sort to dally before bedtime; no doubt she was already making herself comfortable out in the stables—or as comfortable as she was able.

Suddenly, she leapt up from the bed, curious to explore Carrie's closet. She jiggled the knob, and, found, much to her delight, and contrary to Mr. Pitagowan's claims, the door was unlocked. Only one look inside and she gasped over the grizzly display—it was a shrine full of wartime accoutrements: shields, swords, coats, cuffs, spurs, pistols, hats—much of which she suspected was still encrusted with blood. Certainly, the scent of the room was ghastly. And although it wasn't a small room by most standards, there was little doubt Mrs. Grace would prefer the stables. With a hand to her breast, she closed the door again and, resolved to make it a night—vittles could wait until the morrow, when everyone else was sleeping off hangovers.

Chapter Two

CALLUM MACKINNON WAS close enough to home now that he could taste the tang of pine in the air. Unfortunately, the carriageway was impassible—vehicles stalled along the roadway, some parked on the embankments, fresh snow piled high against their rutted wheels.

He frowned at the sight, considering that he might be able to slide through the blockade by abandoning the roadway, but, even eight months later, the area was still crawling with Sassenachs soldiers.

Bloody hell.

At this point, neither he nor his horse were particularly enjoying the bite of the wind, and the snow had already dampened his cloak. The last thing he wished to do was to arrive home looking like the walking dead, and scare his sister into pissing her bed.

And anyway, he was still far enough that, even if he managed to get through the crush, his aching bones might not make it through the night. His wounds were still raw—those on his body, and the one in his heart. Not only was his clan forever divided—some had fought for the Stuart King—he was returning home a traitor, pardoned only so long as he forfeited title and lands.

Decision made, he grunted his annoyance, although, in truth, he couldn't blame it on the weather. He was perpetually disgruntled these days, mourning that bright-hearted self he'd lost on a blood-soaked field at Culloden.

Ach, now, why shouldn't he be sour as sorrel?

He had an Englishman to thank for saving his miserable life, and considering that it was that same bloody Englishman who'd put a ball between his father's eyes, none of it sat well in his gut.

Bloody rotten bastards.

Even despite the fact that they'd already surrendered, General Hawley had ordered both Callum and his father executed, then, to make sure it was done, he stood by as one Major James Wolfe had fired the first ball. That his man wasn't too thrilled to end a life of a prisoner off the battlefield wasn't much of a comfort to Callum's father. Young as he was, the major was an excellent marksman, although once Hawley departed, Wolfe put the next two volleys into Callum—one through his shoulder, the other his thigh—then ordered Callum to run. And run, he had, by God. Only now he sometimes wished he too had taken a ball to the head rather than be forced to relive the memory of his father's twitching corpse and piddled plaid.

Even now, the heinous memory brought an unmanly sting to Callum's tired blue eyes, and he vowed to carry the ignoble image to his grave. So far as his brothers were all concerned, all they ever needed to know was that Angus MacKinnon died like a man—unlike his eldest son, who'd scurried away from the specter of death like a rat from a torch.

As for Wolfe… the sorry bastard…

If he'd meant for Callum to survive, a shoulder wound would have sufficed. How he'd made it so far as he had without succumbing to fever, Callum might never know. The memory of his final days on the run only resurfaced with a blur. Ever since, he'd spent months convalescing, two of those he couldn't even recall.

In the meantime, he had three young brothers and a wee sister waiting at home and, considering that he had very likely been pronounced a traitor to the Crown, he hadn't dared to apprise anyone he was still alive. Unfortunately, it was long past time to do so.

Consequently, and once again because of Major Wolfe, he was here on the Yuletide, stopping short of his destination, dawdling like a coward on the eve of a new year.

God's teeth, it was enough to sour any man's mood, and not even the promise of Mrs. Pitagowan's cranachan managed to lift his spirits.

With some effort, he slid down from his horse—a borrowed mare he'd have to return as soon as he was able. Wincing over the pain in his leg, ignoring the one in his heart, he handed the reins to a young lad, scarcely older than his brother Lachlan. He recognized the youth as one of Pitagowan's nephews, a bright haired lad with more freckles than the night had stars.

"Good tae see ye, lai—sir," said the youth, dressed as a proper Sassenach. And yet, despite that they'd gone and outlawed the clans, and forbade them to carry weapons, no one could mistake the boy's brogue. He was Scots through and through, and Callum knew his father well. The poor soul had fought beside him at Culloden, and died, so he'd been told. His cousin Carrie had since taken to scouring the battlefields for proof of life… or death.

"Uncle John'll be pleased tae see ye," said the lad brightly.

Callum gave the boy a nod, then fished out a full crown, handing it to him. It was New Year's Eve after all, the beginning of Hogmanay, and he trusted John to serve him on credit till he could chance to repay him. In the meantime, Little Joe and his brother needed all the help they could get.

Inside the inn, Pitagowan's wife had decorated the place in good Scot's style—festooning the hearth and trim with boughs of holly. She'd also lit a Yule log for the holiday—a hefty block of birch sprinkled with saltpeter to give it that violet hue. The smoke it emitted tickled the back of Callum's throat, and he'd warrant those men drinking and singing in the puffed up tavern would wake on the morrow with double the ache in their heads.

Better them, than me, he thought.

All he wanted for the instant was a good nights' rest, and nevertheless, he feared, not even that was bound to soothe his soul.

He found John Pitagowan behind his bar, doing what he liked doing best—combing his thick, white beard. Callum smiled over the all-too familiar sight and shook his head, a barb rising to his tongue. "Too bad you've no hair remaining on your head," he said, with a grin, and Pitagowan's comb halted midair. His, thick wiry brows collided, and then he slapped a hand to his burly breast.

"Is it you?"

Callum nodded, and the old man grinned.

Pitagowan had been a good friend of his Da's. During the most difficult of times, it was his father who'd given John Pitagowan the coin to go south and settle in Calvine.

John pulled the hat from his head, scrunching it, then brought a finger to his crusty old lips. "Call me Balthazar," he said. "Folks here don't know me as Pitagowan."

"Yes, they do!" said Bess, coming up behind Callum. "Dinna fool yourself into thinking they don't, husband." And then she craned her neck back to peer up at Callum. "Ain't ye a sight for sore eyes, Callum MacKinnon! We thought ye'd gone and swallowed a bullet!"

"Not me," Callum said, frowning.

The twinkle immediately extinguished from Bess Pitagowan's eyes and she said a little more dourly, "Alas, we heard." Her hand reached out to squeeze Callum's forearm. "We were right sorry to hear it, don't y' know. My Carrie keeps going up to see what she can find. My brother himself didn't show up on the rosters, and neither did he come home." She shook her head sadly. But, then, just as suddenly as it had vanished, her smile returned. "My sweet girl will be so sorry she missed you."

Callum raised a brow. Carrie was a lot of things, though she wasn't particularly sweet, nor was she little anymore. She was a wee bit loud, a wee bit crude, and a wee bit of a tease. One of these days it was going to get her in a lot of trouble. Callum had found himself, on more than one occasion, fending off the flame-haired vixen with the saucer eyes and freckled nose—a trait all the Pitagowans shared.

"Alas, I'll be gone come morn," Callum said. "I was only hoping ye'd have a room to let for the night?"

"Oh, dear, no," lamented Bess, "We've just rented the last—"

Pitagowan's eyes suddenly lit up. "Ho!" he said. "As it so happens to your very lovely bride!"

"Bride?" said Callum, taken aback.

"Aye! She's already here!" announced Pitagowan. "Snapped up the very last room! Come," he demanded, seizing Callum by the arm, and ushering him quickly through the scullery, as Bess wandered back to her guests.

Callum hadn't a moment to set the man straight.

"She's a bit like Carrie," he said. "Though I'm guessing you already know. Here we thought you'd been laid six-feet under, and all the while you were out hunting for a wife. It all makes sense," he said. "Being she's a Sassenach. You cunning devil!" he said. "Just like yer Da. In fact, I wouldn't be too surprised if Angus showed up here tonight as well."

Callum felt the proclamation like a punch to his gut. There was no way his father was still alive. He was dead as the iron nails in Carrie's bedroom door—dead as his heart had been for going on six months, until it was replaced by this bone-deep fury he couldn't shake.

To his utter dismay, he could scarcely keep up with a sixty year old man, but Pitagowan didn't notice, or was too polite to say so. He pulled

Callum before Carrie's door, shoved in a ready key, then pushed Callum inside, barking with laughter.

"I'll send in a hot bath," he said, winking. "Looks like you need it. Oh! And something to eat." He laughed again, as he gave the other occupant of the room a raised thumb and then pointed to Callum and turned about with another chortle. "Love me a good miracle," he said, and then happily closed the door with an exuberant, "Ta ta!"

Chapter Three

"TA TA?"

The sight that greeted Callum as he entered Carrie's room—certainly not Carrie—effectively silenced any protest he might have uttered. A lovely, tawny-haired beauty sat wide-eyed on the bed, in little more than a delicate chemise.

The firelight caught the hint of red in her tresses, giving her pale, golden hair a soft, burnished hue. Her clearly defined cheeks bloomed with color, and he couldn't help himself; fascinated, he watched the blush spread down her long, delicate neckline, into her décolletage.

All his physical pain was forgotten, if only for the instant, and he was slow to remember his tongue as John closed the door behind him.

"I beg pardon," the woman said, rising from the bed. "There *must* be some mistake. This is *my* room!" And then she suddenly cocked her head, her golden brows colliding, as she asked, "Did I hear him say he would draw you a bath?"

Callum nodded, bemused.

"Insufferable! He told me there was no one available to draw one for me! And what's more, he insisted I eat out in that tavern with that randy lot of men; therefore, I was quite prepared to go to bed without supping."

She was English, by her accent, of that there was no doubt.

Wellborn, too, he decided.

And spoiled.

Callum blinked as she crossed her arms, her silken chemise entirely too revealing as she stood before the hearth fire. In her pique, she mustn't even realize, and God knew, it had been far too long since Callum had even seen a woman of her ilk, much less stood before one half-dressed. Swallowing convulsively, he lifted a hand to cover his eyes, as though to shield himself from the bright light of the sun—and that she was, bright as a sweltering noon-day sun, burning him up with her too-close proximity. No matter that *she* was the one blushing, Callum felt the heat of embarrassment creep over him as well—so bloody hot that, for a moment, he feared the return of his fever. "I-I'm sorry," he said, and he meant to turn and go, but she thrust a hand against the curve of her hip and glowered fiercely, shocking him with her pronouncement—not to mention, that bold way she puffed up her chest, revealing the soft moons of her bosom rising above her neckline.

"I am to wed Lord MacKinnon," she apprised him. "Do not doubt he'll have word of this from me, and both you and that tonsured innkeeper will have the devil to pay!"

Callum blinked thrice, trying to make sense of her words.

She was to marry *who*?

Not his father for certain, not him, and certainly it couldn't be young Lachlan, who'd only last year sprouted hairs on his bollocks.

"Mind you, I gave that man half a crown for this room," she was saying, "and if anyone should be sharing this room with me, it should be my chaperone, not you!"

Again, he blinked. "You're tae wed the MacKinnon?" he asked dubiously.

"*Lord* MacKinnon," she corrected him. "Need I remind—"

"Nay, my lady. You need remind me of anything," Callum said furiously, and, with the spell suddenly broken, he limped into the room, moving past the other occupant, and straight toward *his* bed. "I assure you I am reminded daily of what we Scots have lost. I don't need any bleedin' Sassenach to advise me."

"Oh!" she exclaimed, sounding alarmed, instead of angry. "Are you hurt?"

He was acutely aware that she moved behind him, her hand hovering behind his elbow as though he were some feeble old man in need of help. "I am fine," he snapped. "Dinna fash yourself, my lady!"

"Oh, but you are not!" she insisted.

"Yes, I am," Callum argued, although he wasn't. Every bone in his body ached, and none more than his heart. The physician had said he was fortunate. Part of his femur had shattered with the impact of the ball, and, unfortunately, the doctor hadn't arrived in time to remove it so the wound wouldn't fester. By the time the bullet was extracted, he was left with a raging fever that persisted for weeks. However, he didn't remember any of that.

Evidently, the wound in his shoulder had fared only a little better. At least it hadn't gotten infected. Still, he reached for his shoulder as he sat upon the bed, grimacing, one hand on his leg, the other crossing his chest to clutch at his aching flesh.

Like some lady of the lamp, the woman advanced upon him, offering her hands to steady him as he sat, and some angry, raging part of Callum wanted nothing more than to seize her, drag her into his embrace and kiss her punitively—half out of some primal need to ease his ravaged soul, half out of a fierce desire to punish someone for the crimes of her countrymen.

And nevertheless… none of it was her fault.

He realized that as much as he did the simple fact that she was trying to help. And nevertheless, he said again, through gritted teeth, "I am fine."

She stepped back to assess him, looking perfectly stricken although she knew him not at all. Nor did she know what injuries he'd sustained beneath his shirt and trews.

He looked up at her then, grateful that they'd switched places, because, at least now, he could no longer see her fine form limned by the light of the fire.

She was beautiful, certainly, although as fierce as she had been standing up to him, raging against Balthazar, her eyes were now filled with kindness and compassion, and it was nearly his undoing. God's truth, any man would be fortunate simply to know her, much less wed her—a woman unfettered by her emotions, and brave enough to stand up to a stranger, yet tender-hearted enough to consider his wellbeing.

Suddenly, Callum was bone tired, ready to be home in his own bed, wishing he could forget the hell he'd encountered at Culloden and the pain of his injuries since.

For a long, long moment, he didn't know what else to say… so he said nothing…

THE MAN WAS clearly in pain.

There was nothing about his demeanor that decried this fact, and Elizabeth was utterly torn, both incensed that the innkeeper had let her room to some man not of her acquaintance, and now entirely horrified to find him at sixes and sevens.

"Please… won't you allow me to help?" she asked, and before he could think to refuse her, she seized up the shawl she'd lain over her valise and rushed out the door, straight through the adjoining chamber, and into the scullery, fully intending to find the man a proper doctor.

"Pardon!" she said loudly.

A number of eyes flicked in her direction, although, considering the holiday crush, the majority returned to their given tasks, except for the young man who'd lit her hearth fire.

"My lady?" he said.

"Is there a doctor about?"

"No, my lady."

"A midwife?"

"No my lady."

"Well!" Elizabeth donned her most haughty demeanor, taking a cue from her aunt Celeste. No one *ever* dared gainsay Aunt Celeste, and come to think of it, if her Uncle didn't appreciate strong women, he certainly surrounded himself with more than enough of them. "I would like to speak to the proprietor, at once!"

The young man scratched his head. "You mean, Balthazar?"

"Mr. Pitagowan. Balthazar—whatever his name is!"

"E's—" The lad pointed, and never got the chance to finish his statement, because Elizabeth didn't wait. She turned her back to the kitchen and marched into the adjoining room, where the innkeeper stood, once again, combing his infernal beard.

"Good sir," she said. "There's a man in my room who requires your immediate attention!"

The innkeeper looked confused, and said, "MacKinnon?"

"Yes, as I've said. I am Lord MacKinnon's betrothed, and I really must insist you bring in a physician at once. And, please, please, don't worry, I will accept the charges."

The innkeeper pocketed his comb, but he furrowed his brow, and just at that instant, one of the tavern guests raked back a chair and approached the bar.

"Well, well," said the guest "What's this?" He turned to his acquaintances at the table behind him and said, "Loud as a cannon, but pretty as ye please. I'll help ye, sweet dove. You need a doctor, you say?"

A voice boomed at her back.

"Mind your own affairs, Douglass. Put your fat nose back in your cup, else I'll gi' ye a reason to drink!"

The man visibly shrank from the man at her back. "Callum!" he exclaimed. "We all thought ye were dead."

"I nearly was, but believe me, I'm hale enough to keep my word. Didn't ye hear the lady say she was MacKinnnon's bride?"

The Scotsman—Douglass—lifted a hand in surrender and Elizabeth turned to assess the man at her back. If he was still in pain, there was nothing about his demeanor now that betrayed the fact. He did, indeed, look hale as anyone she had ever met.

In fact, the sight of him stole her breath…

And nevertheless, she didn't need his defense. She could fend for herself. There were British guards posted out in the yard. This was no longer a lawless country. She would have told Mister Douglass so, but this man—Callum—didn't give her the chance. The scowl on his face darkened as he advanced on her and slid his arm about her waist, drawing her close. She gasped with shock, as he bent to whisper in her ear.

Chapter Four

"YE LOOK LIKE a doxy," he said for her ears alone, and with another gasp of outrage, she tried to extricate herself from his arms, but Callum wouldn't oblige her.

"How dare you!" she said, and then, perhaps remembering her state of undress, she went limp in his arms. Clearly, she'd been so concerned over his wellbeing that she'd forgotten what she was wearing. No doubt her dress covered all her fine bits, and her shawl hid the most tempting features. Thankfully, without the firelight to illume her, she was nearly concealed, except for those bare ankles and toes—more than enough nudity to tempt a grizzled old man whose greatest pleasure on the new year was to pour ale down his gob whilst watching the Mirrie Dancers in Bess Pitagowan's hearth fire.

Only for good measure, perhaps out of some misplaced sense of spite, Callum bent to nuzzle her neck, and then he couldn't help himself; he sniffed her hair, before meeting auld Douglass's curious gaze.

The faintest scent of roses caught his breath…

"Go back to your pints," he demanded of Douglass, his tone brook-ing no argument. Then, willy-nilly, he dragged "Lord MacKinnon's plucky bride" back to the room.

God's bloody bones, he should have been too tired and far too nettled to sport an arousal, but she smelled so fine. It was all he could do not to resort to some primitive yearning to toss the lady over his shoulders and tote her back to his bed—his bed.

Damn him to perdition, he was too bloody tired to argue over it, but for both their sakes, he released her the instant they entered the room, then kicked the door shut behind them.

Once safely inside, his angel of mercy wasted very little time in finding her mettle, retreating behind her tiny valise as though it were Hadrian's Wall. "How dare you!" she said again, and her expression was furious.

"Ach, lass. Didn't ye say ye were wedding *the* MacKinnon?"

"*Lord* MacKinnon," she corrected him again. But the simple fact was that no Act of Proscription could strip Callum of his birthright. They might brand him a traitor, but he was still the rightful heir of Clan MacKinnon. As the eldest surviving member of a clan that was descended of Kenneth MacAlpin, he was now chieftain, and he'd be damned if he'd let his title go without a fight, particularly if this woman was somehow to be his prize.

"I *am* laird MacKinnon," he announced, as he found and sat on the bed, with a sudden new ache to worry about—one that was beginning to form a tent of his breeches. Callum hid the evidence of his *discomfort* from her delicate view, suddenly reticent although he'd never been bashful a day in his life. However, at the moment, he bloody well wished he had her shawl.

Adjusting himself appropriately, he cast the woman a sour glance, finding her staring, open-mouthed, and he nearly asked her if she was looking to catch flies.

"But it can't be."

"I assure you I am who I say I am," he insisted.

"But… h-he's…"

"Dead?"

"No, he's not dead. Though he's just a boy!"

"He is fifteen," said Callum. "I'm the eldest, by far, but if you prefer my younger brother, I can still arrange it."

Open-mouthed still, she pinched her shawl before her, looking every bit as though she might swoon. "B-But… I don't understand."

Callum heaved a sigh. "Ach, lass. What's there tae understand? I'm back from the dead. Ye're among the first tae know it." Then he narrowed his eyes. "In fact, I'm on my way home—a rather convenient coincidence, I might add."

She blinked disbelievingly. "Are you really?"

"Really what?"

"Lord MacKinnon?"

"I am now," he said with no small measure of disgust. "My Da took a bullet at Falkirk. I would ha'e, as well… were it not for the bloody bastard who shot my Da. So, ye see, here I am by the good graces of a Wolfe."

"Hmmm," she said, casting her head down to assess her wiggling toes. She looked as though she had something more to say… but, for the moment, Callum was heartily relieved she wasn't looking directly at him. Even now, he held back tears that longed to be shed. Only once, after rousing from his fever, had he cried… for the father who'd raised him so honorably and died so ignobly. God's truth, it was no way to meet one's end—with a gob full of muck. War, indeed, was hell.

"Bloody Sassenach," he said, with equal parts anger and confusion. How in the name of St. Andrew was it possible to feel so much hatred and gratitude at once?

He knew well enough that Wolfe hadn't wanted to do it, and the instant he'd had another option, he'd taken it, but it didn't change the fact that his father was dead.

DESPITE HER CONFUSION, Elizabeth recognized truth when she heard it.

For a moment, she stared at her bare feet, unable to find even a modicum of chagrin over their nudity. For some odd reason, she felt entirely comfortable in this man's presence. "So then," she said. "If you are…"

"I am."

"Then… I suppose…"

He gave her a nod. "You're betrothed to me," he finished.

She blushed hotly.

"That… is… indeed…"

"Convenient?"

Elizabeth nodded, wondering how much James had had to do with this very awkward happenstance. Without a bit of help, it seemed entirely unbelievable that she would discover herself ensconced here at this very inn only to be thrust into the same room with her intended—unless, it was… planned?

Or… by some miracle, the fates had intervened.

But nay… Elizabeth blinked with dawning comprehension: Her cousin had returned from Culloden in the dourest of moods. He'd ensconced himself for hours and hours with his father, then emerged from Uncle Edward's office with renewed purpose.

It wasn't very long after that meeting that Elizabeth had been told about her betrothal—to a Highlander, no less. When she'd protested, James had privately reassured her that she would be well pleased with the match, and what was more, he'd said: It would serve her sensibilities far, far better than it would to marry some fat, greasy English lord.

In fact, she wasn't particularly well endowed, and her most recent inquiry had been from an elderly gentleman whose gout hadn't allowed him to serve in the King's army.

Naturally, with James' reassurances, she'd acquiesced. It was only later—much later—when she'd discovered she was actually betrothed to a boy, that she'd felt like socking her cousin in the nose. She'd been irate all over again, although she took some small comfort in the fact that through their affiliation she might, indeed, be able to save a venerable clan.

James was right after all; It spoke to her inner crusader.

Even despite that she didn't entirely understand the political upheaval, or the Scot's lament, she knew enough to know that it was not entirely fair to call these men traitors—men who'd fought, not so much for Bonnie Prince Charlie as they had for their way of life.

In the end, James must also have felt the same, because the walls were not so thick as her uncle liked to believe. She knew her cousin had defied a direct order and freed a Scotman…

That man, she realized, must be Callum MacKinnon.

She opened her mouth to ask him a question, then closed it again, realizing that this was no act of God. Was Mrs. Grace also aware of the circumstances, or was she not part of the plot?

She had a difficult time believing Mrs. Grace would go along with such a farce. Nor could she fathom that James trusted Mrs. Grace more than he trusted Elizabeth.

Therefore, it stood to reason that if he hadn't revealed the sham to her, no doubt he'd never deign to tell such a proper woman as Mrs. Grace.

And then, too… what excuse had James provided for not being able to travel with them? He'd said only that he had some debt of honor to see to. And now, she had a good suspicion as to what that debt of honor must be.

Really, her cousin was a very well-respected man; there was no wonder he'd achieved the rank of brigade major by the age of eighteen, but he wasn't a bootlicker.

Her uncle Edward like to say that it would either gain James a place in history, or it would get him to an early grave. Right now, Elizabeth suspected it might prove to be an early grave—particularly if she ever got hold of him.

"James," she said crossly, and the hint of a crooked smile that was beginning to form on Callum MacKinnon's face suddenly fled—and, yes, he was handsome, she decided. Ruggedly so.

"What did ye say?"

Elizabeth arched a brow. "Please tell me, who shot your father?"

"Major James Wolfe," he said, eying her pointedly.

"But of course," she said, fidgeting under his scrutiny, and then she sighed and confessed, "That blackguard is my cousin."

Chapter Five

AS IT WERE, the only true angel at work this holiday was James.

It was, indeed, Callum MacKinnon he owed the debt to and evidently, after leaving Westerham, he'd tracked Callum to some blackhouse in Alyth, offering him a horse and enough money to travel with, along with papers to carry, all signed and sealed by her Uncle Edward.

The proof was all there; Callum showed her all the documents—all quite official.

And then, with an undeniably heavy heart, he told Elizabeth the rest of his tale—all of it, sparing nothing, not even the manner of his father's death.

They were both ordered to be executed under General Hawley's custody. His father was shot with hands bound, and neither man was armed. Her cousin James had pulled the trigger, but then, after Hawley left, he let Callum go.

Elizabeth could have relayed the rest of the story herself...

James had returned home in a terrible state. She had never seen him so downcast, and, in truth, she had suspected something of this magnitude, because, along with those bits and pieces she'd overheard, she knew her cousin well enough that, if he had kept the truth from her, he was likely ashamed. But she didn't wish to interrupt Callum, so she let him purge his grief, taking his hand when it seemed he might weep. It was a very humbling experience to watch a grown man grieve. And yet, he did not cry; although his bottom lip quivered ever so slightly, he remained strong, and all the while Elizabeth listened patiently until their conversation was interrupted by the innkeeper, who finally arrived bearing a wooden tub.

As Callum stood to converse with Mr. Pitagowan, Elizabeth laid his papers down on the bed, studying the man…

She could do worse.

He was a fine, fine specimen—no boy in him at all.

His thick, broad shoulders bespoke a lifetime of hard labor, and his skin, though pale in the midst of winter, and after an epoch of healing, was still a shade of bronze.

Evidently, he was a friend to Pitagowan family. They spoke with an ease borne of familiarity, and the elder man gave Callum his regrets, telling him of Carrie's mission to recover her Uncle's belongings, which were lost or stolen after he fell. The room, so Elizabeth discerned, was her "Chamber of Sorrows," filled with items belonging to the brave men who fell at Culloden. Every now and again, against his and her mother's wishes, the plucky young lady took a horse and cart north. That was the only reason that her room was empty.

As promised, Mr. Pitagowan left Little Joe to fill the bath, and he went to retrieve not one, but two bowls of Scotch broth with bannocks.

Immediately on the heels of Little Joe's departure arrived yet another stack of firewood for the hearth, along with soap, towels, a pitcher of ale and two cups.

But that wasn't all; Bess arrived with a dessert that consisted of oats, raspberries, cream and whisky—made especially for Callum.

"It's time to celebrate!" she announced as she laid her whisky drenched cranachan down upon a small table. "Back from the dead, with a bride no less!"

She winked at Elizabeth, and said, "Callum won't be sayin' so, mind ye, but 'e always had the ladies in a swoon. You're a lucky lady!"

Elizabeth nodded dumbly, as she accepted a brimming cup of ale, then gulped it down, grateful for the alcohol's calming effect. After a moment, Bess, too, departed, leaving her alone with her "betrothed."

Only now, wondering over the particulars, Elizabeth considered whether she ought to go apprise Mrs. Grace of the shocking turn of events.

"It all makes sense now," she told Callum as he spooned the steaming broth into his mouth. "James insisted I leave for Dunmore at once. And then, he departed without so much as a by your leave. Naturally, I wondered where he was off to in such haste. Now, I know."

Callum nodded very soberly, setting down his bowl, although he didn't yet sit. Her hand drifted into the spot on the bed he had occupied before, feeling for his fading warmth.

"So it seems," he said. "He came to assure me my passage was safe, and then he also insisted I leave at once. He apprised me the precise route to take, and then gave me papers to show in case I should need them."

Elizabeth tilted her head. "But he didn't tell you to stop here, did he? What made you do that?" she asked, curiously.

Callum shrugged. "I don't know. I was damp to my bones. I knew Bess and John well enough to know they'd give me a bed for the night, and a thick bowl of stew. But most of all, I suppose the thought of arriving home wasn't entirely without its sorrow."

"I can only imagine," she said, and now he came and sat beside her on the bed, but not *too* close. He hesitated a moment, then removed a ribbon of tartan from his pocket to show her.

"They burned the rest of his plaid along with his body, and mine as well, but the lady who tended me cut me a piece. She gave it to me before I left."

Red, green with a hint of white.

"The MacKinnon plaid?" she surmised.

He nodded glumly, looking for the moment like a wee little boy.

Elizabeth didn't understand what it was about a small scrap of cloth that the Scot's found so worthy of dying for. And nevertheless, she didn't need to understand to appreciate the fervor with which they applied themselves. They loved their tartans as fiercely as they loved their families… and their land… and now, so it seemed, it wasn't legal to have either…

But she needn't marry the man for pity's sake. There were English guards out in the yard; and knowing what she knew, she could call upon them, and they would arrive with due force, and very likely execute Callum for merely possessing that small scrap.

"I'm sorry," she said.

He shrugged, and said, "In the end, I suppose I wasn't looking forward to providing details." He winced, as though the memory offered him a new blow to the gut.

Elizabeth asked gently, without intending injury, "Don't you think they should know by now?"

"Aye," he said. "But it's the *how* of it I'm dreading, lass."

Elizabeth reached over to lay a few fingers on his bare arm, and the touch gave her a shock, startling her. She pulled her hand away as he peered up at her, his blue eyes glittering, oh so fiercely. The silence that fell between them stretched interminably…

"So, then… are ye keen for the match?" he asked, finally. "With my brother, Lachlan—I must assume it's Lachlan?"

Elizabeth lifted a shoulder. "I wasn't opposed, if that's what you're asking."

"Aye, lass, but is it Lachlan ye're wanting?"

Elizabeth shrugged. "I have never met him."

He lifted a brow then, and said, "I am guessing your cousin's intention was that *I* would return in time tae take his place at the altar. Tis as heavy-handed a scheme as I've ever encountered."

Elizabeth nodded. "And yet… I'm certain he meant well."

He peered down at the ribbon, pulling it between his thumb and forefinger. "Aye, lass… I'm sure he did. Canny lad," he said, smiling ruefully. "For a Sassenach…" His smile widened then, and Elizabeth's heart tripped a few beats.

He lifted his brow. "I'm also guessing he knew, as my brother must have known, that the only chance of us getting through this with our lands is to align ourselves with the English. Your uncle, precisely?"

"Elizabeth nodded, picking nervously at a thumbnail, understanding the implication. "Yes, well… I can assure you my uncle Edward hasn't the least intent to profit from your lands."

"Mayhap not," said Callum, "And yet he will."

Alas, it was Elizabeth's turn to sigh, because, of course, it was true. It would be dishonest to deny it. Some lands were already being appropriated, and forfeited to the Crown. Callum's lands, all but a portion, would be assigned to her uncle and leased to his family. All produce attained from MacKinnon lands would be offered first to the King's regiments, who were bound to be permanent fixtures about Scotland in order to keep the King's peace. "I could… go… home," she offered, realizing she didn't want to.

His smile persisted. "Or you could marry my brother?" he said.

Elizabeth met his gaze, sensing a question in his eyes even as they softened to regard her, and she felt…

Something…

Chapter Six

SOMETHING ABOUT THE way she'd slid her hand across the bed… into the warm spot he'd left behind… it spoke to Callum like nothing ever had. He'd found himself wishing he was still seated there beside her, if only to find her hand… The thought ignited a fire in his veins that he suddenly realized he didn't want to go out.

For a moment, Callum merely stared at her, wondering how the devil to propose, and whether he truly wanted to…

On the one hand, he loathed being manipulated; it would serve that wretch right if his cousin married his brother as planned, but poor Lachlan wouldn't know what to do with her. Although he'd very clearly already accepted the betrothal on behalf of the family, he'd probably done so without ever knowing what his bride even looked like or how fiery her spirit—and, oh, that she was. He sensed it keenly, even as she sat so primly beside him, her thumbs twirling nervously in her lap. The gesture endeared her to him as surely as did the blush in her cheeks… and the flowering of hope in her eyes.

So then, he recognized the boon he'd been offered, and… yes, indeed, there must be such a thing as miracles, because here sat one beside him—with golden-red hair, and eyes as blue as cornflowers. And suddenly, he couldn't bear the thought of her marrying his brother. She was a woman, through and through, and shouldn't be wasted on a boy.

And anyway, he knew Lachlan well enough to know that the burden of leadership would be too much for him to bear. Callum was eldest by thirteen years, and Lachlan was scarcely fifteen. The rest of his brothers were eleven, eight and four, and their wee sister's birth saw their mother gone from this world, barely a year before the Forty Five Rebellion.

Therefore, this was the only logical conclusion…

"Else… you could… marry me," he said, and found he meant it. He knew a good thing when he saw one, no matter how conspiratorially it was delivered.

Indeed, whatever feelings he had about her cousin, they were already growing ambivalent—on the one hand loathing James for killing his father, on the other, grateful as hell for, not only setting him free, but for seeing to it that he had safe passage home to his family… and a future and home to return to…

"You never gave me your name…"

"Elizabeth Louise," she said, and Callum smiled, because the name didn't suit her. It was far too conventional and he had a sense she was anything but.

"Aye, well, Elizabeth Louise…"

He slid from the bed and fell to his knee, hitching up his chin. "If you'll do me the honor of becoming my bride, I shall promise to provide for you to the best of my ability and I will honor and cherish you as a man should honor and cherish his wife."

ELIZABETH BLINKED.

Was he truly asking her to marry him?

On his knees?

The gesture was so intensely sweet that she felt a sting of tears spring to her eyes. Long, long ago, when she was still just a wee girl… she'd dreamt of a moment like this. And with every year that passed, without a proper suitor, nor prospects that weren't stodgy and old, she'd lost all hope of love with marriage. And though it seemed she mustn't truly have a choice, this man… this stranger… was giving her one…

She *could* return home, even to the dismay of her uncle and her cousin.

Her father had never cared one whit what her desires might be, and even now, he was traveling God knew where. Her uncle wouldn't like it if she muddled his plans, but neither would he disown her. In fact, he had given her this choice to begin with, as distasteful as it might have seemed, and Elizabeth had chosen to come here of her own free will, in order to help restore a family's good name. So why shouldn't she still do so?

Simply because it no longer seemed a matter of charity?

Even as Callum knelt before her, asking for her hand, she knew he would honor whatever decision she arrived at. If she asked him to allow it, he would send her back to Westerham, and he would… *what*? *Return home to face his own dispossession?*

And what about her cousin? She knew well enough that the only reason James wasn't being court marshaled for having freed his charge was because, first of all, until now, there hadn't been proof. Callum MacKinnon hadn't yet returned from the dead. Although her cousin was now commissioned to his father's regimen, and he was under Uncle Edward's protection, it wouldn't suit either of them if it became known… unless, James and Uncle Edward had some way to reassure the Crown that its interests were being met. Unfortunately for Callum, it was only their marriage contract that could save him from the gibbet. Eventually, unless he too had her Uncle's protection, he would answer for his participation at Culloden…

Elizabeth studied his face… handsome, despite the small scar on the right side of his chin. She hadn't the first inkling what his brother Lachlan looked like, but it didn't matter, because he was just a boy and Callum was a man…

"Very well," she said. "I will marry you."

He grinned suddenly, clearly pleased with her answer, and now, again, he pulled the ribbon through his fingers and took her gently by the hand.

"There's an old Scot's tradition," he explained as he laid the ribbon over her wrist, and then he peered up into her eyes long enough to explain. "A man and a woman pledge vows to remain faithful for a year and a day. At the end of such time, according to our laws, ye would be free tae leave me if it be your choice… However… if ye'll have me, Elizabeth Louise, I will promise tae gi' ye no cause tae go."

Elizabeth's heart pounded fiercely; she feared he must hear it as well. She nodded, and said, "I will."

And now, again, his smile unfurled in the most stunning display of startling white teeth as he looped his ribbon about her wrist, then tied it carefully, covering her hand with his own. He said, "As this knot is tied, so, too, will our lives be bound."

And then he nodded as though she was supposed to say something as well.

"Is that all?"

He chuckled richly. "For now," he said. "Only one more thing…" He reached up to touch her lightly upon the chin, tapping it gently, and said, "May I kiss my bride?"

Chapter Seven

ELIZABETH SUCKED IN a startled breath.

The unanticipated question gave her a dizzy feeling in her head and a warm gush in the pit of her belly that didn't have a thing to do with the hearth fire, nor the ale she'd drunk, nor even the whisky in her cranachan.

How had she come to this moment so unexpectedly?

She had left home intending to become a wife and mother to a young man, but here she was, feeling like a naive little girl… seated before a grown man… who was asking sincerely for her hand in matrimony. Nay, she corrected herself… they were already "*handfasted*"—married in the eyes of Scot's law. Barbaric, perhaps, but simple, honest and sweet—as sweet as the promises he'd made her.

If you'll do me the honor of becoming my bride, I shall promise to provide for you to the best of my ability and I will honor and cherish you as a man should honor and cherish his wife…

Nodding jerkily, Elizabeth held her breath as he lifted himself up from one knee to press his warm lips against her trembling mouth, and if she feared it would escalate to the marriage bed thereafter, she feared for naught. He drew back, smiling at her, and then rose to his feet, and limped over to the still steaming tub, reminding her again of his injury—not one, but two.

"We'll make it proper once we're home," he said, giving her a reprieve, although truly, Elizabeth wasn't overly concerned with propriety. In fact, had she been so, she might have run screaming from the room the minute he'd arrived.

Moreover, she was very well aware that if they didn't consummate this marriage—here, and now—tonight, she was sorely afraid that everything would fall apart. After all, what if they returned "home" only to discover his brother, young as he was, meant to contest it?

And even if he didn't, what about her uncle?

It seemed perfectly obvious to Elizabeth that James had intended for Callum to intercept her before she arrived at his home, but that didn't mean Uncle Edward intended the same. For all she knew, James had carried out the last part of his mission entirely on his own.

All things considered, this "wedding" had turned out better than she'd hoped for, even if it wasn't yet official in the eyes of the law.

There was simply no help for it; if she didn't lie with her... husband... as a woman should lie with a man... it would be too easy to challenge the *handfasting*.

And then a thought occurred to her... a shockingly bold idea that was stunning even for her. She had a very good sense by now that he was too much a gentleman to avail himself of a woman's body simply because he had a right to...

"May I?" she asked nervously, fiddling with the ribbon at her wrist—a wee scrap of cloth she really ought to remove, lest they brand her traitor for wearing it... and nevertheless, she shoved it higher beneath the sleeve of her chemise, emboldened by its presence.

"May ye what?" he asked, sounding confused.

"If you won't call for a doctor, may I... see to your wound?" Her gaze fell again to the slip of ribbon still peeking from beneath her sleeve. "If I can help, I would like to."

CALLUM SWALLOWED, HIS mouth suddenly gone dry.

One wound was on his upper thigh, near his groin, the other on his shoulder. The latter was safe enough to show her, though he wasn't certain he could trust himself to allow her to minister to either. Neither would it change the healing, or the past. Still, he considered her request, reaching down to test the water—warm though cooling by the moment.

God only knew, every part of him longed to wade into that clean, fresh water and inundate himself… It would be a shame to waste Little Joe's efforts, not to mention all those buckets full of water. But the room was entirely too small, with nowhere to conceal himself… and neither would it be easy to partition, even if he dared to appropriate the bedsheets.

Moreover, he was quite certain Pitagowan didn't have spares on a night like tonight. It was the first night of Hogmanay, after all, and the inn was filled with guests.

All the worse yet, he couldn't bring himself to confess the need to conceal himself from the woman who was supposed to be his bride. That wouldn't make a bit of sense, now would it? As far as Pitagowan was concerned, they were betrothed. So, in the end, he said, "Don't worry about it, lass, I am fine."

"But I must insist," she said, standing.

"No," Callum said more firmly, although having said as much, he still wasn't certain how to handle the bath—a surprising quandary, considering that only a few hours ago he hadn't any notion for how to assuage a blushing bride. And, aye… she was blushing—a very lovely shade of pink that he would dearly love to heighten…

Unfortunately, this was neither the time or place.

On the other hand… dirty as he was, he didn't intend to crawl into that bed beside her with a week's worth of stink on his person, and, in truth, if they were going to make this marriage work, there wasn't any point in concealing himself from her. In fact, if he had his druthers, they'd share the bath together, but it only seemed proper he should offer it to her first. "Would you like to take the first bath?"

"Oh, no!" she said quickly. "Thank you. I can wait."

"Sadly, I cannot," Callum confessed. "There's only one bed and I'd no' repulse ye with my scent."

"Y-yes… I-I… understand," she said.

And then, for a very, very long awkward moment, they simply stared at one another—an odd form of checkmate—until there was nothing left to be done, but to show her his bum…

Chapter Eight

TRUTH BE TOLD, Elizabeth wasn't sure why she'd declined the bath—wasn't that that best, most efficient way to get them both undressed?

Indeed, it was.

And still, she didn't know what to do.

Should she stay?

Should she go?

Should she turn her back to him?

Or maybe ask if he needed her help to undress?

In the meantime, there was a bath going to waste; and nevertheless, she wasn't entirely prepared when he shrugged off his shirt and tossed it over to the bed beside her.

She opened her mouth to speak, not at all sure it was a protest, and then closed it again as he began to fumble with his trousers. The heat in her cheeks began to blaze.

"You might like to turn your head," he said with a hint of a smile, and she did, at once, focusing her attention on the door, half anticipating it to fly open and to find Mrs. Grace's disapproving gaze behind it.

At the instant, though she hadn't yet done a bloody thing to initiate her plan, she felt guilty as charged—or rather, as she might be charged. She was behaving like doxy, no less. Would he think her one if she did what she wished to do?

Lordy, she hadn't the nerve.

Where now her fearlessness?

Where now her mettle?

Unwittingly, her gaze fell to the ribbon of tartan peeking out from beneath her sleeve, and she fiddled with the cloth, discombobulated.

"It rather surprises me that your cousin would allow you to travel so far alone," he said conversationally.

"Oh, I'm not alone," she reassured, and then she heard him slip into the tub, and immediately thereafter heard him heave a contented sigh. Sweet lord, the sound was nearly as intoxicating as the whiskey in her belly, though she wished now that she'd asked for more—at least then she might have the nerve to finish what she hadn't yet had the courage to start.

"You're not?"

"Oh, no," she said. "I came with my chaperone—Mrs. Grace. If it's acceptable to you, she would like to stay on to help… when we… er… arrive… home."

"Aye, well, tis ye're home now, as well," he said with a thickening burr, and then he heaved another sigh as he slid more fully into the tub.

"Yes, I suppose that's true," she said.

"It is."

He sounded so sure…

Trying desperately to rein in her nerve, Elizabeth nipped at her bottom lip, making it burn over the self-abuse, nervous, but loathed to confess it. She had always considered herself to be far more… fearless. It was infinitely more difficult than she had ever supposed… to speak to someone whilst in the same room… and not… look into their face—

while they were loitering in a bath. But this wasn't such a shocking thing, was it?

It used to be in the olden days… the lady of the house would bathe, not merely her husband, but his guests as well. It was really very innocent—except… it wasn't. At the moment, she very definitely had an ulterior motive—did he suspect?

By now, the steam from the bath was beginning to thicken in the room… or mayhap it was merely that she felt overheated. The fire in the hearth must be blazing hot, and yet, she couldn't seem to find it within her to even glance at the hearth, since that happened to be on the very same side of the room with her now naked groom.

UNEXPECTED, THOUGH HE found it, Callum was enjoying her company, despite himself. She was endearing, he decided, as he stared at her lovely, round backside.

He couldn't help himself; he grinned, and then, the very act of doing so was startling, because it was the first time he'd smiled so genuinely in eight long months.

Ye gods, they were *handfasted* now, married according to common law. He hadn't lied to her, and indeed, he would allow her the time and space she needed to decide on her own if she wished to remain at Dunmore, and more importantly to remain as his wife.

Lachlan, too, would respect whatever decision she came to, and Callum had every intention of leaving her chaste until they could all get into a room together to decide their fates.

The problem was… Callum wasn't a saint, and though she was no longer revealed before the fire, he could still spy the tantalizing outline of her fine form beneath the diaphanous gown, and he fought a battle with his demons to confess as much.

In the end, he decided she needn't know, since it would indubitably embarrass her. But God help him, she had a fine, fine form… a narrow waist his hands ached to cradle… a pert, round bottom that offered him an intriguing view of the shadow beneath… the very sight made him dizzy, and it wasn't only from the heat of the water…

Really, despite her bashfulness, he sensed an inherent strength in the lass, evident even now in the set of her shoulders. Having committed herself to their union, she didn't dress herself and leave in protest of his nudeness. Nor did she rail at him for having availed himself of the tub. She simply accepted the truth, and, just as he had, she'd honed in on the most favorable outcome.

Nay indeed, he wouldn't rush her, nor push her into anything rash, but that didn't stop his body from hardening, nor did it ease the discomfort of his sudden, unreasonable desire.

Bloody hell… here he was… on the eve of a new year, enjoying a nice, hot bath… in the company of his lovely new bride… and still he was honor bound to keep his todger to himself—hell and damnation.

How he adored those tiny curls at her nape… most likely not the effect of any iron. But rather, having been dampened by the weather, they were naturally curling.

"I was thinking… after my bath, should we summon your chaperone and tell her the good news? Maybe share a pint of ale with her?"

"Hmm," she said, sounding confused. And then she added, "No, I don't think so."

"Why not, lass? Do ye plan to change your mind?" He hadn't a clue why he said it so defiantly, but the very notion curdled the dessert in his belly. "If so, I should warn ye, I mean to hold ye to our bargain…"

Evidently, that was all it took to chase away her shyness; her gaze narrowed and she spun about to pierce him with an angry glower. Only the sight of his smile disarmed her, and whatever it was she was about to say, she thought better of it. "You're jesting," she said, with no small trace of relief.

"Indeed, I am."

"That's a very good thing," she said, with a smile, and Callum lifted his brow, amused.

GOOD HEAVENS.

Elizabeth knew she ought to look away. Propriety dictated as much, and yet… and yet… she couldn't seem to make herself do it.

And now that she was looking, she did so greedily, secretly thrilling to the sight of her husband's male form.

His smile was achingly beautiful and his storm-blue eyes so full of mischief—like a naughty little boy, but there was nothing so little about him.

He couldn't possibly have realized she would take such offense at his suggestion. She was a woman of her honor, and she wouldn't back down—even if she did suddenly feel like flying out the door. At any rate, where would she go?

Not to Mrs. Grace, that much was certain. That was the last thing she would do as she didn't want her chaperone to know anything until their vows were already consummated and there was nothing anyone could do to prevent it.

He scooched down now, with a knee lifted from the water, and otherwise buried to his chin. Steam rose from the tub, like fine ribbons of smoke, and much to Elizabeth's dismay, her gaze found his shoulder and locked on the small puckered wound there. "Does it hurt?" she asked, well aware that his hand slid through the tub, in a direction and fashion she daren't contemplate. "Yes," he said. "Very much."

"It appears to be healing," she said. "What about the one on your leg?"

Chapter Nine

"HEALING," HE SAID.

"Oh."

Every last bit of good will Callum had mustered suddenly vanished with the steam rising from his tub. It had been far too long since he'd been with a woman and even now, as he brushed his hand across his cock to shove it down between his thighs to conceal it… white, hot desire pulsed through his veins, and heat rose into his unshaven face—another thing he meant to remedy. Until now, he hadn't had any good reason to shave, but suddenly he had delightful visions of diving into her soft muff, curious for the taste of his wife.

His wife.

His wife.

His. Wife.

Before he could wrap his brain about that fact, and before he could warn her to stay away, she advanced upon the tub, setting his heart to pounding.

"I am no doctor," she said. "But you might as well show me since I am now your wife. If there is anything at all I can do to ease your pain, I will certainly try."

"You can't," he said, through gritted teeth and he would have thrust up a hand to hold her back, but he daren't release the kraken in his tub. "Elizabeth," he said, as she knelt, and the word came out of his throat with a tortured groan.

"Don't worry, I'll be gentle," she promised.

Callum groaned again, though she'd yet to even touch him.

"Where is it?" she demanded.

"Where is what?" Surely, she didn't mean the beast between his thighs? That was hidden if only for the moment, but not for long, because even as the scent of her reached his nostrils, enhanced by the steam from the tub, his erection thickened and throbbed, threatening to free itself of all restraints.

"Elizabeth!" he protested again, as her hand dove into the water, and Callum twisted uncomfortably as she brushed his thigh.

ELIZABETH DIDN'T KNOW what got into her, but having reassured herself that this was the best course of action, she was now determined.

She didn't wish to marry a boy. She wanted to marry a man—this man.

And neither was she entirely ignorant of what must be done. She understood the dangers of being in such close proximity with a naked man. In fact, that was precisely the end result she anticipated. She merely lacked the skills to know how to get what she wanted without asking for it, and no matter that she had always considered herself to be quite outspoken and yes, even intrepid, she didn't anticipate the words that came out of her mouth.

"What?" she asked innocently. "If you won't allow me to tend to your wound, I must help you wash. Therefore, I am searching for the soap."

"That is my… leg," he said.

"Of course it is—because you blocked my hand."

"The soap," he declared. "Is still in *my* hand."

Elizabeth smiled coyly. "Oh."

"You don't want to wash me," he said.

"Oh, but I do! It's the least I can do."

He frowned. "No, it isn't."

Elizabeth batted her lashes. "Well, I can't very well sit about like an empty headed miss whilst you bathe," she reasoned.

He was still scowling at her. "Of course, you can."

"My lord, in case you didn't realize, that is insulting," Elizabeth said. "Women are not objects to be passively admired. I would therefore like to be of use," she said more firmly.

"Elizabeth," he warned, the sound of her name already achingly familiar on his lips.

Elizabeth's heart beat wildly. The scent of him so close was intoxicating—a combination of sweat, horse and … man. It made her nostrils flare and she inched closer to catch another whiff…

Holy Christ in heaven above, Callum thought.

She's too close—too close!

Neither did he miss the delicate flare of her nostrils as she inhaled his masculine scent and the not-so subtle way it drew her closer for another sniff. Ach, God, she was his wife now, and despite that he'd sworn not to avail himself of her bountiful gifts, it was all he could do to keep his head. "Elizabeth," he said hoarsely, as she moved even closer.

"Callum," she said, and God help him, that single word was like a balm to his wounded heart. It soothed him in a way that the healer's efforts never could.

In fact, at the moment, his greatest ache was not the injury on his shoulder nor the one on his thigh… it was the one in his heart… and the one now throbbing between his legs.

Helplessly caught in the prison of her eyes, he released his hold on his cock and let it slip, to rise to a full salute. At the feel of it cresting the water, he swallowed convulsively, and though she must have heard the thrashing of water, she didn't immediately appear to notice.

He seized her by the wrist, reveling in the feel of his tartan ribbon still bound there. "Elizabeth," he said again, and the sound was as much a plea as he dared.

He wanted to command her to leave the room, but, in truth, deep down he sensed that this woman's affection was exactly what could save him… not only tonight, but for all time.

As he stood there, basking in the promise of her gaze, he was like a drowning man reaching for a line…

THERE NEEDN'T BE any words spoken…

Not now.

Elizabeth had never been more certain of anything in all her life.

Gone was the effort of pretense. Her woman's heart reveled in the feel of his strong hand closed about her wrist. Her nipples pebbled against her gown, fully revealed by the water that had splashed upon her chemise. His gaze was drawn there, as well, and he, too, swallowed, the hunger in his gaze making her feel… empowered.

"Am I not your wife?" she asked softly, sensually, sensing the moment could turn as he attempted to compose himself.

"You are."

"Then make it so, in truth."

He swallowed again, visibly, the apple in his throat bobbing. "Art certain?"

Elizabeth nodded with certainty, and then, if she had second thoughts they fled as he drew her into the tub, soaking her chemise to the flesh. She gasped in surprise, hardly having anticipated this—not quite this. He sat as he embraced her, cradling her in his arms as his lips unerringly found her mouth. Hungrily, they explored her, suckling and lapping in turn, coaxing her to open for him…

SUDDENLY FAMISHED FOR something more than food, Callum held his wife close, reveling in the feel of her in his arms.

She stiffened, though only for a moment, as she settled over his lap, no doubt feeling the heat of his manhood rising to seek her mons—silky, sweet and wet.

He groaned with desire, the sound no longer tortured but ravenous. Her body was like a bounty laid before a wasting man, and he was not strong enough to deny her.

"Elizabeth," he said, once more, if only because honor compelled him. "If we do this now, there will be no turning back. You'll be my wife, in truth."

She smiled mischievously, and he wondered why. Was she already deflowered? Had she come to him with another man's seed in her womb? It wasn't unheard of and she was far too bold to be a virgin, but still…

His hand found and sought the lips he craved. Without warning, he slid a finger between her slick folds, and then once inside, he found the barrier he sought, and stopped, only slightly surprised. She *was* a virgin—a virgin with intelligence and passion. He could see the fire burning in her beautiful blue eyes… undisguised desire with an unbridled honesty to reveal it.

What was more, she knew, as he knew, that a willing consummation of this union meant they would be bound hereafter… so be it.

She moaned softly as his finger continued to explore, and, finally, she sagged into his arms as Callum deepened his kiss, mimicking with his tongue the rhythm he longed to show her elsewhere, knowing in his heart that she was everything he needed.

If, in fact, he'd lost his faith, this woman would restore it—no doubt she had already done so, judging by the lift of his spirit.

He didn't know if the water would make her first time easier, but he was so hard he didn't want to wait. And besides, when they were through, he would bathe her himself, reveal and worship every inch of her body…

Chapter Ten

THIS WASN'T PRECISELY how Elizabeth thought it might go—never had she imagined he would take her right here in the tub. And yet, there was nothing about their union that felt wrong. Somehow, every touch of his hands on her body felt oh, so right. When he found her most private place, and boldly touched her woman's flower, she sagged against him, reveling in the hardness she encountered beneath her, and greedy in a way she had never anticipated. Her body seemed to have a hunger and will of its own, instinctively knowing what it should seek…

She repositioned herself fully over his searing erection, thrilling over the feel of it as it also seemed to find a life of its own, slipping and seeking between them until it found the hollow it sought, nestling itself hotly between her thighs.

"Ye're mine," he said, as though he couldn't believe it. "Mine, mine, mine…"

And then his arms enfolded her greedily, his hands pulling and tugging at her wet chemise, only to give up when he found it irrevocably stuck to her flesh—all the more so with every pass of his soaking hands. The flimsy material melded against Elizabeth's skin.

His gaze clouding with passion, he abandoned the garment, and so did she as his hands fell to both sides of her hips, lifting her ever so gently in order to settle her more conveniently over his arousal, and then, she gasped with new delight at the feel of his shaft pressing slowly, but firmly into her body… claiming her once and for all. Her heart hammered against her ribs in anticipation, and she knew the instant he encountered her maidenhead. Only when it seemed he might hesitate, she wouldn't allow it. She sank down over him, taking him fully into her body, crying out over the thickness of him inside her.

"Oh, my!" she said, and he grinned.

"Ach, lass, I'll have my hands full with you."

Elizabeth smiled because, indeed, he would.

Indeed, he would.

His fingers dug into her waist, clutching her desperately as he rocked against her, until she thought she would die with pleasure.

Oh, my…

This wasn't at all like Mrs. Grace had warned.

She had thought there must be pain, but no, indeed, there was none. There was only pleasure so intense she thought she might weep.

She adored the way his broad chest felt beneath her palms, loved the way his body melted into her own, loved the way he was looking at her right now…

They moved together in the tub, slowly at first, dancing a primal dance, hands exploring, mouths entwined, tongues exploring…

GOD'S TRUTH, THIS was not how Callum had anticipated the holiday might go. It was hardly the way he'd anticipated returning home—with a new wife en tow. And yet, suddenly, in that instant, he knew in his heart that everything would be all right…

I would be a good year, indeed.

He vowed to honor his pledge—to give this woman no reason to leave him, ever, because he suddenly, without any doubt understood that without her he couldn't be whole.

It had been so long since he'd lain with a woman that he came too quickly, giving her his seed, and then, because he knew instinctively that she didn't understand what had happened, he rose from the tub lifting up his beautiful wife to carry her to the bed.

Once there, he made love to her, still hard as stone though he shouldn't be, and he was stunned to discover that, even as he stroked and teased her to fruition, he hardened again. And this time, when he felt her body shudder with release, he covered her mouth with his own, greedy for the taste of her, and jealous enough not to want anyone else to overhear her cries of pleasure.

"Oh, my," she said again, breathlessly, and he grinned down at her, reluctant to separate even still. He couldn't stop, not yet, still sensitive with pleasure though he lifted himself enough so he could fill his eyes with her beauty. And when she smiled at him, her eyes so full of promise he came once more, the culmination so intensely pleasurable that he lifted his head back and stifled a primal howl.

Outside the chamber, all throughout the scullery and tavern, voices rose with huzzahs and shouts of "slàinte mhath!" It took Callum a full moment to realize they weren't shouting hallelujahs for him… The clock must have struck twelve.

The first day of Hogmanay.

The first day of the rest of his life.

"Happy New Year, missus MacKinnon," he said with a grin.

"Happy New Year," she cooed.

Epilogue

One year later…

CALLUM MACKINNON CORNERED his wife at the top of the stairs, sweeping her into an embrace to keep her from going down to corral the children—not their own as yet, though he longed to hold a wee one in his arms, a sweet little girl, like her mother… with darling little freckles on her nose, a mischievous little grin more like his own, and an irrefutable sass she would come by honestly through both her parents.

"Callum," she protested. "First footing will be upon soon… there's still so much so do." He loved that she was developing the barest hint of a brogue.

Together a full year this Hogmanay, he wanted to celebrate a wee moment just the two of them. Alice, their housemaid, along with Mrs. Grace to supervise her, was already well on the way to supplying the entire village with black buns. All he wanted from his lovely wife was two minutes alone to reveal his gift for her—his mother's wedding band, hers to keep as the lady of Dunmore. "The neighbors can wait," he said silkily, dragging her back into his arms when she tried to flee.

"I've something tae give you, my beautiful wife."

Her brows lifted, her attention piqued. They were still in the process of rebuilding Dunmore and their funds were tight as ticks on a dog in winter.

"A gift?" she asked.

He chuckled. "Aye, but dinna be so surprised, mo chroí." The use of his Gaelic tongue still wasn't entirely safe, but he had nothing to hide from his wife. "First I should ask… do ye mean to leave?"

Her brows drew together in confusion. "Leave?"

"Me," he said, hitching his chin at her wrist, at the slip of ribbon she still wore hidden beneath her sleeve, knowing the answer before she gave it.

She squeezed him lovingly, lifting herself up on tippy toes to press her warm lips against his. "No, I'm afraid not, my love; you're stuck with me."

"Ach, then," he said, with feigned disappointment. "In that case…" He fished a small box out of his pocket to hand it to her.

With blooming cheeks and wide blue eyes she accepted it, making short work of the ribbons, opening it to reveal a simple braided band—a silver ring that had been in his family's possession since his ancestor, Iain MacKinnon had it fashioned for his wife to present to her on her sixtieth birthday.

"Oh, my… it's beautiful," she said, fingering the ring, with its delicate etchings—fine Celtic knots. And then she slid the ring on her finger, and lifted her hand to better inspect it.

"It belonged to my mother," explained Callum. "And her mother before her. I wanted ye to have it."

"Thank you," she said, looking up at him with such love that it squeezed at his heart. "I—"

Something exploded, and there was an inexplicable clatter belowstairs in the general vicinity of the drawing room. Nothing good,

Callum thought as he released his wife, and ran down the stairs to find what had transpired.

Elizabeth arrived only seconds behind him.

Lachlan and Rory stood facing the door, with their backs to a smoking hearth. Their faces were blackened with soot, only their wide eyes visible through smoke and ash.

The acrid scent of chemicals wafted from the room.

ELIZABETH BLINKED, STARING aghast at the boys—the young man she'd very nearly wed, and thanked God every day she had not. At Sixteen, Lachlan MacKinnon was no more a man than he was on the day they'd met. All four MacKinnon boys were present and staring at their eldest brother. "It was Lachlan's fault," claimed twelve-year old Rory.

"We wanted the fire tae be blue," explained five-year old Ailbert, with such a sober look that Elizabeth wanted to laugh.

And Fergus, at nine, had little to say. He simply pointed at Lachlan, and, Elizabeth couldn't help it. Although she was grateful that Maggie was in the kitchen with Alice, most likely poking at black buns, she did stifle a laugh.

"All o' ye, out!" demanded Callum. "Get yourselves clean!"

He needn't have said it twice. Like rats, the younger boys fled all together, the only answering sound the patter of their feet as they rushed into the hall, and rumbled up the stairs.

Only Lachlan sauntered by slowly, casting a glinting glance at Elizabeth, and giving her a conspiratorial wink before turning to his brother to say, "I'm sorry, Callum. I wasn't thinking."

"Nay ye werena'," agreed Callum. "What do ye think Isobel Percy might say if I told her what ye did here today?"

He shrugged. "I think she would laugh."

Callum smacked his brother on the back of the head as he passed by. "Aye, well, I can well assure ye her Da wadna, and if ye e'er hope to ask for the girl's hand, ye'd better be thinking twice before ye lead your brothers astray."

"Yes, sir," said Lachlan, with a sheepish grin, and Elizabeth patted him gently on the shoulder as he passed, and said, still smiling, "There's a clean set of clothes on your bed, Lachlan. Isobel and her parents should be here soon. Go wash yourself quick."

"Yes ma'am," he said, with a fond smile.

Once Lachlan was gone, Elizabeth embraced her husband, squeezing him tight. And then she lifted her ring finger again, and whispered for his ears alone, "Remind me to thank you properly once our guests have come and gone."

"Ach, lass," he said. "That's a promise that requires a toast." And with that, he lifted his wife up to sip from the delicate cup of her mouth, drinking deeply of her love.

ꟹ THE END ꟹ

Are you hoping this isn't the end? Stay tuned for a brand new historical romance series. To make sure you don't miss any news, please join my newsletter.

www.tanyaannecrosby.com/subscribe

About Tanya Anne Crosby

Tanya Anne Crosby is the New York Times and USA Today bestselling author of thirty novels. She has been featured in magazines, such as People, Romantic Times and Publisher's Weekly, and her books have been translated into eight languages. Her first novel was published in 1992 by Avon Books, where Tanya was hailed as "one of Avon's fastest rising stars." Her fourth book was chosen to launch the company's Avon Romantic Treasure imprint.

Known for stories charged with emotion and humor and filled with flawed characters Tanya is an award-winning author, journalist, and editor, and her novels have garnered reader praise and glowing critical reviews. She and her writer husband split their time between Charleston, SC, where she was raised, and northern Michigan, where the couple make their home.

Website: www.tanyaannecrosby.com
Facebook: facebook.com/tanyaannecrosby
Twitter: twitter.com/TanyaAnneCrosby
Instagram: instagram.com/tanyaannecrosby

The Legend of a Rogue

By Darcy Burke

Part of A Very Highland Holiday Collection

The Legend of a Rogue

The Legend of a Rogue

When Tavish Crawford learns treasure hunter Elspeth Marshall is on the trail of his family's missing legacy, he swears to prevent her at any cost. As nefarious forces threaten them both, he realizes he must not only protect the mystical sword, but the woman who has stolen his heart.

AUTHOR'S NOTE

The thirteen treasures of Britain are mythical objects that appear in various legends. They have been used in countless stories and in many ways (Harry Potter's Deathly Hallows are somewhat based on them). I adapted them for the Legendary Rogues series and added the Heart of Llanllwch for purely narrative purposes. Llan Dhearg is also my creation but Rhydderch Hael and his son Constantine are historical figures, and they lived in the kingdom of Alt Clut or Strathclyde. Dumbarton, where Tavish lives, was the medieval capital of this region.

To read what happens with Llan Dhearg's twin, Dyrnwyn, don't miss Romancing the Earl.

Prologue

Lammas Fair, August 1744
Dunkeld, Scotland

"AFTER THAT, RANULF carried the dagger with him everywhere he went." Elspeth Marshall looked around at the dozen or so children who were gathered in a semicircle on the lawn listening to her recount the tale of Ranulf and Hilaria.

"And it worked?" one of the older girls asked. "He didn't fall in love with Hilaria?"

"That's correct," Elspeth said. "The dagger prevented it."

"Because the witch Mazelina enchanted the dagger to protect him from the Heart of Llanllwch," another girl, with bright red hair, said with a touch of impatience. Her attempt at the Welsh double-l sound wasn't quite right, but it was very difficult to make. Elspeth had worked years to get it right.

The first girl, a blonde, frowned with disappointment. "But he should be with Hilaria."

"She shouldn't have tried to use the magic heart to win him," the redhead said. "That wasn't fair."

"All is fair in matters of love and war," the blonde argued. "Hilaria loves him, and Maud isn't very nice."

Elspeth smiled at the blonde. "Well, *we* know that, but Ranulf doesn't. She's very nice to him, isn't she?"

The redhead scoffed. "He's blinded by love."

"Will you finish the story?" a boy of about ten asked.

"Of course." Elspeth picked up the thread. "Ranulf was indeed blinded by his love for Maud. He failed to see how much Hilaria cared for him. However, his younger brother, Aldred, was not so foolish. Captivated by the kind and beautiful Hilaria, he fell in love with her instead.

"The cunning Maud used her friendship with Hilaria's sister to encourage their union. She also continued to woo Ranulf. Smitten as he was, he married her, breaking Hilaria's heart."

The blonde gasped and shook her head. A few of the children spoke amongst themselves. Elspeth looked past them and saw that several adults, besides the children's parents, had also gathered. One of them, an exceptionally tall, broad-shouldered gentleman leaned against a tree. His arms were crossed over his chest as he watched Elspeth intently.

"Do not fret," Elspeth soothed the girl. "For Aldred was gentle and charming, and most of all, patient. He asked Hilaria to be his wife and while she refused him at first, she eventually relented."

"Was she trying to make Ranulf jealous?" the blonde asked.

The redhead turned toward her friend. "What would it matter? Ranulf was already married." She looked back to Elspeth. "Please say that Hilaria grew to love Aldred." Her keen expression showed how involved she was in the story, which delighted Elspeth. Telling stories, especially to children, gave her such joy.

Elspeth glanced back at the tall stranger. He was still intently engaged. Something about the way he watched her sent a shiver down her spine. Not a bad, apprehensive shiver, but one that made her heart beat faster with anticipation.

Putting her attention back to the story, Elspeth said, "As a matter of fact, Hilaria did grow to love Aldred. He was a kind and loving husband, and soon Hilaria forgot all about Ranulf. By then, however, Ranulf had learned just how conniving and cold his wife could be. He regretted marrying Maud and not giving Hilaria a chance, especially when he saw how happy Hilaria and Aldred were."

"So did the magic heart even work?" a boy asked. "It was supposed to make Ranulf fall in love with Hilaria, but he didn't. I think it wasn't real."

"But it had already been used to make others fall in love by the time it came to Hilaria." This came from the tall stranger, prompting all the children—and Elspeth—to look in his direction.

The man continued, his gaze on the boy who'd asked about the heart. "If Ranulf hadn't found out she had the heart and gone to the witch Mazelina to ask for a way to stop its magic, he would have been beguiled, just as Hilaria intended."

"I'm glad he wasn't," the redhead said, crossing her arms. "Hilaria shouldn't have wanted to trick him. Either he loved her or he didn't. And he didn't."

"But he was sorry he married Maud," the blonde said. "Maybe he and Hilaria were meant to be."

The redhead gaped at her. "What about Aldred?"

Elspeth chuckled. This story never failed to provoke discussion. Perhaps that was why it was one of her very favorites.

"I liked that story," a younger girl said. "Thank you, Miss Elspeth."

"You're welcome." Elspeth smiled at her, then let her gaze go to the tall man once more. He hadn't been there at the start of the story, but he seemed to know the entire tale.

Before she could find a reason to make her way toward him, he came forward, skirting the children as they stood and returned to their parents.

"You're an excellent storyteller," he said.

"Thank you. And you are familiar with the tale of Ranulf and Hilaria."

"I am indeed."

One of the boys, whom Elspeth knew quite well, came forward without even looking at the gentleman. "Miss Elspeth, are you going to tell us about the rest of the thirteen treasures?"

Elspeth laughed softly. "David, you have heard about the thirteen treasures maybe thirteen times. And I just told you about one of them—the Heart of Llanllwch."

"I'd rather hear about the sword—Dyrnwyn," he said stubbornly, his small mouth turning down.

"Would you like to hear about Dyrnwyn's twin?" the man asked, prompting both David and Elspeth to swing their heads in his direction.

"There's another sword?" David asked, his voice rising and his eyes widening eagerly.

"I am not aware of a twin sword," Elspeth said, her breath catching with excitement. There was nothing she loved more than discovering a new story.

"You are familiar with Rhydderch Hael, of course, since Dyrnwyn, or White-Hilt, belonged to him?"

"He was Rhydderch the Generous," David responded quickly. "Because he loaned Dyrnwyn to anyone who wanted it."

"Most people didn't want it, however," the man said with a chuckle. "At least not then. Now, there are plenty of those who would like to own the sword that flames blue."

David nodded. "I would!"

"Well, eventually, someone *did* take Dyrnwyn. That was the knight, Gareth, to whom Rhydderch gifted the sword on his wedding day.

However, there was a second sword called Lann Dhearg, or red blade. It also fired from tip to hilt, but the flames were an orange-red instead of blue. This blade belonged to Rhydderch's brother, and he was…not so generous." The man winked at David.

"What happened to Lann Dhearg?"

"It was lost, unfortunately," the man said with a touch of sadness. "Just as Dyrnwyn has been lost."

"How come Dyrnwyn is one of the thirteen treasures and Lann Dhearg is not?" David asked.

"Because Dyrnwyn was given to one of Arthur's knights, but you know that, I expect." He looked at Elspeth. "Something tells me *you* know every detail of those treasures." His blue eyes sparked with an inner heat.

"David!" the boy's mother called from several feet away.

Elspeth turned her head to see the woman smiling at her son and gesturing for him to come. David threw his arms around Elspeth for a quick hug. "Thank you, Miss Elspeth." He looked up at the gentleman and said, "And thank you for telling me about Lann Dhearg." He turned and dashed to his mother.

"Are you visiting for the Lammas Fair?" Elspeth asked the man.

"Passing through town on my way to Inverness, but yes, I am spending the night." He spoke in a deep, lowland brogue.

"I ask because David will probably draw a picture of Lann Dhearg and if he sees you again, he'll offer to give it to you."

"He's drawn pictures for you, I take it?"

Elspeth thought of the stack in her library. "Many. My favorite is Dyrnwyn." She paused and contemplated him a moment. "I still can't quite believe you knew of Ranulf and Hilaria and that you had a new story to share. Is there more you can tell me of Lann Dhearg?"

"Not much…Miss Elspeth?"

"Miss Marshall, but the children call me Miss Elspeth."

"I am Roy Williams." He bowed. "Pleased to make your acquaintance." He grinned, and Elspeth's knees felt watery. He was exceptionally handsome. The strong, angular planes of his face were utterly masculine in their shape, from the square set of his jaw to the sharp line of his cheekbones. But it was his interest in her storytelling and his contribution of his own that captivated her.

"How do you know about this twin sword?" she asked. "I've never heard of it, and I go out of my way to hear every story and legend I possibly can."

"Do you?"

She nodded. "I write them down. Someday, I hope to publish them." Her father wished she would marry instead, preferably to the young physician he'd recently hired to join him in tending to the people of Dunkeld as well as Birnam on the other side of the River Tay. Will you please tell me more about Lann Dhearg? And Rhydderch and his brother? I'd love to hear whatever you have to share."

"It would be my privilege. Perhaps in return, you'd agree to show me around the fair?" He offered her his arm.

"I'd be delighted." Elspeth put her hand on his coat sleeve. He was garbed entirely in brown, save the white of his shirt and the slight green tinge to his waistcoat. His clothing was made from fine, quality wool, indicating he was not poor. "What is taking you to Inverness?"

"Visiting family." He guided her from the lawn near the cathedral toward the High Street and the stalls set up there. "Highland games near there, actually."

She looked at his profile, thinking he presented a striking figure with his aristocratic nose and dark sable hair gathered into a queue at the back of his neck. "How exciting. You've been before?"

"Every year since I was small." He peered down at her. "You didn't think I was from there?"

She shook her head. "Not with your accent. In fact, I would say you are from the area of Rhydderch Hael. He was a king of Alt Clut."

"You have a good ear," he said with a hint of admiration.

"I've listened to a great many oral stories. I've become good at detecting where people are from. I'm still waiting for you to tell me about Lann Dhearg. Is there a chance Rhydderch was your ancestor?"

He laughed. "That would be remarkable, wouldn't it? You are correct that I am from that area. Stories of him—and other kings—are still told. You should visit sometime, for there would be much for you to hear."

"I would love to." In truth, she wanted to travel all over Scotland and into Wales and England. But as a young, unmarried woman, she didn't have the ability to do so. Nor would her father approve. He had, however, provided her with space for her growing library and supplied her with ink and parchment.

"In the meantime, I will tell you what I know," Mr. Williams said. "Although, there isn't much more beyond what I already told the young lad. Two swords were made—Dyrnwyn and Lann Dhearg. One was for Rhydderch and the other was for his younger brother, Constantine."

"I thought Constantine was his son."

"He was named for his uncle."

"Did he also inherit Lann Dhearg?" Elspeth asked, her mind working with excitement over finding a new story to record.

"I can't imagine so, since he abdicated the throne and devoted his life to religion."

"Of course." Elspeth knew Rhydderch's son was *Saint* Constantine. "I am getting ahead of myself in my enthusiasm. You said the sword was lost. Do you know what happened to it when Constantine died?"

"Unfortunately, I do not. It is mentioned in a description from the tenth century regarding Owain ap Dyfnwal, who was a King of Strathclyde. He formed an alliance with Alba and Mercia, and was said to have carried a 'red sword.' Many believe that was Lann Dhearg.

However, that is the only mention of it."

"And yet, the legend persisted." Elspeth had learned that stories were easily lost. It was easy to discount one story from over a century ago, harder when there were two stories, as in this case. It was harder still if there were several tales about a person or an object. She tipped her head to look up at him as they entered the market square. "Do you think it is that—a legend?"

He lifted a shoulder. "Probably. But as you say, it has persisted. I suppose a part of me hopes it really exists. Do you think the thirteen treasures do?"

Elspeth exhaled. "Like you and Lann Dhearg, I want to believe they do. Especially the Heart of Llanllwch."

"Why, so you can make someone fall in love with you?" His tone was teasing, but there was something else to it too.

Elspeth paused, and as he drew to a stop beside her, he turned slightly. "No, it's just more appealing to me than a sword or a halter or a cauldron." She named just a few of the treasures.

Mr. Williams laughed, a warm, robust sound that made Elspeth smile. "For me, it's the cloak. I should like to be able to render myself invisible."

"I can definitely understand the benefits of that. Perhaps I might change my mind."

"You cannot, I'm afraid. The cloak has been spoken for—it is mine. You may have the heart. It's made of tourmaline and quite pretty, it's said."

Elspeth grinned. "You're a beast, but fine, I'll take the heart."

They continued to the stalls, where Elspeth introduced him to everyone she knew. They sampled ale and fresh-baked pastry, and watched a trio of musicians. By the time they'd made their way to all the stalls, it was late in the day.

"I must return home to have dinner with my father," Elspeth said reluctantly. She'd enjoyed their afternoon together.

"Would it be wrong of me to ask for one more story?" He grinned. "That makes me sound like a child."

Elspeth was inordinately flattered. "It does not. Must you leave on the morrow?"

He nodded. "I'm afraid so."

"Perhaps you'll stop by again on your return trip. My father is the physician here—you can find us on the other side of town." She gestured past the square toward the road that led to the river.

"I may do that."

They found themselves removed from the stalls, in a quiet area off the road. Elspeth took her hand from his arm and allowed herself to stare up into his striking blue eyes.

"I hope you will," she whispered.

He took her hand. "I did not expect to find you here, Miss Marshall. You are an impressive woman—smart and confident. Most women of your age are already married or nearly so."

"My father would like me to be. I am too interested in books, however. The reading and writing of them." She blushed. "Most men—of any age—find me...odd."

"That is their misfortune," Mr. Williams said softly. "I hope your father won't press you into a union you don't want."

"He won't." Of that, Elspeth was certain. He wanted her to wed, but more than that, he wanted her to be happy. "He knows and accepts that I am content with my library. For now."

For the first time, Elspeth glimpsed a shared future. With a strong man who found her interesting.

"I am glad to hear it, Miss Marshall. Perhaps when I come by again in the future, you will still be unmarried."

What was he saying?

Before she could ask, he shook his head. "Forgive me. That was inappropriate. I shall hope our paths cross again. Until then, be very well, Miss Marshall." He bent his head and brushed his lips across her cheek.

Lightness filled her, as if she might float away. She clasped his hand tightly so that he might anchor her to the earth.

Without thinking, she put her other hand on his neck and held his head down. She moved so she could put her lips to his.

Shocked by her action, she gasped as she pulled back. "My apologies. I don't know what I was thinking. I wasn't, actually."

"Sometimes thought is overrated." His eyes gleamed with heat. "Don't apologize. I am not in the least offended."

Elspeth relaxed slightly, even as a wonderful current of anticipation flowed through her. "I really must go."

"You look as if you don't want to."

"I do not. Maybe just one more—" She cut herself off and wrinkled her nose. "You'll think me a wanton."

"One more kiss?" He leaned close as he steered her toward the side of a shop. Blocked by the stalls, they could not be seen from the square. "If you are a wanton, then I am a rogue."

She smiled up at him. "Oh, I like rogues. Remember, I write down stories. And rogues usually make the best characters."

"How lovely to hear." He swept his mouth over hers, gently at first, then with more pressure, his lips molding against hers.

They were soft and wonderful, and the energy coursing through Elspeth intensified. She put her arms around his neck and stood on her toes as he clasped his arms around her.

His tongue licked along her lower lip. "Open your mouth," he whispered.

She did and was simultaneously shocked and thrilled when his tongue stroked inside. Somehow, she knew to use her tongue too, and the kiss became something far more intimate…and passionate.

His hands moved over her back as she clutched at his neck. She never wanted this moment to end, and yet she knew it must.

And just like that, it was over. He released her and stepped back, his eyes a storm of desire. She knew it because she felt the same.

"You should go." He sounded hoarse, as if the kiss had affected him physically.

"I hope I'll see you soon."

"I hope so too."

Reluctantly, Elspeth turned and walked slowly toward the square. She pivoted before going to the street she would follow home. He stared after her, his gaze smoldering.

Elspeth felt the connection between them deep in her bones. She would count the days until his return.

Chapter One

December 15, 1746
Calvine, Scotland

THE SNOW BEGAN to fall more heavily as the coach rumbled into the yard of Balthazar's Inn, and the ground was already turning white. Some would say it was foolish to travel at this time of year, but Elspeth had no qualms about doing so. Her aunt, whom Elspeth had accompanied to Inverness to visit her daughter, Elspeth's cousin, was less intrepid. Still, she'd been desperate to visit her new grandchild—a cherub-faced boy with bright blue eyes and a particularly loud wail.

The color of his eyes had reminded Elspeth of Roy Williams. Though it had been over two years since she'd met him at the Lammas Fair, she would never forget his eyes. Or his smile. Or his kiss.

Or the fact that he'd never returned to Dunkeld. Not on his return trip from Inverness and not since.

"Even if we hadn't planned to stop here for the night, we would have to," Aunt Leah said, looking out the window of the coach. In her late forties, Aunt Leah often seemed a decade younger, both in her appearance and vigor. "I do hope it stops snowing so we can continue tomorrow."

Aunt Leah lived in Perth. After her husband had died a year and a half ago, she'd taken to visiting her closest relatives—Elspeth and her father—quite often. She'd also invited Elspeth to accompany her when she traveled, an opportunity for which Elspeth was most grateful as it had allowed her to collect new stories to write down. In Inverness, she'd gathered stories about the Battle of Culloden that had been fought—and lost—in April.

The coach drew to a halt, and a moment later, the footman opened the door and helped Aunt Leah to the ground. Next, he offered Elspeth assistance.

The inn, which Elspeth had traveled past several times as she'd journeyed between Dunkeld and Inverness, was three stories and constructed of thick stone. The structure was a few hundred years old and looked it, though some of the windows seemed new.

Aunt Leah preceded her into the common room as the footman followed with their bags and the coachman took care of their vehicle and horses. "Oh my." Aunt Leah stopped short just inside. "This is rather…rustic."

Straw covered the floors in patches and a group of dogs was sprawled near the massive hearth on the left side of the room. Many of the tables in the common room were occupied, including by a pair of English soldiers, their bright red coats making them impossible to miss. Even so, the atmosphere was boisterous and welcoming, but then Elspeth loved to hear people talk.

"I'll go speak to the innkeeper," Aunt Leah said as she perused the common room with her assessing blue gaze. "Do you want to sit down? I can tell you're desperate to hear anything of interest."

Elspeth smiled and ducked her chin. "You know me too well, Aunt. Thank you." She went to find a table surrounded by people so that she could listen to all the conversations around her.

As she sat and removed her hat and gloves, she perused the common room. She faced the wall where the fireplace was located.

In the corner to the right of the hearth, his back to the wall, sat a solitary man with a hood drawn up over his head. Perhaps he was cold. Elspeth felt bad that he was alone. She was certain he had a story. Everyone had a story.

Continuing her survey along the back wall where there was a small counter, she saw Aunt Leah speaking with a man who must be the innkeeper. He sported a knit cap stretched atop his head and an impressively bushy beard. As he directed their footman upstairs, Aunt Leah came to join her at the table.

"Because we stopped and paid to reserve our lodging on our way north, Mr. Pitagowan—rather, Balthazar, as he prefers to be called—made sure to give us a suite of adjoined rooms." Aunt Leah removed her hat, revealing her glossy dark hair. Her gloves followed, and she deposited her items on the vacant chair where Elspeth had placed hers.

"How pleasant," Elspeth said. Aunt Leah preferred to sleep in her own bed and her own chamber whenever possible. A restless sleeper, she snored so loudly that Elspeth could often hear her even from the next room. Her aunt hated disturbing people.

"I asked for tea," Aunt Leah continued. "And for dinner to be delivered to our rooms. I'm rather tired. I hope you don't mind." She flashed Elspeth an apologetic smile.

"Not at all." Elspeth hid her disappointment. She would just have to soak up the atmosphere before they went upstairs. She listened intently to the conversations humming around her. One rose above the others. She wasn't sure it was due to the volume or the content. The words "flaming sword" drew her instant and rapt attention.

The man who'd uttered the phrase sat to her left. He shared his small table with a second man, who appeared as captivated by his words as Elspeth. She leaned in their direction as she strained to hear more.

Thankfully, they did not speak quietly.

"Was it a torch?" the other man, a younger fellow but still older than Elspeth, asked.

"I said it was a sword, did I not?" the first man said crossly. With a shock of bright blond hair, he was perhaps five years older than the other.

The younger man, who had a hooked nose, waved his hand. "Bah, ye weren't there. How could ye know?"

The blond man, who was about thirty, narrowed his eyes at the other. "I heard it from Russell."

"He heard it too." A man at the next table over—between the two men and the solitary man in the corner—gestured to his tablemate. "His brother fought at Culloden." He looked to the man whose face had turned gray. "Didna ye say he saw a sword that burst inta bright orange flame?"

Elspeth didn't bother trying to hide her interest any longer. In fact, half the common room now seemed riveted to the discussion.

"What's this about a flaming sword?" Aunt Leah asked only to Elspeth as she leaned across the table.

Elspeth set her jaw with determination. "I don't know yet, but I'm going to find out."

"Oh, here's the tea." Aunt Leah thanked the serving maid who set the pot and cups on the table.

"We don't get many requests for tea," the young woman said, her bright red curls bouncing against her temples.

"I can't imagine you do, dear," Aunt Leah murmured.

Elspeth ignored the rest of their conversation as she focused on the far more interesting one going on to her left.

One of the English soldiers stood and glowered at the men who were discussing the sword. "Eh now, enough talk of Culloden!"

The blond man at the table next to Elspeth curled his lip. "Ye can't keep us from talking."

"I most certainly can. On your feet, Highlander!"

The common room fell silent as fear raced across the blond man's features. Elspeth's gut clenched.

The hooded man in the corner leapt to his feet and weaved through the tables to where the soldier stood. "Now then, Captain, I don't think these men mean any harm. They're drinking ale and sharing fantastical stories. Surely there's no trouble in that?"

"Sedition is a crime," the captain said, glaring at the men who remained seated.

"It is indeed," the hooded man agreed in a smooth, placating tone. "But they aren't doing that. Are you?" He turned his head to look at the men, and the movement caused the hood to fall.

Elspeth's eyes nearly popped out. Though the man's loose sable hair was shorter, probably just long enough to be tied back, there was no mistaking his blue gaze. It was *him*. Roy Bloody Williams.

The men shook their heads.

"We didn't fight," the blond man said, his eyes wide and fixed on the soldiers.

"See?" Williams said. "Let us all return to our ale."

Ale? Elspeth wanted to hear about the flaming sword. No, she wanted to interrogate Mr. Williams as to why he'd never returned to Dunkeld. She'd thought the kisses they'd shared meant something.

She covertly watched him as he sat back down in the corner. He didn't pull the hood back up over his head. His gaze swept the room and didn't even pause on Elspeth. There was no look of recognition, no hesitation, nothing.

Elspeth sucked in a breath and stirred sugar into her tea before taking a sip. She glowered at the liquid before setting the cup back onto the saucer.

"Is something amiss, Elspeth?" Aunt Leah asked.

"The man in the corner is Mr. Williams," she said quietly with barely contained anger—and hurt.

Aunt Leah's gaze strayed toward him before snapping back to Elspeth. "*That* Mr. Williams?"

Elspeth had told her aunt about him, in part because Aunt Leah kept questioning when Elspeth might consider marriage. It wasn't that Elspeth wasn't considering that she should wed, it was that she fancied she'd already met the man she wanted to. Which was foolish since they'd spent only a matter of hours in each other's company. It hadn't *felt* foolish, however. Not until today.

Clearly, she was the only one who'd been affected by their time together. He didn't even appear to remember her.

"Yes, him," Elspeth said tightly. She sat up straighter and took a deep breath. "Ignore him. I shall. I have much more important things to attend to."

Aunt Leah arched a dark brow. "Such as?" She shot another glance toward Williams in the corner.

"Such as learning everything I can about this flaming sword that was seen at Culloden."

"You don't think it's real?" Aunt Leah's blue eyes narrowed slightly as her brow creased with confusion. "I know you like stories, but it's absurd."

"No, I don't think it's real." Probably. "But it's reminiscent of one of the Thirteen Treasures of Britain." Which were also likely not real. This flaming sword sounded like the one Roy Williams had told her about—Lann Dhearg. What did he think of these stories and rumors flying around the common room? "You know I can't turn my back on a story. It doesn't have to be true."

Aunt Leah smiled warmly. "Sounds like you have work to do." She glanced around. "Should we invite someone to join us?"

"Perhaps. But first…" Elspeth turned to the two men seated at the table next to theirs. "Excuse me, might I trouble you to tell me what you specifically heard about this flaming sword at Culloden? I record oral stories, and this sounds like an amazing tale."

The blond man eyed the soldiers apprehensively, then scooted his chair closer to Elspeth's. "My cousin was there. He told me all about it. Ye want to write it down?"

"I would. What can you tell me? Starting with your name, so I can give you credit for the information."

The man flicked another guarded glance toward the soldiers. He spoke in a low voice. "I don't think I want to give ye my name. But ye could just call me…George." That he used the name of the king wasn't lost on Elspeth. "My cousin fought for the Jacobites. He was injured in the battle, but he saw a man wielding a sword that lit with an orange flame."

Elspeth leaned toward the man. "Was it a fellow Jacobite?" She understood their cause and felt sorry for their devastating loss, but her father had been careful not to align himself with them. Even so, he'd helped more than a few wounded Jacobites as they'd passed through Dunkeld—secretly, of course.

George sent another furtive look toward the soldiers. "Yes." The word was barely audible.

A Jacobite had wielded Lann Dhearg. Elspeth couldn't help but look briefly toward Williams. "Do you know what happened to the man with the sword?"

He shook his head. "As far as I know, no one has seen it since the battle."

It would be easy to think George's cousin had seen something that wasn't real in the heat of battle. But that other man's brother had seen it too. Elspeth looked toward the table where the other pair of men had been sitting, but they were gone. Had they left?

She frowned, wishing she'd had the chance to talk to the brother. As it was, this was barely a story. That didn't mean she couldn't investigate further.

"Thank you." She smiled at George. "If you hear of anything else, I do hope you'll let me know. I'd love to record the story. I've been writing down many recollections from Culloden. I'll add this one."

The man inclined his head toward her. "That's well done of ye, miss."

Elspeth gave him a single nod, then returned her attention to her aunt. "Well, now I have something to research."

"So it would seem. What a fantastical tale." Aunt Leah blinked at her. "You still don't think it's real, do you?"

"No. The myth likely started with one person fabricating the tale." That was the way stories originated. Someone exaggerated or made something up outright, such as with the thirteen treasures or with King Arthur, who was often tied to them. Arthur probably existed, or someone like him. Had he pulled a sword from a stone? That hardly seemed possible. Tracing those stories to a single source *was* impossible, especially after more than a thousand years since Arthur had purportedly lived in the sixth century.

Aunt Leah picked up her cup. "Can you find that person? That seems unlikely." She sipped her tea.

"It is, but since the event happened recently, I may get lucky." She waggled her brows at Aunt Leah, who laughed softly.

"If anyone can find the source, it's you."

Unless it really was multiple sources. So far, two different parties had attested to the same rumor. The story either came from that single source exaggerating or outright fabricating the sword, or those multiple parties really had seen a flaming sword. Or something that *looked* like a flaming sword. What could that be?

Elspeth's mind worked as they finished their tea. She nearly forgot about Mr. Williams.

No, that wasn't true. She'd just latched on to the distraction that kept her from thinking about him.

"Are you ready to go upstairs?" Aunt Leah asked.

"Yes." Elspeth wasn't really, but perhaps she'd steal back down later after Aunt Leah fell asleep. As she rose, hat and gloves in hand, she looked toward Mr. Williams. His gaze met hers, and for a moment, she felt an invisible connection stretch between them. The light of recognition was still absent in his expression, but there was something else. Briefly, she wondered if she'd been wrong, that he wasn't really Williams. But no, she wasn't wrong—she'd never forget his eyes.

What she wanted to know was if he truly didn't recognize her or he was pretending not to. That was the mystery—one she planned to solve.

Chapter Two

TAVISH CRAWFORD EYED the pair of English soldiers who remained in the common room. He'd been waiting for the right moment to approach them. After watching them drink an excessive amount of ale over the past few hours, the time was near.

The innkeeper's red-haired daughter, Carrie, as she'd introduced herself hours earlier, bustled to his table. "Finished?"

"I am, thank you. The stew was delicious." Tavish gestured to his empty tankard. "Another ale, if you please."

"Finally. Ye're the slowest drinker in the entire inn. Can't believe it given yer size." She eyed him with stark interest. "Ye talk like ye're a lord or summat. Are ye?"

Tavish gave her a bland smile. He was many things. "I'm just John MacLean, I'm afraid." Tonight. He couldn't help but think of Elspeth Marshall and how he was someone else to her. He'd seen the confusion and then anger in her expression when he'd failed to acknowledge her.

But he couldn't. Besides, she was better off not knowing him—as Roy Williams, John MacLean, or Tavish Crawford.

"Where are ye from?" Carrie asked as she scooped up his trencher and empty mug. "Not the Highlands."

"Near Glasgow."

"It's not England, but it'd be an improvement," she said with a sigh. "I'll fetch ye another ale." Then she turned and swept back toward the kitchen.

As she passed the soldiers, they asked for more ale. It was time.

Tavish stood and made his way to their table. "'Evening. I hope you don't mind that I stepped in earlier. I probably should have let you pummel them." He shook his head with faux regret. "There's no place for talk of Culloden unless it's to remind them how badly they lost." Tavish softened his brogue so that he almost sounded English.

"Damn right," the captain who'd made the earlier threat said with a sharp nod. His small dark eyes surveyed Tavish. "Did you fight?"

"I'm not a soldier." Not officially. "What brings you men to the middle of nowhere?"

"On our way home on leave," the captain responded. "I'm Fowler. This is Sergeant Boyd."

"Not sure we'll make it home for Christmas, but we're going to try our damnedest," Boyd said as Carrie delivered their ale. "We're fortunate to be able to go home since you heathens don't even celebrate the season." He snorted.

Fowler nodded in agreement. "We'll make it. Unless we find any fugitives."

"You're on the hunt for Jacobites?" Tavish asked casually before taking a sip of ale.

Boyd spat on the floor. "Bloody criminals. We'll catch every last one and see 'em hang."

"Or in jail," Fowler said with more restraint. But then his lip curled and a feral gleam blistered his gaze.

Tavish tensed. He hoped they could leave tomorrow. He didn't need them hanging about, not when he was also on the hunt for

Jacobites. But for a wholly different purpose. He didn't think there was anyone in Calvine who needed his help, but he was ever mindful and would offer assistance where it was wanted.

"You're looking for someone in particular, then?" Tavish asked.

Fowler nodded. "Several someones. Know anyone named McCloud or Williams? Those are the two I'd most like to find. McCloud's a skinny fellow with black hair and a jagged scar across his brow. Williams is larger—about your size, I'd say—with long hair and a thick beard."

"Can't say I do," Tavish lied. "But I'll keep an ear out." McCloud was a friend and currently in hiding. His injuries had been extensive. Tavish had recovered more quickly—after shaving his beard and lopping his hair off. He was, most likely, the Williams they wanted.

"There you are."

The feminine voice drew all three men to turn their heads. Standing next to the table, her dusky green eyes flashing with ire, was Elspeth Marshall.

She'd wound her red-blonde hair atop her head, save a few wispy curls that grazed her cheeks. She wore a dark green gown that laced across the front of her bodice beneath a square neckline. Putting one hand on her slender waist, she fixed her angry stare on Tavish.

He swallowed. "I'm sorry, I don't think we've met." This could go very, very badly.

Her lips parted. "You really don't remember me?"

Tavish allowed a lazy smile as he glanced toward the soldiers. "I think I would. Ergo, you must be mistaken. No matter, I'm delighted to meet you now." Before he could say his name and show her it *wasn't* Williams, she spoke.

"Oh, I know you already, Mr. Williams. And you know me. What I'd like to know is why—"

Tavish couldn't let her continue. "My name is not Williams. You are mistaken, miss." He hardened his gaze and prayed she would go.

"Williams?" Fowler asked, his eyes focusing—and narrowing—on Tavish.

"As I said, I'm MacLean." Tavish looked directly at Miss Marshall. "John MacLean. Now, if you'll excuse us, miss, we are drinking ale and discussing things that don't involve a young lady such as yourself." He turned his attention to his tablemates even as he heard her sharp intake of breath.

Miss Marshall didn't immediately leave. Tavish felt her presence and her outrage like a stiff, cold wind. Still, he refused to be buffeted.

With a small sound of indignation, she spun on her heel and left. Inwardly, Tavish winced. Outwardly, he lifted his ale and muttered, "Good riddance."

Fowler scrutinized him across the table. "You really aren't Williams?"

"A Jacobite?" Tavish snorted in disdain. "No. But I'd be happy to help you find him. He ought to be strung up with the rest of the traitors."

"Hear, hear!" Boyd banged his tankard on the table before taking a long drink.

Fowler hesitated, but eventually did the same. Then he leaned back in his chair, still holding the mug. "Good, because I'm not in the mood for a fight tonight. I just want to get home to my family. Is that too much to ask?" He sounded weary. Tavish could understand that. They all wanted comfort after the nightmare of Culloden.

"Amen to that," Tavish said.

"What do you make of that silly story about a flaming sword?" Boyd sniggered. "These bloody Highlanders will believe anything."

Today wasn't the first time Tavish had heard rumors about the sword. He knew they weren't rumors, of course. The sword had been used at Culloden, and he needed to find it. While he was always looking for Jacobite survivors of Culloden, his primary concern at the moment was locating Lann Dhearg before it fell into the wrong hands. And if it already had, well, he'd have to get it back.

"They particularly appreciate legend and fantasy," Tavish said derisively.

Fowler pressed his lips together. "I've heard about this fiery sword before. For a fallacy, it is remarkably persistent."

Boyd let out a snort. "That doesn't make it true. I didn't see anything of the sort that day. Can you imagine it, though? A sword that burst into flame. That would be very useful in the dark." He laughed before taking another drink.

"Seems like I've heard the rumor too," Tavish mused. "Can't remember where exactly." He pretended to think and hoped one of the other men would play along.

"The first time I heard about it was just outside Inverness," Fowler said. "A month or so after Culloden."

Tavish looked at the captain over the rim of his tankard. "You've heard the tale multiple times?"

"Indeed. I've heard its flames took out a dozen men, that it's a broadsword, and that the man wielding it was seven feet tall." His tone was droll.

Tavish smiled into his ale before taking a drink. He was tall, but not that tall…

"Nonsense, but at least it's entertaining!" Boyd set his mug onto the table with a thud. "I need to take a piss." He stood and left the common room, going out the front door.

Fowler glanced toward the stairs in the corner. "Too bad you didn't really know that pretty thing. But then if you did, I'd have to take you into custody." The edge of his mouth ticked up in an arrogant half smile.

"*If* I were Williams, I wouldn't be sitting here with you. And I sure as hell wouldn't allow you to take me anywhere." Tavish let a brief moment pass before he let out a low, dark laugh, which Fowler joined.

"We'll find him," Fowler said with great confidence. "One by one, we're rounding them all up. They can't hide forever."

"You'll be back up here, then—after your holiday?"

Nodding, Fowler took another drink. "Right after Epiphany."

Tavish wondered if all the soldiers scouting for Jacobite stragglers were doing the same. Not that it mattered overmuch—those who'd fought or supported the Jacobites mustn't let down their guard.

Fowler's dark brows drew together as he cast a look at the front door. "Hell, Boyd is taking a long time. The other night, he fell over when he went out to piss. I'd better go check on him."

"I think I'll turn in." Tavish stood along with the captain and bid him good night.

When he got to the stairs, he looked to make sure Fowler had left. When the front door was closed, Tavish walked upstairs. As soon as he hit the landing, a figure jumped out in front of him.

Hands on her hips, Elspeth Marshall glared at him, her eyes ablaze. "You're a lying blackguard." Then she drove her fist into his gut.

As Williams doubled over, Elspeth considered delivering another injury. He deserved at least that.

"I deserved that," he said, echoing her thoughts. His voice was muffled from his bent position.

"You saying that doesn't make you less guilty." It did steal a bit of her outrage, however.

He straightened and grasped her hand, dragging her along the narrow corridor to a door at the end. Opening it, she saw another flight of stairs.

She dug her feet into the floorboards. "Where are you taking me?"

"We can't stand here out in the open." He tossed a look toward the landing at the top of the stairs from the common room where she'd been waiting for him. His dark brows were drawn low over his eyes. "We can go to your room or mine, which is upstairs. Choose. And be quick."

"Mine." She turned across from the door he'd just opened and unlatched the one to her room. "Here."

She stepped inside and pulled her hand from his.

He closed the door firmly behind them and faced her. His cloak from earlier was gone, leaving him dressed in a rather drab suit of brown, not unlike the one he'd worn when they'd met. No, not drab. He was far too arresting—from his dark hair to his supple lips and square jaw to the way his muscular form filled out his clothing.

Elspeth stood in the middle of the small chamber and folded her arms over her chest. "I'm waiting."

Williams or MacLean or whatever his name was glanced about. "Where's your companion?"

A loud snore answered him. His eyes widened, and he looked to the left, where there was another door—which led to Aunt Leah's chamber.

"In the next room."

"That's not an animal?"

Elspeth pursed her lips so she wouldn't laugh. "My aunt snores." She stared at him expectantly.

He went to the hearth and crouched to stoke the fire, then added another piece of wood. "I had to lie. Those soldiers were looking for me."

Dropping her arms to her sides, Elspeth exhaled some of her ire. Most of it, really. "They found you."

He turned his head from the fire. "They're looking for a man called

Williams—a Jacobite. They don't particularly know what he looks like."

Shock replaced the remains of her anger. "You're a Jacobite?"

Setting the poker back on the hearth, he stood and faced her once more. "I believe in Scotland and in my family. I have cousins who are—*were*—Jacobites."

She moved to stand near the hearth. Not near him—she wanted the warmth of the fire. "You fought at Culloden?"

Stepping to the side, he gestured for her to take the spot in front of the fireplace. "I did. As Roy Williams."

"But now you go by John MacLean."

"Yes. However, my real name is Tavish Crawford." He gave her a lopsided smile that made her heart skip even as he pricked her outrage once more.

"You lied about who you were when we met?"

"It was necessary, I'm afraid. At the time, I was on my way to Inverness to meet with Jacobites." He didn't seem the least bit sorry. "I had to be Roy Williams."

"So Roy Williams is a Jacobite and a soldier. What is John MacLean?"

"A man who helps those in need. Particularly those wounded at Culloden."

She had trouble retaining her anger given his desire to help people. "A Jacobite sympathizer, then."

He lifted a shoulder. "I sympathize with those who have suffered and seek to provide aid where I can." He took a step toward her. "I apologize for lying downstairs and for my rude behavior toward you."

"I recognized you as soon as your hood fell away."

His blue gaze held hers. "I recognized you as soon as you walked into the common room."

The ripple of awareness or whatever it was that she'd felt downstairs when she'd looked at him returned with greater force. She was glad to know she hadn't imagined the connection she'd felt to him two years ago. And that it hadn't diminished. If anything, the attraction felt stronger.

Elspeth's breath caught. She'd given up on him. Well, she'd tried to, anyway. "You said you'd come back." Her words were barely above a whisper.

"I said I *hoped* to see you again. I was still hoping." The crooked smile returned, as did the answering trip of Elspeth's heart. "On this very trip, in fact."

"You planned to stop in Dunkeld?"

"I did."

Elspeth couldn't help but feel a rush of pleasure. Still, she was a trifle hurt. "Perhaps I am betrothed."

His gaze remained steady. "Since you said perhaps, I will take that to mean you are not."

She blew out a breath. "No, I am not. Angus Macintosh did ask me last year, however."

"You said no." Of course he knew she had, but the confidence with which he uttered the words gave her a slight pause.

"It was at the Lammas Fair. He wanted to handfast, as was common in the past." She rolled her eyes. "I was the third woman he'd asked."

Williams—no, MacLean—no, *Crawford* laughed.

She put her hands on her hips. "What am I to call you? I feel as though I don't know you at all." And really, she didn't. A few hours' acquaintance over two years ago barely signified, attraction or not.

"How about Tavish? Unless you see a British soldier, then I'd prefer you call me John."

"Mr. MacLean is probably more appropriate." She realized they were alone together in a room, which would draw raised eyebrows, if not plain outrage, from some.

"Whatever makes you most comfortable, Miss Marshall. I should be devastated if you remained angry with me. Am I forgiven for my behavior downstairs?"

"And for not visiting Dunkeld in the past two years?"

He bowed slightly. "And for that."

She looked him in the eye. "That depends. What do you know about this flaming sword that was seen at Culloden? Since you were there and you're the one who told me about Lann Dhearg in the first place, I must presume you know something."

"You're still writing stories?"

"Always."

"Then you must want to write this one. I wish I could help you." His tone held a touch of regret. "I didn't see it, but I have heard it mentioned several times before today."

"I was just in Inverness visiting my cousin and listened to a few stories of the battle, one of them from a firsthand account. No one mentioned the sword."

"As I said, I didn't see it, and no one I knew who was at Culloden mentioned it."

Elspeth paced to the small table where her stack of parchment sat. She'd dashed off the information she'd heard earlier in the common room. "I can't decide if it's one person's fiction—a fantasy in the midst of a horrid event—or if someone, or multiple someones, actually saw something they thought was a flaming sword. In the absence of a firsthand source, I have to think it's fiction."

"Either way, just seeing a flaming sword isn't much of a story, is it?"

She exhaled. "Not really. While I might use a superlative to tell a story, I try not to embellish what I've actually heard."

"So you won't position the sword as the turning point in the battle?" he asked wryly.

She smiled. "Not unless someone tells me that. I always write down my sources and whether they were firsthand."

"Do you get many of those?"

She shook her head. "Not until lately as I've begun traveling to collect stories." She'd accompanied Aunt Leah on trips to visit family and friends over the past year. "It's much different from writing down a legend or a myth that's been retold countlessly across time and space."

"I can imagine." He looked at her with a light in his eye. Was that admiration? "How wonderful to spend time talking with people and recording the history of our land through their eyes as they are living it."

Elspeth hadn't thought about it in that way, but she supposed that was what she was doing. "I find it fascinating, but I wasn't sure anyone else would."

He glanced toward the parchment on the table. "Miss Marshall, I wonder if you might allow me to read one of your stories."

"Oh." She hadn't expected that. No one asked to read her stories except her father and her aunt. Children and even some adults asked her to *tell* them, but no one asked to read them.

"Nearly all of them are at home in Dunkeld. I do have one that I finished in Inverness. It was told to me by a man who lives near my cousin. Her husband was at Culloden. He didn't fight. He was there to help care for anyone who was wounded."

"Is he a physician like your father?" Tavish—since he'd asked her to call him that, she would—knew from their first meeting that her father was a doctor and that her mother had died. At the time, it had been only six years since her mother had been gone. Elspeth's grief had lessened, but the sense of loss, especially at this time of year, was still keen. She, on the other hand, knew very little about him. She realized in retrospect that she'd done much more sharing during their time together in Dunkeld. Probably because he'd been hiding who he really was.

Elspeth returned her focus to their conversation and replied to his question. "No, he isn't, but he'd like to be. I think my father is going to help him get to the University of Edinburgh to study." She shuffled through the parchment and found the few pieces that held the story she'd recorded.

"Is that it?" Tavish asked, coming toward her from the hearth.

She held the papers in one hand up to her chest. "Yes. However, you'll have to trade me for it."

He stopped and arched a brow. "What do you want?"

"Information. You know I collect that, and I am especially interested in people I know—or those who have misrepresented themselves." She hardened her gaze at him for a moment. "I told you a great many things about myself when we met, while you revealed next to nothing, not even your true name."

"I've told you my name," he said slowly.

She shook her head. "Not good enough. I want more. I *require* more if you want to read my story." She lifted her shoulder and gave him a saucy look before setting the papers back on the table—facedown—and sitting in one of the pair of chairs.

"You drive a steep bargain, Miss Marshall."

"Is it so hard to reveal something about yourself?" She looked up at him expectantly.

Exhaling, he sat opposite her. "When you are going about clandestine activities such as supporting Jacobites, saving them, or hiding them, *yes*."

"Why do you do that?"

"That is where things become difficult." A fleeting smile dashed across his mouth, then his eyes narrowed as he frowned at the table. "My father was not a Jacobite. My mother's family was. She angered them when she married my father."

"The cousins are your mother's family?"

He nodded. "After my father died—that was fifteen years ago—I finally got to meet my mother's family. Without any siblings, I was rather thrilled to meet my cousins. We became close. That's why I supported them in their endeavors. It gave me a sense of belonging."

"Of family," she whispered. "I understand. I don't have any siblings either."

"Then of course you understand." He smiled at her. "Do I get my story now?"

She laughed softy. "Yes, but I do hope you'll tell me more about yourself. If not now, then…later." She handed him the papers.

He took them from her, his fingers grazing hers. "Does that mean you forgive me."

"It means I'm giving you another opportunity." She gave him a dark, direct stare. "Don't squander it."

"I won't. Not this time." He touched the papers to his chest. "Thank you." He rose and she did the same.

"I don't suppose we'll be leaving tomorrow," she said, glancing toward the window, not that she could see anything in the dark night outside. "The snow looked quite thick."

"I went out not too long ago, and you are correct. If you want to leave, you must do it on horseback or foot. I imagine you have a coach."

"Yes." She hesitated to say more, but ultimately said, "I can't say I'm disappointed for the extra day here. Unless you are on horseback?"

"I am. However, I think I'd rather stay too." He rattled the papers gently. "As it happens, I have reading to do." He grinned at her.

She walked with him to the door. "I will hope to see you at breakfast."

"Count on it. And I mean that most sincerely." His blue eyes gleamed with promise before she closed the door behind him.

Pressing her back to the wood, Elspeth took a deep breath to try to calm the racing of her heart. Morning couldn't come soon enough.

Chapter Three

TAVISH HAD ARISEN early. He wanted to make sure the soldiers left on horseback. Once they were gone, he breathed more easily. Now he could focus on finding Lann Dhearg.

To that end, he went in search of the innkeeper, Mr. Pitagowan, and found him behind the bar in the common room. It was still early, but his daughter was busy preparing the room for breakfast. The innkeeper perched on a stool, his bald pate gleaming as he brushed—brushed?—his full auburn beard.

"Good morning, Mr. Pitagowan," Tavish said cheerfully, trying not to fixate on the man's odd behavior. He supposed brushing a beard of that volume was a necessity—Tavish's hadn't been that…bushy—but he wondered if there might be a better place to conduct such matters.

"Ye must call me Balthazar," the innkeeper said as he set his brush beneath the bar. "How did you pass your night, MacLean?"

"Quite well, thank you." He'd devoured every word of Miss Marshall's story before seeking his rest. She was as gifted a storyteller in writing as she was in the spoken word, which he'd heard when they'd met. In fact, if not for her storytelling, he might not have stopped and made her acquaintance at all.

Tavish continued, "I hope you won't mind if I stay another night. I'd rather not travel in the snow."

Balthazar grunted. "Ye can stay as long as ye like. I'm happy ta take yer money."

Tavish chuckled. "I won't be staying indefinitely." He wanted to get home before the new year. It had been some time since he'd seen his grandmother. As Miss Marshall had pointed out, family was important.

Miss Marshall. If he found Lann Dhearg today, would he still leave tomorrow, knowing he could spend one more day in her company?

"Carrie said ye were from Glasgow. Is that right?"

That was close enough. "Yes." It was time to obtain the information he needed to track down Lann Dhearg, starting with the man whose brother had seen it at Culloden. "I wonder if you might tell me where I can find one of the men who was here yesterday. We chatted briefly, and I found him quite interesting. He left before we could continue our conversation. Shorter fellow with wide shoulders and brown hair? Perhaps twenty-five years or so?"

Balthazar stroked his impressive—and tidy—beard. "Ye must mean Dougal. Dougal Kerr. Lives in a cottage on the northeast edge of town."

"By himself?" Tavish liked to know what to expect.

"Now he does. His brother seems to have moved on." He shook his head sadly.

"I'm sorry to hear that," Tavish said.

Balthazar's gaze moved past him toward the stairs. He jumped off the stool. "Time for breakfast!" He bustled back toward the kitchen.

Tavish turned to see Miss Marshall step into the common room. Gowned in a blue wool dress, she looked fresh and lovely. She surveyed the surroundings until her gaze found him. Her heart-shaped face lit as a smile pushed at her pink lips.

She was not alone. A more petite woman with dark hair stood at her side. That must be her aunt.

Tavish left the bar and went toward them. "Good morning, ladies."

"Good morning, Mr. MacLean," Miss Marshall said smoothly. Tavish inclined his head slightly in appreciation that she went along with his alias. She flicked a glance toward the woman at her side. "Aunt Leah, this is Mr. MacLean, whom I told you about. Mr. MacLean, this is my aunt, Leah Craig."

Tavish took her hand and bowed. "I'm pleased to make your acquaintance, Mrs. Craig."

"Oh, he is as charming as you said, dear." Mrs. Craig gave her niece an approving wink.

Carrie had arrived and was now staring at Tavish with something that might have been desire. "Very charming," she murmured.

Miss Marshall, her aunt, and Tavish all looked at the serving maid.

"Do ye want breakfast?" she asked.

"We do," Miss Marshall answered.

"Take a seat, then." Carrie waved toward the tables.

"Shall we sit near the fire?" Tavish asked. "The dogs are not about."

"That would be lovely," Aunt Leah said.

Tavish offered his arms to both ladies and then guided them to the table. He held a chair for Miss Marshall's aunt first and then Miss Marshall.

"It looks like we're going to be here another day," Mrs. Craig said. "What about you, Mr. MacLean?"

"The same, but I can't say I mind." He smiled at Miss Marshall, whose cheeks tinged pink. "I enjoyed your story about Culloden very much." He wanted to say more, that her descriptions had evoked his memory of the day in a visceral way. Hopefully, he would have a chance to tell her so later. Reading it had made him want to tell her his story of the day. Perhaps someday he would.

Mrs. Craig looked between them. "You read Elspeth's story?"

"I gave it to him last night," Miss Marshall explained. "We encountered each other on the landing and spoke for a while." Which was the truth. At least part of it.

It wasn't as if they had something to hide. Yes, he'd gone into her chamber, but nothing untoward had happened. That didn't mean he hadn't considered it. Standing with her in the small quarters, the firelight making the reddish strands in her blonde hair glow and her spicy floral scent taunting his senses, he'd almost been moved to kiss her. Indeed, he'd had to talk himself out of it.

Carrie arrived at their table with a tray of food. She placed trenchers of kippers, fried eggs, and oatcakes in front of each of them. Then she deposited a crock of raspberry jam in the center of the table. "Fer yer oatcakes," she said. "I'll bring ye some ale."

"And tea, please," Mrs. Craig requested.

Nodding in response, Carrie took her leave.

"The jam looks delicious." Miss Marshall reached for the pot just as Tavish did the same, intending to move it closer to her. Their fingers touched, prompting their gazes to connect.

A frisson of longing swept through him along with a jolt of electricity. She was the first to look away, and she withdrew her hand.

Tavish picked up the crock and set it near her trencher. "My grandmother adores raspberry jam. She has a recipe for it that she refuses to share."

"That's too bad," Miss Marshall said as she dolloped some of the bright red jam on one of her oatcakes. "If she changes her mind, you must let me know."

"You make jam?"

"I've helped our cook, Mrs. Fisher, on occasion. However, I think I'd prefer to collect recipes and stories about them and combine them into a book." Her eyes twinkled with enthusiasm.

"What a wonderful idea," Mrs. Craig said. "Have you started this project?"

"No. I thought of it recently, and Mr. MacLean's mention of his grandmother's recipe has reminded me. Perhaps I will pursue it."

Tavish thought it a brilliant idea. "I hope you do. You've a gift with words. While the recipes will be helpful, the stories behind them will make the book a treasure."

Mrs. Craig cast a loving look at her niece. "Our Elspeth can do anything she puts her mind to."

Tavish didn't doubt that. Though he had only known her briefly, she had a sense of purpose and an inner strength that were impossible to miss. He recognized those things because he possessed them himself. "And what is it you put your mind to, Miss Marshall?" He took a bite of the smoked kippers.

"Hearing stories and writing them down, mostly."

"Her father and I wish she would set her mind on marriage." Mrs. Craig laughed softly as she helped herself to the jam.

Carrie arrived with the tea and ale and arranged the various items atop the table. "Did I not tell ye the jam was excellent?"

"It is delicious," Miss Marshall said.

With a satisfied smile, Carrie winked at Tavish before turning and departing.

Though Carrie's arrival had interrupted their conversation, Tavish hadn't lost the thread. Miss Marshall's family wished for her to wed. He could understand that—his grandmother wanted him to do the same.

Mrs. Craig looked toward him with interest. "Do you have a profession, Mr. MacLean?"

Tavish chose his words carefully. "Farming, mostly." That was true. He glanced toward Miss Marshall, who was watching him intently. She, of course, knew of his other activities. At least some of them. He should tell her the full truth. Later, he would. He was apparently counting rather heavily on spending time with her today.

They continued to eat and share pleasant conversation, all while Tavish kept stealing looks at Miss Marshall. On occasion, he caught her doing the same, until he felt as if the energy between them was perhaps visible to everyone else who'd entered the common room. Let alone Mrs. Craig, who must surely be aware of whatever was simmering between them.

"Elspeth is hoping to track down a story today," Mrs. Craig said. "I suppose it's fortuitous that we must stay here."

"It is indeed," Miss Marshall said with a grin. She had to mean Lann Dhearg. Of course she would try to find more information—she'd indicated as much last night.

Tavish considered what he should tell her. If he told her the truth about who he was, he ought to include all of it. But would her need to tell the story be too powerful to resist? He didn't yet know her well enough to say, and the answer was crucially important. This was not a story she could reveal.

"I wonder if we might dine together tonight?" Mrs. Craig asked. "Elspeth can share what she learns today."

"I look forward to that." Tavish suddenly itched to leave. It wasn't just that he was eager to question Kerr, but that he was afraid Mrs. Craig would next ask him what he planned to do today. He was getting the sense that she *was* noticing the…connection between him and Miss Marshall and hoped to encourage it.

"Excellent," Mrs. Craig said.

Tavish decided it was time to depart. "And now, if you'll excuse me, I must check on my horse."

"Of course," Miss Marshall said. "We'll see you later." She gave him a look that said something a bit different, something that didn't include the pronoun "we."

Tavish stood and bowed to them, his gaze lingering on Miss Marshall. With more reluctance than he cared to recognize, he turned and left the inn.

ELSPETH WATCHED TAVISH leave the common room. Cold air drifted from the door, sending a slight chill up her spine as she finished the last of her tea. She wished she could have accompanied him.

"I'm so pleased you found Mr. Will—MacLean again." Aunt Leah sent her an apologetic grimace.

That morning, when Elspeth had told Aunt Leah about meeting Tavish for breakfast, she'd explained his aliases. Actually, she hadn't given her his real name. That seemed as though it would confuse an already complicated situation. "I am too." She lowered her voice and leaned closer to her aunt. "And thank you for understanding about his names."

"Of course," she whispered in response. "He sounds like such a kindhearted man—a farmer who helps people in need after that horrid battle. Don't you think so?"

"That he's kindhearted? Yes, he seems to be." Elspeth wasn't entirely certain. She barely knew the man. But she wanted to. Hopefully, she'd get the chance. She glanced longingly toward the door, again wishing she'd been able to go with him to the stable. Perhaps she could "check" on their coach and horses. After all, their coachman had family in town and was visiting with them. Aunt Leah had already said she would have one of the inn's grooms take a message to him to let him know they'd be staying another day.

But Elspeth had something else to focus on—chasing her story. Turning her head, she looked for the innkeeper's daughter but didn't see her in the common room.

"What's the matter, dear?" Aunt Leah asked.

"Nothing's the matter. I want to speak with Carrie."

"About your story, of course. I'll go speak with Balthazar about having a groom deliver a message to Fisk." Aunt Leah stood. "I'm sure he'll be delighted to have another day with his mother."

"Indeed he will," Elspeth said with a smile.

Elspeth rose, intending to look for Carrie. She and Aunt Leah walked toward the bar as Carrie appeared from the kitchen with a plate of food. After she deposited it on a table, she walked back toward the kitchen.

"Carrie, is your father busy? My aunt would like to make a request."

"He's in the kitchen." Carrie wiped her hand on her apron and looked to Aunt Leah. "Can I help?"

Aunt Leah explained what she needed, and Carrie said she'd see it was taken care of. Satisfied, Aunt Leah left to go upstairs.

Before Carrie could return to the kitchen, Elspeth stopped her. "May I ask you a question?"

Carrie stuck her hip out and rested her fist against it. "All right."

"I'm looking for a gentleman who was here yesterday. He left just after the commotion with the English soldiers."

"Ye mean Dougal Kerr. He doesna like the English. Canna say I blame him." She stepped closer so that Elspeth could see Carrie's freckles in great detail. "His brother fought at Culloden." The serving maid looked away. "Forget I said that, please. It's not something to be known—who fought there."

"I wouldn't blame him for not liking the English either," Elspeth said softly.

Carrie eyed Elspeth cautiously. "Why de ye want ta speak with Dougal?"

"He mentioned something yesterday that I want to ask him about. I record stories, and he said something intriguing." Her breath caught as she waited to see if Carrie would help her find the man.

"He may not want ta talk ta ye, but ye can try. He lives on the northeast corner of town—small cottage that needs some repair on the roof. Ye'll know what I mean."

Relief flooded Elspeth along with anticipation. "Thank you, Carrie. I appreciate this so much."

Elspeth rushed upstairs to tell Aunt Leah where she was going and hoped her aunt wouldn't want to come along. She was relieved when her aunt said she preferred to remain at the inn. As Elspeth donned her cloak and gloves, she hoped she might find a way to encounter Tavish when she returned.

Outside, the sun peeked through the clouds. Elspeth's boots squished in the melting snow, and she felt a flash of disappointment. She would have no quarrel being trapped at an inn with Tavish for longer—then she'd be assured of getting to know him better.

Looking on the bright side, Elspeth was glad for the dry weather in which to walk through the small village to find Mr. Kerr's cottage. There wasn't much to Calvine, but it was a busy stop on the road between Perth and Inverness.

Carrie had been right—Elspeth had no trouble determining which cottage belonged to Mr. Kerr. Feeling optimistic, she walked to his door and knocked.

A moment later, the man she'd seen yesterday answered, his dark eyes blinking in surprise. "Ye're from the inn," he blurted.

"I am, yes." She smiled warmly. "I'm Miss Elspeth Marshall. I was hoping to speak with you about—" A movement behind the man caught Elspeth's eye and stole the words from her mouth.

Tavish was here?

"Come in," Mr. Kerr invited as he pulled the door open wider and stepped back.

"I see you already have a guest," she said, staring at Tavish. What was he doing here?

Tavish stood at the table where he'd just risen. He watched her intently but said nothing.

"This is Mr. MacLean," Mr. Kerr said. "He also came from the inn. I have to wonder if ye've both come for the same reason."

Elspeth wondered the same thing. She also wondered why Tavish hadn't mentioned his intentions. He knew she wanted to learn more about the sword. Narrowing her eyes at him, she said, "I don't know. Why are you here, Mr. MacLean?"

Tavish swallowed, but he didn't look away from her. "I came to ask about Mr. Kerr's brother, whom he mentioned yesterday."

Had he come in search of the brother? Guilt washed over her.

"And about the flaming sword," Mr. Kerr added, looking from Tavish to Elspeth.

The guilt vanished beneath a stinging wave of disappointment. Elspeth pressed her lips together before focusing on Mr. Kerr. "I came to ask about the sword. I write down oral stories that are told to me. I've heard a few about Culloden, and this sounded like one that should be recorded."

Why did Tavish want to know about it? She looked at him and silently asked the question as if he could hear her and answer.

His lips parted briefly, but he said nothing. His eyes said plenty, however—he looked like a man caught in a lie. One who was sorry for it, which, on its own, did nothing to soothe her ire. No, she wasn't angry. She was hurt. And she shouldn't be. They were hardly more than acquaintances. Furthermore, he'd already demonstrated his penchant for half-truths or outright deception.

"Would ye like to sit with us?" Mr. Kerr asked. "I'll tell ye what I was just saying to Mr. MacLean." He flicked a glance toward Tavish, who nodded slightly. Was he asking Tavish for permission?

Elspeth wanted to know what was going on here. She also wanted to hear about the sword. "Yes, thank you."

It appeared Mr. Kerr and Tavish had been seated across from each other, which meant she had to take one of the other sides of the square table and sit next to Tavish.

Pursing her lips, Elspeth moved to one of the chairs. Tavish rushed to hold it for her. "It's a pleasure to see you, Miss Marshall."

"Ye ken each other?" Mr. Kerr asked, sounding relieved.

"We met briefly at the inn," Elspeth said tightly.

"She is someone you can trust," Tavish said, and finally Elspeth understood Mr. Kerr's anxiety as well as the unspoken communication between the two men. "Like me." It appeared Tavish had already persuaded Mr. Kerr he was trustworthy. Well, Elspeth wasn't convinced.

Mr. Kerr nodded at Tavish, then offered to take her cloak. After undoing the clasp, Elspeth handed the garment to him, and he went to hang it on a hook near the door.

While he was completing the task, Tavish bent his head toward hers. "I'm sorry I didn't tell you I was coming here."

"Later," she whispered before giving him a dark stare. "And you will tell me *everything*."

He held her chair as she sat. Her back brushed against his fingers, and she bristled.

Tavish withdrew his hands and retook his chair. He did not look in her direction. He did, however, take a drink of ale, his body completely relaxed as if nothing was amiss. Why did he have to look so calm and collected? His dark hair was pulled back today in a neat queue, and he wore a burgundy waistcoat that made the brown of his coat far less drab. In fact, she almost thought it was a different garment altogether.

She jerked her gaze away lest he catch her studying him.

Mr. Kerr returned to the table. "Would ye care for ale, Miss Marshall?"

"Yes, thank you."

Their host went to the small kitchen area and, a moment later, returned with a small cup of ale. "I get it from Balthazar at the inn, so ye may recognize it." He took his chair and glanced between them. "It's a bit odd that ye both came here today."

"Your story is a bit odd," Elspeth said. "I would be more surprised if no one questioned you further about what was said yesterday regarding your brother." She took a sip of the ale.

Kerr ran a hand through his dark hair, tousling the strands atop his head. His face creased with worry. "Ye really just want to know about the sword?" Mr. Kerr asked her, his tone dubious.

"Yes, nothing more. I only want to hear the story as your brother told it to you—if that's acceptable to you. If not, I will take my leave and understand completely." She tipped her head toward Tavish. "Mr. MacLean desires other information?"

"I wish to help his brother," Tavish said. He had said he helped other soldiers from Culloden. Was that actually true?

Mr. Kerr angled himself to face Elspeth. "I was just explaining to Mr. MacLean that my brother, Neil, came home from Culloden and told me the story about seeing the flaming sword. He said those that saw it stopped fighting. The man who was wielding it fell, and the flame stopped."

"Was the man killed?" Elspeth asked.

"I asked Neil the same thing, but he didna ken. He was wounded a few minutes later and barely dragged himself from the battlefield. Someone cared for him afterward, and he managed to find his way here a few weeks later."

"Where is he now?" Tavish asked.

"Right, that is what we were getting to when Miss Marshall arrived." Mr. Kerr sent a quick glance in her direction. His brow was still furrowed. Elspeth could sense his agitation.

"You can trust me, Mr. Kerr. I am not going to share your brother's location with anyone." Tavish put his hand on the table, his palm flat. "As I said earlier, that is not my intent either. I'd like to help your brother if I can. I've helped other Jacobites from Culloden."

"How?" Mr. Kerr asked what Elspeth wanted to know too.

"I hide them—sometimes far away. We change their names and sometimes their appearances, as much as we can."

Mr. Kerr looked at Tavish intently. "How far away?"

"I've helped several sail to the American colonies."

How had he done that? Had they signed a contract to work for a number of years in exchange for the transport?

Mr. Kerr's eyes widened. "Do they sign indentures?"

"No." The single word carried a weight that snaked up Elspeth's spine.

"I've considered doing that," Mr. Kerr admitted before taking a drink of ale.

Elspeth's chest ached. She supposed it was an opportunity for some who were looking to change their fortune.

"How do ye help them get ta America, then?" Mr. Kerr asked.

"I have...contacts," Tavish answered rather enigmatically. Elspeth added that question to the several bouncing around in her head that she intended to ask him when they left. "Do you know where your brother is? I could help him."

Mr. Kerr cupped his hands around his ale and looked down. "I dinna ken. He was here with me for a fortnight, until he felt strong enough to leave. Soldiers were looking for those who had fought. He didna want ta be caught here with me." Mr. Kerr lifted his gaze, and it was filled with stark pain. "I didna fight, because I was a coward. My brother is younger, taller, stronger. I have no skills useful in battle. Still, I should have gone." His head dropped as he fixed on the table once more.

Elspeth reached over and touched his forearm. "Not everyone is a soldier."

"No, but I could have done something else. I could have helped tend ta the wounded, perhaps."

"Miss Marshall is right," Tavish said quietly. "Not everyone can—or should—be a soldier. Do you have any idea where your brother might have gone? Family, a friend, something else?"

Mr. Kerr lifted his gaze. "Ye really do just want to help him? Ye aren't an English soldier in disguise?"

"I am not," Tavish assured him.

"I heard ye were talking to those soldiers last night," Mr. Kerr said, his gaze narrowing.

Tavish didn't look at all bothered by Mr. Kerr's doubt. "I was, but only to ascertain their movements. They are on leave and going back to England. They were not looking for difficulty—or lost Jacobites." He leaned slightly forward. "I promise you can trust me, Mr. Kerr. I was at Culloden too. I have the scars to prove it."

He did? Elspeth turned her head to stare at him, wondering—rather inappropriately—where those scars were.

"Ye seem like a kind man, Mr. MacLean."

"I try to be, Mr. Kerr. If you can think of anything that might help me find your brother, it would be my honor to see him safe. He can come with me to Glasgow. I've had success finding work for a few men there."

"We dinna have any other family, and our friends are here. I think I'd ken if he were in Calvine."

Tavish smiled with understanding. "Probably. It's a rather small village. I'll be at the inn for at least one more night should you think of something." He looked toward Elspeth and almost imperceptibly inclined his head toward the door.

Elspeth took another drink of ale. "Thank you for your hospitality, Mr. Kerr. If I do write about the flaming sword, I'll be sure to keep your and your brother's name out of the story."

"I'd appreciate that, miss, thank ye." Mr. Kerr got to his feet.

Tavish stood and offered her his hand. Elspeth ignored his gesture and rose unaided. She smiled warmly at Mr. Kerr, who went to fetch her cloak. She walked to the door, where he draped it about her shoulders.

Elspeth fastened the clasp at her throat, then walked outside. She did not wait for Tavish, but strode to the lane, where she turned toward the inn.

Tavish caught up to her on her left. "I'm sorry I didn't tell you I was coming here."

"You already said that. You really came here because you thought you could help Mr. Kerr's brother?"

"I did."

She kept walking, her pace increasing. "Except Mr. Kerr exposed your other purpose—the sword." She stopped abruptly and turned to glare at him. "You know I wanted to learn more about the sword."

"Yes." His tone was annoyingly calm. "I would have shared what I learned with you."

Elspeth looked up into his eyes. "Would you? I would like to believe that, but so far, you've given me little reason to trust you. Change my mind, or our acquaintance ends right now."

Chapter Four

MISS MARSHALL'S DARK green eyes gleamed with indignation. Tavish was captivated.

"You're quite beautiful when you're angry."

Her lips parted, and Tavish fell even more under her spell. Then she grunted and turned.

He clasped her arm and shook himself out of his idiocy. "My apologies. I'm not at all used to feeling…drawn to someone." He didn't know how else to describe it. No one had ever gotten under his skin the way Miss Marshall had.

"Will you let me explain?"

She pulled her arm from his grasp and pivoted to face him once more. "I told you to change my mind. Do it quickly."

"The flaming sword—Lann Dhearg—is a dark tool. There's a reason it was hidden while its twin, Dryrnwyn, was not. Dyrnwyn flames for the worthy. Lann Dhearg feeds on fear and strife. Anyone can wield it in the presence of hatred, of darkness, of despair."

Her eyes narrowed slightly. "How do you know all this?"

He exhaled. It was time—past time—to tell her the truth. "Because it belongs to me."

She gasped, her eyes widening.

He offered her his arm. "Let us walk, please."

She curled her hand around his sleeve, and they made their way along the slushy ground. The snow had melted somewhat, but the clouds had also thickened once more, indicating it might snow again.

"It belongs to *you*?"

"I should probably tell you the one name I haven't yet revealed." He tensed. "I am the Lord Strathclyde."

She stopped once more and tried to take her hand from his arm, but he covered it with his and held her fast. "Strathclyde?!"

"Stay with me, please." He kept walking, pulling her along with him. "Yes, Strathclyde. And to answer what you surely must be thinking, yes, I'm a descendant of Rhydderch Hael. More importantly, I'm a direct descendant of his younger brother, Constantine. Lann Dhearg was his sword. Once he learned how dangerous it could be, that it would flame for anyone and grow even more powerful through hatred and anger, he hid it away. Our family has done so for centuries."

"That's why no one has heard of it," she breathed.

He could hear the fascination in her tone, the curiosity. "And why no one ever will. I foolishly took the damn thing to Culloden."

"Why would you do that?" The disappointment in her voice matched his own. No, nothing could do that. He was positively livid with himself.

"Because I thought I could control it. I don't feel angry or afraid when I hold it—because I am supposed to wield it."

"You are?"

"Anyone from my line—my father, my son."

This time, she took her hand from his arm so quickly, he wasn't able to keep hold of her. "You have a son?" She turned and glared up at him.

"No! I meant a future son. I have told you everything—I have no children, no wife, no family at all, save my grandmother."

She eyed him skeptically. "Why should I believe you?"

"Because I won't lie to you ever again. About anything."

She pulled her gaze from his and stared off to the right, her jaw working. He could practically see the anguish in her brain and loathed himself for it. Just as he'd stupidly thought Lann Dhearg would make him invincible in battle, he somehow believed he could keep her from knowing about it. About the sword or about his idiocy?

She glanced toward him. "I don't know if I should trust you. You deceived me—on more than one occasion. On *every* occasion."

"Never again." He took her hand. "I swear it."

"You're a bloody lord. You should have honor to spare."

Her words stung, as they should. "I try to. I'm afraid I allowed my mistake and the ensuing humiliation I feel because of it to drive my actions." He took a deep breath as he tried to think of how to say what else needed to be said. "I was also concerned about sharing the details with someone like you."

"What does that mean, someone like me?"

"A born storyteller. You want to share the story of Lann Dhearg—it's a completely unknown legend."

"It isn't a legend, apparently," she said with disdain. "It's history."

"For my family, but not for everyone else." He frowned. "This is why I didn't tell you. You want to share the story."

"Then why tell me—and David—about Lann Dhearg at all two years ago?"

"Because I was smitten." Afterward, he'd berated himself for revealing his family's secret legacy. "I shouldn't have shared it, but I was trying to impress you."

She blew out a breath and looked away for a moment before pinning him with an earnest stare. "Yes, I want to tell the story. It proves

Dyrnwyn—and perhaps the rest of the Thirteen Treasures of Britain—are real."

"And then countless numbers will search for it just as they do for Dyrnwyn and the rest of the treasures. As they do for Excalibur. Or the holy grail." He stepped toward her so that they were close enough to…kiss. "Do you know the lengths men will go to in order to find and own such objects? There is a secret organization full of dangerous men who spend their lives trying to hunt them down." He stared at her. "Let me ask you something, and please be as honest as possible—I won't think less of you." Certainly no less than he thought of his own behavior. "Do you want to tell the story because you think it's important for people to know, or because it will gain you notoriety for learning it?"

Her eyes widened slightly and her brows rose. She looked away from him, pulling her cloak more tightly around herself as the wind picked up.

"We should get back to the inn," he said softly.

She nodded and took his arm once more, which gave him comfort—and hope.

At length, she said, "You're right. I want to tell the story because it would be the greatest story of our generation. Perhaps the century."

"I'm not right. I didn't know the answer. That's why I asked. I should have asked sooner."

She looked at him askance. "Is there really a secret organization that searches for the treasures?"

"Yes. And they're dangerous." He met her gaze. "I promised I wouldn't lie—that's the truth as I know it. My uncle liked to tell tales about our family. It got him killed, or so my father told me when I was young." How he missed his father, lost to illness more than a decade past.

Miss Marshall sucked in a breath and squeezed his arm. "I'm so sorry. I believe you. About all of it. And I…understand why you didn't tell me." Her brow furrowed, then she pushed her shoulders back and her face smoothed. "You can trust me to keep your family's secret. I promise. We are in league together now, my lord."

He stopped and faced her. "Please don't. I'm still Tavish—to you."

"Will you tell me something else?"

"Anything."

"How do you really help these Jacobites?"

He hesitated and saw her reaction—a darkening of her eyes and stiffening of her hand on his arm. "The only reason I'm reluctant to tell you—and I realize the same is true of Lann Dhearg and who I really am—is because the more you know, the more danger that knowledge presents for you. If an English soldier thought you could help him find Jacobite soldiers, he might go to any length to get that information out of you."

She lifted her free hand to her mouth. "That's—" She didn't finish her thought. Instead, she lifted her chin. "I would still like to know, but I'll understand if you don't tell me in order to keep these men safe."

"That is my primary concern." He gave her a slight smile. "If I tell you, I'll just have to keep you close."

The darkness in her gaze shifted, heating as she edged closer to him. "Like this?"

"Perhaps a trifle closer." He put his free hand on her waist.

"Don't tell me," she breathed as she put her hand on his chest. "I would hate to be the cause of putting someone in danger. Especially after all you've done to help them." She pushed her hand up and cupped the side of his neck.

"Someday, I will," he whispered just before he put his lips on hers.

He took his arm from beneath her hand and clasped her back, drawing her against him. She tipped her head back as he plundered her mouth. With every brush of her lips and sweep of her tongue, he recalled the kisses they'd shared in Dunkeld, kisses that had owned his dreams these past two years.

After several long moments, they parted. His heart beat a rapid pace. Her lips were kiss reddened, her pupils dilated.

"You are a sorcerer, I think," she whispered. "Are you sure you aren't descended from Merlin?"

He chuckled. "I am sure." Then he stroked his thumb along her cheek. "I really am sorry."

A snowflake fell and landed on her nose. He licked it off, and she laughed. "We should get back to the inn."

He didn't disagree, but he had a goal to accomplish. "I need to find the sword."

"Oh! Of course. We didn't get to that part, did we? There were too many things to share."

"Particularly the kisses."

She blushed. Then she took a step back, and cold air swept between them. "What happened to you and the sword at Culloden?"

He offered her his arm once more. "I was wounded, and I lost consciousness. When I awoke, someone had dragged me from the battlefield. I went back the next day, but of course, Lann Dhearg was gone."

She put her hand on his sleeve, and they continued toward the inn. "You've been looking for it ever since."

He nodded. "In the wrong hands, it can cause incalculable destruction. The fire it can cause is particularly hard to extinguish. If someone with evil intent were to wield it, there's no telling what could happen."

"Is Neil Kerr the only person with a firsthand account?"

"As far as I've found. Everyone else who has heard of it was either lying about having seen it, or it's the same as the other men from the inn—someone they knew saw it." He wanted to make sure she understood his intent. "Let me be clear: I want to find Neil Kerr to keep him safe. If he can help me locate the sword, I will be grateful. But that is not a requirement for my assistance."

"I didn't think it was. I'm the one who demanded a trade." She grimaced.

"I thought you were flirting."

She laughed, a lovely sound that encircled his heart with warmth and joy. "I probably was. I don't have much experience with that, I'm afraid."

"Good."

She jerked her head to the side and blinked at him. "Jealous?"

"Maybe. When I accompany you to Dunkeld on the morrow—or the next day, if it snows too much tonight—I may want to find this cretin who wanted to handfast."

A sardonic smile lifted her lips. "Don't bother. He found a willing party. Their year was up in August, and neither wanted to continue. He decided to leave Dunkeld."

"How fortunate for him."

"What would you have done?"

He shrugged. "Just made sure he didn't bother you again."

"Oh, I quite took care of that." She gave him a confident smile.

He let out a loud laugh. "I would have liked to have seen that. And I am not the least surprised. I should have known you wouldn't need my protection."

"It's still nice to know you would have given it."

"Any time, Miss Marshall."

As they neared the inn, it seemed their gait slowed.

"You may call me Elspeth. And probably should if you plan to continue kissing me."

"Will you allow me to?"

"So long as you don't lie."

"I meant what I said." He bent his head and spoke next to her ear. "I look forward to more kisses." He felt the tremor that ran through her and smiled.

She exhaled. "They shall have to wait as I must go check on my aunt. I'll see you at dinner?"

"Yes. I think I may do a little exploring and see if I can learn anything about Neil Kerr. I do wonder if Dougal wasn't entirely truthful, not that I blame him. He is clearly worried for his brother, as he should be."

They walked into Balthazar's yard, and she took her hand from his arm. "You'll find him. I suspect you're exceptionally good at that."

He turned toward her, his body thrumming with desire. "I'm good at whatever I put my mind to, Elspeth. I hope you'll remember that."

Chapter Five

AFTER DROPPING HER gloves and cloak in her chamber, Elspeth knocked on the adjoining door to her aunt's room. She was still working on reining in the tumult of emotions and thoughts rioting in her brain.

"Come in!" Aunt Leah called. "How was your walk?"

"Very nice, but I'm afraid it's started to snow again." Elspeth crossed to the window. "So far it's light, but that could change."

Aunt Leah sat in a cushioned chair positioned in front of the fireplace. Her room was larger and had a bit more furniture than Elspeth's. "Do you think we'll be able to leave tomorrow?"

"I don't know. Mr. MacLean wasn't sure either."

One of Aunt Leah's sable brows arched with interest. "Oh, you saw Mr. MacLean?"

"On my walk, yes." He was already taking up a good portion of space in her head, and now talking about him almost made it seem he was here in the room. Which was silly.

Yet why else would her body be tingling? It seemed to only do that when he was around. Or when she was thinking about him, apparently.

All of this was ridiculous. She should still be angry with him, shouldn't she? He'd lied about, well, nearly everything.

He'd also had reasonable explanations for why he'd done so.

"I like him," Aunt Leah was saying as Elspeth dragged herself from the distraction of thinking of Tavish. Rather, *Lord* bloody Strathclyde. "It seems you do too. Also, that he likes you in return. Would I be wrong to hope for a match? I admit I would hate for you to move to Glasgow, but it would be so lovely to see you wed. My brother—your father, that is—would think so too."

Oh dear, Elspeth wasn't sure how she felt about Aunt Leah trying to marry her off to Tavish—Lord Strathclyde. "I think it's too soon to think of such things, let alone discuss them." Sharing kisses was one thing, but Elspeth couldn't see where a lord would marry someone like her. Surely, he'd wed a daughter of an earl or someone similar.

And yet, if that were the case, why would he be kissing her? A seed of hope burrowed itself into her chest. Then she promptly thrust the thought from her mind in favor of something far more important: finding Lann Dhearg.

"Would you like some tea, Aunt?" Elspeth asked.

"Why yes, that would be lovely."

"I'll go and ask Carrie." Elspeth went downstairs in search of the innkeeper's daughter.

Upon entering the common room, she saw Balthazar himself perched on a stool behind the bar, brushing his beard. She didn't particularly want to interrupt his toilet, so she ducked behind the stairs and found a narrow corridor that presumably led to the rooms where Balthazar and Carrie lived.

"Miss Marshall," Carrie said with a touch of surprise as she came from the kitchen. She wiped her hands on her apron. "Do ye need something?"

"Yes, please. My aunt would like some tea."

Carrie nodded. "Ye're back from visiting Dougal, then?"

"I am."

"Did ye get the story ye wanted?"

Not even close. Elspeth recalled her conversation with Carrie that morning. It seemed she might know Neil Kerr. Perhaps she had information that could help them find him. "Partially," Elspeth answered. "I would love to speak with his brother."

Carrie looked away, as she'd done that morning. She also fidgeted with her apron. "I dinna ken where he is."

Elspeth hadn't even asked, which made her wonder if Carrie *did* in fact know where Neil was. Perhaps if she knew Tavish wanted to help him, she might reveal his location. Before Elspeth could think of how to tell Carrie about Tavish, Carrie said she'd fetch the tea for Aunt Leah and took herself off.

Frowning after the redhead, Elspeth considered following her to the kitchen. Except the woman was nervous, perhaps even frightened. If she feared Neil would be captured, that would make sense.

Elspeth turned and went back toward the stairs. She wanted to tell Tavish what she'd learned. Perhaps together they could talk to Carrie.

But where was Tavish now? Pausing at the bottom of the stairs, Elspeth considered looking for him outside. Surely he'd come in by now? His room was on the second floor… She'd try there first.

After climbing two flights of stairs, she emerged onto a small landing. There were only two doors, one to her right and one straight ahead at the end of the narrow corridor. Which one was his?

Taking a deep breath, she went to the door on the right. She lifted her hand to knock, but didn't. Looking at the positions of the doors and taking her knowledge of the inn's layout into account, she surmised this room was probably about the same size as hers, whereas the one at the end of the corridor would be quite large. What if that wasn't a single room at all, but a door to more rooms?

She didn't have time to dither. She was going to try this chamber first. Before she could knock, the door creaked open. Tavish stood on the other side, his eyes widening with surprise. "Elspeth."

She exhaled with relief. "This *is* your room."

"It is indeed. I heard a creak outside the door and thought someone must be here. Come in."

Elspeth swept inside and surveyed the chamber. There was a narrow bed and small table with a single chair situated in front of the hearth. The pitched roof and dormer window made the room seem cramped. "Do you have to crouch in here?"

"Somewhat. I mostly stick to the taller side of the room. It's not as if I've spent much time here."

"You could probably move downstairs. The inn isn't full as it was last night." In addition to the soldiers, a few other guests had left on horseback after breakfast.

"I considered that, but as I am not spending much time in here, I didn't want to trouble Balthazar or Carrie." He lifted a shoulder. "Besides, the room is rather cozy."

She didn't disagree, especially with the cheery fire, which actually made the chamber a touch warm. Or, she realized, that could be the result of his presence. That thrilling sensation she'd felt earlier when she'd been speaking to Aunt Leah returned far more intensely.

"What brings you up here?" he asked.

Elspeth blinked. Yes, she had a purpose here that didn't involve beguilement. "I wanted to tell you about Carrie."

A crease formed between his brows. "The serving maid?"

Elspeth nodded. "When I asked her how to find Mr. Kerr this morning, she seemed slightly agitated. I credited that to her concern for someone who was perhaps trying to evade capture. Then I just spoke with her again—she asked me if I'd found him and gotten my story—and she was as nervous as before. She said she didn't know where Mr.

Kerr's brother is, but, and this is the really strange part, I didn't even ask her if she knew."

Tavish stroked his chin, his brows dipping pensively. "That certainly sounds like she *might* know where he is."

"I had the sense she was afraid. Or worried. If she does know where Neil is, I don't think she'll reveal where he's hiding." Elspeth moved closer to where Tavish stood where the ceiling was tall enough to accommodate his height. "I thought perhaps we could persuade her to tell us if she knew you planned to help him remain safe from capture."

He grinned, his eyes lighting with admiration. "That's a brilliant idea."

Elspeth felt inordinately flattered. "Thank you."

"You are an excellent partner," he said softly, taking her hand. Anticipation curled through her.

"I do want to help you find Lann Dhearg, and not just because I want the story."

"I know that." He lifted her hand to his chest, his fingers stroking and tangling with hers. His gaze drifted toward the window, and the crease between his brows returned. "The sun has come out again."

Elspeth couldn't tear her eyes from his. "The snow stopped?"

"Sadly."

"Sadly?"

"I admit I was looking forward to having to spend at least one more night—in addition to tonight—here. With you."

The sensation she felt was far more than flattery. "Were you?" The question was quiet but daring, almost breathless.

"Mmm, yes." He lifted his other hand and caressed her temple, her cheek, her jaw.

Elspeth nearly closed her eyes. His touch stirred a pulse deep within her, a desire she'd never known. She swayed toward him so that their hands were trapped between their chests. "You probably shouldn't kiss me again."

"Why not?" His thumb stroked her lower lip.

She sucked in a breath and nearly brought the digit into her mouth. She was an utter wanton. "You're a—" She fought to retain her control lest she throw all the caution she had out the window to her right. "You're a lord."

His eyes narrowed, and the tone of his voice changed. "Do you think I would take advantage? That I would expect—"

Elspeth took her hand from between them and put her fingertips on his mouth. She shook her head. "No, I don't think that. I meant that we are from different backgrounds. While I enjoy kissing you—very much—we probably should not."

A slow smile curled across his mouth. "You enjoy kissing me?"

She nodded, her heart clenching at how handsome he was when he smiled.

"Your background is immaterial." He grimaced. "I don't mean that it's not important. I mean that my being a lord is…" He exhaled. "I am utterly botching this. Let me start again." He cupped the side of her head. "Any difference of background between us is of no consequence to me. If you're wondering whether a lord might consider a future with you, the answer is that *this lord* absolutely would."

"Oh." Joy bubbled up inside her. She couldn't stop herself from smiling rather giddily.

"As to whether we should kiss, I suppose you have a point. It's bad enough that you're up here in my room alone with—"

Elspeth curled her hands around his neck and pulled his head down to kiss him. The moment his mouth met hers, her body seemed to melt. She fell against him, and he caught her, sweeping his hands to her back and holding her tightly. Their lips molded together, sealing in a delicious kiss that burned through her.

Strangely, she thought of who he really was—not a lord, but the descendant of a legendary king, a man about whom stories had been told for over a millennium. To someone like her, the realization was almost heady, as if she herself had stepped into a legend.

Or perhaps she was merely kissing one.

Elspeth was more than aware that they were alone in his chamber, where there was a bed. She was not so innocent that she'd never been kissed before, that she didn't know what went on in a bed. She'd just never met anyone who'd made her want to experience it for herself.

Heat and desire seared through her as he deepened their kisses. Despite the clothing between them, she felt the hard planes of his body, and the hard bulge of his sex pressed to her. An ache began in her core and spread up her abdomen, swelling her breasts. Then, almost as if conjured by her thoughts, his hand moved under her arm and cupped her breast through her clothes.

She gasped as he took his lips from hers and kissed along her jaw. The bliss of his mouth against her flesh pushed her to cast her head back so he could have his fill of her if he wanted. She desperately hoped he wanted.

"Elspeth," he whispered against her, his tongue swirling over her earlobe and then lower along her neck. All the while, his hand cupped and caressed her breast. How she longed to feel his flesh bare against her. Wanton was perhaps not a strong enough word to describe her behavior, but she didn't care. She wanted this. She wanted him.

"We should stop," he murmured even as he did nothing of the sort. His mouth trailed down to the hollow at the base of her throat.

He abruptly stepped back from her. "It's best if we pause our, uh, this."

"Pause? Does that mean we can continue later?" Her body screamed for something.

"Perhaps. We should probably go question Carrie."

"I imagine she's preparing for dinner. I think it must wait until later."

"Elspeth, are you trying to coax me to continue…this?"

"Would that be bad?"

He chuckled and took her hand once more. Pressing a kiss to her fingertips, he looked into her eyes with unabashed desire. "Not to me, but we are not wed, and I would not have you thinking I would take advantage."

"We could handfast." She flinched. "I'm no better than Angus."

"I can guess who Angus is, and don't you dare compare yourself to him. Unless you've asked other men to handfast today?"

She smiled at his dry tone. "Not today." She sobered and squeezed his hand. "Not ever."

"You tempt me, Elspeth. In every way." He swept his lips over hers once more. The kiss was brief, but her body reacted, curling toward him like a plant seeking the sun.

He stepped back once more. "You should go prepare for dinner." His tone was gruff, while his eyes were hot with desire.

"All right." She didn't hide the reluctance or disappointment from her voice. "I'll see you downstairs. After, we'll speak with Carrie."

He nodded. "And after that… Well, we'll see what happens."

Elspeth slitted her eyes at him, then dashed forward to brush a kiss against his cheek before turning and taking her leave. It was as if she walked on air.

She never wanted to come down.

Chapter Six

TAVISH WAS THE first to arrive in the common room for dinner. He could attribute it to hoping to catch Carrie so he could question her, but the truth was that he was eager to see Elspeth.

He'd nearly asked her to be his wife. The only thing that had stopped him was the short length of their acquaintance—that they'd met over two years ago didn't count. How was it, then, that he felt as if he'd known her at least that long?

Because she'd inhabited his mind. From the moment he'd been drawn into her story in Dunkeld, he'd been enchanted. That she'd abandoned her need to tell a story to join him in his quest to find Lann Dhearg made her that much more enticing.

There was also her laugh, her sharp intelligence, and the undeniable way she felt in his arms—*right*. He was already halfway in love with her, at least, so why not propose marriage? After all, she was the one who'd suggested handfasting, and what was that beyond a step to marriage?

It allowed for a temporary union, one in which they didn't have to stop what they'd been doing earlier. Was that all she wanted?

Carrie emerged from the kitchen just as the front door opened. A swell of cold air filled the common room just before a man fell forward. The dogs rushed over from the hearth, barking and sniffing at him.

Tavish hurried to the man as Carrie ran to close the door. Kneeling beside the prone form, Tavish tilted the man's head and sucked in air through his teeth. Though he was battered and bleeding, there was no mistaking his identity: Dougal Kerr.

Carrie gasped. "Dougal!"

"Where can I take him?" Tavish asked.

"Bring him to my room so ye dinna have ta carry him upstairs."

Tavish hefted the man into his arms and followed Carrie to a narrow corridor behind the stairs. She went through a doorway to the left, and they stepped into a snug chamber. Tavish deposited Kerr on the bed in the corner.

"I'll fetch some medicine and cloth." Carrie gestured to a washbasin against the far wall. "There's water."

Kerr groaned as his eyes fluttered open. He tried to focus on Tavish, but his features were creased with fear.

"It's John MacLean," Tavish said soothingly. "You made it to Balthazar's. What happened?"

"There were men." He closed his eyes once more and lifted his hand to his head. Wincing, he let out a sharp gasp. "Hurts so much."

"Carrie will be back with something to help you." Tavish went to the washbasin and found a small cloth there. After wetting it, he returned to the bed and gently dabbed at the worst of Kerr's wounds—a bleeding gash on the side of his head.

"I thought they were good men," Kerr rasped, his eyes still closed. "They said they would help Neil too. I asked if they ken ye, and they said they did."

What the devil? Tavish didn't work with anyone, especially when it came to assisting Jacobites. Could it have been men he'd helped in the past who wanted to return the favor? That didn't make sense. His blood went cold—they'd mentioned Neil. They were after Lann Dhearg. They had to be.

Before he could ask, Carrie returned. She shooed Tavish aside as she put the items she'd gathered on the table beside the bed. "Fetch me the washbasin, Mr. MacLean." She tore strips of cloth and set them on the table as Tavish brought the pottery and put it down next to her implements. There was a bottle and a jar, salve, perhaps.

Tavish handed her the cloth he'd used to dab at Kerr's head. "Here."

She didn't spare a look for Tavish as she took the cloth and set to work cleaning Kerr's face to the best of her ability. The patient grimaced and moaned, but she worked quickly and efficiently.

"You might consider a new occupation as a healer," Tavish noted.

Carrie snorted. "As if my father would permit that." She poured the liquid from the bottle onto a clean cloth, and the scent of witch hazel rose in the air. She applied the medicine to Dougal's cuts. "Better now?" she asked.

"Yes, thank you." Kerr opened one eye—the other was beginning to swell shut—and looked up at Tavish. "They want the sword. I heard them talking about it after they thought I was unconscious. They think Neil can lead them to it."

Dammit. Tavish ran his hand over the side of his neck.

Carrie had picked up the jar of salve and then immediately dropped it. Muttering a curse, she picked it up and removed the lid, setting it on the table.

"How many men?" Tavish asked.

"Three came into the cottage. But there were more outside."

"Can you tell me exactly what they said about the sword?"

"Ow!" Kerr yelped and Carrie apologized.

Tavish noted her hands were shaking. He recalled what Elspeth had told him. It seemed Carrie knew something. "Carrie, are you all right?" he asked gently.

"I'm fine," she snapped, indicating she was perhaps not. "I'm not the one who was thrashed."

He looked back to Kerr. "Have you any idea where the men might have gone?"

"Good question," Carrie said. "I hope they don't come here."

That drew Tavish's entire attention. "Carrie, is there something you know about these men?" Tavish had a fair idea who they were and would be shocked if she knew them.

She stood, brushing her hands on her apron and glaring at Tavish. "Why would I ken these men? I just don't want them showing up here. It's bad for business!"

"Carrie, do you happen to know where Neil Kerr is hiding?"

Her bright green eyes widened, and she darted a look at Dougal, who rose up on his elbow, then promptly fell back on the bed with a groan.

"Ye can trust Mr. MacLean," Dougal said between sucking in breaths and squeezing his one good eye shut.

Carrie bit her lip as she surveyed Tavish, her expression heavy with doubt.

"You *can* trust me." Tavish gave her an encouraging nod. "I am trying to find Neil so that I may keep him safe from the English soldiers."

A bit of her skepticism seemed to fade, but they were interrupted by the arrival of her father. Balthazar stood in the doorway, his hands on his hips. "There ye are, daughter! I need ye in the common room!" His gaze fell on her bed. "What the bloody hell happened to him?"

Tavish opened his mouth to answer, but Balthazar waved his hand. "Later. We've got customers who want ale. Get yerself going, Carrie!" he bellowed before turning and striding away toward the common room.

"I'll check on ye later!" Carrie hurried from the room without so much as a glance toward Tavish.

Tavish frowned in deep disappointment. He was sure Carrie knew more than she was saying. After dinner, he would find out what.

Approaching the bed, Tavish realized Kerr had fallen asleep, his even breathing matching the rise and fall of his chest. Tavish muttered a frustrated curse, then departed. On his way to the common room, he ran into Elspeth.

She'd changed for dinner and wore a fetching gown of cream silk with an embroidered stomacher. He momentarily forgot everything but her loveliness.

"You look beautiful," he breathed.

She blushed as she skimmed her palms over the skirt of her gown. "Thank you. It's my finest dress. I wore it to a dinner with my cousins and their neighbors in Inverness." She shook her head. "Never mind, that hardly signifies. I heard there was a commotion."

Tavish pulled himself back to what was happening. "Dougal Kerr was attacked." He pressed his lips together as the anger he'd held at bay began to simmer.

Elspeth lifted her hand to her throat, where a pearl necklace lay against her flesh. "Is he all right?"

"He will be." While Tavish hadn't investigated Kerr's wounds, he assumed the man had more injuries than to his face.

She clasped her hands, squeezing them together as her face darkened with concern. "I am not a physician like my father, but I can take a look at him and offer some suggestions."

"You are very kind." Tavish smiled, thinking this was yet another reason he could see himself with her…

Once again, he shook himself from his reverie. This was no time to be distracted. "The men who attacked him were looking for Neil—and the sword."

The color left Elspeth's face. "You told me there were dangerous groups who would seek the sword. Is this…one of them?"

"I'm afraid it might be. It's the only thing that makes sense. If they'd just been looking for Neil, I might think they were English soldiers out of uniform, which would be awful, or perhaps mercenaries they hired to hunt down Jacobites. However, since they were in search of the sword, I have to believe they are from one of these groups. If that's true, Kerr should be glad he escaped with his life." Tavish glanced back toward Carrie's chamber where he slept.

"You have to find the sword before they do," Elspeth said fiercely.

"Yes." He stepped toward her and clasped her waist. "And I think you're right about Carrie—she knows something. She tended to Kerr's injuries, and when he told me about the sword, she grew very agitated."

"Did she tell you anything?"

He shook his head. "Her father interrupted, but I intend to get answers later."

Elspeth touched his cheek. "Where do you think those men are now?"

"I don't know, but I'm going to investigate Kerr's cottage to see if I can learn anything."

"Now?" At his answering nod, she said, "But what about dinner? Aunt Leah is looking forward to seeing you."

He squeezed her waist. "Please give her my apologies. We will simply have to delay our congregation until breakfast."

"Does that include you and me?" Elspeth asked softly, her dusky green gaze sweeping over him with unmasked desire.

Tavish's body hardened. "I'll come see you later."

She stood on her toes and kissed his cheek near his ear, then whispered, "So you can tell me about what you learn, or for some other…activity?"

He groaned softly, wishing he could take her upstairs right that very moment for an activity that involved both of them naked in front of the fire. "We should probably question Carrie."

Elspeth sighed as her fingers pressed into his nape, and she kissed the spot beneath his ear. "I suppose. But perhaps I'll have done so before you return."

His thoughts were beginning to cloud in a haze of want. He couldn't help but bring her hips flush against his. His cock strained in his breeches as he reveled in the sweet torture of her proximity—so close and yet so far. "That would be most, ah, efficient of you."

"I'll do my best." She dragged her lips across his jaw and kissed him.

He wrapped his arms about her with a harsh moan and swept her around to the wall, pressing her against it and settling his hips between her legs—or trying to anyway. He'd have to lift her to get the position just right, and her panniers, narrow as they were, would likely prevent that. She licked her tongue into his mouth as she held his head, their kiss turning wild.

With great effort, he pulled his mouth from hers, his breath coming hard and fast. "Elspeth, I'm sorely tempted to toss your skirts up right here, but that will not be the first way we come together, do you understand?"

She nodded, her eyes dark with desire.

"When I take you, it will be in a bed, with your glorious body spread before me, nude and aroused."

"I think I've mastered the aroused part."

A laugh burst from his lips, and he kissed her again, smiling the whole while. "Get back to your aunt. I'll see you soon." He released her and stepped back, smoothing his hand over his hair.

"Be careful, please." She stared at him intently before pivoting and returning to the common room.

He would be more than careful. He'd never had more reason to be.

ALL DURING DINNER, Elspeth watched the door, hopeful for Tavish's return, and not just so he could join them for dinner. No, that wasn't nearly as troublesome as whether he was safe. What if the men who'd attacked Dougal Kerr were watching the cottage and Tavish had walked right into their trap?

Even now, he could be lying unconscious at the cottage. Or worse, he could be—

Elspeth shoved the thought away. She wasn't going to consider such a thing, not when she'd just found him.

After drinking a glass of madeira with Aunt Leah, who truly was disappointed that Tavish wasn't able to join them, Elspeth made her way back downstairs with the intention of speaking with Carrie. Elspeth surveyed the common room, but Tavish wasn't there.

Carrie came from the kitchen and delivered stew to a couple near the fireplace. Wiping her hands on her apron, she went to a table that had clearly been recently vacated and began to gather the empty tankards and trenchers.

Elspeth approached her cautiously. She'd rehearsed what she planned to say, but didn't get a chance to utter a word as Carrie met her gaze right away. "Might I ask ye a favor, Miss Marshall? I don't know if ye heard, but Dougal Kerr was attacked and is asleep in my chamber."

Taken aback, Elspeth struggled to respond, "I, ah—"

"You didn't know? I assumed Mr. MacLean would have told you." She lifted a shoulder. "Seems like you two are cozy."

It did? "Yes, he mentioned it. I'd be happy to check on Mr. Kerr."

"Thank ye, Miss Marshall. I'm just so very busy. Papa insists all the tables be clean and available for customers." Carrie inclined her head toward the stairs, and red curls brushed her temple. "My room's past the stairs, on the left."

Elspeth wanted to question her, but again, it seemed that would have to wait.

Carrie hurriedly wiped the table. "Will ye let me know if he's awake? I'll bring him some dinner."

Elspeth nodded. "I will."

She made her way to Elspeth's chamber, finding it easily, and slipped quietly inside. Mr. Kerr lay prone on the bed, his lips parted and eyes closed. One didn't look as if it *could* open.

Elspeth bent over the man, her concern for Tavish growing as she inspected Kerr's injuries. Her heart began to beat faster, and she felt as if the room was closing in around her.

He's a soldier. He's capable. And he's smart. He'll be fine.

She repeated the words over and over in her mind until she began to calm. Then she collapsed in a chair in the corner, exhaling as she wiped her hand over her brow.

Why was she so very concerned about Tavish? Had she come to care for him so much in this incredibly short time? Even after he'd deceived her?

She understood why he'd done so, and he'd apologized. Repeatedly. And if she truly believed him, she accepted what he said about helping Jacobites, about keeping some number of men safe from capture and harm. She recalled his behavior with the English soldiers yesterday, how he'd leapt to the defense of the men discussing Culloden.

And the sword.

The sword she'd hoped to write about but now couldn't. It existed! She could still scarcely believe that fact.

She suddenly realized she was in Carrie's room. Alone. Her gaze drifted to the man on the bed. Well, not alone, but close enough.

Elspeth stood hastily and poked around the chamber, looking for any clue that might lead her and Tavish to Neil or the sword. Not that

Carrie would know where the sword was. But maybe she did.

The room wasn't large, but it was well lived in, with a bed, dresser, small table, and chair, and, of course, the hearth. There was also a narrow door at the end of the bed.

Elspeth slipped the latch and slowly pushed it open. "I hope this doesn't lead to someone else's chamber, and that they're inside," she murmured to herself.

The room was dark, so she had to fetch a candle from Carrie's room. Armed with flickering light, Elspeth stepped into the other chamber and instantly froze. It was rather small, but it was full of…things. What drew her eye most were the weapons—swords, daggers, a pair of shields. One shelf held an odd assortment of badges and brooches as well as a necklace and a ring.

Elspeth ran her fingers over one of the brooches, a gold lion with an intricate design. What was all this? She turned in a complete circle, moving slowly, as she surveyed the items. The door blocked part of a shield, so she pushed it nearly closed.

Her gaze arrested on a sword standing in the corner behind the door. It was quite long, the blade broad. But it was the hilt that drew her attention. Made of gold, the upper and lower guards bore interesting markings.

Elspeth went to look more closely. The markings were runes, she thought, and upon closer inspection, the blade had a herringbone pattern. It didn't look like any sword she'd seen. The longer she studied it, the faster her heart raced.

She held the candle closer and crouched down to use the light to study the hilt.

"What are ye doing in here?"

Carrie's shrill question startled Elspeth, causing her to drop the sword. It clanged against the floorboards, and the candle sputtered.

Elspeth stood. "My goodness, you frightened me. I'm so sorry. I didn't mean to intrude."

Carrie's green eyes flashed with annoyance. "And yet ye are." She didn't move to pick up the sword. Probably because it was nearly impossible to do so. How did she even get it here?

"I really am sorry. I was…curious. This is quite a collection."

"It's my Chamber of Sorrow." She walked to the shelf and fingered the necklace. "Everything here is from Culloden."

"From…the battle?" Elspeth whispered in wonder as she once again perused the room.

Carrie nodded. "I've gone a few times. I felt like I had to. The first time, I found this." She held up the necklace. "And that dagger there." She pointed to a short, well-worn dagger that was missing the very tip. "As well as a few other tidbits. Sometimes people come through Calvine and give me something for the chamber."

Elspeth gestured to the sword. "How did you come to possess this?" She felt like she already knew, but wanted to be sure.

"A friend gave it to me."

"Do you know what this sword is?" Again, Elspeth didn't know for certain, but she was willing to wager all the stories she'd written that she was right.

"It isna mine," Carrie said, sounding frightened. Her gaze was guarded once more, as it had been when Elspeth had talked to her about Neil Kerr.

"Is it Neil's?" Elspeth asked softly.

Sniffing, Carrie nodded. She wiped the back of her hand over her nose. "He asked me to hold it for him, said I couldna keep it even though I wanted to. It's unlike anything else in my collection."

"Did he tell you what it would do?"

Carrie sucked in a breath, and even in the dim light, Elspeth could see that she'd gone pale. She chewed on her lip but didn't answer.

"It's all right, Carrie. I know what it does, and I know who it really belongs to."

"Not Neil?" Lines furrowed across Carrie's brow.

"No. I think he must have found it at Culloden." Elspeth considered what to reveal. "The owner lost it in the battle, and he would like it back."

"Is that why ye and Mr. MacLean were both asking me about him. About Neil, I mean?"

Elspeth hesitated but ultimately answered. "Yes."

"It belongs to Mr. MacLean, then?"

"It's not for me to say," Elspeth said. The less Carrie knew the better. She now understood why Tavish hadn't told her about Lann Dhearg. It wasn't something anyone should have to bear. That he'd revealed the sword and his true identity to her showed her just how much he valued her. Didn't it?

"Why did Neil ask you to hold on to it?" Elspeth asked.

"He said men were after him, that they wanted it. He left it here a few weeks ago."

So recently? "And you truly don't know where he is?"

She shook her head.

"That's unfortunate, because Mr. MacLean wants to help keep him safe. He hides Jacobites." The moment the words left her mouth, Elspeth wondered if she shouldn't have told the serving maid. She was so gregarious in the common room. What if she divulged Tavish's secrets to someone?

She stared at Elspeth in disbelief. "That's what he does? Dougal said I could trust him, that he wanted to help."

"He can even take this sword for you and keep it safe." Elspeth held her breath, hoping Carrie would agree. It wasn't as if Elspeth could pick it up and flee. Not only did she have nowhere to go, she could hardly lift the bloody thing.

In fact, how she was she going to get it up to Tavish's chamber?

"He will take Neil's sword?" Carrie asked, drawing Elspeth back to their exchange.

"I'm certain of it."

"Yes, please." Carrie looked at her with a mixture of relief and joy. "Thank you."

Elspeth squinted one eye at Lann Dhearg. Tavish must be incredibly strong to be able to wield such a weapon.

Carrie came to stand beside Elspeth. "It's very heavy."

Elspeth looked over at the serving maid. "I don't suppose you'll help me carry it upstairs to my chamber?"

"Not to Mr. MacLean's?"

"No," Elspeth said with a short laugh. "I don't think we can do that, not even together."

Carrie smiled briefly. "I'll get something to wrap it in." She disappeared into her chamber for a moment, then returned with a blanket, which she spread on the floor. Together, they moved the sword on top of it, then wrapped the wool around the weapon.

Each taking an end, they hefted Lann Dhearg and rose. "I'll go first," Carrie said. "We'll take the backstairs."

Carrie led the way, and they made it halfway up before they had to stop and rest. After catching their breath, they continued, taking one more rest at the top before they made it to Elspeth's chamber.

"We could never have made it up to Mr. MacLean's chamber!" Carrie exclaimed as they wrestled the sword into Elspeth's room.

When it was resting on the floor next to the bed, Elspeth wiped her hands on her skirt. Perspiration dappled her brow. "Thank you for helping me," Elspeth said. "And for trusting Mr. MacLean."

"I'm glad to be rid of it, especially if the men who hurt Dougal are looking for it." She pivoted toward the door. "I'd best be getting back to Dougal. And the common room before my father has a fit of apoplexy."

Elspeth thanked her again and closed the door behind the redhead after she left. Glancing at the bundled-up sword, she strode to the window. Light from the inn spilled into the yard, but there was no sign of Tavish.

Where was he? Elspeth prayed he was safe and that he would be here soon. He would be elated when he learned she had Lann Dhearg.

And then what would happen? Would he escort her and Aunt Leah to Dunkeld and then continue home? Where was his home? She knew it was near Glasgow, but wanted specifics. She wanted to know everything about him.

As she stared out into the black night, she hoped she would have the chance to find out.

Chapter Seven

KERR'S COTTAGE HAD been ransacked. Whoever had attacked him had made sure the sword wasn't hidden in the cottage. Still, Tavish had picked over everything with meticulous care. Then he'd left the same way he'd arrived—stealing through the shadows to avoid detection, in case the men from the order were watching.

The Order of the Round Table. The secret organization that sought to control the Thirteen Treasures of Britain. Although Lann Dhearg wasn't one of them, it was related to one, and apparently, they felt they should obtain it.

Tavish planned to disabuse them of that idea, should he get the opportunity. He hoped he would. More than that, he wanted to find his damned sword.

He'd been such an utter fool. His grandmother had been distraught when he'd told her what he'd done. But then she'd consoled him and assured him he would find Lann Dhearg and set things right. Her faith in him meant everything. He would not let her down.

After finishing at Kerr's cottage, Tavish had looked around the surrounding area. He'd been fortunate enough to encounter a couple of people who lived nearby. Neither had seen anything, much to his disappointment.

Now, as he stepped into the inn, he couldn't help but feel frustrated. However, buried beneath that was an anticipation that had burned within him all night.

Elspeth.

A few tables in the common room were still occupied, and a pair of the dogs came to greet Tavish as he entered. He stroked their heads briefly before striding to the stairs. After taking them two at a time, he found himself in front of Elspeth's door rather quickly.

He hesitated. What if her aunt was there? Or perhaps Elspeth was in her aunt's room? There was one way to find out.

Tavish went to the next room and listened. A soft snore reached his ears, followed by a loud one that made him twitch. Smiling, he went back to Elspeth's room and rapped softly.

He'd barely lowered his hand before the door came open. She pulled him inside so swiftly that he nearly toppled into her. Apparently, he wasn't the only one eager for their reunion.

Elspeth cupped his face, her green eyes glossy with relief. "You're safe."

"You were worried?"

She gave him a look that said she was. "You saw Dougal Kerr, did you not?"

"You saw him too?" It was no wonder she'd been concerned.

"Carrie asked me to check on him while she was busy in the common room. He was still sleeping, but I could see the injury to his face." A shiver ran through her.

Tavish put his hands on her hips and pulled her to him. "I'm fine. I didn't encounter any trouble at all."

She smiled. "I'm so glad."

While he was thoroughly enjoying this moment with Elspeth, he couldn't ignore the dark sense of failure needling him. "I'm disappointed I wasn't able to find any clues regarding these men. Or the sword."

Her entire face lit like fireworks illuminating the night sky. "I found it."

He stared at her. "You…found it? I don't understand."

She lowered her hands from his face and turned from him. As she moved toward the bed, he grew even more perplexed. Then she knelt next to a blanket on the floor. She unwrapped the wool plaid, and there, lying in the middle of it, was Lann Dhearg.

She gave him a beatific smile. "I'd hand it to you, but I can barely lift it."

"My God. Elspeth, however did you…" He didn't finish the question as he quickly lowered to his knees on the other side of the sword from her.

"You will never believe it, but it was here the entire time. Well, not the *entire* time—not since Culloden. Carrie said Neil left it with her a few weeks ago."

Tavish ran his fingers over the familiar ancient runic symbols on upper and lower guards of the hilt. The weapon hummed beneath his touch, as it always did for him or others in his family. He looked over at her. "Will you start at the beginning, please?"

"Yes, of course." She blushed and let out a soft laugh. "I'm afraid I was quite thrilled to find it. I was excited to tell you."

He wrapped his palm around the grip. "I still can't believe it."

"When I went to check on Mr. Kerr, he was asleep, so I thought I would investigate Carrie's room for clues about Neil." She shrugged. "I honestly didn't expect to find anything."

"Yet you did."

"There was a door, so I opened it. She has a room filled with items collected from Culloden field. Weapons, jewelry, shields. She calls it her Chamber of Sorrow."

Tavish let go of the sword and sat back on his heels. "That's…incredible."

"It was somewhat unsettling, to tell you the truth. It's a small room, and it was filled with these objects."

"That's where you found Lann Dhearg?" At her nod, he asked, "How did you know what it was?"

"It just looked…different from any sword I've ever seen. Because of the herringbone pattern and the markings. Are those runes?"

He glanced down at the markings. "Yes. We aren't exactly sure what they mean, but the upper guard is something like 'burn bright' while the lower is akin to 'flame eternal.' And the herringbone pattern is due to the manner in which it was forged."

Her eyes gleamed with wonder. "That's fascinating. So this isn't the Cumbric language?"

That she was aware of the dead language of his ancestors was more than impressive. Tavish leaned over the sword and kissed her. "You are brilliant. I can't say for certain since there are no surviving texts of the Cumbric language. How do you even know about Cumbric?" He sat back, smiling.

She shrugged. "As a writer, I've sought to learn about Celtic languages. I don't know if that makes me brilliant, however. I'm just glad to have found your sword. Except for the part when I had to bring it upstairs." She made a face.

"It would be quite heavy for you. How did you manage it?"

"Carrie helped me, thank goodness. But we agreed that taking it up to your room was beyond our ability." She laughed, and he laughed with her, amazed at how joyful he felt. It was more than just finding the sword. That was a relief. It was sharing this moment with her, knowing she'd worked to help him, that without her, he might not have found it.

"Thank you for finding my sword," he said softly.

"Why is it so bloody heavy?"

Tavish easily picked up the weapon, feeling its vibration through his hand and up into his arm.

She gaped at him. "You're unfathomably strong."

He chuckled as he got to his feet. "No, it isn't heavy for me. It's part of the magic of the sword. Dyrnwyn is the same, but slightly different. Dyrnwyn is heavy for everyone but those who are worthy. Lann Dhearg is heavy for everyone until someone from our bloodline deems them worthy. More simply, I can give it to someone to use, but it's a very specific act and, once done, can't be reversed."

She began to rise, and he quickly offered his hand to aid her. Putting her fingers in his, she said, "So you'd better be sure that person won't use it for ill purposes."

He tipped Lann Dhearg down but didn't let go of her hand. "Exactly. As far as I know, no one in my family has given—or loaned—it to someone else in hundreds of years. But then, it's been hidden at Dumbarton. Until I was idiot enough to take it with me to Culloden."

"You weren't an idiot." Her voice was gentle, understanding. He almost believed her.

"I thought it would be safe because no one can wield it without my granting them the ability. I didn't imagine someone would steal it, even if it was difficult to do so."

"It had to have been *incredibly* difficult. I had a hard enough time getting it upstairs. And I had help."

Tavish let go of her hand and went to set Lann Dhearg in the corner. When he returned to his room, he'd reunite it with its scabbard. "Do you know how to use a sword?"

"No. A paring knife is about the extent of my skill with blades."

Tavish smiled, wondering if she was trying to lighten his mood. "I suppose you could protect yourself with that if you had to."

She took a deep breath, moving toward the fire as she did so. "What will you do now that you have the sword?"

He should go home immediately and return the sword to its hiding place, where it would remain. "Well, when I was out tonight, it seems the snow melted enough today to allow for travel."

"Did it?" She sounded as disappointed by that assessment as he felt. "For horses only, or also for vehicles?"

Crossing the room, he joined her in front of the hearth. "Either. I imagine you and your aunt will wish to continue to Dunkeld."

Elspeth tipped her head back to look up at him. The firelight danced across the arch of her brow and the curve of her cheek. "Yes, I'm sure she will."

He couldn't look away from her, not just because of her beauty, but because of the way she looked at him. As if he were more than he was. "But not you?"

"No." She blinked. "I mean, I do want to return. I also don't want to leave."

He half smiled. "Because the inn is so inviting?"

She stepped toward him, closing the gap between them. "It's nothing to do with the inn, and I think you know that."

"I wasn't completely certain, but I am now." He itched to touch her, to claim her. He flexed his hands against his thighs. "May I accompany you to Dunkeld?"

"Yes." She wetted her lips with her tongue. Tavish nearly groaned.

"I won't be able to stay long. I promised my grandmother I'd be home for the new year."

"You can't disappoint her," she whispered with a hint of sadness.

"No." He lifted his hand to her cheek, then tucked a red-gold lock of hair behind her ear. Grazing his fingers along the outer edge, he felt her tremble. His body reacted, twitching with need for her. "I don't wish to disappoint you either."

She pushed her hands up his chest and clutched his coat. "Then I think you'd better kiss me."

Tavish curled his hand around her head, cupping her as his mouth claimed hers. She pulled at him as her lips and tongue met his in a fierce dance of desire. He put his other hand on the small of her back and pressed so that their hips came together.

His fingers met a pin in her hair, so he pulled it free. Then another and another. Her curls began to tumble over his hand. He continued until there was nothing left but the feel of her silken tresses between his fingers. Pulling back, he gazed down at her. "Beautiful," he murmured.

She twined her hands around his neck and tugged until their lips met once more. The heat of the fire to his left combined with the scorching need lighting through him. He wanted to peel her clothes away until she was bare before him. Then he would worship her body with his hands and mouth until she quivered with desire. Then he would bring her pleasure until she cried his name and came apart.

Summoning a strength he wasn't sure he possessed, Tavish broke the kiss. "Elspeth, I should go."

She didn't release him. In fact, her grip tightened around his neck. "Don't. Please. I want you to stay."

"If I stay..." He stared down at her. "If I stay, I'm going to take you over to that bed."

An exhalation of relief passed through her kiss-swollen lips. "Good."

"Should we handfast, then?" he asked.

"What is handfasting but a promise to try to determine if we are suitable for marriage? I promise to expend every effort."

Tavish couldn't help but grin. "You are a singular woman, Elspeth. I promise to do the same. Starting right now." He looked down at her ivory gown with its embroidered stomacher, assessing how to undress her.

Elspeth plucked the pins from her stomacher and took them to the table, where she set them down. Tavish joined her as she removed the stomacher and placed it atop the pins. Then she turned to him. "Better?"

"Slightly," he said wryly.

She gave him an apologetic smile as she untied the front at her waist. "This is the one dress I own that requires help."

"Why did you wear it here?"

"Because I wanted to impress you." The statement was so simple, so honest, he couldn't think of what to say. So he kissed her instead.

"You look beautiful."

"Help me take it off," she whispered.

He lifted the gown over her head and laid it over the back of one of the chairs. She was already untying the quilted petticoat, and a moment later, he swept that from her in the same fashion. After depositing it on the chair, he helped her remove the panniers, grateful they were a rather narrow variety and saying so.

"I am thankful I have no need for the wider kind." She stopped and stared at him. "You're a lord. If we are handfasted, will I need wider panniers?"

He laughed softly. "No."

She smiled in relief as she began to unlace her stays.

Arrested by the sight of her in stays, shift, and stockings—she'd apparently removed her shoes earlier—it took a moment for Tavish to act. He took her hands and gently pushed them aside. Taking over the task of loosening her stays, he pulled at the laces, the sound of them coming free an erotic whisper in the air.

When he was finished, she turned. "You'll need to loosen the back." She swept her hair over her shoulder, giving him access.

Distracted by the pale column of her neck, he managed to coax his fingers to work, plucking at the laces until the stays were sufficiently loose. Then he gave in to temptation and pressed his lips to her nape. He kissed along her neck and shoulder, then down across the blade of her back until he met her spine. She shivered.

Gripping the stays, he pulled them over her head and dropped them to the floor. Her shift was made of a thick linen, likely because it was December. Thus, the fabric wasn't sheer enough to see through it. No matter since she wasn't going to wear it much longer. He picked her up, prompting a gasp from her as she put her arms around his neck.

It was a short walk to the bed—too short, for he loved holding her—where he set her on the edge. Intending to finish undressing her, he froze when she shook her head.

"Your turn. You're wearing too many clothes." She slid back on the bed and watched him as he undressed.

Tavish couldn't remember a woman ever looking at him the way she did. He resisted the urge to strip everything away as quickly as possible since she seemed to be enjoying watching him. Instead, he went slowly until he was wearing just his shirt and breeches. "Should I keep going?"

"I think you must." Her voice had darkened to a sensual rasp.

His body thrumming with desire, Tavish drew the shirt over his head and let it fall to the floor. She answered by removing her shift. He held his breath as each inch of her flesh was exposed.

Unable to help himself, he reached for her, his fingers gliding up her thigh and across her hip. Then up along her ribs until he met the swell of her breast. Her rose-hued nipples went taut as he cupped her. He leaned forward and put his mouth on her, taking his time to go slowly as he used his lips and tongue to caress her.

She closed her eyes and cast her head back with a soft moan. He withdrew long enough to remove his breeches, then moved onto the bed. Returning to his task, he suckled her breast once more. She pulled the tie holding his hair back, freeing the mass to graze his shoulders, and ran her fingers through it.

He moved between her legs, skimming his hand down over the

smooth slope of her belly until he found the curls at her sex. He stroked her folds, drawing a gasp from her as she arched up from the bed. She clutched at his head, her soft whimpers sharpening his desire.

"Tavish," she breathed.

He lifted his head and looked down at her. Eyes closed, red-gold hair splayed across the pillow, lips damp and parted, she was exquisite. He teased her clitoris and with each touch of his fingers, she moved with him, her body begging wordlessly for more. He slipped his finger into her, and she clasped his shoulders. Moving between stroking her clitoris and filling her sheath, he coaxed her response until she was coming up from the bed to meet his thrusts. On and on he worked as her cries intensified.

"I don't know what to do. I feel something…" She moaned as he filled her with two fingers.

"Let go, Elspeth," he whispered against her cheek. "You're so tight for me. You're ready. Let yourself fall. I'll catch you."

He increased his pace, and her body began to shudder. Her muscles clenched around him. She cried out his name. Spasms racked her thighs as she dug her fingers into his back.

Though he wanted so badly to bury himself inside her, Tavish knew he should stop. They were not wed, nor were they really handfasted. She deserved to know that he wouldn't leave her.

He rolled to his side. "Elspeth."

Her eyes opened, but just barely. "Where are you going?"

"Nowhere. I'm right here."

"But we aren't finished." She put her hand on his hip, then slid it down to curl her palm around his cock.

Tavish groaned softly. This was not helping his resolve. "Elspeth," he rasped. "We should wait."

She turned her head toward him. "Wait? For what?"

He cupped her cheek. "Will you marry me?"

Chapter Eight

ELSPETH FROZE IN shock. Had she heard him right?

"What did you say?"

He cracked that half smile that never failed to squeeze her heart. "I asked if you would marry me. And I swear it's not because you're touching my cock."

She couldn't help it, she laughed. So hard that she put her other hand over her mouth. "I'm sorry."

"Forgive me for not joining in your amusement. I'm afraid that while you're touching me like that, laughter is not the reaction that comes to mind."

She slitted her eyes again and stroked her hand along his length. "What is?"

He closed his eyes briefly. "Good Lord, woman, are you trying to torture me?"

"No, I'm trying to arouse you. Is it working?"

"Quite. But, truly, we should wait."

"Why? If we're to be wed, I see no reason for us not to consummate our union right now."

He rolled over on top of her, settling between her legs, which she bent to accommodate him. "Does that mean you'll be my wife?"

She hesitated. "We really could handfast, instead of pretending to. We've hardly known each other."

"As you said, handfasting is little more than a temporary arrangement—or something like that." His eyes darkened, sending a flush of longing through her. "And I wasn't pretending. I want you, Elspeth. In my bed, in my life, in my heart."

She'd been afraid to admit that she was falling in love with him. What if he didn't feel the same? Yet here he was, proposing marriage, and not just because she was touching his sex. "Yes," she said softly, joy and wonder filling her. "I'll marry you. Now, will you finish?"

He laughed finally, just before he kissed her again. He took his time exploring her mouth as he pressed between her thighs. She still held him, and began to move her hand along his shaft.

He put his hand over hers. "Take me into you," he said against her mouth.

Together, they guided him into her sheath, already sensitive from the pleasure he'd given her. He went slowly, filling and stretching her, until he was completely inside. She moved her hand to his backside, skimming her palm over him as he moved. Sliding from her, he pressed forward again, the muscles of his backside growing taut.

"I think I could just enjoy fondling your arse," she said before she nipped his ear with her teeth.

"*Elspeth.*" He gathered her in his arms. "Wrap your legs around me—tight." Then he truly began to move, his hips thrusting as he filled her again and again.

She held him close, kissing his neck and squeezing her legs around him as the release she'd found a short time ago began to coil within her once more. She hadn't known what to expect before, but now she did.

"Come with me, Elspeth." He kissed her as her muscles tightened again. He'd told her to fall, and she had. Now she dove off the edge willingly, plunging herself into the darkness, knowing he would do as he'd promised and catch her.

He moaned as he drove into her, then cried out. She dug her fingers into his flesh and clutched him as the storm raged within and around them. Eventually, the air calmed. He kissed her cheek, her lips, her neck, then slid from her body, rolling to his back.

Elspeth smiled as she brushed her hair back from her face. Before she could open her eyes, the sound of a door crashing open jolted her upright. Tavish did the same.

She looked toward the door to her chamber, but the sound hadn't been that close. Loud voices filtered from somewhere downstairs—the common room, most likely, which was below her room.

Tavish leapt from the bed and ran to the window. He pushed the curtain aside and looked down.

"What is it?" Elspeth asked, sliding to the edge of the bed.

He swore, then came back to her and immediately began to dress. Elspeth left the bed and found her shift, then pulled it on.

"I'll go investigate," Tavish said after he had his breeches on. He dragged his shirt over his head. The sound of men yelling from the landing made them both freeze.

Tavish swore again, then raced for Lann Dhearg on the other side of the bed. "There's no time. They're here for the sword."

He went to the window. "Thank God these are newer windows." He opened the sash, then turned his head. "I'll make sure you're safe. Don't tell them I'm here. I need to be able to surprise them."

Fear sliced through Elspeth—not just for her, but for him. For Aunt Leah. For everyone at the inn. She ran to the window. "You think it's the men who attacked Dougal Kerr?"

"I do. There's a knife in my boot. Close this behind me." He stared at her intently, a determined fire burning in his gaze. "Don't be afraid."

And then he was gone through the window.

She wanted to watch what he did, but the sound of men outside her door made her close the window. Before she could find some clothing to throw on or grab Tavish's knife, the door flew open, crashing against the wall.

A man came over the threshold. He was tall with dark, clubbed hair, though lank strands hung against the sides of his thin face. "Look here, I've found myself a right Scottish lass, haven't I?" He spoke in an English accent—southwestern, if Elspeth had to guess.

The door adjoining her room with Aunt Leah's opened. Another man steered Aunt Leah into Elspeth's room. Aunt Leah, sobbing, ran to embrace her.

Elspeth held her tightly. "It's going to be all right," she whispered.

"Let's get downstairs," the other man, who was shorter, with a scar across his cheek and nose and also an Englishman, said.

"Surely you can let me dress," Elspeth demanded.

The thin-faced man came toward her, his gaze menacing. "Move!" He narrowed his eyes. "Is the window open?" He checked the sash, then touched the curtain. "The fabric is cool." He looked around at Elspeth's clothing strewn about. "Was there someone in here with you?"

"No." Elspeth lifted her chin and prayed he believed her.

He squeezed her arm, his strong fingers digging mercilessly into her flesh. "Don't lie to me. Who was here?"

"No one."

He pulled her from Aunt Leah's arms and brought her face close to his so that she could smell his stale, whisky-laden breath. "I'm not supposed to touch you, but I will." He let his gaze drift over her barely clad body.

Elspeth twitched with revulsion.

"Stop it, Marley," the other man said.

Aunt Leah grabbed Elspeth's hand and pulled her away from Marley.

"Downstairs, then," the scar-faced man said.

"You let me put on a banyan," Aunt Leah said. "Let my niece do the same."

Marley took a pistol from his waistband and waved it at them. "Go!"

Elspeth put her arm around Aunt Leah and started toward the door. "It will be all right." She was at least grateful she was still wearing her stockings so that her feet weren't bare.

When they arrived in the common room, their situation became wholly and horribly apparent. Several villains stood around the perimeter of the room while the inn's guests, Balthazar, and Carrie sat in the middle.

Balthazar sat at a table with Carrie, his brow furrowed and his eyes spitting fury. Carrie sat stiff and straight beside him. Elspeth decided she and Leah should sit with them. She wanted to somehow communicate to them that Tavish was going to save them.

Weaving through the tables, Elspeth led her aunt to the innkeeper and his daughter and helped her to sit. "I promise—everything will be fine," she whispered before kissing Aunt Leah's soft cheek. It was damp from her tears, and Elspeth wanted to lash out at the men who'd caused her distress. She settled for glowering at them before sitting down herself.

The men who'd brought them downstairs went to the fireplace, where a handsome man with loose, shoulder-length dark hair and a close-cropped beard stood. While they spoke quietly to one another, Elspeth leaned over to talk to Carrie and Balthazar.

"Mr. MacLean is outside," she whispered. "He will save us."

Balthazar grunted as he tossed a hate-filled stare toward the fireplace. "They said they have the stables, and the grooms have been dealt with." He sniffed. "It's likely MacLean has already suffered the same fate. They won't tell me what they did with my dogs." He blinked and sniffed again, then wiped the back of his hand over his nose.

Elspeth's insides twisted, and her breath stuck in her lungs. She tried to breathe but couldn't.

Aunt Leah reached over and took her hand but said nothing. While Elspeth appreciated the attempt at comfort, it didn't stop the terrible cold spreading through her.

"We shouldn't tell them about MacLean," Carrie said quietly from Elspeth's right.

Elspeth looked to the other woman and nodded. Carrie clasped her hands on the table, and it seemed to Elspeth that she was perhaps shaking.

Elspeth glanced around, taking stock of who was in the room. "What about Dougal?" she whispered.

Carrie gripped her hands tighter so that her fingers started to turn white. "They tied him to the bed in my chamber."

They were interrupted from further conversation by the voice of the handsome man at the fireplace. "Good evening, friends." He spoke in a crisp, slightly foreign accent, perhaps Dutch, but Elspeth couldn't be sure.

"We aren't your friends," Elspeth spat.

He looked pointedly at Elspeth. His mouth curved into a beguiling smile. "Perhaps it's too soon to expect that, but I hope that will change." He lifted his gaze to survey everyone. "We are here to find something. Help us do that, and we will leave immediately."

Lann Dhearg. Elspeth exchanged a look with Carrie, then was careful to turn her attention toward the man at the fireplace.

"I think one or more of you probably already know what we seek." He slowly perused the room, his gaze boring into each person in turn. "Come forward now, and you can go about your evening."

Elspeth's heart beat so fast, she was sure someone would notice. She worked to keep her outward appearance relaxed, but feared she was squeezing Aunt Leah's hand rather tightly. Giving her an encouraging smile, Elspeth loosened her grip.

The silence in the common room grew. Everyone looked around, mostly in fear. In addition to Elspeth and her aunt, the guests were one single man, a married couple, and three women.

"I'm disappointed no one will speak," the man said, frowning. He inclined his head to a man standing not too far to his right. Then he pointed at Elspeth. "Her."

"No!" Aunt Leah grabbed Elspeth's arm.

"Don't fret, Aunt Leah," Elspeth said with a calm she didn't feel.

The man came toward her. He was very tall, with wild, straw-colored hair and small, intense eyes. He held a flintlock pistol and had a sword strapped to his hip.

Elspeth stood and squared her shoulders, hoping the posture would give her some much-needed courage. "What do you want with me?"

The man at the fireplace gestured for her to come forward. "Kent, bring her."

Kent reached for her, but Elspeth hurried around another table and went to the man who was apparently their leader. She gave him a defiant stare as she arrived at his side.

The leader's eyes glittered with impatience. "My men said your room was cold. Tell me why."

"I was overheated. I had the window open."

"Then why were there men's boots in your room?"

Oh, hell. She hadn't even had time to consider that. Heat rushed to her face, and she didn't think it was possible he wouldn't notice.

"They're mine," she said with only the barest hesitation. "I sometimes dress as a man. Undoubtedly, they also saw my coat."

Pulling back his lips in an exaggerated smile, the leader bared his teeth. "I find that hard to believe, Miss…?"

"Why does my name matter? Besides, I don't know yours."

"I am Hurst Grover. I work for an organization, and we are here to find a sword that rightfully belongs to us."

No, it didn't! Elspeth pressed her lips together.

He stepped toward her. "Now, you are…?"

She felt the breath of the other man—Kent—behind her. "Miss Marshall."

"Lovely. Now, Miss Marshall, where is the man who was in your room?"

"I told you, the boots and coat are—"

She didn't get to finish because Grover's hand shot out, striking her across the mouth. Pain streaked through her lips and cheek. She tasted blood. Her aunt's cry filled the common room, and Elspeth could hear others murmuring. But she didn't turn her head to look. She kept her gaze—and all her fury—directed at Grover.

"I know where it is."

Now Elspeth swung her head, as did Grover, toward the person who had spoken.

Carrie looked at him, her eyes devoid of their usual brightness.

"Carrie, don't," Elspeth said.

She turned her gaze to Elspeth and pushed herself up from the table. "I'm sorry."

Chapter Nine

LEAVING FROM ELSPETH'S window proved more difficult once Tavish got outside. He'd found a footing in the stonework, then a gust of cold wind had nearly blown him to the ground. The sound of voices in Elspeth's room nearly drove him back inside, but he didn't know how many men he would face. Better to assess the situation and hopefully recruit the pair of grooms in the stable to help him.

As he made his way along the stones toward the corner of the building, he was simultaneously grateful for his bare feet and annoyed. He was able to use his toes to grip the stones, but they were absolutely freezing, and the wind was fierce, so that by the time he rounded the edge of the building and dropped onto the roof of the lean-to, his feet were quite cold.

Ignoring his discomfort, he lowered himself from the roof, then pivoted toward the stable. Lanterns hung on either side of the wide entryway. In the middle stood a man—not one of the grooms—with a musket. *Bloody hell.*

Tavish waited until the man's head was turned, then dashed over to the building, pressing himself against the icy stone. Moving quickly, he crept along the shadows. Damn, he wished he had his boots, and not just because his feet were cold. He wanted his knife. Except that he hoped Elspeth had been able to grab it.

He couldn't use the sword because it would flame as soon as Tavish was threatened. The last thing he wanted to do was set his opponent on fire and have that fire spread to the stables. Lann Dhearg was a powerful weapon, but in some instances, it was a nuisance that only compounded an already dangerous situation.

Except…his grandfather had once told him that the flame could be controlled, but he didn't know how. Tavish wished he knew. He tried to think of something that made sense, but he didn't have time. Also, his mind was too stressed.

He continued along the building and felt a surge of relief as he reached the wide opening of the building where the man stood. A pitchfork stood against the edge of the entryway.

In one quick move, Tavish grabbed the implement and raced toward the man. He used the pitchfork to knock the musket out of his hand. The weapon flew out, and Tavish dove to catch it, nearly losing his balance. He swept around and used the butt to hit the man in the head. The villain crumpled to the ground.

Tavish searched the man and found a knife at his waist. Removing the weapon, Tavish considered how he could take it with him. He had no pockets or any other way to carry it. He was already burdened with the sword since he didn't have the scabbard.

He tossed the knife away and dragged the unconscious man just inside the stable.

"Fitz?" a man called from deeper in the stable to Tavish's right.

Tavish pressed himself against the side of a stall. Dammit. He needed that pitchfork. Or the musket. Or the bloody knife. Having none of them, he waited, his breath coming hard.

The man rounded the corner of the stall. Tavish knew the moment he realized Fitz was no longer at his post. The villain unsheathed his sword and swung around.

There was no help for it. Tavish had to use Lann Dhearg. He hefted the sword, and red-orange flame started at the base, licking its way upward as the other man's eyes widened. Tavish launched, and their swords clashed.

The other man was a good swordsman. They thrust and parried, circling each other several times before Tavish knocked the other man's blade away. It would be too easy to finish him, but his body would go up in flames and the stable would catch fire.

Instead, Tavish threw Lann Dhearg aside and dove for the other man's sword. The villain did the same, and they both got there at the same time, hitting the ground on top of the sword.

They tussled over the weapon, but the villain got his hand around it first. It was too big and bulky to wield as they tangled together, but he brought the pommel down hard against Tavish's temple. Pain exploded in his head, but he ignored it as he continued to fight for the weapon.

Tavish wrapped his hand around the man's wrist and squeezed. The villain put his hand on Tavish's neck, his fingers digging into the flesh and threatening Tavish's airway. Tavish rolled and pushed the man's hand away as his opponent tried desperately to use the sword.

The light from the lanterns glinted off something else to Tavish's left. The knife he'd cast aside.

Tavish released the villain's wrist and rolled. He reached out, then closed his fingers around the knife and picked it up. The man was already on his knees, his eyes intent, his lip curled. Unsheathing the dagger, Tavish threw it at the man, catching him just below his collarbone. Without hesitation, Tavish grabbed the sword from the man and drove the blade into his gut.

Chest heaving, Tavish wiped at the blood streaming down the side of his face. He got to his feet, sweat trickling down his back despite the frigid air.

He swept up Lann Dhearg and rushed deeper into the stable in search of more of the miscreants and for the grooms. These men had to be from the Order of the Round Table.

Another lantern hung at this end of the building. Its light illuminated the pair of grooms tied together in a heap in an unused stall, both unconscious.

"Damn," he muttered. He'd been hoping to use their help. After ensuring there were no more villains, Tavish quickly untied their bonds, then raced back to the inn while he madly tried to come up with a plan.

Two villains in the stables. How many inside? One had come into Elspeth's room, but there had to be more.

Clinging to the shadows along the outside of the inn, Tavish made his way to the first window into the common room. He crouched low and peered in through the corner.

It seemed everyone had been gathered—they sat at tables while six men armed with guns and swords encircled them. Tavish noted Balthazar's knitted cap atop his bald head as well as the fiery curls of his daughter. Then his breath caught as he saw Elspeth, also seated at their table along with her aunt.

Tavish no longer felt the cold on his feet, but his blood turned to ice as a tall blond man started toward her. She got up and avoided him, going to the fireplace, where she stood beside another man. His close-cropped beard was familiar…Tavish recognized him from earlier in the day when he'd gone to visit Kerr. He'd passed the man on his way.

That made nine—the two in the stable and seven in the common room. But were there more anywhere else?

How he wished he could hear what they were saying. Then the man hit Elspeth across the mouth. Tavish leapt up, Lann Dhearg tight in his grip, as fury tore through him.

Reason won out. If he charged inside now, he would lose. He counted seven men, most with pistols. He needed to split them up somehow so he could even the numbers.

He watched as the man who'd hit Elspeth—and would surely pay for it before the night was finished—and two others took her and Carrie toward the back of the inn. Toward Carrie's chamber.

That left four men. Forming a plan, he ran around to the back of the inn to the kitchen door, which was, as expected, locked. "Had to try," he muttered.

Using Lann Dhearg's pommel, he broke through the window and quickly scrambled inside, cutting his arm on a shard of glass. The door from the common room swung open and in ran one of the men—directly toward Tavish. He moved quickly, slicing his feet on the glass scattered about the floor. He'd hoped to draw two of the men, not one.

He'd take what he could get. When he lifted Lann Dhearg, the sword flamed. Once again, he had to consider how his actions might set the whole bloody place on fire. The sword was becoming a liability. Still, he couldn't put it down.

The other man yelled as soon as the flames took over the blade and lifted his pistol. Glancing about, Tavish saw a knife on a table used for preparing food. As he'd done in the stable, he threw the weapon. This man, however, provided a much better target. The knife landed in the hollow of his neck, silencing him as he crumpled to the floor.

"Go and shoot him!"

The directive came from the common room. Scarcely a second later, the muzzle of a musket peeked around the door. Tavish threw himself toward the back door and pushed the bolt aside. The musket fired, and wood splintered over his head. He considered facing the man, but others had guns. He'd taken one of them, anyway.

Tavish opened the door and ran into the cold night, his mind already churning with another plan.

GROVER HELD ELSPETH'S arm as Carrie, held by Kent, led them toward the back corner of the inn. A third man named Thane came with them. He appeared to be the youngest of the brigands and wore spectacles.

Once Carrie had told them to follow her, Elspeth had relaxed. Carrie couldn't lead them to Tavish or the sword.

Carrie took them to her room, where they all crammed inside. Dougal Kerr was still on the bed asleep. However, there were bindings keeping him there, just as Carrie had said.

"What the bloody hell is this?" Grover growled. He let go of Elspeth and stepped toward Carrie.

"The sword is there." She pointed at the door to her Chamber of Sorrow.

Grover nodded toward Kent, who directed his pistol at Carrie. "Open it."

Carrie sent a glance toward Elspeth before going to push open the door. She went inside, and Grover followed.

"Go," Kent said, pushing at Elspeth. She joined them in the small chamber, as did Kent. The room was quite cramped with all of them inside.

"What the devil is all this?" Grover asked.

Carrie shrugged. "I collect things. The sword is there." She pointed to a sword hanging on the wall.

Elspeth's breath caught. It was a risk... Hopefully none of them would know it wasn't truly Lann Dhearg. Did they know it had runes on the hilt or a herringbone pattern on the blade? Did they know it wouldn't flame for them? Were they expecting it to be too heavy to carry? The sword on the wall possessed none of those traits.

She looked toward Carrie, who gave her an almost imperceptible nod as her eyes shot to a spot just behind Elspeth. Turning her head slightly, Elspeth saw a small dirk with a hollow circle at its base hanging on a hook on the wall. What did Carrie mean to do? Elspeth's pulse sped.

Grover removed the sword from where it hung and lifted it up. "Thane! Come look at this."

Thane squeezed into the room, his gaze instantly landing on the sword in Grover's hand.

"What's that?"

"Supposedly Dyrnwyn."

They thought this was the sword of Rhydderch Hael? If they were from the organization Tavish had mentioned, and it seemed they were, it made sense they were looking for one of the thirteen treasures. Were they even aware of Lann Dhearg?

Thane took the sword from Grover and turned it in his hand before laughing with youthful exuberance. "The hilt is all wrong. Dyrnwyn has a red jewel in the pommel. But that wasn't its original form. It was gold, with runes—"

"Enough," Grover snapped.

Thane nodded as he pressed his lips together.

Grover pivoted toward Carrie, snarling. She grabbed a mace from the wall and swung it at Thane, who was closest to her.

The second Carrie attacked, Elspeth grabbed the dirk and struck out at the nearest man, which was Grover. He dodged the knife and hit her in the forearm. Carrie cried out, distracting Elspeth. She lost hold of the dirk, and it flew from her grip.

Elspeth watched in horror as Carrie fell to the floor in a heap next to a seemingly unconscious Thane. "Carrie!" She tried to go to the fallen woman, but Grover grabbed her upper arm.

He screamed in her face, his spittle showering her cheek. "Bitch!" He shoved her toward Kent. "Take her!"

Kent put his arm around Elspeth's middle and hauled her from the Chamber of Sorrow. Something inside her snapped. She kicked at him and tried to wrest free of his hold.

One of the villains from the common room appeared in the doorway to Carrie's room. His gaze flicked nervously toward Kent. "Tomlin is dead. Fitz came from the stable—he was hit in the head and fell unconscious. Ed is taking care of him."

Grover had come out of the Chamber of Sorrow and now swore viciously. Kent began to throw things—a pitcher, a basin. Then he went into the Chamber of Sorrow, where he pulled things from the walls, all the while shouting and cursing. Elspeth could clearly see him from where she stood.

"Kent!" Grover went back into the Chamber of Sorrow and grabbed the man's shoulder. "You can't save him now. But you can kill the man who did this."

Kent stopped and turned, his expression cold and terrifying. He combed his hand through his hair. "I will see him dead."

Elspeth's blood turned to ice. She didn't doubt he would try to kill Tavish at the earliest possible moment. Assuming Tavish was still alive. Her insides went colder still.

"Yes, you will kill him," Grover assured Kent. "You will have revenge for your brother." He turned suddenly and came back into Carrie's room. "You." He clasped Elspeth's forearm, then turned his head to the man who'd come to inform them of Tomlin's death. Grover pointed toward the Chamber of Sorrow. "Jackson, tie up the serving maid and bring Thane."

Jackson nodded and stepped into the room. Grover dragged Elspeth into the corridor and shoved her against the opposite wall. "You know this man who killed Tomlin. Tell me who he is."

Kent had come out behind them and now moved to Grover's side. He wound his hand in Elspeth's hair and pulled until her scalp burned.

"Tell me!"

Elspeth fought to keep her panic at bay as tears of pain burned her eyes. "I don't know him."

"You lie." Grover bared his teeth at her again as he leaned close. "Does he have the sword?"

"I don't know anything about a sword." Elspeth wanted to pull away from Kent's hold, but to try would only increase the agony in her head.

"She lies," Kent spat. "They knew about the sword."

"We don't. Carrie—she was just trying to appease you with one of the swords in her collection. *You're* the one who mentioned a sword."

Grover stared at her. "I know you're lying about knowing him. It seems reasonable you'd lie about the sword too." Grover tipped his head in the direction of Carrie's room. "Perhaps I should have Ed kill the serving maid to find out what you know."

Kent pulled on Elspeth's hair. Hysteria rose in her throat. She struggled to breathe as the blistering ache in her scalp persisted. "His name is John MacLean. I swear I don't know anything about a sword." She wanted to say he didn't either, but how could she know unless they'd discussed it? And that would quite negate the entire lie.

Grover frowned. "We'll see." He looked over at Kent. "Time to lure Mr. MacLean to us."

He wrapped his hand around Elspeth's arm once more and stalked toward the common room, pulling her along with him. Thankfully, Kent had let go of her hair. A tear snaked down her cheek, and she used her free hand to wipe it away. She didn't want Aunt Leah to see her distress.

Grover pulled her back toward the fireplace. Kent was hard on their heels.

Balthazar stood, his eyes moving from them toward the back of the inn and back again. "Where's Carrie? Where's my daughter?" His voice held a dark frenzy that tore at Elspeth's heart.

Elspeth wanted to assure him that she was fine, but couldn't.

"If ye hurt her—" Balthazar cut himself off with a sob.

Aunt Leah reached for his hand and pulled him to sit back down. She kept hold of him as her gaze met Elspeth's. Elspeth gave her a small encouraging nod that was completely at odds with her fear.

Grover cleared his throat. "It's come to my attention that there is a guest missing from this gathering. A Mr. MacLean. I'm beginning to think he has something I want." He strolled toward Balthazar, who twisted in his chair as Grover approached.

"Mr. Pitagowan," Grover said pleasantly, standing next to Balthazar's chair. "What can you tell me of Mr. MacLean?"

"Nothing. He's just a guest."

"You must be able to tell me where he's from or what he's doing here, whether he went to see anyone—that sort of thing."

"He's from Glasgow. That's all I know."

Grover turned in a slow circle. "Can no one tell me why this man went to see Dougal Kerr?"

"Why would any of us know that?" Balthazar took his hand from Aunt Leah's and rose, his brows pitching low over his eyes in anger. "Ye come in here and threaten everyone. Ye strike Miss Marshall and ye did Lord knows what to my daughter." He looked around at the other guests. "There are more of us than them!"

Exhaling, Grover nodded toward Kent. He came forward and slammed the butt of his pistol into the side of Balthazar's head, sending him sprawling to the floor. Aunt Leah shrieked, and the other women did the same.

"Tie him up and gag him," Grover said. "Tie them all up!"

Chapter Ten

SCREAMS FROM THE inn drew Tavish to run to the common room window, his bloodied feet protesting as they hit the near-frozen ground, particularly when he ran over a large rock. He crouched low as he'd done before and peered inside. A pair of the villains were tying the guests to chairs, while others held pistols to keep anyone from rebelling. Tavish noted that Elspeth wasn't among them but was standing with the leader.

He swore and stood up from the window, going to pace in the shadows of the corner of the building. Holding Lann Dhearg in one hand, he scrubbed the other over his face. He needed to set these people free.

Going back to the window, he counted the villains again. Five. But shit, one of them was the man he'd knocked out with the musket in the stable. Five in the common room, two dead, two missing. He realized Carrie was missing too and swore again.

He should just charge inside. One of them might shoot him, but if he could get to one of the male hostages and untie him so that he could then untie others, perhaps they could launch a revolt and retake the inn. He knew Elspeth would help. He had no doubt of her courage.

Tavish studied the five men and tried to assess their abilities. It was nearly impossible since he hadn't seen them fight. One was exceptionally tall and rather vicious looking—the one with the blond hair. Tavish would wager he was the one who would give Tavish the most trouble.

The two missing brigands came from the rear of the inn. One was leaning on the other, his hand cradling the side of his face, which was covered in blood. A hostage had done that to him. Tavish wanted to cheer.

A moment later, two of the villains walked to the door. Tavish pressed himself back against the frigid stone.

"MacLean!" one of them called. "Come inside and give us the sword, or we're going to start killing the hostages!"

Did they really know he had the sword? Tavish gripped Lann Dhearg as the two men walked out into the yard. One was smaller than the other. Tavish decided he'd take out the larger one first. He inched backward, skimming his free hand over the ground in search of the rock he'd found with his injured foot.

"We know you have the sword! Bring it in and save these people!"

Something in his tone told Tavish they *didn't* know—as well as the fact that he'd said, "We know you have" it. To him, that indicated they didn't actually know, which made more sense to him. Elspeth wouldn't have told them, and Carrie wouldn't know for sure.

Recalling that Carrie was not with the others, Tavish renewed his resolve and continued searching for the rock. At last, his fingers closed around it. Fist sized, the rock filled his palm as he picked it up. He had one chance.

Lanterns on the outside of the inn cast a glow over the yard. Tavish kept himself low and dashed out along the perimeter until he was closer to the larger of the two men. Standing, he quickly took aim and launched the rock. It hit the man square in the back of the head, driving him to his knees with a loud cry.

Tavish's breath caught—he'd wanted to knock him out. Then the man pitched forward onto the ground, and Tavish exhaled. He threw himself on the ground as the smaller man spun around, looking for the threat.

His gaze landed on Tavish, and he sprinted forward. Tavish barely got to his feet before the man raised his pistol. But nothing happened. Cursing, the man threw the weapon away and drew his sword.

Raising Lann Dhearg, Tavish realized he could use the sword to its full potential out here without worrying about setting the inn or stable on fire. He narrowed his eyes at his opponent. "Let the hostages go."

Red-orange flame licked up the blade and cast bright light over the other man's face, clearly revealing his fear as his gaze locked on the sword. He took a step back.

"I don't want to hurt you," Tavish said, advancing. "But I will save those people."

"Just as we'll get that sword." The man surprised Tavish by lunging forward. Their weapons clashed. Then they circled each other a moment before the smaller man again tried an offensive strike.

Tavish easily parried the blow. "This is your last chance. Surrender."

The man answered by pushing forward. But Tavish didn't retreat. He was taller and bigger, and so was his sword. Plus, it was on fire. He pressed his advantage, driving the man back with thrust after thrust.

Faltering, the man dropped his sword. Tavish wanted to let him go, but then he pulled a knife from his boot. Gritting his teeth, Tavish lunged, sinking the blade into the man's chest. His eyes widened as his body caught fire. He screamed and ran.

Tavish didn't watch what happened next. He dashed to the first man he'd taken down with the rock, intending to drag him to the stable to tie him up.

But the man was already rising to his knees. His face was pale, his eyes wide with terror. He looked from the flaming man to Tavish, then jumped to his feet and sprinted into the night.

Tavish let him go. Then he ran back to the inn and pressed himself next to the window. He peered inside. The villains seemed agitated. Perhaps they'd heard the screams of the man who'd caught fire.

That left five of them, two of whom were injured. For the first time, Tavish liked these odds. A plan formed in his mind. He dashed to the stable to set it in motion.

"HE HAS THE bloody sword!" Grover stalked back to the fireplace from the window, his eyes blazing.

The screams from outside echoed in Elspeth's ears. She prayed the sounds hadn't come from Tavish. When no one came back into the inn, she exhaled in relief. If Tavish had been the one hurt—or worse—the brigands would have returned.

Grover paced beside her in front of the fireplace. His face was drawn tight with tension. He stopped abruptly and came toward her, not stopping until there were just inches between them. "MacLean has become a problem for me. Perhaps what I need to do is dangle you from a window upstairs and threaten to drop you unless he comes in."

Elspeth swallowed. She couldn't look away from the malevolence in his eyes.

"At least now we know he has the sword." He slitted his eyes and stroked his hand along his jaw.

Elspeth wanted to know how they'd tracked the sword to the inn, but to do so would show she knew more than she'd admitted.

Kent approached. "Let's burn the inn with these people inside. That will draw MacLean out, and we can take him easily—even with that damned sword. I will do it myself, in fact." The craven hunger in his eyes made it clear he wanted to try.

Grover grabbed Elspeth's arm once more and dragged her to the front door. Opening it, he yelled outside, "I'm going to kill your Miss Marshall! You have five minutes to bring the sword to me!"

After slamming the door, he strode back to the fireplace, pulling Elspeth along with him. Once there, he released her with such force that she went sprawling on the floor, hitting her shoulder as she landed.

Huffing out a breath, Grover offered her his hand. "Look what you made me do."

Elspeth sat up but scooted away from him. Suddenly, the front door of the inn opened. Grover turned his head, and Elspeth did the same.

Tavish appeared, closing the door behind him.

Blood caked the left side of his face from temple to jaw. His white shirt was smeared with dirt and blood, and one sleeve had a gaping hole. There was more blood on his feet. So much blood.

A cry tore from Elspeth's lips as she scrambled to her feet. Before she could go to him, Grover clasped her arm and pulled her to his side.

The two uninjured brigands trained their flintlocks on Tavish. He lifted his hands in the air. Where was Lann Dhearg? Had he hidden the sword to prevent them from obtaining it? She hoped so.

"At last," Grover said, sounding pleased. And calm—though Elspeth could feel the tension radiating from him. "Where is Dyrnwyn?"

Elspeth caught the flicker of surprise that dashed across Tavish's brow. He clearly hadn't known they thought the sword was its twin.

"You can't have it," Tavish said calmly. "I know who you are."

Grover smiled. "Do you?"

"Not you specifically—and that doesn't matter to me one whit." Elspeth felt Grover twitch. "But I know your organization, and I'll say it again—you can't have the sword."

Grover looked toward Kent, who tossed him the flintlock he held. Catching the pistol, Grover turned it on Elspeth, leveling it against her temple. "Then you can't have Miss Marshall."

"No!" Tavish thrust his arms up higher. He reached his right hand behind his head. When he brought it back up, Lann Dhearg was there. As he brandished it before him, bright red-orange fire danced along the blade.

Everyone gasped. The sound of a pistol firing drew another cry from Elspeth. She watched in horror as it struck Tavish's left bicep, tearing another hole in his shirt. The grimy white linen began to turn red with his blood.

Another pistol fired as Tavish advanced on one of the men. Elspeth tried to break free from Grover, but he squeezed more tightly. She had to help Tavish!

"Kent, upstairs!" Grover called before he tugged Elspeth toward the stairs. The sounds of everyone yelling or screaming and swords clashing filled her ears as they ascended to the landing.

The last thing she heard was Aunt Leah sobbing her name, and the last thing she saw was the three villains, including Thane and Fitz, driving Tavish into a corner with their swords. She screamed as Grover pulled her around the corner, certain that Tavish would be lost.

ELSPETH'S SCREAM DISTRACTED Tavish just enough so that one of his opponents was able to nick his side with his sword. Pain slicing through him, he drove forward.

"Don't start a fire!" someone yelled.

Tavish didn't want to set a fire, but he also needed to finish these men so he could get to Elspeth. He knew they were luring him upstairs.

Perhaps if he started a fire, he would force them down…

Suddenly, he had help. One of the guests, a spry lad in his early twenties, was free from his bonds. He used a chair to engage one of the men. The married man joined him—he'd grabbed a poker from the fireplace.

A musket fired, and the uninjured villain fell. Tavish looked over to see Balthazar standing behind the bar with the flintlock in his grip, his lip curled. Then he worked to reload it.

One of the remaining villains, a younger man with spectacles, shrieked and dropped his sword.

"Go!" the young guest yelled to Tavish as he jerked his head toward the stairs.

Tavish didn't need further urging. He sprinted upstairs and kicked the first door open in search of Elspeth.

A feminine shriek sounded from the direction of her room. Tavish ran but had to stop short as the man called Kent came into the corridor. Brandishing his broadsword, he strode toward Tavish. The light was dim, but Tavish could see the menace cut into the lines of the man's face.

Bloody hell. Tavish couldn't use Lann Dhearg. He'd set the inn on fire for certain. Yet, if he didn't use it, how could he combat the man? And he *must* fight to get to Elspeth. No, he must *win* to get to her. He'd just found love, and he'd do anything to keep her.

Lann Dhearg's flame diminished as he moved forward. By the time he faced Kent, it had died.

Kent narrowed his eyes. "What happened to the fire?"

Tavish thought he knew—it was the love he felt. Lann Dhearg thrived on darker emotion. The key, it seemed, to controlling the flame was to feel something better. He focused on love and hope, letting the joy of finding Elspeth and their plans for a future guide him. He swung the blade with all his might.

Kent fell back as he parried. Tavish didn't give him a chance to respond and struck out again. Pivoting, Kent caught Tavish's blade on his. Tavish pushed him against the wall, their swords clashing between them. Kent's pale blue eyes narrowed just before he spit in Tavish's face. Then he shoved Tavish so that he sprawled against the opposite wall.

Tavish wiped his hand over his face and launched away from the wall as Kent turned, reversing their original positions so that Elspeth's room was now behind Tavish. He was tempted to go and ensure she was safe, but he had to finish this first.

With a loud cry, Kent drove forward, swinging his sword. Tavish parried the blow, clenching his jaw as the blades struck, igniting a spark that Tavish feared was the sword starting to flame once more. He was relieved when it did not and concentrated on the love in his heart.

"No!" Elspeth's cry from inside her room spurred Tavish into greater action. With renewed fervor, he attacked, pushing Kent backward toward the stairs. He was relentless in his pursuit, thrusting and swinging until he finally met the man's flesh. Lann Dhearg cut into Kent's shoulder.

The man screamed and dropped his sword. The blade clattered down the stairs. Tavish kicked out and sent Kent tumbling after.

The married guest, carrying another sword, ran to the fallen Kent. It was all Tavish needed to see. He spun around and raced to Elspeth's room.

Elspeth's lower half was outside the window. She clutched at the leader's hand as he started to turn. "Grover!" she shouted.

"Don't you let her fall," Tavish said. "Not if you want this sword."

Grover held a pistol, which Tavish hadn't realized he possessed. He leveled it at Tavish. "I will have that sword, whether she falls or not."

"It's not Dyrnwyn." Tavish felt a rush of satisfaction at the surprise in Grover's eyes. "Your order wants Dyrnwyn. I'd tell you to inform them of their mistake, but you won't be able to do that." Tavish hadn't wanted to kill anyone, but this man had made it clear he'd go to any length to get what he wanted. And Tavish still didn't know what had happened to Carrie.

Grover's dark eyes glittered in the light from the fireplace. "It may not be Dyrnwyn, but I will have it." He let go of Elspeth. She wildly reached for purchase.

Tavish pitched himself toward her as Grover fired. Dropping Lann Dhearg, Tavish grabbed her hands and pulled her back through the window. They landed together on the floor, with him taking the brunt of their fall.

He looked into her wide green eyes. "Are you all right?"

She nodded, then pushed herself off him. Tavish leapt up and helped her to do the same. Grover had picked up the sword.

He frowned. "Why is it so bloody heavy?"

Tavish advanced on him. "Because it wasn't made for you."

"Get the sword!" Elspeth rushed at Grover and lifted her arm.

Tavish saw the glint of a blade in her hand, but couldn't see what she did to Grover. He could guess, however, as Grover's eyes rounded. The villain gasped, and Lann Dhearg fell to the floor.

Grover stumbled back. Elspeth stepped away. Tavish plucked up the sword, then saw blood staining the front of Grover's clothing. The knife Tavish had left in his boot protruded from his chest. Grover fell against the window opening. Elspeth pushed him through.

The villain opened his mouth, but nothing came out. He fell to the earth below.

Elspeth threw her arms around Tavish's neck. "You're safe."

"So are you." Clasping her, he buried his face in her hair and closed his eyes. Suddenly, all the injuries he'd suffered decided to remind him they were there. He winced. "Ow."

She let him go and pulled back. He opened his eyes to see her looking over him intently. "You need help."

"Soon. I want to make sure everyone downstairs is safe and that the rest of the villains are in hand."

She nodded, taking his free hand. "I've got you."

"Yes, and I'm never letting you go."

Chapter Eleven

As Elspeth helped Tavish walk downstairs, she was aware of every ache and pain he suffered. "You need to sit as soon as possible so I can tend to your feet. What happened?"

"Glass in the kitchen. I had to break a window to get in."

"So you decided to dance all over it?"

Tavish was surprised he could laugh, but he did. "I had to fight someone."

"What happened to him?"

"Same as Grover, minus falling from a window." Tavish kissed her forehead. "You are a formidable woman, Elspeth."

"He was evil."

"Yes, he was."

She guided him down the stairs and immediately surveyed the common room. Kent and Thane were bound together near the bar, while the other two were off to the side. One was the victim of Balthazar's musket, and the other had been gutted by someone's sword.

Aunt Leah rushed to meet Elspeth, hugging her tightly. "I'm so glad you're all right." Then she looked at Tavish and gasped. "You look terrible."

Tavish gave her his lopsided smile before turning his attention to the other guests. "I see you all have everything well in hand."

The young guest who'd sprung into action inclined his head toward the sword in Tavish's hand. "Is that what they wanted?"

Tavish nodded. "Yes. As I'm sure you could all see, it's a rather special weapon. Because of that, I would beg just one thing of you—and I know I don't have a right to ask anything at all. However, there are many people who would like to get their hands on this sword for nefarious purposes. Men like Grover and his band. It would be best for everyone if this sword and its…abilities remained a whispered story, a myth." He glanced at Elspeth.

She'd already agreed she wouldn't write about it, and she never would.

"No one but those here tonight would believe it anyway," the married man said, clutching his wife to his side.

Balthazar burst into the common room at that moment, his arm around Carrie. "She's all right!"

Elspeth felt Tavish relax beside her. In fact, it was as if all the tension left his body. He began to slump against her so that she had to prop him up. "Help me," she said to no one in particular.

Aunt Leah moved to Tavish's other side, and together, she and Elspeth guided him to the nearest chair.

Elspeth knelt before him, then glanced up at Aunt Leah. "His feet…"

"I'll fetch water and cloth."

"And medicine," Carrie said.

Elspeth looked to the serving maid. "You're truly all right?"

Carrie smiled. "Yes."

"That was a brilliant plan," Elspeth said.

"Thank you." Carrie notched her chin up with pride, then looked to

Tavish. "Have you any idea how these brigands knew to come here in search of the sword?"

"I don't, but I wonder if Dougal might be able to tell us when he awakens."

Carrie nodded, then left the common room, presumably to fetch medicine.

Tavish let out a groan. "Are all the villains accounted for?"

"The grooms?" Balthazar asked worriedly.

"Unconscious," Tavish said.

The sound of loud barking drew everyone to turn their heads. The front door opened, and the dogs rushed inside, followed by the grooms. Balthazar rushed to the animals, who swarmed around him.

"There is one villain missing," Tavish said to Elspeth. "One of them ran off after the man outside caught fire."

Elspeth picked up one of his feet and winced at the damage. Several jagged cuts tore his flesh. "Is there glass stuck in there?"

"I don't think so. I pulled out a few pieces after I left the kitchen."

She wrapped her hand around his ankle and looked up at him. "I'll take care of you."

He smiled. "My feet appreciate that."

"Not just your feet, but all of you. That's what wives do."

"Wives?" Aunt Leah had arrived with a basin of water. She set it down next to Elspeth and stared at her. Another guest set down a small stack of cloths.

"Mr. MacLean has asked me to marry him, and I said yes."

Aunt Leah put her hand on her mouth. "Oh my, well, that's wonderful. I just hope it's not a hasty decision after everything…" She shook her head. "On second thought, it seems as though he *should* propose." She gave Elspeth a pointed look. Aunt Leah had seen his clothing littered about Elspeth's room as well as her state of undress, and she was no fool.

"He asked earlier, before any of this happened." Elspeth smiled up at him as she wetted a cloth.

Tavish turned his head toward Aunt Leah. "Truth be known, I started to fall in love with your niece two years ago. Seeing her again ensured I fell the rest of the way." He moved his warm gaze to Elspeth. "I'm only sorry I didn't make that happen sooner."

Elspeth dabbed at his foot, and he flinched. "Sorry!"

"It's quite all right," he said. "Necessary, in fact. Do your worst."

"I will do my *best*—with love."

He grinned at her. "That is all I can hope for."

Epilogue

December 29

ELSPETH COULD SCARCELY believe it had just been over a week since the terrifying events at Balthazar's Inn. Everyone that had endured that evening had promised to gather at the inn in the summer to make a new, better memory. And Elspeth and Tavish would do it as the Lord and Lady Strathclyde.

They'd stopped in Dunkeld to collect her father, who'd been shocked to hear of what had occurred, especially that his daughter was to be wed, and continued to Dumbarton. They'd arrived just two days ago and had been married the day before, much to the tearful delight of Aunt Leah, Elspeth's father, and Tavish's grandmother. Elspeth looked forward to spending the day with them. As soon as the sun came up.

For now, she snuggled against her husband's side in his wide bed, a smile stretching her cheeks.

"Methinks you are awake," Tavish murmured as his lips caressed her forehead.

"Yes. I didn't think you were, however."

"I wasn't, but when you wiggle against me like that, I can't remain asleep."

She laughed before kissing his chest. "I'll remember that. I was just thinking about the day ahead and how lovely it will be to celebrate with everyone. I'm glad Dougal and Neil arrived yesterday."

It turned out that Carrie had, in fact, known how to find Neil. He'd been hiding out not far from Calvine. She'd sent word to him, and, at Tavish's invitation, he and his brother had come here to Dumbarton. The first thing he'd done when he'd arrived was apologize to Tavish for stealing his sword and causing this mess.

Then Neil had explained that he'd written a note to Dougal about the sword being hidden at the inn, which the men from the order had found when they'd searched Dougal's cottage. Dougal had lied about not knowing about the sword out of fear for his brother. At last, they'd learned how the brigands had known to come to the inn.

"Do you think they'll accept your offer of going to the colonies?" Elspeth had been astounded to learn that Tavish not only owned three ships on which he transported Jacobites to America, but that he owned property in a place called North Carolina, where many of them had settled and would build farms.

Tavish stroked her shoulder. "I think they will. Neil was quite excited by the prospect, and I think Dougal is just glad to have his brother safe."

"I am glad to have all of us safe." Elspeth shuddered when she recalled what they'd had to do at the inn.

Tavish took his arm from her and started to slip from the bed. Elspeth reached for him. "Where are you going?"

He smiled at her. "Nowhere, but I need to do something." He left the bed and stoked the fire, then returned carrying Lann Dhearg of all things.

She bolted upright. "What are you doing with that? Please don't set the bed on fire!"

He chuckled as he climbed onto the bed. "That won't happen. I didn't have a chance to tell you the true secret of this sword. We've scarcely had a moment alone since we left the inn, and last night, well, I had other, more pressing matters to attend to."

Heat sparked in Elspeth's core as she arched a brow at him. "What secret?"

"How I kept it from bursting into flame when I fought Kent outside your room. My grandfather had told me there was a way to control the flame, but he didn't know what it was. We knew that anger and despair and other negative emotions made the sword more powerful. When I was fighting to save you, I knew I loved you—more than anything. That love and the hope for our future together extinguished the flame. Even now, I can feel that love vibrating through the sword."

Love tingled through Elspeth's chest and spread to her limbs. "Your love for me saved us all?"

His eyes gleamed with mirth. "That, in addition to your quick thinking and expert paring knife skills."

Elspeth laughed. "What a wonderful secret for such a terrible weapon. You're still going to hide it in the morning?"

He nodded. "As soon as it's light. First, however, I want to do something. Elspeth, I grant you the use of Lann Dhearg." He held out the sword.

She frowned. "You know I can't lift that."

"Try." The corner of his mouth ticked up.

Still frowning, she closed her hand around the handle and tentatively took it from him. It wasn't exactly light—it was still a sword—but she *could* lift it. "Because you gave it to me?"

He nodded again. "Do you feel the way it sings in your grip?"

"I'm not sure I'd describe it like that. Perhaps more of a low hum." She tipped her head to the side. "Why did you want to give it to me?"

"Because after I hide it in a few hours, it will be lost forever. I wanted it to know the love we share from both of us. This will sound strange, but I think it was…content once I learned how to control it."

"You talk as if it's a living thing."

"Of course, it's not, but it has power."

She could feel it. "Yes, it does." Concentrating, she thought she could feel the love the blade now held. But perhaps that was just the love she felt for Tavish, which was almost overwhelming. She looked up at him a bit shyly. "I can't believe how happy I am."

He leaned over and kissed her, his lips lingering against hers. "Believe it. And believe how very much I love you."

"It can't be as much as I love you." She gasped as the sword truly *sang* in her grip. Her eyes met his. "I think I felt what you meant!"

He grinned. "See?" He took the sword from her and set it down beside the bed. Then he gathered her against him and buried his face in her hair. "If someone were to write this legend, they'd have to include the story of our love—of how we tamed the sword."

"You tamed it."

He pulled back and looked down into her eyes. "We did it together. If not for the sword and our shared passion for legends, we may never have met. I would not have stopped to listen to your story at the Lammas Fair."

"I suppose that is true. You did take a rather long time to pursue me, however."

"Only because I was committed to supporting my mother's family." Even so, she saw the regret in his gaze.

She rushed to reassure him, putting her hand on his cheek. "I know. That's all behind us, and it doesn't matter because everything has turned out as it should. I am grateful we found our way to one another."

"As am I." He bent his head and kissed her collarbone, then her neck, then the hollow of her throat. "Allow me to show you." He pressed her back onto the bed and settled between her thighs.

"Shouldn't I be on top again?" she asked, tracing the scar that stretched across his shoulder blade that he'd sustained at Culloden. "I realize your wounds are mostly healed, but I'd hate for you to tear the stitches in your arm."

He let out a throaty laugh. "If you insist. Or, if you'd care to move to your side, I can show you another way." He rolled away from her, and she turned to face him.

He shook his head. "Other way."

Desire pulsed in her core as she rolled over and presented her back to him. "Like this?"

"Just like that." He stroked his hand up her back as he pushed her hair aside and kissed her nape. Then he trailed his hand down her collarbone and cupped her breast. She gasped as he rolled her nipple between his thumb and forefinger.

"You are the story I always hoped my life might be," she said softly, arching into his touch.

He kissed the side of her ear and whispered, "Then let us write it."

THE END

About Darcy Burke

Want to read more about the Thirteen Treasures of Britain and one family's quest to find and protect them? Don't miss the Legendary Rogues series: four intrepid heroines and adventurous heroes embark on exciting quests across Regency England and Wales! Start with Lady of Desire!

Darcy Burke is the USA Today Bestselling Author of sexy, emotional historical and contemporary romance. A native Oregonian, Darcy lives on the edge of wine country with her guitar-strumming husband, artist daughter, and imaginative son who will almost certainly out-write her one day (that may be tomorrow). Would you like to know when Darcy's next book is available and to hear about sales and deals? Sign up for the Darcy's Reader Club newsletter, visit her darcyburke.com, and follow her on social media:

Facebook: facebook.com/DarcyBurkeFans
Facebook Group – Darcy's Duchesses:
facebook.com/groups/DarcysDuchesses
Instagram at darcyburkeauthor

The Highlander Who Stole Christmas

By Eliza Knight

Part of A Very Highland Holiday Collection

The Highlander Who Stole Christmas

For eight months, Thane Shaw has patiently waited to enact his revenge against the Campbells, and finally he can't resist the opportunity that's presented itself: stealing their most precious treasure for his own—Lady Sarah.

AUTHOR'S NOTE

Dear Reader,

I'm very excited to be a part of A Very Highland Holiday collection. My story, The Highlander Who Stole Christmas, is a fun tale loosely based on How the Grinch Stole Christmas by Dr. Seuss. It's one of my very favorite Christmas stories, and I thought it would be a lot of fun to use some of the themes from it in writing this Highland holiday tale.

Thane is quite bitter when he heads down south from his clan's holding to Campbell lands where he plans to ruin their Christmas festivities and all of the holiday season by stealing Lady Sarah. But he may just find his heart growing by three, as did the Grinch.

While it's true that Christmas wasn't widely celebrated in the Highlands after being banned, and frowned upon even when the ban was lifted, there were some small pockets where traditions were maintained (probably in secret), perhaps a bit more quiet than how I portray celebrations in my story.

After all, it is said that the Christmas Carol, "O, Come All Ye Faithful" was written as a call to rebel arms after the birth of Bonnie Prince Charlie. How else would such a call be passed if rebels weren't singing in secret?

I wish you all a very merry holiday season, and a wonderful New Year.

Happy Highland Reading!

XO,
Eliza

DEDICATION

To Andrea, because you always bring me Christmas cheer!

Chapter One

REVENGE WAS A dish best served on a cold, snowy platter.

At least, that was what Laird Thane Shaw told himself as he headed out into the darkness just after nightfall, ignoring how the clouds covered the stars in the inky black sky. A blustery wind blew, and a man with less hate in his bones might have frozen to death. But his thirst for revenge was enough to keep him warm.

This was for his twin sister, Thea. If no one else felt the need to exact revenge on her behalf, then he would gladly take up the mantle. Thea deserved no less—in fact, she deserved so much more. Life, for one.

Damn his clan for fearing the wrath of the Campbells. The bloody bastards deserved to feel the same pain the Shaw clan endured. No matter their size, no matter their might, the Campbells couldn't get away with *murder*.

And he was going to teach them just that.

An eye for an eye—or rather, a sister for a sister.

Lady Sarah Campbell was about to become collateral damage in a war waged between clans, and while he did feel a twinge of guilt at putting her life in danger for the sake of his bloodlust, at least he wasn't going to kill her. Unlike the Campbells who had violently stolen his sister's life.

And so, Thane ignored the warnings of the weather and rode out into the night before anyone could stop him.

Wrapped in his plaid to ward off the cold along with an extra riding blanket on his horse, Destiny, he rode over the moors. His horse's hooves knocked against the frozen, packed earth. White clouds puffed from his mouth and the horse's muzzle, and with each gust of wind, the ice on the tree limbs tinkled like musical wind chimes.

Eight long months had passed since the Battle of Culloden, which had not only changed the landscape of Scotland but the landscape of his clan. His entire life. And ended his sister's.

He'd been one of the lucky ones. Hell, if one could call him lucky. He felt cursed. Vexed with life, and guilt for surviving, when so many others had died for the cause. More than half of the Shaw warriors had been annihilated in battle. And those who'd made it were filled with such anguish and fear. Not to mention they'd had to hide from those who sought to kill them ever since. The Duke of Cumberland had orchestrated the catastrophic battle, and when it had ended, he'd put out the order for all Jacobite rebels to be murdered.

And still, Thane was here. But without his twin sister in the world, what more did he have to live for?

When he returned to his castle with Lady Sarah in tow, it would raise the morale of his people. Seeing that Thea's death was being avenged would bring them hope for a brighter future. Or in some way present a future that was less bleak. Even the dogs looked dejected these days. All of the clan's crops had been burned or stolen by dragoons, and what little stores they'd been able to hide were quickly dwindling. Neighboring clans were all in the same boat. The population itself was dwindling because of it, as some fled to the New World and parts of

Europe. Escaping starvation, fear and grief.

At the very least, he might be able to extort some supplies from the Campbells when they came looking for Sarah. A ransom paid was better than a silly chit who required rations.

Lady Sarah Campbell…He'd not seen her since Thea had been wed to the Chief of Clan Campbell, but his memory of her was sharp. The lass had a confidence about her that came with the privilege of belonging to a powerful clan. One that had not seemed to fair as badly as the rest of the nation.

Trailing in undulating waves down her back and threaded with little white flowers, her red locks screamed out to the sun. Her lips were a perfect pink bow, accented by a beauty mark on the indentation of her creamy, dimpled cheek. But most noteworthy were her brown eyes, the kind that saw straight into a man's soul, disturbing him enough that he'd dreamt of them for months after their meeting.

What sort of things had a lass like that seen?

He hardly had to guess, given the brutality of her brothers. It crossed his mind then that perhaps Lady Sarah had witnessed his sister's death. A shudder passed through him, imagining what Thea had gone through. Why had their da arranged to marry her off? If Thane had been laird at the time, he'd not have agreed. But the responsibility had only fallen to his shoulders after the great battle, which had also stolen his da's life. And what was done was done.

Thane thrust aside those melancholy thoughts, or else he might guide his horse right off a cliff. Instead, he focused on his plan for infiltrating the Campbell stronghold and finding Lady Sarah as fast as he could.

Recognizing her was the least of his worries. Och, but Thane could pick her out of a crowd of a thousand fiery-headed beauties, of that he was certain.

What he worried about most was blending in with those in residence.

He planned to infiltrate the castle during their annual Christmas feast, which took place on the eve of the holiday, and steal her away while everyone was distracted by the celebration. Word had leached out across the Highlands that the Campbells still planned to celebrate despite the death and destruction that had hit their country. Another great blow to those who were still suffering.

Bloody bastards would be drunk on ale and wine and spiced cider, dining on the blood and guts of their peers.

The Campbells hardly suffered enough during the battle.

Of course, he knew that wasn't generous of him. All the clans had suffered. However, after learning that Thea had been left with little protection at the castle while the warriors had gone off to fight for Bonnie Prince Charlie and that when the ransom for Thea was demanded, the Campbells had refused, he wasn't feeling very charitable.

Oh, how his sister must have suffered at the hands of the butcher of the loyalist government army—also known as the Duke of Cumberland, son to King George who'd exacted his revenge on the Scottish rebels in favor of Bonnie Prince Charlie. Knowing that had made him harden his heart. Not just to the bloody *Sassenachs* who'd murdered her, but to those bastard Campbells, who might as well have been a party to it for they hadn't done much to protect her.

The place in his chest that used to burn a fire for a cause, had now frozen over, beating only for revenge.

BEFORE THIS MOMENT, Lady Sarah Campbell had considered herself to be quite beloved by her family.

But now, as she backed against the wall in the darkened corridor, she realized what a complete fool she'd been. How easily she'd allowed herself to live in a bubble of pure fantasy. For it was evident now, considering the conversation happening on the other side of the tightly closed door, that she was only a commodity to be traded.

Her heart pounded in her ears, threatening to drown out the rest of the conversation happening within.

"There will be dozens of them present." This was the distinctive deep voice of her younger brother Edward.

"Ye were smart, brother, to invite everyone for the Christmas feast. No one will guess that we're actually brokering a deal." And that had been her other youngest brother Ellyson's reply.

Both her brothers chuckled, following by the sound of clinking. Were they giving cheers to selling her off?

Sarah fumed, hands fisted at her side, and her jaw clenched so tight she risked breaking a tooth. To them, she was a deal to be brokered, and neither of them seemed to care one wit that she was human, and until a few moments ago, their much-beloved sister.

Alas, that had all been in her mind, for it was evident now that she didn't mean as much to them as she thought she did. What an absolutely pathetic idiot she'd been.

The Christmas feast that she'd been helping to prepare for weeks—had in fact planned most of—was just a ruse to auction her off to the highest bidder. Why did they even bother with the feast to begin with? They could have saved themselves a lot of trouble and resources if they'd simply tossed her naked out into the moors for the quickest man to grab.

The clans were all hurting for money and staples since the Battle of Culloden, and though their clan was larger and richer than others, their size was the problem. They were large, *too large*, and had a lot of mouths to feed. So why not get rid of her and collect coin in the process?

She was nothing but a piece of property.

Jon was so busy with the rebellion these last few years that he'd put off arranging a marriage for her, and she'd been glad for it. Now that she was five and twenty, she thought for certain she'd be too long in the tooth for anyone to want her. Apparently not.

Sarah reached forward, preparing to bang on the door to tell them exactly what she thought of their disgusting plan, but what they said next stilled her.

"Northumberland's son will be there, as well."

"English bastards," cursed her brother Edward.

"Aye. We'll rob him blind if he's willing to take her."

Selling her to a bloody *Sassenach* made her stomach curdle, and she dropped her hand, pressing it to her gut, willing herself not to vomit. Northumberland…The same man who'd killed their brother and cousins on the field of battle.

Oh, dear God, she could not be wed to a *Sassenach*! Especially one who'd led a red-coated regiment against her own kin. What had got into her brothers?

Greed.

Sarah pinched her forearm, hoping this was a dream, but the pain radiating from the spot between her thumb and forefinger was very real.

They rattled off a few other names—all men she knew to be violent, and several more that were in league with the government, having gone against Bonnie Prince Charlie. Was that it then? After having fought for the prince at Culloden, her brothers were now prepared to sell their souls, and hers, to the highest bidder?

This wouldn't do. *It couldn't.*

Again, she raised her hand to rap on the door, to barge inside and tell them that they were crazy, but something stopped her. What if they denied her argument? What if they were so desperate for coin that they locked her up until the deed was done, the papers signed, and she was no longer a Campbell, but the wife of an Englishman?

Sarah backed away from the door, fear snaking its way down her spine. Her entire body started to tremble, and she bit her knuckles to keep from screaming.

There was so little she had control over. So little, indeed.

Except for one thing. Edward and Ellyson didn't need to know she was aware of their plans. If they weren't privy to her knowledge, and they continued with the charade of a festive Christmas celebration, they would have no idea that she was planning to escape, for that was what she must do.

Get as far away as possible.

Sarah would not wed any of the dozen or so men her brothers had invited into their home to steal her away. Never. And she wasn't against marriage—but she was against being sold to butchers.

She needed to escape, and perhaps the night of the feast was the perfect time. Her brothers would be so distracted sorting through the proposals, counting the coins that would soon line their coffers, they wouldn't notice she'd gone missing.

Blinded by tears, Sarah rushed back to her chamber and quietly shut the door. She leaned against the cool wood, sucking in a breath on a sob.

So much had changed in the last eight months. So much had changed in the last eight *minutes.*

This time last year, they'd been celebrating the holiday season with their clan. Singing, dancing. There had been so much hope for a better future with Jon as their new leader. Edward and Ellyson had been eager to join their comrades in the Jacobite rebellion, to bring honor to the clan. Their eldest brother Jon had been wooing his new wife, Thea.

Standing in the center of the great hall last Christmas, Sarah never would have guessed that she'd be where she was now. Jon and Thea dead. Her, escaping the family she'd once loved so fiercely.

Och, not once, but *still.* She loved them even now when they were tearing her apart on the inside.

Pushing away from the door, Sarah marched toward her wardrobe and wrenched it open. She pulled her leather traveling satchel out from behind the hanging gowns and stuffed her winter cloak inside, along with a gown, a pair of riding boots and a spare chemise. Then she opened the tiny box her father had carved for her and stared inside at the ring that had once belonged to her mother—the Campbell crest surrounded by rubies. It was her prized possession. If her brothers realized that she had it, they would steal it for certain.

But the ring had been given to her in private by her and Jon's mother just before she'd passed when she'd been barely five years old, and she doubted they were even aware of its existence. She put that into the satchel with her other belongings.

This was all she could take with her.

Where she would go, she'd not yet decided. Tonight, when it was dark, she would hide the satchel in the barn so that it was there when she was ready to leave. She prayed the feast tomorrow evening would give her some answers.

Until then, she'd need to come up with a plan—any plan, as long as she was gone before midnight struck on Christmas.

Chapter Two

"THANKS FOR THE borrow, sir. Though ye dinna know it yet, ye've done a great service to your fellow Scot." Thane gave a salute to the unconscious man at his feet, speaking as he divested the costumed Father Christmas from his garments and pulled them on himself.

He'd not had any idea of how he was going to sneak into Campbell castle until he'd happened upon the festively dressed man, and then he'd known exactly. Once inside, with Sarah held captive, he could divest himself of the costume and be about his business of abduction.

The old red velvet cloak smelled of must and horses, and other unmentionable things. Probably hadn't seen a wash since the Christmas before, but he tried not to think about that. Served these traitorous bastards right. They might have fought with the Scots on the field of battle, but Thane had to wonder if deep in their hearts, they were English loving all along.

Father Christmas was distinctly un-Scottish.

He tugged on the makeshift beard and curly, woolen hair that had once been white but now was yellowed with age. Good lord, but it smelled like sour, not so well-preserved, ale.

Dressed, he hopped back onto Destiny's back and rode casually right through the gates, shouting messages of good tidings to those he passed and tossing little wrapped sweets that had been prepared for the occasion. All the while, in his mind, he recited a prayer for their traitorous deaths. The bastards.

In the bailey, a young lad came forward to take his mount by the reins. He was tall and lanky, hungry-looking. Eyes haunted. Poor bairn had likely been ill-treated by his clansmen.

"Och, wee laddie, I've a task for ye."

The lad cocked his head, interest in his eyes, especially when Thane passed him a coin.

"Rub him down, but then, if ye would, saddle him right back up again and keep him tied to the outside of the barn by the trough." Thane made an exaggerated look about the bailey teeming with people, some of whom appeared already to be quite into their cups. "I dinna think I'll be staying as long as I had anticipated." He gave a slow, exaggerated wink. "And if ye're a good lad, there's another coin where the first one came from."

"Och, Father Christmas, I'd do it for free." The lad beamed, looking as though the coin were the first that he'd ever seen, and likely the best gift he'd ever received in his entire life.

Thane regretted disappointing the lad when he found out who Thane truly was—the enemy. Would he trade the coin for Lady Sarah's life? Thane was willing to bet the lad would not.

Guilt ebbed at his conscience. But feeling sorry had no place in his plan, else he might as well walk right out the castle gates and back to where he came from. There was no time for regrets.

As Thane walked about the bailey, tossing out good cheer, sometimes through gritted teeth, he noted the various ways of escape and studied every female he passed in hopes of finding the red-haired beauty. The castle walls were being protected by guards. A good number of them, in fact, but they were all holding various cups likely filled with ale, wine or spirits, and they were all laughing and jesting instead of looking out over the snow-covered moors.

The winds had died down, and the massive bonfires in the bailey warmed the air. People danced and lazed about as if it were the height of summer rather than the middle of winter.

A tug at the bottom of his coat had Thane whirling about a little too exuberantly, afraid that he'd been caught. Much to his horror, the sudden movement sent a small child flying. The wee lass was sprawled on her backside, a look of alarm on her face. That expression alone was enough to make him want to abandon his cause. He'd not set out to frighten children. But her fear was quickly erased when she spied his beard and velvet coat. A tentative smile curved her tiny mouth.

Thane rushed forward, extending his hand. "My dear, I am so verra sorry."

The wee lass grasped onto his outstretched hand with wide, blameless eyes.

Forcing a smile, he said, "Why do ye no' tell this clumsy Father Christmas what it is ye wish for."

The bairn stood before him, blinking upward with large eyes, hands clasped in front of her, and without preamble said, "I wish to have our lady and laird back."

The lass could not have done more damage if she'd thrust a dagger into the center of Thane's heart. Her request broke his heart, and he found it hard to breathe for a moment. What innocence…

"Lady Thea was helping my ma with the new bairn in her belly. 'Tis being quite troublesome. And the laird, my da said he was twice the laird as these new ones. Says only the weak need to rule together." Truth out of the mouths of bairns.

Thane choked on his heart, which seemed to have removed itself from his chest and thrust its way up into his throat. He, too, had thought it odd that Edward and Ellyson Campbell had made a pact to share the lairdship.

He swallowed and then patted the lass on the head. "How old are ye?"

"Six summers."

"Well then, ye're practically grown. I bet ye can be a great help to your ma with the bairn."

The lass beamed up at him. "I think I can. But…" She shook her head and bit her lip. "What if she doesna want my help?" The wee thing looked so worried.

Thane knelt before her at eye level. "All mothers want help from their older bairns with the younger set. Trust me."

The lass held her hands to her chest, a beaming smile cutting across her face. "Oh, thank ye, Father Christmas. Ye've given me a great gift."

She hugged him tightly, her little arms barely reaching around his middle, and Thane awkwardly patted her back.

"Go on now, afore ye're missed."

She skipped off, and again he felt that perhaps his plan had been misguided. The wee lass missed Thea.

God, he missed his amazing sister too.

And that was why he needed to avenge her death. He was not the only one suffering from Thea's loss—the people were missing their mistress, their healer.

A tap on his shoulder had him startling once more. He turned around a bit more carefully to avoid knocking down someone else. Only this time, he found himself staring into a pair of inquisitive brown eyes, with an equally inquisitive pair of red arched brows.

"A word, Father Christmas?" Her voice was low and silky as she made her request.

Finding Lady Sarah Campbell had been a lot simpler than he thought, for she had been the one to locate him.

SARAH HELD HER shock in well by masking it with curiosity.

Just what was Thane Shaw doing here, and dressed as Father Christmas of all things?

The man had a death wish to be certain, for why else would he appear here, apparently unarmed and unaided? She glanced around surreptitiously. No one seemed to recognize him just yet, but that didn't mean they wouldn't soon. His face was quite distinctive. Blue eyes that were flickering in the bonfire light, the same shade as Thea's. His golden locks were hidden beneath the decrepit wig, but she'd bet all the grain in the storehouse that it was him.

"Is that your wish, my lady? I'm only giving away one to each soul."

She rolled her eyes. "Ye dinna seem to grasp just what your position here is, sir."

"Father Christmas," he insisted.

"As ye say." Miraculously, she kept from rolling her eyes at him.

"Is over there fine?" He indicated the barn. "Ye can tell me what ye would rather see as my position."

He handed her a sweet from his satchel, but she pushed it back. "Nay, thank ye."

Thane held out his arm to her. She considered arguing about going toward the barn with the man, but then she realized perhaps now was the exact moment she needed to make her move. No one would care if they saw her walking about with Father Christmas. She might easily be able to slip away with him as a distraction.

Besides, she had to find out just what the devil he was doing here.

The soft velvet of the red coat was straining from the breadth of his muscular arms, and she wouldn't be surprised if, at any moment, there was a tearing sound as his body gained its freedom from the restrictive garment. Normally a red coat would scare the devil out of everyone, fearing for their lives that the dragoons were back and ready to murder them all. Father Christmas was the only one who could get away with it. But Thane Shaw was *not* the man she'd hired to play the part.

At the barn, she let her hand drop, and when he faced her fully, his thoughts shuttered from his face.

"I am ready for my lesson." There was a teasing note to his words that she found surprising, given the intensity of how much she knew he disliked her family. That had been evident at Thea and Jon's wedding, and even more so after her death.

"Father Christmas doesna grant wishes to souls," Sarah mused. "Ye're confusing too many ideologies."

Thane wiped his hand down the neck of a sleek black horse that did not belong to the Campbell clan. She guessed it was his, judging from the familiar way he stroked the mane.

"He's a beauty," she said, adding her hand to the mix. "My brother had one just like it. Though truth be told the horse preferred his wife."

He stiffened beside her, catching on that she spoke of Thea. Oh, how she missed her. Wanted to talk to Thane about his sister, but knew that broaching the subject now when he was trying for anonymity would likely be the wrong course of action. Then again, if she was going to get what she wanted, there was no time like the present.

"What is it ye wished to speak to me about?" he asked.

"I know who ye are."

"Then ye must know why I've come."

"I have an idea, but I dinna think it will work," she said.

His gaze met hers, steel blue. "Just what is it ye think I'm here to do?"

"Lay siege." She shrugged. "Some sort of revenge."

"Ye have the latter right, but I'm afraid ye've got the execution wrong."

The way he said "execution" with a bite to it had her flinching. Was that what he thought had happened to Thea? No doubt.

"I dinna deny that our clan likely is in need of some sort of punishment for what happened to your sister, but if ye should die too, ye will be of no help to your people."

"I think ye're wrong," he said, a menacing undertone. "I think what I've got planned will be a massive help."

Sarah sighed. "What is it ye have planned then?"

He winged a brow in challenge. "Climb onto my horse, and I'll tell ye all about it."

"Climb onto your horse?" She let out a short laugh and narrowed her gaze, the realization of his plot dawning. "Ah, so ye wish to abduct me."

He pressed his hand to his chest. "That is *my* Christmas wish."

Sarah sucked in a heady breath. Here was a gift placed right before her. The means to her escape. And he had no idea. They could kill two birds with one stone. He'd get his revenge, and she'd get her freedom.

She didn't even bother putting up a fight. "Can I get something from the barn first?"

Thane looked taken aback. "As I'm certain ye've no' been abducted before, I feel obliged to let ye know that will no' be possible."

Sarah leaned in close enough that she could smell the stink of the rotting wool beard. "But, you see, I have already packed a bag."

"What?" he sounded exasperated.

"I..." She licked her lips. "I was going to run away."

"Why?"

She glanced around, wondering if anyone had taken note of just how long she'd been talking with Father Christmas, but everyone was enjoying the drinks and food and paid them no attention. At least not yet.

"My brothers have arranged for several men to make offers for my hand this evening. One of whom is English. Nay, thank ye."

Thane groaned. "Fine. Get your bag, but I'm coming with ye. And just so we're clear, this is still me taking ye, no' me saving ye."

"Aye, of course," she nodded emphatically, grateful he was letting her get the satchel.

THEY ENTERED THE barn, and she spoke to the same wee lad Thane had given a coin to. "Just getting a sack of gifts for Father Christmas," she explained.

Thane tossed the lad another coin, which quickly distracted him from their task.

A second later, she emerged with the satchel, beaming a smile at the lad and avoiding eye contact with Thane.

"Here we are. Thank ye, Georgie, for all ye've done with the horses tonight. I know it's been quite an ordeal with Harry sick."

The lad blushed and kicked at the barn floor. "Thank ye, my lady. I'm more than happy to help."

The lad glanced down at the coin in his hand, and Thane could practically see the thoughts about what he'd spend it on popping from his mind.

Outside of the barn, Thane took Sarah's satchel and attached it to his saddle.

"Wait." She touched his arm, and he ignored the frisson of heat that shot through him. "I need my cloak so that no one will see me."

This was ludicrous. She was actually helping him abduct her. This chore could not have been any easier. He was a little disappointed.

"Good idea." With his mount blocking him from the crowd in the bailey, he tossed the beard and wig, took off the red jacket, hanging it on the trough and then put on his own cloak.

A few minutes later, they were riding outside of the gates with no one the wiser that Father Christmas had just stolen the best prize of all.

Chapter Three

THOUGH THE SNOWFALL had ebbed before Thane arrived on Campbell lands, the storm had steadily picked up since they'd ridden away the night before. Save for a few short breaks to rest Destiny and relieve themselves, they'd ridden through the night. At times Sarah was alert, leaning away from him, and at other times her body sagged against him.

He'd pulled her onto his lap and given her the extra blanket he had, and she'd buried herself inside of it so much that he could barely see her. If not for the weight of her body against him and the unintelligible words he could hear her murmur in her sleep, he might not have known she was even there.

They were at least another day's ride from his holding south of Inverness, but with exhaustion setting in along with the renewed storm on this Christmas morning, they had nothing for it save to stop at the same place he'd stayed the night before on his way to Campbell lands—Balthazar's.

Good God, it had been a mess…But at least no one would come looking for them there.

All through the night with Sarah on his lap, he'd followed the same northern star, keeping him on the right path. The lass had been quiet, thankfully, because he'd not wanted to talk, but rather concentrate on the horrible weather and the road ahead. Not to mention any sounds from behind them.

If no one had realized she was gone the night before, they'd certainly be noticing now with the sun rising on the horizon. Christmas morning, the lass would have been expected to wed, or at the very least, woken in her own bed and joined her clan for breakfast.

Knowing that he had many hours lead and the storm to protect them, a stopover at Balthazar's, though it seemed a risky move, would not be as dangerous for them.

"Are ye awake, lass?" he asked.

She stirred in his arms, stretching her arms out and then tucking herself quickly back into the blanket. "Aye. Where are we?"

Thane glanced toward the smoke curling into the sky just ahead, his stomach souring. This was the last place he wanted to be. Well, not the last—that would be Campbells's dungeon. "Balthazar's Tavern."

"Well, this will be a new Christmas adventure." There was a bit of excitement in her tone that he found alarming.

"Nay, lass. 'Tis no' that kind of place. We'll need to be on our guard. Dinna mention your name," he warned. "And I'm no' a Shaw while we're here, and ye're no' a Campbell, understand?"

Sarah stiffened in his arms. "Who might ye be, then?"

"Munros. Headed home from the clan wedding of our cousins near Lindsay lands."

"All right…Is there a reason ye've named clans who fought with the dragoons at Culloden?" She sat up a little farther, her bottom rubbing against his thighs.

Thane groaned at her movement. "Aye, we're headed into the snake pit."

"Oh," she breathed out, the excitement gone from her voice. There was a long pause, and he could practically hear the questions racking up in her mind. "And are we brother and sister for this journey?"

"Nay." He clamped his mouth closed, shifting a little farther back on his saddle. "Ye're my wife. Then none of the bastards will see fit to mess with ye."

"That kind of a crowd, eh?"

"The patrons of Balthazar's fought on the other side of the battlefield, lass. And they are no'...friends of ours. They are rough about the edges. But stick with me, and ye'll be safe."

"Oh." There was fear and sadness in her sigh.

"We'll stay only as long as the weather demands," he said.

She nodded, the top of her head tapping against his chin, nearly making him bite his tongue. The snake pit was going to be a reprieve away from this temptress. She didn't even realize how much she was...*bothering* him. Perhaps it was just that it had been so long since he'd been with a woman. Not that he found the adventurous lass in his lap to be of any interest at all.

"'Tis there." He indicated the tavern just a stone's throw away to get his mind off her squirming, enticing body.

The tavern was built of thick, heavy stones. Tiny windows barely emitted any candlelight now that it was morning, but come night, the wee squares of light would lure in weary travelers.

The thatched roof was covered in thick snow, and Thane wondered how long it would take before a part of it collapsed in on the inhabitants. Given the state of the inside, he'd hazard to guess very soon.

Thane led Destiny on a path that had been recently cleared around the back of the tavern to where the stable was located. A young lad stood in the doorway, rubbing his hands together. A shovel leaned on the side of the stone building beside him. Clearly, he was the one who had shoveled the path. Another lad shoved him aside with an armload of wood. They'd have a nice fire going on inside to keep themselves and the horses warm. A small curl of smoke leached from the ceiling, which was good. At least they'd managed to keep the chimney clear.

"Got room for another?" Thane called.

The lad nodded and hopped forward on feet that were probably frozen. He reached for the reins, holding tight while they dismounted, each of them grabbing their respective satchels.

"Gonna cost ye, but Balthazar will collect inside," the lad said, teeth chattering.

"Thanks, lad." Thane reached into his sporran and pulled out a coin. "For ye and the others in the stables. Keep my mount well."

"Aye, sir. Thank ye." The lad led Destiny inside, telling him exuberantly how much oats he was about to have for his breakfast. He called over his shoulder, "Ye can go in the door to the kitchens rather than trudge about."

"Thank ye." He took Sarah by the hand. Her fingers were small, slim and freezing. "Goodness, ye should have told me how cold ye were."

"No' my place to complain, though, is it?"

Saints, did she really think he meant to torture her on top of the abduction? "'Tis no' complaining. I dinna want ye to lose a finger."

"Ye dinna?" She glanced up at him, and he could figure out the rest of what she meant, that a finger was a lot smaller of a thing to lose than one's life.

The truth was he didn't want her to lose a finger—not even a hair on her head.

"Remember what we discussed," Thane said gruffly. "Munros on the way back from Lindsey lands."

"I'll no' forget." She shuddered, and he had a feeling it was not from the cold.

THE KITCHENS WERE smoky and filled with shouted orders as scullions rushed to follow the head cook's demands. It smelled enticing, rich with herbs and baking scones. There was a savory scent that belied the large pot of porridge being ladled into bowls from the hearth fire. All of the aromas reminded Sarah how little she'd eaten in the last few days, since she'd been so worried about the Christmas Eve celebration and subsequent auction of her life.

Thane had offered her nothing but a canteen of water on their ride here, and she hadn't asked for more. It had been the middle of the night, after all, and he wasn't responsible for her having missed supper. Besides, she'd spent most of the time sleeping, keeping warm and trying to refrain from annoying him so he wouldn't change his mind and take her back to her brothers.

"Get out, ye rapscallions!" shouted the cook, swinging a ladle in their direction. A few speckles of porridge hit Sarah's cheeks. "Food will come when 'tis good and ready."

Thane ducked the swinging utensil, and the second fling of oats. Barely having time to wipe her face, Sarah followed suit, rushing from the kitchens. However, they went the wrong way and ended up in the scullery room, where they were met by a buxom redhead who greeted them with a saucy grin, her hands buried in a wash bin full of dishes.

"Och, but ye'll no' be doing your dirty business in here, ye two." She pointed toward the door, droplets of water flinging in their direction. "Back to the common room with ye."

Sarah's face heated, and she was sure it flamed as red as her own hair at what the woman suggest with that line about "dirty business." She might not be as worldly as some, but she knew exactly what that referenced.

"We got turned around," Thane explained. "We just arrived and came in the back door."

The irritation dissipated from the woman's face. "Well, in that case, welcome to Balthazar's. He's my da. I'm Carrie, and this is our tavern. Will ye be taking a room?"

"Aye, that would be verra much appreciated," Thane said.

"Of course, I'm just back here helping out while I waited for my own room to be tidied up after it was let out to someone else." The woman narrowed her eyes, wet, red hands on her hips. "Ye wouldna be here causin' trouble, would ye? We've had a few troublemakers about the past fortnight or so."

"Oh, nay," they both answered at the same time. Then as if they'd been playing this game for more than a few minutes, they glanced at each other and laughed like two lovebirds.

"Sorry," Sarah said with a giggle. "Newlyweds. I'm S—Samantha Lindsey, I mean Samantha Munro now. This is my husband—Tobias Munro."

"Och, I see. Welcome, welcome and congratulations. Ye'll have a round of ale on us, I'll see to that. Go on out to the common room, and in the meantime, I'll have a room set up. Oh," she squealed. "And one more thing. I've go' a special room here, my Chamber of Sorrow, if ye'd like to pay respects to anyone that ye lost in the battle. Doesna matter the side. We all lost that day."

Carrie had a whole chamber devoted to prayer for the dead Scots and traitorous dragoons? Immediately she wondered if anything belonging to her brother would be in that room.

It was a mighty task to hide her horror, but Sarah managed it. "Thank ye kindly, Carrie. I'm sure we'd love to enjoy it later today."

"Excellent. Now go on with ye. Cook is going to begin serving soon, and if ye miss out on the meal, it will be a while before supper."

Carrie ushered them out of the scullery through the kitchen, where this time they dodged scraps of cabbage tossed their way and finally made it into the common room. The tiny windows barely let in any light, and the ceiling was low. The floors were made of dirt, strewn with straw, which was a shock to Sarah, given the only taverns she'd ever been in had either wood or slate flooring. What were they trying to hide beneath the straw? But she needn't have wondered, for the stench in the commons quickly dispelled the delicious scents from the kitchen. It smelled like…

Dog excrement.

Sarah tried not to gag at the overpowering smell. She glanced up at Thane to see if he'd noticed, but he was busy scanning the patrons and available tables. Several dogs lounged by the hearth sleeping, but there was one who'd taken up the telltale curved back pose of disposing of his bowels.

"Dear God," Thane muttered to her under his breath. "We'll take our meal in a chamber. Hopefully, the private rooms are better."

"Good idea." She leaned closer to him as if that would somehow make her feel better.

A large, bald, older man slapped his hand on a table with a friend, shouting for the dog to cease his business, before addressing them. "Welcome, newcomers. I'm Balthazar."

His beard looked similar to the fake one Thane had been sporting at Campbell castle, and if she had to guess, Sarah thought it probably smelled worse.

"Thank ye, sir. We're waiting on a room your daughter is having prepared for us," Thane said. "And if we could have our meals served there? Newlyweds." He added a wink for emphasis, which got a round of cheers from those in residence and started the hounds to howling.

Sarah was not against dogs; she loved them dearly. Her own sweet Mildred had just passed the month before. But these hounds were unruly, and she guessed it had something to do with the tavern owner himself, who seemed something of a wild man.

"Come, come. I've got one already set up." Balthazar ushered them through a series of chambers. "Will this do?"

But before they could reply, Carrie shouted, "Da, I've got another one prepared for the newlyweds."

She took them to a door across from the one her father had suggested. Before opening it, she leaned in a little close, speaking conspiratorially. "On the other side of this wall is my Chamber of Sorrow." Carrie glanced down at her feet, then back up at them brightly with her green eyes. "I'm hoping the souls whose possessions I've got displayed there will bless your union. And that it will bring me good luck in finding my own gentleman husband."

And what type of gentleman would that be—an English dragoon or a Jacobite rebel? Somehow, she managed to mask her musings and offer her thanks enthusiastically.

"Gave ye the best bed in the tavern. Sheets have been cleaned recently. Dinna mind about the table, it will make do."

As soon as Carrie and Balthazar shut the door behind them, Sarah turned to Thane. His handsome features were masked with indifference, but then his brooding gaze latched onto hers.

Mildly teasing, but partly serious, Sarah said, "Just where in blazes have ye brought me, sir? I promised to behave. Ye need no' have added torture to your abduction."

Thane raised his brows, arms crossing over the wide expanse of his muscled chest. "I could leave ye here. Maybe Cook will stop swinging her ladle long enough to offer ye a position?"

Chapter Four

SARAH LAUGHED. "WERE ye sotted on your last sojourn? Or is this what I should expect of the Shaw holding?"

Thane grunted, smirking at her joke, before quickly wiping away his mirth. They were supposed to be enemies. They *were* enemies. He'd abducted her, even if she had come willingly.

"I wish I could say I was, and no, Shaw is an oasis of calm," he drawled, turning his gaze to their private hell. The chamber was not as unwelcoming as the common area of the tavern, and Thane was more than happy to take it for the night. Hopefully, that was all they would need it for.

"Ha! I'll believe that when I see it!"

Though this floor was also dirt-packed, a carpet that appeared recently beaten lay on the floor beside the bed, which was shoved against a wall.

The wooden bed frame sagged from the lumpy straw mattress that appeared to weigh an unfathomably vast amount, and tossed on top of it was a plain wool blanket. At least it did look clean, as Carrie had said. She and her father seemed like they aimed to please. If he'd been on better terms with them, perhaps a regular, Thane might have told them a simple redecorating of the main tavern room would bring in more guests. But they seemed smart enough to have figured that out on their own, which meant they probably purposefully kept it…*rustic.*

Two stools flanked a small table that was missing half a leg, but an upside-down bucket had been placed to steady it. Best rented chamber in the place—that was saying a lot. He kind of wished that Balthazar had opened the other chamber door, so he'd have something to compare it to.

Perhaps there was a certain charm in providing such a medieval tavern to those looking to go back in time. A time when Scotland had not been trampled over by dragoons. Saints, but he could not remember such a time ever having existed.

Thane turned away from the bed to investigate a crumbling iron brazier that had seen better days. The room was chilly and could do with a bit of heat. He picked up the poker resting on the rim and jabbed at the half-burned logs in the cavern. One of them crumbled to ash, sending up a plumb of dust, which had them both waving in front of their faces and coughing.

"I'm no' that cold," Sarah said with a cough and a laugh.

Thane groaned and dropped the poker. "Good. I'm afraid if I light it, the whole room will blaze."

"It might go to flame anyhow with the way it was roaring in the kitchen and the common room." She giggled and backed away from the brazier. Either she was daft, or she was the type of person who always seemed to look on the bright side of the coin. While he wanted to think it was the former, he was fairly certain it was the latter, which only ended up endearing her to him.

"I hardly noticed," he quipped. "Though I did wonder if ye were going to lick the oats off your face."

"Ha! Maybe I should have, for I am starving." Sarah tossed her satchel onto the bed, and surprisingly a plume of dust did not rise with it.

Carrie had not fibbed about cleaning the bedding. Well, that boded well for their sleep. Och, but they would have to share a bed. There was barely even any room on the floor for Sarah to curl up on, and he wasn't going to make her sleep on the dirt-packed earth, despite there being a rug tossed down.

Sarah pulled out one of the stools and sat on it, wobbling a little and catching herself on the uneven table, nearly dislodging the bucket. "Whoa," she said, finally managing to catch her balance.

This only seemed to make her laugh, and Thane couldn't help but notice her dimple and the beauty mark that winked in and out with her humor.

She was beautiful, and it wasn't fair. Under the circumstances, he should not find her so attractive and fascinating. Instead of taking the stool opposite her, Thane leaned against the door, arms crossed, one ankle over the other, and stared in her direction. He told himself he was doing as an abductor would, but truly, it was to put distance between them because the way she was wriggling her bottom on that stool reminded him all too well of their journey on Destiny.

Sarah cocked her head, a tease in her dark eyes. She stared back at him, a bit of humor dancing about her mouth too. "Goodness, but ye sure are brooding. If ye're doing that for my benefit so that I remember ye're my captor, I assure ye, I am well aware, and I dinna plan to go anywhere."

A knock vibrated the door at his back, and Thane pushed away from it, opening it to see who would interrupt them.

Carrie stood in the hallway with a tray of food, and one of the lads from the stable behind her held a jug and two cups.

"We've brought your breakfast, a bit standard for us, but I assure ye supper will be delightful. And we've got a mid-morning Christmas treat too. Are ye planning to dine in your chamber this evening as well?"

"Aye." Thane's mouth watered at the simple fair. Lord, but he was starving. If he recalled correctly, the butter here last time was surprisingly good.

"All right, good then. When ye finish, if ye like, I can show ye the Chamber of Sorrow." Carrie beamed a smile at them and shifted on her feet.

"Hmm," Thane said. "We'll consider it."

Sarah was beside him then, her hand on his arm. "We'd love to see it. Perhaps with a bit of food, my husband will be more cheerful." She nudged him in the elbow as if she were the one in charge of their current circumstances.

Thane raised a brow and forced a smile that appeared genuine. "I do apologize. I'm starved, and I tend to get a bit grouchy when I'm hungry," he explained.

"Och, dinna we all," Carrie said with a laugh. She pushed past them into their chamber and placed the tray of food on the table, then took the jug and cups from the lad. "Feel free to leave the tray on the floor outside the chamber when ye're done. The lads will come by soon to collect it."

When Carrie had left, Thane shut the door and stared at Sarah, who was pouring ale into the cups and setting out the food.

"Why are ye being so agreeable?" he asked. "I abducted ye. I am dangerous."

SARAH GLANCED UP from where she'd placed a spoon in Thane's porridge, beside the melting ball of butter.

"Why are ye dangerous?" she asked, studying him from head to toe.

He was large; there was no doubt. Tall and muscular, where his sister had been small. A few faint scars, and a nose that had been broken more than once, showed he was a warrior, and the mere fact that he was still alive was proof he could handle himself. But that didn't frighten her. If anything, it made her feel safe.

Mayhap she was mad. For he did have a point.

He stalked forward, the way a predator hunted prey.

Instead of being scared, she found herself wanting to meet him halfway. Mayhap they weren't getting enough air in this chamber.

"Your family is responsible for Thea's death."

Sarah nodded. She'd been waiting for him to say those words. They gave her something else to focus on besides the way her heart was beating wildly against her ribs. "Come, let's eat while we talk."

The way he grimaced, she thought he would disagree, and her stomach growled in protest, but he did come forward and take the stool opposite the one she'd claimed.

"Thea was—" she started, but he interrupted her.

"How dare ye say her name?" He stabbed his spoon into the nearly melted butter.

"She was my friend." Sarah boldly met his gaze. "My brother, Jon, loved her."

Pain flickered in Thane's eyes, and doubt. He likely didn't know whether or not he could believe her, and she understood why.

Sarah swirled the golden, dissolving lump of butter around her porridge. "I loved her, too. She brought life to our clan. Added light where there was darkness. Jon had been so disparaged by what was happening in Scotland—we all were—but she gave him hope."

She put down her spoon, suddenly unable to take a bite. Instead, she took a sip of bitter ale.

Thane did the same, gulping the entire contents of his cup and then refilling it. "What happened?"

The fact that he asked her that showed he expected to hear the truth from her, and she was more than willing to give it.

"I might be a traitor to Edward and Ellyson for telling ye this, Thane, but I dinna believe that I'd be betraying Jon, or Thea or our clan for that matter. After we lost Jon at the Battle of Culloden, my brothers…they decided to rule the clan together. One in charge of the common people and one in charge of our soldiers." Here she paused. "But it started even before then. They were always arguing with Jon over edicts he'd implemented or new ways of doing things. They hated that Thea was beloved by the clan, that a lot of the changes happening had started with her. She was brilliant, but ye know that. Edward and Ellyson were jealous, really."

This was the part that Sarah didn't want to talk about, but she knew she had to tell him. He needed to understand that what happened to Thea was not on the entire clans' heads.

"They were increasingly hard on her after Jon died. Worried, I think, that she might be with child and that child would eventually take the place they'd claimed. So, when Thea was taken by the dragoons while gathering various herbs and roots just outside the castle walls, they declined to pay the ransom. They thought it better to be rid of her." Sarah shook her head. "I pleaded with them, but they refused. I dinna think they believed she'd be killed, just taken away and married off to some English general."

"But she *was* killed." Thane's voice was low and fueled by anger and pain.

She reached for his hand then but pulled back at the way he curled his fingers into the wood of the table. Comfort from her could come in the form of truth, but not yet from touch. That was the more appropriate form, anyhow.

"Aye. Right in front of us as we stood on the battlements." Sarah choked on a sob, bringing her hands to her mouth. "She didna deserve it. There was no retaliation. And I waited every day for ye to come and avenge her. I would have given ye the keys to the castle if ye'd asked."

Thane's anger shifted to suffering. "And that is why ye came so willingly? Because ye think ye deserve to bear the brunt of whatever revenge I've got planned?"

Sarah shook her head, shifted forward in her chair and then locked her gaze on his. "I told ye they were selling me off to the highest bidder."

"And ye think ye might have suffered Thea's fate."

She shrugged. "I could have."

He was quiet a long time, staring into his porridge as he slowly spun his cup of ale on the table. Time ticked silently for so long she worried that he wasn't going to speak again. Sarah sat on the edge of her seat, willing him to speak, to at least look up. He had to believe her.

When he finally did, his voice was tight with emotion. "I dinna place blame on ye, Sarah. But knowing what ye've told me, it would be impossible for me no' to bring war to your clan."

This she knew, but she was desperate to find a way out of it. To protect her people, even if her brothers wouldn't. "If I could beg ye no' to…If there were some way to punish Edward and Ellyson for what they've done without bringing pain to the people. They loved Thea, and she loved them."

Thane's eyes were hard, the line of his mouth unbending. "I canna see a way out of it."

Chapter Five

THANE WAS TORN.

He'd known already that his sister had suffered. The vague and unemotional missive that he'd received after her death from the new lairds of Campbell had been terse and to the point. Over the months, his mind had embellished what had happened, creating the torment in his mind that was his beloved sister's demise.

But even his own imaginings hadn't culled that she might have been with child. That those two devils had been jealous enough of a potential bairn that they'd given away her life. He flexed his fists, wishing he had those two bastards in front of him right then and there.

Oh, how he would murder them…

Sarah might not have understood what would have been Thea's fate, but Edward and Ellyson would have been very aware. There wasn't a clan in Scotland that had been untouched by the ravages of the dragoons and the Duke of Cumberland's orders to show no mercy. Men, women, children. It mattered not; they all suffered.

He did not place blame on Sarah. In fact, she'd been trying to escape her brothers as well, and he'd provided the perfect avenue. As it turned out, his mission to abduct her for revenge had turned into a rescue mission. Some of his guilt assuaged, for he'd not truly intended on harming her. A scare perhaps in being abducted, but never would he have put her through what happened to Thea.

Damn.

He thought back to the lad in the stables at Campbell Castle, so grateful for a little kindness. To the wee lass who said she wanted her mistress back, that her mother needed her, how Thea had meant so much to them. Sarah was right that an entire clan should not have to suffer for the misdeeds of their conniving and selfish leaders.

That was not the type of man he was, to make innocents suffer.

"We should eat before it gets cold," he said, needing to think a lot more before he spoke again.

They ate in silence as his mind ruminated on one plan after another. A number of scenarios played out, but not one seemed more perfect over the other. They could infiltrate the walls and abduct Edward and Ellyson, execute them in the woods. The Shaw clan could appeal to the rest of Clan Chattan, the cooperative confederate between the twelve clans to which the Shaws were a member. He could call upon the other rebel leaders who he'd fought with at Culloden. But the thing was other clans might not want to be involved. The Campbells were massive in size and power. He had to find a way to hit them where it hurt. Which he'd already started by abducting Sarah.

When he'd finished eating, she began to gather their things on the tray, but he stilled her hand. "I'll get it," he offered and took the tray himself to place it outside the door.

"Thank ye," she called out to him.

He stood by the door, his fingers resting on the handle. "Ye're welcome."

Thane felt the heat of her presence before he saw her from the side of his eye, standing by his side. Her fingers brushed his. Tiny flames danced on the skin of his knuckles.

"I'm truly verra verra sorry for your loss, Thane."

He turned to face her, seeing the tears, how much she too was heartbroken, in eyes that were the color of peat. "And I'm verra sorry for yours."

"We have all lost so much in this rebellion," she whispered.

"Shh…" He held his finger to his lips and nodded his head at the empty corridor. "Never know who's listening."

Sarah bit her lip, peering out into the empty corridor. When she leaned back, her arm brushed his, and they both stared down at the spot. "How about we check out the Chamber of Sorrow?" she suggested in a welcome change of subject.

"No' certain that's a very festive thing to do on Christmas morning, but I'm willing to try if ye like."

Sarah shrugged, grimacing slightly. "Better to see what we are fighting for than to sit here wallowing in our grief."

"Excellent point."

Thane took her hand in his, her small, warm fingers sliding comfortably against his. Their palms flattened against one another. He gritted his teeth at the contact and how it sent tiny shivers racing down his spine. As much as touching her excited him, he was also keenly aware of how easy it was to be with her. Thane would have thought it torture, but instead, he was quite calm around her.

Sarah stopped suddenly. "Perhaps ye should leave your weapons here?" Her gaze was on his belt, where a pistol was holstered on one side and a dagger on the other.

"Why would I do that?"

She shrugged. "For the safety of others?"

Thane chuckled at her humor. "I like the way ye think."

Sarah grinned, that impish dimple flashing at him, and he found himself mesmerized for a moment, his gaze tracing the outline of her lips. She looked nothing like her younger brothers. Acted nothing like them, either.

"How are ye possibly related to Edward and Ellyson?" he mused, stopping them in the center of the corridor and glancing down at her.

"They are my brothers," she answered quite literally. "Though Jon and I share a different mother."

"Was their mother unkind?"

Sarah frowned, the crease between her brow tiny, and he had the sudden urge to kiss her there.

"She was not particularly *unkind* to me," she said. "Ignored me mostly. I didna know her well. She died birthing Ellyson. The midwife, after the birth of Edward, warned that she should wait several years, allowing her body to heal after such a traumatic birthing, but she didna wait a month. Not even enough time to be clean in the eyes of the church. I remember her getting my da deep in his cups and having her way with him. She must have conceived that night. Edward and Ellyson are so close in age, less than a year, they could almost be twins."

Thane could not imagine Sarah pulling a trick like that. She just didn't seem the type. "I wonder at her urgency."

Sarah released a long sigh and tugged at his hand, resuming their walk toward the Chamber of Sorrow by way of the tavern common area. "I've speculated on it over the years. She was a cousin of my mother. I think she was desperate to give my da two sons, while my mama had only been able to give him one."

"There are no guarantees. She risked her life when her second child could have been another lass."

"Aye. But jealousy does strange things to people." Sadness edged her words.

He was instantly reminded of her brothers and how they'd left Thea to her fate for their resentful reasons. "Seems it ran in her blood."

"Aye."

They reached the common room, which had taken on a more pleasant odor than before. Bows of holly had been spread near the hearth, ropes of pine on the mantel, and the dogs were gone, as were their messy piles. Platters of currant scones were in the centers of the tables, and jugs of what smelled like cider were beside them.

"Och, but ye've come out," Carrie said. "Have a scone. Cook's specialty on Christmas morn."

"Perhaps after we see your Chamber of Sorrow?" Sarah said. "Unless Tobias, would enjoy one now?"

For a moment, he forgot that she'd renamed him for the sake of their anonymity. Sarah indicated the table to Thane where a steaming pile of scones rested.

"Will they still be here when we come back?" he asked Carrie.

"Of course, and if they're looking to get a bit low, I'll set one aside for ye."

He flashed the woman a grateful smile, working hard to endear themselves to their hosts, so when the Campbells eventually came by, Thane and Sarah would be the last ones from their minds. A happy, jovial couple, versus a villain with an abducted lass, was not likely to be mentioned. "Our thanks."

"We aim to please at Balthazar's." She waved them to follow, leading them back through the various chambers until they reached her own bedchamber. "I keep it back here so no one can sneak in."

THE DOOR TO the Chamber of Sorrow was not locked, Sarah noted.

Carrie pushed the door open, which creaked and groaned, revealing a black cavern and swish of air that felt every bit as heavy as Sarah had imagined it would. Their host disappeared into the yawning dark, and

Sarah had the intense urge to run. Nothing about this place felt good.

There was a spark as Carrie lit a candle, the flash illuminating her pale, freckled face and the weapons behind her. Several more bursts, and then finally, she brought the chamber to glow, exposing the contents of the room.

And with it, whether real or imagined, the scent of death.

Dawning horror rained down on Sarah, prickling her skin, seizing her throat. When she made a move to enter, her feet remained rooted in place as if her subconscious were fearful of entering. She gripped onto Thane's arm like an anchor, and he led her inside.

"Gathered these up from the battlefield." Carrie swept the candle high, revealing weapons that hung on the plastered walls with crude hooks. "And when others realized what I was doing here, they've brought me more."

A claymore, distinctly a rebel weapon, and above it a musket with a bayonet on the end—dragoon. Here at odds for eternity. They'd at least been cleaned before being put on display.

"Been a few times now. I take the wagon with me." She moved about the room, showing broken arrow shafts, a bow with the string snapped.

An English sword, and another claymore. Sarah studied every weapon for signs of familiarity.

"Is the battlefield close to here?" Sarah asked. If so, she'd ask Thane to take her when the weather dissipated. She wanted to pay respects to the place where her brother had died.

"Och, nay," Carried fluttered her hand as if it weren't a big deal. "Several days ride in the wagon." Her voice had taken on a somber tone. "So many were lost in the battle. This is my shrine to their memory."

Sarah suppressed a shudder as her eyes caught on a Highland cap, the white rosette cockade stained red with blood.

"Did ye lose someone close to ye?" Sarah asked. It was increasingly difficult to conceal her emotions from Carrie, and she was glad for the shadows in the room that hid her expression.

"Aye." But Carrie did not expound on that, and Sarah was afraid of delving too deep.

Afraid she might reveal something about herself and Thane. "I'm verra sorry for your loss," she managed.

Carrie made a non-committal sound but did not return the sentiment. "I'll leave the two of ye alone to mourn. I just ask ye close the door on your way out."

"We will." Sarah took the candleholder from Carrie and stood in the center of the room for several moments before she lifted it high to reveal more of the walls.

Swords, shields, spurs. A pair of roughly used boots. The sleeve of a jacket, the pattern distinctly plaid, and beside it, the sleeve of one that was red. More examples of the battle that waged between two factions. On the floor, beside a table full of coins, rings, and fragments of metal, were two cannonballs. She'd been told that was how Jon had died, torn apart by the blast of a cannon.

Tears came to her eyes, and Sarah wrenched herself away from seeing anymore, running smack into Thane. His arms were around her instantly, holding her tight. His warmth was a comfort she needed. Wanted to bury herself inside.

"This is…" She couldn't even finish her sentence to say how awful the room made her feel.

"Aye," was all he murmured in return, stroking her hair.

Thane took the candle from her, setting it down on the table before she lit his coat on fire.

"This is no' a Chamber of Sorrow," Sarah said. "This is a Chamber of Horrors."

"Do ye want me to destroy it?"

Sarah shook her head, leaning back to look up at him. It felt so good to be in his arms that she didn't want to move away. His face was shadowed like hers, but she could see that he was not jesting.

"As much as I want to say aye, if ye did, we'd both likely be killed. Or cursed."

"Possibly." He tilted his head. "We might be able to escape quickly. The lad out back seemed eager to please."

Sarah smiled. Some of her sorrow ebbed with his teasing. "I'm no' willing to risk your life for a petty thing. But before we leave, I might come in here and steal something. Maybe all of the dragoon items, so no one can mourn them."

"Oh, a thief. Ye have no' mentioned before that ye have the skill."

She shrugged, enjoying the sensation of their arms around each other, and neither seemed inclined to withdraw. "I grew up with three brothers. I learned a few things to survive."

"Do ye recognize anything in here?" He maneuvered them toward the table, his arm still around her waist.

Sarah examined the rings, touching the various items, imagining who the owners might be. Thankfully, nothing struck her as familiar. "I dinna. What about ye?"

"Nothing," he said quietly.

Sarah glanced up at him. "How many did ye lose?"

"Nearly half our men in the battle. A dozen or more in the retreat. More that were routed out as rebels after." He swallowed hard enough that she could see the lump bob in his throat. "We'll rebuild."

Goodness, they'd lost so many. They were a smaller clan to begin with. But his note of hope filled her with the same sentiment. Though she'd barely known him when his sister had joined her family, now she felt like she'd known him for years, when in reality, less than twenty-four hours had passed.

They had a connection. Mutual loss. Mutual sorrow. And a common goal.

Plus, he'd opened up to her, revealing his strength and integrity. All men should want to be like Thane Shaw.

Without thinking, she leaned up on her tiptoes and pressed her lips to his.

Chapter Six

THANE HAD NOT seen this coming. A fantasy or two, sure, but actually kissing Sarah?

Softness and heat pressed against him in body and lips. Desire flooded his veins, and even though he knew he should stop kissing her, he couldn't bring himself to pull away.

With a slant of his head, Thane kissed her deeper. The scent of her surrounded him, and her tiny hands clutched to the front of him, right over the place his heart pounded. He flicked his tongue against her lips, tasting the butter from their breakfast, and then dipping between them when she opened on a gasp.

Tentatively, she touched her tongue to his. Her grip tightened on his shirt, and she let out a little mewl as he stroked his tongue slowly, languidly along hers. She tasted of heaven and sweetness, anything but what he would have thought of someone that should be his enemy.

But he knew she wasn't. That much had been made clear already.

Thane stroked her face, ending the kiss as softly as it had begun, his gaze locked on hers.

"Why did ye do that?" he asked, curious about her motives.

Sarah bit her lip and started to move away, but he held her close. "I'm no' sure. I just…It felt right."

She wasn't wrong. Kissing her had felt very right.

Before the battle at Culloden, he'd been thinking that he needed to take a wife; had flirted with many women, kissed a few. But after the battle, he'd kept everyone at arm's length or longer. No more was his priority to wed, but to keep his clan alive and out of the clutches of the men who would see them all executed for treason.

It had been nearly a year since he'd kissed a lass, and he was certain that any kisses before now had meant little. Why was this one so different? In his gut, he felt that there was something special about this woman. Something to be discovered, once her layers peeled away. And not just her garments, but *her*, the very essence of her.

"I'm…I'm sorry." Sarah shook her head and again tried to pull away. "Ye told me from the beginning that we should be enemies, that I should remember just why we're here together. And I…" She sucked in a breath, pressed her hands to her cheeks, clearly mortified when she needn't have been. "I think the emotion of this room, it—I just could no'—" She broke off then, shaking her head even more.

"Lass, I didna mind the kiss," he soothed, stroking his hand over hers and gently tugging it from her pinkened cheeks. "I would kiss ye again, but no' here. No' in this place of sorrow."

"Horror."

"Both." He took her hand and led her out of the chamber, closing the door behind them as they'd been instructed. Then he guided her back through the common room, nodding to fellow patrons.

Balthazar accosted them along the way, much to Thane's irritation, which he couldn't' show. "Carrie says ye were in her Chamber of Sorrow, and I see it has greatly affected your lass." The man frowned. "Take extra scones with ye back to your room. 'Twill make ye feel better."

That was a ridiculous notion. How were food and drink going to make them feel better when they'd both lost family to a massacre that should never have taken place?

But Thane didn't say that. Instead, he nodded, lifted a tray from a table with at least half a dozen scones on it and a jug of cider. Their host looked ready to balk, but Sarah took that moment to give an all-body shudder, and the old man clamped his lips closed over his rotting teeth.

In their chamber, he poured them each a glass of cider, and they ate the scones sitting on the edge of the bed, each of them trying to absorb all that had happened.

"Balthazar's Tavern may be akin to a type of Hell for me," Sarah said, following a long gulp of cider. So many dreadful and wretched memories flooded her.

"Only parts of it," Thane said. "It would seem our chamber is no' haunted or filled with mad people."

"'Tis true. Unless one of us is mad," she offered with a lift of her shoulders and popped the last of her scone into her mouth.

Thane eyed the tray with four more scones on it. They had been delicious. He could eat the entire tray. But he didn't want to get up, not when it felt so good to be sitting beside her.

"This Christmas is so much different than last." Sarah's shoulders slumped with that admission.

"Oh?" he urged.

"Aye. Last Christmas, Thea decorated the entire great hall with holly and pinecones and sweet-smelling herbs. We had a massive feast, dancing, and games and singing. Thea had a spectacular singing voice. She went to great lengths to make it wonderful for us all." She flashed him a smile.

"That is surprising." Thane pursed his lips in thought. "We didna do all that at Tordarroch Castle. My clan much prefers celebrating the holidays of old. Yule and the winter solstice."

She smiled up at him. "Perhaps that is why she went all out then, because it was so new and magical to her."

"There is something to be said about new traditions." Thane grinned. "Thank ye for sharing your memories of Thea with me."

"'Tis nice to relive them." Her little finger danced over his, where their hands were braced on the edge of the bed. "I'm glad we can share them together."

"Me too." And then, before he could change his mind, Thane bent to kiss her once more.

SARAH WAS PLAYING with fire.

Already she'd crossed too many lines. Her brothers would have her head if they knew she was behaving this way. Kissing a man she barely knew in a chamber they were meant to share for the night. A man she'd willingly allowed to abduct her. If they'd knew she'd packed the bag before he'd ever arrived—Lord, but they would kill her.

And she'd be fine with it, for she'd had a chance to feel Thane's lips on hers. A man worthy of a kiss. A man worthy of so much more.

Their fingers entwined, his thumb brushing over her knuckles. What would it be like to kiss him every day like this? To glory in the soft sweep of his lips, the sensual stroke of his tongue?

That was when the idea came to her. She needed to be ruined. And who better for the task than Thane? Should her brothers catch up to them, it would make it impossible for her to partner with anyone else. Whoever they sold her to would not pay for a woman who'd already been claimed by another.

But Thane...He was honorable. Felt guilty at having abducted her. Even the tough attitude he tried to have with her was seen through easily enough. The man was formidable when he needed to be and in the next breath filled with heart. Much like his sister had been. Which meant that he would not simply steal her virginity if she asked him, too. She'd have to *make* him take it.

Sarah threaded her free hand in his hair, kissing him deeper, and he enjoyed it, judging from the sound in the back of his throat. She had no practice at wooing or seducing. Though Thane was not the first man she'd ever kissed, she'd done nothing more than that. And the only knowledge she had of what happened between a man and a woman was what she'd overheard the maids talking about after a feast that had seen plenty of them deep in their cups. But from what she'd heard, she thought she could piece together a fairly decent seduction.

And she'd not know until she tried.

With that in mind, and the confidence of someone well versed in lovemaking, she lifted herself up and straddled Thane's lap. The crux of her thighs pressed to the hardened length of him, sending a shudder of pleasure through her.

Oh, my...The maids had not been jesting about that part. Frissons of wicked decadence raced through her, and when she rubbed herself back and forth, yet more intense quivers followed.

No wonder they did this. It actually felt rather good. Better than good. Not the stories she'd been told as a girl by her da. That to rut with a lad would only lead to unbearable pain and was best saved for marriage, when the blessing of God would lessen the torment.

Da was wrong, it would seem. Or he'd lied.

Thane's hands came around her backside, gripping her arse and massaging, and he too moved beneath her, increasing the friction as his arousal stroked against hers. She moaned against his mouth, a little surprised at the sounds she was making. Then he was flipping her around so her back was flush to the mattress, and he was over her, between her thighs.

He kissed her harder, with more vigor and passion, tossing all her sensations into the air like fairy dust until she felt like she was in a magical dream. His hand swept up her ribs, clutching at her breast, and then he tore his mouth from hers and traveled heatedly over her neck and downward until his lips clamped over her nipple.

Sarah cried out at that, bucking upward. *Goodness...*She'd not thought touching could feel any better, but it just kept getting more intense and more pleasurable.

"Dear God, I love the way ye respond," he said, panting, his eyes on her. Desire filled his gaze, made his eyelids dip.

Sarah grinned encouragingly. This was going quite well. "Your touch is magic."

He kissed her again, caressing her everywhere until she was floating in a sea of delicious awareness she never wanted to be rescued from.

"I want ye," he groaned against her lips.

His words, spoken so passionately, pinged off all the right spots in her mind and body.

Seduction had been so easy. And so exciting. "Ye can have me. I give myself willingly."

There, she'd said it. And soon she would be ruined, and it would be wonderful.

Thane pushed her skirts up, fumbled with his breeches, and then she felt the very heat of him at her core.

"Are ye certain?" he asked, gaze locked on hers, eyes filled with question.

"Aye," she said with a confidence she'd never felt so keenly before.

Thane let out a satisfied groan and surged forward, the invasion accompanied by a sharp clamp of pain. Sarah cried out unbidden at the ache, surprised that it should have felt that way when everything else had been so wonderful.

Thane stilled, letting out a curse, the force of which blew the hair from her forehead. Sarah's eyes had been clamped closed, but his angry tone made her snap open her lids.

"Ye were a virgin," he accused, a thunderstorm clouding his expression. Gone was the heady look of his lowered lids.

Tears sprang to her eyes. "Aye," she whispered.

"Why did ye no' bloody tell me?"

Sarah swallowed hard. Perhaps tricking him into taking her virginity had been stupid, but she had given her full permission. "I did no' think it mattered. I consented."

Thane cursed, withdrawing from her body, leaving her feeling empty and lost. She reached for him as he climbed off, but he backed away from the bed and shoved himself back into his breeches. "I would no' have done that. 'Tis no' honorable."

Exactly as she'd imagined he would act if he'd known. Tears fell in earnest now, hot waves down her cheeks. "It was no' your choice to make." She shoved her skirts back down, pulling her legs up tight to her chest, aching all the more.

"Why?" There was true anguish in his tone.

"Because if my brothers come for me, and they *will*, I can be of no use to them if I am spoiled. I dinna want to be their pawn."

"But why would ye have me be the one to spoil ye?" He pressed his fist to his chest.

Without hesitation, she answered, "Because ye're so honorable. A good man."

"And so ye wished to trick me into marriage then?"

She shook her head vigorously, everything spinning out of control. That had been the last thing on her mind. And she hated the way his anger had turned to pain. "Nay, I thought…If I were to ruin myself, I'd want to do with it a man like ye, rather than just anyone."

All the anger dissipated from him now, his shoulders sagging, and he trudged back toward her. Thane sighed and sat down on the bed next to her, gathering her in his arms. He was quiet for a long time, and she remained very still. Afraid if he remembered that he was holding her, he'd walk away. "If I had known, I would have taken my time. Made sure ye were ready."

"I am ready."

"I mean, your body."

"Oh." She sucked in a weary breath and stared up at him, meeting his gaze head-on, wanting him to see the truth in her eyes. "I was no' trying to trick ye, I swear. I dinna seek marriage. I only sought to rid myself of the bargaining chip my brothers are trying to sell."

Thane stroked her hair, wiped away her tears. The pain in his expression receded and returned the man she'd fallen for. Oh, dear heavens…Aye, she had fallen for him. Swept up and deposited right on the shores of his affection, should he want her.

"I will marry ye." Conviction powered each syllable.

"What?" She pushed away from him then. Had he not understood her? "I told ye that's no' what I seek."

"I know, lass. But it is the only way to make certain they canna sell ye. Your brothers will lie about your virginity for the riches it will bring them. I'll protect ye because I was no' able to protect my sister."

Sarah glanced down at the rug on the dirt floor. "I canna ask ye to do that." Keeping her safe wouldn't bring Thea back, and she didn't want him to feel obligated to her for the rest of their lives. For eternity.

"Ye didna." He tipped her chin up. "I offered. Of my own free will, I consent." He pressed his lips to hers softly. Saints, but it felt so good. "Besides, I like the idea of being able to kiss ye more."

"Truly?" His embrace was warm, comforting, and she felt safe with him, cared for.

"Aye." He kissed her again and then left the bed once more, though this time he only went to the basin where he took a loose rag and dipped it in water.

She watched, curious, as he came back to her and then gentle as he could washed between her legs. His ministrations were perhaps the most considerate of any she'd ever had.

"To soothe the ache," he murmured.

"Thank ye," she said.

"If ye'll still have me…I'd like to finish what we started, only make it better this time."

Tentatively, she nodded. But then she knew he'd want to hear her say it aloud. "Ye have my permission to make love to me."

And then he was laying her back down on the bed, and once more she was melting into the sheets and sighing with pleasure. He kissed his way down the length of her body until he hovered over the very center of her.

"I want to kiss ye here."

"That is…" That had not been discussed by the maids. "It sounds…"

But she couldn't find the words, and it didn't matter anyway because he robbed her of all sense as his tongue stroked the sensitive folds of her sex. Again and again, he stroked until she was clutching at the sheets and crying out in pleasure. Wave after delicious heady wave crashed over her. *Oh my…*Thane was a skilled lover. Made her feel powerful one moment and weak in the knees the next. And pleasure, there was so much of it.

"That was what I meant before," he said, crawling up the length of her still-shuddering body. "Now, ye're ready."

This time when he pushed inside her, there was no pain, only more pleasure. She gasped, letting the last vestiges of control go. Wrapping herself around him, she followed his lead, kissed his shoulders, his mouth. Gripped his arse, stroked his back. Cried out when he somehow made her body break apart once more and drank in the sounds of his rapture as he whispered her name over and over again.

"Ye're mine forever now, lass," he said, nuzzling against her neck before meeting her gaze. There was not even an inkling of regret in his words or eyes.

Sarah grinned, placing her arms around his neck and threading her fingers into his hair. "Who knew revenge and abduction could be so…satisfying?"

Thane let out a roar of laughter and gently bit her lip. "*Ye* are satisfying."

Chapter Seven

THEY LAY IN bliss for an hour or so, whispering, touching and eating the rest of the scones. This was the first time Thane had ever done this with a woman. Just lying there languidly sharing stories from their childhood. Their likes and dislikes. Exploring one another, both in mind and body.

In the span of an hour, he'd learned more about Sarah than he knew about any other person—even his twin sister Thea.

Sarah was ticklish behind her knees and at her ankles, but not on her ribs. She loved sunrise more than sunset, and her favorite time of year was in spring when dewdrops dripped from trees onto the tip of her tongue. The lass had a penchant for sweets and disliked spirits, but she'd drink them if she must and agreed to taste the whisky he distilled himself at Tordarroch.

They'd both learned to play the lute when they were young, but he was the only one who'd continued to play. He told her about how he and Thea would combine their musical talents to entertain the clan, to which Sarah belted out in the most angelic voice he'd ever heard a ballad of winter and the spring that was to come.

When they were willing to brave the cold, they pulled on their cloaks on the pretense of checking on the horses, but in reality, it was to check the weather.

The crowd in the common area had slimmed now that the scones were gone. In the corner, an older man sung and played his lute. The brim of his hat pulled low, casting a shadow on his face. The two of them were very tempted to join him, but at that moment, Balthazar came barreling into the room, demanding the man change his Christmas tune to one of battle.

Rather than brave the kitchens and more of Cook's ladle flinging, they went out the front door, the cold of winter slapping against their cheeks, along with a gust that brought with it dustings of snow from the ground. They slammed the door shut to keep it from entering the tavern, though it was likely too late.

The snow was easily above their ankles, but the lads had shoveled a path leading from the front door around the back of the tavern toward the stable.

"Still coming down," Thane mused.

"Aye, but at least the sky is not only white with clouds. A bit of blue peeking through the white means we may yet get a reprieve." The wind whipped against them, and Sarah tripped then clutched at his arm to keep from falling. And good thing, because right then, a massive icicle fell from the thatched roof, stabbing into the snow where she'd just been. Both of them leapt back, he as though to protect her and she because her life was flashing before her eyes.

"We'll need a good two or three days reprieve if we're to make it back in decent time. Might have to stop along the way at another tavern or two."

"Additional adventures then." She grinned up at him, excitement in the creases about her eyes. What had transpired between the two of them was almost enough to erase the reasons they'd got together to begin with. Almost.

"Aye, but also more possibility of your brothers finding us," he reminded her grimly.

The light left her eyes then, and she seemed to remember that she'd been running from them suddenly. "Do ye think they've left yet?"

Thane nodded. "They'd no' wait too long to come after ye. And our tracks may yet be visible in the snow, though with the way it fell through the night, I'm hoping most were covered. At any rate, they'll have lost us by the time they get to the road, given all the others who've traversed."

"But they would guess it was ye?" She glanced around nervously as if expecting to see her brothers leap out.

"Does your clan have any other enemies?" That was a silly question, and he knew it.

"Of course."

"Then maybe we have a chance yet." He offered that as hope.

Sarah shivered, and he took her hand, looping her arm in his and rubbing vigorously at the exposed skin of her fingers. They made their way to the stables and poked their heads inside when no lads were seen lurking about.

The stable was long and smoky, with the telltale sounds of horse snuffling and stomping.

"Destiny, we've come to greet ye," Thane called out, and his horse stuck his head out from one of the stalls, letting out a hearty neigh.

They made their way down until they reached him, observing a clean stall, a bucket of water and another filled with hay.

"I see ye're being properly spoiled." Thane stroked his hand over his horse's soft muzzle.

"Why did ye name him Destiny?" Sarah asked.

"I found him on the battlefield. Or rather, he found me." He'd never told anyone this story before, but with Sarah, it came out easily. He would need to keep some of the details vague, so if anyone were listening in, they wouldn't realize which side he fought on. He also kept to himself that Destiny's previous master had been a dragoon, evident from the contents he found in the attached satchel, and the crest stamped into the saddle. Wasn't it ironic that the horse of his enemy had saved his life?

"This is going to be intriguing," Sarah said, wiggling her brows.

"The enemy was surrounding me, knocking me back. My own horse had already been massacred, and so I was on foot, in danger of joining my brethren in the beyond. Then from behind me comes this massive warhorse. He nuzzles me in the back as men advance on me, taking aim. I leapt up into the saddle, and he took off, with shots fired at us from behind. He saved my life, and the fact that we found each other on the field like that, well, it felt like Destiny."

Sarah leaned against him, her hand joining his in stroking the horse. "That is an incredible story. And the perfect name. I'm glad for my sake that he found ye."

Thane grinned. "He's a good horse. And for that reason, he should be spoiled for the rest of his days."

SARAH LEANED HER head against Thane's shoulder, so glad that he'd come to Campbell lands. Even if his intent had been to abduct her, which now seemed like a massive jest. He'd rescued her from a fate that could have been horrible. And to think she was now going to be linked to her dearest friend's brother—a man of honor and integrity—she couldn't have dreamed up a better scenario.

They left the stable, agreeing to spend one more night at the tavern, and then hopefully be on their way the following morning.

By the time they made it back to their chamber, the delicious stew they'd been smelling all day waited for them on the table, along with wine and thick brown bread. They ate with gusto, having worked up an appetite earlier in the day, and when their meal was complete, they made love again and again.

When morning finally broke, a slim crack of light was seen through where the wall met the roof, and so they rose with tired eyes. Sarah prayed the weather had waned, and they could be on their way from this tavern of sorrow. And yet, she'd always remember it fondly for being the place where she'd given herself to Thane.

"That sun is a good sign." Thane climbed from the bed, giving her arse a gentle pat.

Sarah giggled and rolled over. "Ye think we can leave?"

"Aye, we can try." He tugged back the covers, and she squealed at the cold blast of air.

They dressed quickly and exited the chamber, skipping the porridge in favor of a hunk of bread with butter, and then before the sun had fully risen, they climbed onto Destiny's back and took off at a trot down the road. Some of the snow had started to melt, and with the morning sun the twinkling white moors took on more of a glistening shine.

Just as they had the night they escaped Campbell Castle, they stopped every few hours to rest Destiny and relieve themselves. They packed their canteen with snow to keep it full. No one seemed to be following them, and indeed they did not pass anyone of note on the road.

In the distance, the clanging of kirk bells could be heard coming from a small village.

"I think we need to make it official," Thane said.

"What's that?" Sarah mused sleepily.

"Our union. Would ye, Sarah Campbell, consent to being my wife?"

She sat up a little straighter, nodding as she looked into his quite serious gaze. Though she'd agreed before, the fact that he asked her once more warmed her heart. "Every day for the rest of my life."

They rode into the village and to the kirk, where they found a priest more than willing to wed them for a small fortune.

"I dinna have a ring for ye." Thane frowned as they stood on the stairs out front of the kirk.

"Wait," she said. "I have one."

Sarah pulled the small box from her satchel, revealing the ring that had once been her mother's. The rubies glistened in the sunlight. "My ma gave me this. 'Twas hers."

"'Tis perfect, just like ye."

Sarah's face heated at his words. He made her feel so special. She passed the jewelry box to Thane, and when it came time to place the ring on her finger, he did so slowly, eyes locked on hers. So much emotion was conveyed there, so much trust, and anticipation.

They were in this together. Them against the injustices of the world.

She couldn't help but smile with joy, for even though destiny had brought them together, it would seem the two of them had forged their own path from there on.

When the priest said the groom could kiss his bride, Sarah didn't wait. She tossed herself into his arms and pressed her lips to his, startling the priest and their witnesses by her boldness. But Thane was not surprised at all. By the way he wrapped his arms around her, she knew he relished her.

"That's my lass," Thane said with a chuckle.

They left the kirk and took a room in the village tavern. Regaled by singing and festive games, which they joined in this time, not feeling threatened or haunted, but amid company they could revel in. They feasted on roasted pheasant and stewed turnips in a thick brown sauce that was perfect for dipping bread into. And that night, when Thane made love to her, Sarah felt a deep emotion for him all the way to her soul…

Love. Wholly and passionately. Everything tingled inside and out, and not just from his touch, but his gaze, his presence, the idea of a future together.

As they lay in the dark, fingers and legs entwined, their breaths in sync, she whispered, "I love ye."

Thane rolled toward her, tugging her close against him. "I love ye, too, lass. I canna believe that I set out to steal ye, and instead, ye've stolen my heart."

Epilogue

Several months later...

THE PRISONERS ARRIVED just before sunset, shackled on top of their mounts, shackled and gagged, so no one had to hear them speak.

"They are here," Sarah said quietly. Her eyes were riveted on the two men who'd been willing to sell her. The two men who had been responsible for Thane's sister's death.

"We dinna have to go through with this." Thane tucked his arm around her shoulders. She was beautiful in winter, but even more so in spring. Especially with his bairn rounding out her belly. Sarah had taken to the Shaw clan as if she'd been a member all along. They loved her dearly, and she loved them. "There is always an execution or exile. I can put them on a ship to the Americas."

She shook her head. "I canna have the guilt of their deaths on my conscience or the guilt for it being on yours. Nor do I want to unleash them on anyone else."

Thane cupped her chin, brushed his lips over hers. "I will do whatever ye want, my love."

"Your plans for their imprisonment are perfect. Perhaps in time, they will be reformed and can be set free. But for now, they will be punished." Sarah wrapped her arms around his middle and tucked her body close to his. "Thank ye for all ye've done."

"I couldna have done it without ye." And that was the truth. They'd worked as a team from Christmas Eve until now, securing the safety of the Campbell clan, and the men responsible for Thea's death, and it had been glorious. "Both our clans will thrive from here on out."

Hand in hand, they met Angus Campbell, the new Campbell laird, outside Tordarroch gates, eyeing Edward and Ellyson, who glared down at them.

"Thank ye, Angus." Sarah embraced her uncle. "The clan will be in excellent hands with ye."

"Nay lass, thank ye, and your husband." Her uncle glanced down at her rounded belly. "And I see we may yet have an heir to Jon's seat growing in your womb."

Sarah pressed her hand over her middle. "We would be honored for our child to have such a choice."

"Your father would want that."

Angus nodded to Thane and reached out his hand, grasping Thane's arm and shaking it. "We owe ye a great debt."

"Ye owe me nothing, I did my duty." And he meant it.

Sarah, Thane and Angus made a deal, surreptitiously. A coup, really. With Thane and Sarah's assistance, Angus had been able to take over his clan. A task which had not been too hard, given how everyone had felt about Edward and Ellyson's rule. Not to mention they did not want a war on their head, which Thane might have exaggerated slightly, with the help of his Chattan clan confederate.

"Ye'll make an excellent leader," Sarah said. "My da and Jon would be so proud of ye."

Angus was Sarah's uncle, the much younger brother of her father, and the natural and best choice for the clan's new rule. He'd graciously accepted the appointment after a secret vote by the elders. Part of the plan was that Edward and Ellyson would be brought to Shaw lands, where they would be held prisoner for the remainder of their days, unless it was deemed safe for them to be let out. Sarah did not want to execute her brothers, though they deserved it. And Thane wanted to make her happy. He supposed death in this case would not make right what had been done in the past. Thea wasn't coming back. But at least they could honor her memory every day in having freed the Campbells from the rotten brothers' rule.

"Will ye join us for supper, Uncle?" Sarah asked.

"Gladly." Angus offered Sarah his arm, and they walked into Tordarroch ahead of Thane, who waited behind to escort his prisoners to their new quarters.

When Sarah was out of earshot, Thane turned on the two bastard brothers. "I'm going to make your lives a living hell, lads. Ye took my sister and possibly her child from this world without a care. My wife has seen fit to let ye live because she is a merciful and good woman. But that does no' mean ye get to live free and well."

Thane dragged the shackled men to the dungeon of Tordarroch and grinned widely. In the end, he'd gotten more than he bargained for, retribution, love and a bigger family. Glancing down at the two men who glared fire and hate at him, Thane said, "Welcome home. I like to call this the Chamber of Sorrow."

THE END

About Eliza Knight

Eliza Knight is an award-winning and *USA Today* bestselling author of over fifty sizzling historical romance and erotic romance. Under the name E. Knight, she pens rip-your-heart-out historical fiction. While not reading, writing or researching for her latest book, she chases after her three children. In her spare time (if there is such a thing…) she likes daydreaming, wine-tasting, traveling, hiking, staring at the stars, watching movies, shopping and visiting with family and friends. She lives atop a small mountain with her own knight in shining armor, three princesses and two very naughty puppies.

For a book list, visit Eliza at www.elizaknight.com or her historical blog History Undressed: www.historyundressed.com. Sign up for her newsletter to get news about books, events, contests and sneak peaks!

eepurl.com/CSFFD

Follow Eliza on:
Facebook: facebook.com/elizaknightfiction
BookBub: bookbub.com/authors/eliza-knight
Instagram: @elizaknightfiction
Twitter: @ElizaKnight
Goodreads: goodreads.com/elizaknight

Printed in Great Britain
by Amazon

49943073R00301